Praise for Sulari Gentill

After She Wrote Him
(previously published as *Crossing the Lines*)

2018 Winner of the Ned Kelly Awards, Best Crime Fiction

"A pure delight, a swift yet psychologically complex read, cleverly conceived and brilliantly executed."
> —Dean Koontz, *New York Times* bestselling author

"A tour de force! A brilliant blend of mystery, gut-wrenching psychological suspense, and literary storytelling. The novel stands as a shining (and refreshing) example of metafiction at its best— witty and wry, stylish and a joy to read."
> —Jeffery Deaver, *New York Times* bestselling author

"A delightful, cerebral novel featuring a crime writer who grows dangerously enamored with her main character. As the interplay between creator and created reaches Russian-nesting-doll complexity, it forced us to question the nature of fiction itself."
> —Gregg Hurwitz, *New York Times* bestselling author

"This is an elegant exploration of the creative process, as well as a strong defense of the crime-fiction genre, as Gentill illustrates the crossing of lines between imagination and reality."
> —*Booklist*

"In this intriguing and unusual tale, a stunning departure from Gentill's period mysteries, the question is not whodunit but who's real and who's a figment of someone's vivid imagination."
> —*Kirkus Reviews*

"Fans of postmodern fiction will enjoy this departure from Gentill's 1930s series. It's an exploration, as one character puts it, of 'an author's relationship with her protagonist, an examination of the tenuous line between belief and reality, imagination and self, and what happens when that line is crossed.'"

—*Publishers Weekly*

"Literary or pop fiction lovers will enjoy."

—*Library Journal*

Shanghai Secrets
The Ninth Rowland Sinclair WWII Mystery

"A frothy retro cocktail with a whodunit chaser."

—*Kirkus Reviews*

A Dangerous Language
The Eighth Rowland Sinclair WWII Mystery

"A thrilling eighth mystery."

—*Publishers Weekly*

"Fans of historical fiction and murder mysteries will consider her treasure trove of novels to be a rich discovery."

—*Bookreporter*

Give the Devil His Due
The Seventh Rowland Sinclair WWII Mystery

"This is a great addition to a fun Australian mystery series...a fast-paced and captivating novel set during a turbulent period in Australia's history. Containing an intriguing mystery, a unique sense of humour, and a range of historical characters, this is a highly recommended read for lovers of Australian fiction."

—Sydney Morning Herald

"[D]evil of a good read."

—Herald Sun

"This 1930s Sydney is vibrant and authentic, and the inclusion of a relevant newspaper cutting at the beginning of each chapter is a neat touch... In order to get the best value out of this highly original series with its quirky characters...seek out the earlier titles and follow them in sequence."

—Historical Novel Society

A Murder Unmentioned
The Sixth Rowland Sinclair WWII Mystery

Shortlisted for the Davitt Award for Best Adult Novel for 2015
Shortlisted for the Ned Kelly Award for Best Crime Novel 2015

"Each chapter begins with a brief excerpt from an Australian publication, such as the *Camperdown Chronicle*, that offers insights into the popular culture of the times. Fans of historical mysteries will find a lot to savor."

—Publishers Weekly

"A charmingly complex hero whose adventures continue to highlight many worldly problems between the great wars."

—Kirkus Reviews

"This sixth entry in the Rowland Sinclair series, which blends historical figures seamlessly with fictional ones, clarifies and advances the family dynamics of its appealing protagonist, which should delight fans and win new readers."

—Booklist

"Sulari Gentill likes to tease, blithely slotting real people and events into a crime series set in the 1930s relating the fictional adventures of artist and gentleman of leisure, Rowland Sinclair... The sixth book in the series and by far the most interesting... As always, every chapter opens with a relevant snippet from a periodical of the time. Once again, telling the fictional from the real is part of the fun... Clever Gentill. Investigating the past has never been more fun."

—Sydney Morning Herald

Gentlemen Formerly Dressed
The Fifth Rowland Sinclair WWII Mystery

"This book has it all: intrigue among the British aristocracy, the Nazi threat, and a dashing Australian hero. I didn't want it to end!"

—Rhys Bowen, author of the New York Times
bestselling Royal Spyness and Molly Murphy mysteries,
and the #1 Kindle bestseller, In Farleigh Field

"Rowland's determined attempts to open British eyes to the gathering storm combine mystery, rousing adventure, and chance meetings with eminent figures from Churchill to Evelyn Waugh."

—Kirkus Reviews

"The pleasure of this novel lies...in observing Rowland at dinner with Evelyn Waugh, trading insights with H. G. Wells, and setting Winston Churchill straight on the evils of nationalism. Fans of upper-class sleuths will be in their element."

—Publishers Weekly

"With fast pacing, madcap characters and intriguing historical personages like H. G. Wells, Evelyn Waugh, and Winston Churchill making appearances, *Gentlemen Formerly Dressed* is historical mystery at its most fun. Sulari Gentill has managed to capture the odd decadence of the British upper classes, in stark contrast to the rising fascist factions in both Germany and England. Fascinating history, entertaining characters, and a hint of romance make *Gentlemen Formerly Dressed* irresistible."

—*Shelf Awareness*

Paving the New Road
The Fourth Rowland Sinclair WWII Mystery

Shortlisted for the Davitt Award for Best Adult Crime Fiction for 2013

"The combination of famous historical figures, detailed descriptions of a troubling time, and plenty of action makes for a tale as rousing as it is relevant."

—*Kirkus Reviews*

"This installment takes the aristocratic Sinclair into a much darker place than did the previous three entries in the series but does so without losing the stylish prose and the easy way with character that have given the novels their appeal."

—*Booklist*

"Stylish, well-paced murder mystery…cheeky plotline… This tale is told with such flair and feeling for those extraordinary times… Verdict: thrilling."

—*Herald Sun*

Miles Off Course
The Third Rowland Sinclair WWII Mystery

"Gentill's third reads like a superior Western, alternating high adventure with social and political observations about prewar Australia."
—*Kirkus Reviews*

"Set in Australia in 1933, Gentill's entertaining third mystery featuring portrait artist Rowland Sinclair will appeal to fans of Greenwood's Phryne Fisher... Gentill matches Greenwood's skill at blending suspense with a light touch."
—*Publishers Weekly*

"Rowland is an especially interesting character: at first he comes off as a bit of a layabout, a guy who feels he's entitled to a cushy life by virtue of his aristocratic roots, but, as the story moves along, we realize he has a strong moral center and a compulsion to finish a job once he's started it. A great addition to a strong series and a fine read-alike for fans of Kerry Greenwood's Phryne Fisher novels."
—*Booklist*

A Decline in Prophets
The Second Rowland Sinclair WWII Mystery

Winner of the Davitt Award for Best Adult Crime Fiction for 2012

"I thoroughly enjoyed the glamour of the ocean voyage, the warmth and wit among the friends, and yet all the time, simmering beneath the surface, was the real and savage violence, waiting to erupt. The 1930s are a marvelous period. We know what lies ahead! This is beautifully drawn, with all its fragile hope and looming tragedy. I am delighted this is a series. I want them all."
—Anne Perry, *New York Times* bestselling author

"Set in late 1932, Gentill's lively second mystery featuring dashing Australian millionaire Rowland 'Rowly' Sinclair takes place initially aboard the luxury cruise ship *Aquitania*, as it steams along toward Sydney... The witty and insightful glimpses of the Australian bourgeoisie of this period keep this mystery afloat."

—*Publishers Weekly*

"A delightful period piece."

—*Kirkus Reviews*

"Rowland Sinclair is a gentleman artist who comes from a privileged background but whose sympathies are with bohemians, lefties, and ratbags. It's a rich political and cultural era to explore, and Gentill has a lot of fun with a hero who is always getting paint on his immaculate tailoring."

—*Sydney Morning Herald*

A House Divided
(formerly *A Few Right Thinking Men*)
The First Rowland Sinclair WWII Mystery

Shortlisted for Best First Book for the Commonwealth Writers' Price for 2011

"As series-launching novels go, this one is especially successful: the plot effectively plays Sinclair's aristocratic bearing and involvement in the arts against the Depression setting, fraught with radical politics, both of which he becomes involves in as he turns sleuth. And Sinclair himself is a delight: winning us over completely and making us feel as though he's an old friend."

—*Booklist,* Starred Review

Also by Sulari Gentill

The Rowland Sinclair WWII Mysteries
A House Divided
A Decline in Prophets
Miles Off Course
Paving the New Road
Gentlemen Formerly Dressed
A Murder Unmentioned
Give the Devil His Due
A Dangerous Language
Shanghai Secrets

The Hero Trilogy
Chasing Odysseus
Trying War
The Blood of Wolves

Standalone Novel
After She Wrote Him

WHERE THERE'S
A WILL

WHERE THERE'S A WILL

A Rowland Sinclair WWII *Mystery*

SULARI GENTILL

Poisoned Pen

PRESS

Published by Poisoned Pen Press, an imprint of Sourcebooks
P.O. Box 4410, Naperville, Illinois 60567-4410
(630) 961-3900
sourcebooks.com

Originally published as *A Testament of Character* in 2020 by Pantera Press.

Cataloging-in-Publication Data is on file with the Library of Congress.

Printed and bound in the United States of America.
KP 10 9 8 7 6 5 4 3 2 1

For Larry Vincent, who showed me around
Boston at great personal risk.

And Leith Henry, who didn't let me chicken out of writing that scene.

Chapter One

SINGAPORE BASE

LONDON, Tuesday: Speaking at the 1912 Club, Lord Halisham's private secretary, Captain Grahame said: "If we lose Singapore as a base, we lose every part of the Empire east and south of Singapore."

—*Goulburn Evening Penny Post*,
13 February 1935

The doors leading out to the suite's balcony were open to the brewing storm outside. Heavy clouds churned overhead without releasing their burden, but the wind already carried the scent of rain and jasmine. The gentleman who leant on the railing wore a dinner suit—traditional black, as opposed to the white jackets that were popular in the tropics. The sharp part of his dark hair had been lost in the building gusts. Yet he seemed oblivious to the oncoming tempest.

Rowland Sinclair unknotted his bow tie with one hand

as he read the letter he held in the other. The missive summoning him back to Sydney at the earliest convenience had been issued by his elder brother, Wilfred, upon whom the mantle and burden of family power had settled. The letter mentioned that there were papers and affairs that required his attention. Rowland doubted that was true—the commercial machinations of the Sinclair fortune had been designed by Wilfred to require little from Rowland beyond an occasional directed signature. It was an arrangement with which they were both happy.

Pulling the tie free of his collar, Rowland folded the page and shoved both into his pocket. Rowland and his friends had been in the East for six months now, most of it in Shanghai, the last four weeks here in Singapore.

The animosity which had made his exit from Australia to China seem expedient and timely, would, by now, have settled…surely. Clearly, Wilfred believed so, or he would have sent his brother on some other errand abroad. Of course, the sojourn to Shanghai had not proved to be as effective in keeping Rowland out of harm's way as Wilfred had hoped— the treaty port was rife with violence and treachery, in which they'd found themselves embroiled. But they had come out of it more or less intact.

They'd lingered in Singapore longer than intended. Wilfred had asked his brother to look into the progress of the massive naval base being built on the island. The construction, begun well over a decade before, had been fraught with delays and changes in policy, but had, with the increase in Japanese aggression in the region, been given new priority. Rowland was not sure of the exact nature of Wilfred's interest in the massive dry dock, but he had toured the facility, gaining access via his brother's connections, and reported back as asked. It had not been uninteresting, and he had found himself fascinated with the engineering might behind the build.

Throughout their time in Singapore, the Raffles Hotel had provided a very comfortable place of repose, with pleasant evenings of cards and conversation fuelled by gin-slings, but Rowland had been ready to go home for some time. Of course that was impossible now. He reached into his other pocket and extracted the telegram he had received at the same time as Wilfred's letter. The thin paper was creased, crumpled in grief and shock. But now here, alone, he allowed the impact of its message to wind him with loss.

A tentative knock on the door to the suite, was followed by a head peering cautiously around it—long hair for a man, dark features, and a white dinner jacket embellished with a feathered buttonhole of the flamboyant wearer's own making. "Rowly, are you alone?" Milton Isaacs came in. The poet shook his head in disgust to find that Rowland was indeed on his own. "Where is—?"

Rowland's gaze remained fixed on the impending squall. "I accompanied Lady Woolridge to her room and said good-night," he replied vaguely. He'd been handed both envelopes as he and Persephone Woolridge had left the Long Bar in search of somewhere more private. Naturally, Rowland had read the telegram immediately. And Persephone had been somewhat unhappy when he'd withdrawn from their plans for the evening.

Milton heard something in Rowland's voice that startled him. He noticed now the distinctive pink leaf of telegram paper. "What's happened?"

Two more people entered the suite before Rowland could answer, laughing as they stepped into the room.

Brawny Clyde Watson Jones, who even after all these years in Rowland Sinclair's company looked out of place in formal attire—his sun-lined face spoke of a much harder life than that experienced in the luxury of hotels such as Raffles—and Miss Edna Higgins, the beautiful, uninhibited sculptress who had been Rowland's muse since the day they met. They made up the rest of Rowland's party—a tight, loyal set who lived and created and played together under the benevolence and almost incomprehensible wealth of the Sinclairs. It was not to any of their minds an uneven relationship. They all shared everything they had, it was just that Rowland had so much more.

Milton shot Clyde a glance. Something was wrong. Edna didn't need Milton's warning. She sensed it immediately. The laughter fell silent, and she unhooked her arm from Clyde's to go to Rowland. She reached up to turn his face towards hers. Rowland's dark blue eyes seemed grey—like the storm; there was a kind of restrained anguish in his face.

"Rowly," Edna said, frightened now, "what is it?" She looked down at the telegram. "Who is it?"

Rowland handed her the page. "Danny."

"Cartwright?" Edna read—*We regret to inform you that Daniel Fullerton Cartwright died this morning...* There was more, but she could not see because of the tears—for Danny Cartwright, who years ago had welcomed them into his home in New York, who had been kind and generous and absurd. And for Rowland, who had known him for years before that and who carried his friendships close to his heart. "Oh, Rowly, I'm so sorry."

He placed his arm around her shoulders.

Clyde took the telegram from Edna, and he and Milton read the notice in dismay.

"Cartwright! God! Had he been ill, Rowly?"

Rowland shook his head. "Not as far as I know. But I haven't had a letter from him in a while."

Milton went to the drinks cabinet to find something that might dull the sharp edge of this news. Daniel Cartwright had been distinctly odd—a Francophile artist who only painted himself—but they had all genuinely liked him. Cartwright had been perhaps five years older than Rowland, thirty-five at the most, fond of comfort and not given to dangerous pursuits. This was most unexpected news.

Edna pulled Rowland in from the balcony onto the settee beside her. He handed her a handkerchief, strangely comforted by the impulsive honesty of her tears. Daniel Cartwright had been a good friend. They'd navigated Oxford society together as outsiders, an American and a Colonial, both despised to some degree. Cartwright had introduced him to painting and, once it had been established that they did not share the same proclivities, to girls. They had not seen each other very often since Cartwright had returned to New York and Rowland to Sydney, but he would miss him nonetheless. Quite terribly.

Milton distributed tall glasses of gin, and raised a sombre toast to the late artist. "Farewell to thee, but not farewell to all my fondest thoughts of thee: Within my heart they still shall dwell; and they shall cheer and comfort me."

Rowland smiled faintly. The words were not Milton's, whose reputation as a poet had been gained through his ability to repurpose the works of the great romantic bards without attribution, guilt, or hesitation. Still the selection was apt. Rowland did have many fond memories of Daniel Cartwright. "Brontë," he said quietly.

For a while they sat silently, until Rowland spoke again. "I must go to America."

"Will you make it for the funeral?" Clyde asked sceptically. Even flying it would take at least two weeks. Two months by ocean liner.

Rowland sighed. "Apparently, Danny cannot be buried till I get there." He nodded at the telegram still in Clyde's hand. "It seems Danny made me his executor."

Clyde looked back at the paper and read beyond the statement that Daniel Cartwright was deceased. The telegram had been despatched by lawyers and informed Mr. Rowland Sinclair that he had been named as the sole executor of Daniel Cartwright's considerable estate. And that Daniel's body could only be released to him. "Did you know about this?"

Rowland shook his head. "No."

"Didn't Danny have any family?" Edna asked. It seemed strange to appoint an old friend who lived abroad.

Rowland frowned. "They're from Boston, I believe." He rubbed his face. "There was a falling out some years ago. I don't know that Danny had a lot to do with them since."

Clyde groaned. "So he appointed you to spite his family?"

"Or to disinherit them," Milton added darkly. "Either way, he's sending you to war."

Edna took Rowland's hand, but she said nothing.

Rowland swirled the gin his glass. His friends were probably right, but what choice did he have? "I don't know why Danny appointed me his executor," he said, draining the glass. "What's more, I've no idea why his body can only be released to me...or who has his body, for that matter. It's all a bit of a blow, to be honest. But I owe Danny a lot, and if this is what he—"

"Of course." Edna pressed his hand. "We have to go."

Milton stood. "I'll speak to the concierge now about booking our passages." He braced Rowland's shoulder as he passed on his way to the door. "I assume you want to fly, comrade?"

Rowland nodded. "You know you don't have to—" he began half-heartedly. He knew they had all been thinking of home lately, and this was his duty alone.

"Danny was a good bloke," Clyde said firmly. "We'd like to send him off, mate. It's the very least we could do."

Chapter Two

Reputation and Character

By William Hersey Davis

The circumstances amid which you live determine your reputation; the truth you believe determines your character.

Reputation is what you are supposed to be; character is what you are.

Reputation is the photograph; character is the face.

Reputation is a manufactured thing, rolled and plated and hammered and brazed and bolted; character is a growth.

Reputation comes over one from without; character grows up from within.

Reputation is what you have when you come to a new community; character is what you have when you go away.

Your reputation is learned in an hour; your character does not come to light for a year.

Reputation is made in a moment; character is built in a lifetime.

Reputation grows like the mushroom; character grows like the oak.

Reputation goes like the mushroom; character lasts like eternity.

A single newspaper report gives you your reputation; a life of toil gives you your character.

If you want to get a position, you need a reputation; if you want to keep it, you need a character.

Reputation makes you rich or makes you poor; character makes you happy or makes you miserable.

Reputation is what men say about you on your tombstone; character is what the angels say about you before the throne of God.

Reputation is the basis of the temporal judgment of men; character is the basis of the eternal judgment of God.

—*Word and Way*
(Kansas City, Missouri), January 3, 1935

The Douglas DC-2—American Airlines' daily flight from New York—touched down at the East Boston Airfield and taxied to a stop. Four Australians disembarked for the last time after a journey which had brought them from Singapore in a series of hops. Still, it had taken only fourteen days.

Rowland was the first to step out onto the muddy airfield and turned to offer Edna his hand. The autumn wind was bracing and cut like a wet lash. Edna clamped a sage-green cloche to her head and smiled as she accepted his hand. Rowland inhaled. In the grey of the day, she was sunshine. Warm, and welcome, and belonging to no man.

Clyde and Milton climbed out of the DC-2's cabin. Milton nudged Edna down the steps. "Hurry up, Ed. It's too wet to make an entrance."

Edna rolled her eyes, but she made her way down the last two rungs quickly. Rowland held his umbrella out to shield her from the rain, and they proceeded into the airport building, invigorated by the fact that there was no new leg on which to embark, that they would sleep that night in beds.

There was a party to receive them at the airport. Rowland was surprised by just how many gentlemen were lined up to shake their hands and welcome them to Boston. He had expected one of Daniel Cartwright's lawyers to meet them, perhaps two, but this was a reception committee in great coats and scarves. The first to introduce himself was a gentleman of advanced years who sported the mutton-chop whiskers that had been popular in the previous century. Oliver Burr of Burr, Mayfair and Wilkes, who had once had the privilege of representing the late Mr. Cartwright and now discharged that duty for his estate. He introduced John Mayfair, Lawrence Wilkes, George Burden, and Percy Herbert, all of whom had some experience dealing with Mr. Cartwright's holdings and would be at Rowland Sinclair's disposal in the administration of the estate. Rowland introduced his companions.

"We took the liberty of making reservations for you at the Copley Plaza Hotel," Burr said. "I'm sure you'll find it very comfortable."

Rowland thanked him. He'd not been to Boston before, and they'd embarked from Singapore so quickly that there'd been no time to make arrangements. Cartwright had based himself in New York for as long as Rowland had known him and had rarely even spoken of Boston. When he had, it had been brief and with bitterness. They'd never discussed the falling out which seemed to have estranged him from his hometown and his family.

Perhaps it was that which had connected Rowland and Daniel Cartwright so strongly—they'd both been exiles. Rowland had been sent to England, and Cartwright, it seemed, had fled to it.

They were shown to waiting cars. Uniformed chauffeurs jumped out to load luggage and open doors. Clyde and Milton went in the first; Edna and Rowland climbed into the second with Oliver Burr.

"Tell me, Mr. Burr," Rowland said slowly as the Buick pulled out, "how did Danny die?"

Burr cleared his throat and glanced nervously at Edna. "Perhaps this is not a conversation suited to present company, Mr. Sinclair."

"Please do not be concerned about my constitution, Mr. Burr," Edna insisted. "It is not as delicate as you might expect, and we have all been wondering what happened to poor Mr. Cartwright. He was not an old man."

"No, indeed he was not, Miss Higgins." Burr turned again to Rowland, as if he was looking for leave.

"Was he ill?" Edna pressed.

"Mr. Cartwright's body was found beside the Charles River." Rowland tensed. "He drowned?"

"No, sir. It appears he was shot."

A moment. "By whom?" Rowland asked.

Burr shook his head. "A vagrant, perhaps, or a tramp, or a robber of some sort who waylaid Mr. Cartwright."

"I take it that no one has been arrested, Mr. Burr?"

"I fear not, Mr. Sinclair."

Rowland exhaled. He wasn't sure what he'd thought, what he'd hoped about the manner in which his old friend had died. The anger that had lurked unsaid since the first telegram had reached him, that had been held in check by grief, seemed to focus now on an unknown murderer. He could feel the press of Edna's palm against his, a reminder that she was there. "Do the police have any suspects at all, Mr. Burr?"

"We are not privy to that, Mr. Sinclair, but if you wish, we can arrange for you to talk to the detective in charge of the case."

"I do wish that."

Rowland looked out the window. They were crossing a bridge. He shook his head. "Forgive me, Mr. Burr. This news is something of a shock."

"Of course," Burr said gravely.

"Do you have any reason to believe Mr. Cartwright was concerned for his safety?" Rowland asked suddenly.

Burr was startled. "No," he said carefully. "But you must understand, Burr, Mayfair and Wilkes were the late gentleman's attorneys, not his confidants. I can tell you that if Mr. Cartwright was concerned, he did not respond to that concern by putting his affairs in order."

"He died intestate?" Rowland asked confused.

"Not at all. I didn't mean to imply..." Burr sighed. "You may find, Mr. Sinclair, that the family—and we are talking about one of Boston's best families—are somewhat surprised by the fact that the late Mr. Cartwright named you as his executor."

"How long ago did Mr. Cartwright make his will?" Rowland asked.

"Mr. Cartwright finalised his most recent will and testament two months ago"—Burr guessed what Rowland was thinking—"at which time he appointed you his executor."

Rowland decided to just ask. "Do you have any idea why, Mr. Burr?"

Burr stroked his whiskers. "He was adamant it be you. To be honest, I advised Mr. Cartwright that a member of his family or even a Boston-based firm might be a more practical and judicious choice, but he would have none of it." The solicitor removed his spectacles and misted them with his breath. "To be frank, he trusted you, Mr. Sinclair."

"Are you telling me there was no one else he could trust, Mr. Burr?"

"I expect Mr. Cartwright did not believe so."

Rowland heard Edna inhale. "That's so very sad," the sculptress said softly.

They had turned into Arlington Street and were now proceeding past the Boston Public Garden in the heart of the city. For a while they kept their own counsel. Rowland was struck by a sense of having failed his friend already. If he had known that he had been made Cartwright's executor, he might have recognised that there was something wrong.

Copley Plaza was in the Boston district of Back Bay. The grand public square was bordered by some of Boston's most prestigious and beautiful buildings, among which the Copley Plaza Hotel was not embarrassed.

The Buicks pulled up and the lawyers accompanied them into the hotel foyer.

"The Copley was raised on what was originally the site of the Museum of Fine Arts and named to honour John Singleton Copley, the eminent American portrait artist," Burr said as they walked through the entrance hallway into a vast lobby with a high coffered ceiling, gilded and painted with clouds and sky. "Mr. Cartwright thought you'd find it fitting?"

"Danny?" Rowland asked perplexed.

"Mr. Cartwright left instructions that should we ever have call to find you, then we were to put you up here. All accommodation, costs, and expenses will naturally be borne by the estate."

Rowland smiled faintly. It did sound like the kind of ridiculous thing with which Daniel would concern himself. Rowland took in the marble columns, the matching Empire-style crystal chandeliers. In them, he could see his old friend's love of opulence and detail.

Burr, Mayfair and Wilkes had arranged two adjoining suites on their behalf. Once they'd checked in, Oliver Burr requested a moment, for which he arranged a private room off the foyer. Therein Percy Herbert produced a tape measure and took their measurements. "We expect you did not have the time or opportunity to acquire attire for the funeral," Burr explained. "With your permission, we have tailors and dressmakers standing by to alter appropriate garments for your use and convenience."

"Oh...yes," Rowland said, as Edna commandeered the tape from a flustered Herbert and took her own measurements. Burr was right, of course. They had been travelling in the tropics. They did not have attire suitable for a funeral in the Boston autumn. "That's remarkably thoughtful, sir. Thank you."

Burr held out a briefcase. "Some documents for your perusal. I've taken the liberty of outlining the particulars of the Cartwright estate and holdings," he said. "You'll find a copy of Mr. Cartwright's last will and testament. The family is already in Boston, so if you have no objection, we'll schedule the official reading tomorrow, immediately after the funeral."

"The funeral is tomorrow?"

"Mr. Cartwright has been deceased for over a month. We thought—"

"Yes, by all means. Danny should be laid to rest as soon as possible."

"We presume you will want to deliver the eulogy."

"His brothers—"

"Have declined."

Rowland breathed. "Then, yes." He took the briefcase from Burr. "I should express my condolences to the family personally, in any case."

"There are also a number of letters, one addressed to you. They were on the tray, for posting when Mr. Cartwright died. His butler was unsure what to do and so they have been retained as part of the estate."

"Thank you, Mr. Burr. I shall attend to them directly."

Burr nodded approvingly. The lawyer had feared that his client's mysterious executor would prove to be a fool, or indolent, or at the very least reluctant. But Sinclair appeared none of those things, and he seemed genuinely grieved by the loss of Daniel Cartwright. "You will doubtless have questions, Mr. Sinclair. I shall return tomorrow to answer them if I can." He turned to include Edna, Milton, and Clyde. "We'll leave you to get settled." He handed Rowland a card. "If there is anything at all. Good evening, Miss Higgins, gentlemen."

The gentlemen of Burr, Mayfair and Wilkes offered their hands and good wishes in turn, and returned to the Buicks, leaving the concierge to take the Australians to their suites. Each of the premier suites had two bedrooms, a spacious sitting and dining room, and a study, all furnished in a manner that was as elegant if more subtle than they had seen in the spectacular foyer. The suites were connected by a door which Edna wedged open before they selected their bedrooms. Bellhops brought up their trunks; chambermaids unpacked with practiced efficiency, and soon the wardrobes were hung with suits and shirts and, in Edna's bedroom, frocks and gowns. Some items were sent for pressing and shoes put out for polishing. It was something of a quiet relief when the staff finally departed, having seen to the settling in of the Copley Plaza's Australian guests.

Rowland observed the square through the window. Boston in the late afternoon: city workers heading home— collars turned up, metered strides; couples strolling arm in arm, leaning into each other against the late autumn chill; the architectural magnificence of Trinity Church. It was the kind of outlook he preferred to water or mountain views. A vista of human life. But today his gaze was directed more out of habit than any real interest, his mind preoccupied.

He opened the letter that Burr had given him, and read the florid and familiar hand of Daniel Cartwright.

"Mon ami."

The American had delighted in the French language, though its correct usage had often eluded him. The salutation was followed by a confession.

"Je suis ivre, Rowly." (I am drunk right now, Rowly.)

As Rowland read, his memory gave Cartwright's voice to the words. He was still reading when he heard a sharp tapping on the suite's door. Clyde had admitted the callers before he looked up.

Two gentlemen, grey double-breasted suits, wing-tipped shoes. One carried the silver-handled walking stick he'd used to announce their arrival. His hair had receded quite severely, a fact he sought to disguise by combing long strands over the naked territory. Even so, he was the younger, a year or two older than Rowland at most. The other had a full head of ash grey hair, a small moustache to match.

Rowland slipped Cartwright's letter into his breast pocket.

"Geoffrey Cartwright, sir," said the younger. "My brother, Frank. We are—"

"Danny's brothers," Rowland finished. He offered his hand. "Rowland Sinclair. How d'you do? My sincere condolences, gentlemen. Danny was an outstanding chap. I will... I do miss him."

The Cartwrights accepted his commiserations, and those of his companions.

"You were all acquainted with Danny?" Frank ventured uncertainly.

"We all enjoyed the hospitality of your late brother in New York, Mr. Cartwright," Edna said gently.

"We wonder if we might have a word, Sinclair," Geoffrey Cartwright said brusquely.

"Certainly." Rowland invited them to take seats and offered the customary liquid refreshments. They took the former and declined the latter.

"This is a matter of some sensitivity," Frank said, looking pointedly at Edna and then moving that gaze to Milton and Clyde.

"If you'll excuse me, I must finish unpacking," Edna said diplomatically. Clyde followed suit, but Milton remained in his seat with a glass of Scotch, until Edna, exasperated, asked him to assist her with her trunk. The poet obliged reluctantly. He had always been predisposed to distrust the establishment and he suspected that the purpose of the Cartwright brothers' visit was not necessarily friendly. There was an air of disgust in the way they regarded Rowland Sinclair that Milton recognised. It probably had a different cause, of course, but it made the poet uneasy nonetheless.

All this, Rowland didn't seem to notice. "Is there anything in particular you wish to discuss, gentlemen?"

"May we speak frankly, sir?"

"You may."

"It is our opinion that our dear brother was not in his right mind, that he had succumbed to certain weaknesses of character and the influence of degenerates—in particular, degenerate men."

Rowland sat back. "I see."

"We would like to inspect and verify our brother's last will."

"As I'm sure Mr. Burr has informed you," Rowland replied evenly, "the details of Danny's will shall be read tomorrow."

"Let me ask you this, Sinclair." Geoffrey pressed his fingertips together. "How exactly do you intend to distribute my brother's estate?"

Rowland regarded him, a single brow arched quizzically. "I intend to distribute it according to his instructions, Mr. Cartwright."

"And if those instructions are perverse?"

"As I understand it, gentlemen, my own opinion of his instructions is irrelevant. My duty is simply to implement them."

Frank sat back in his armchair. "You should know that we will not stand for this."

"Stand for what, exactly?"

Geoffrey sighed. "We have no desire to besmirch your reputation, Sinclair. Nor Danny's, such as it is."

"I'm not sure I understand, gentlemen."

"Do you not?" Frank snarled.

Rowland's face gave nothing away. "Are you threatening me, Mr. Cartwright?"

"We are, sir!"

"With what, precisely?"

"With exposure! With ruin!" Frank emphasised each with his fist against the scrolled arm of the chair. "The world would know what you are."

Rowland did not flinch. He did not ask what the Cartwrights believed they might expose. "Gentlemen, as you may imagine, it's been a long journey, and we have only just arrived in Boston. Again, my condolences for the loss of your brother, who in my opinion was the best of men." He stood. "I look forward to seeing you tomorrow. In the meantime, please feel at liberty to direct any enquiries to Burr, Mayfair and Wilkes."

For a moment the Cartwrights did not move, and the carriage clock on the mantle counted the passing moments, the ratcheting tension.

Finally, they stood. "Consider your position carefully, Sinclair," Geoffrey warned. "We will not allow Danny's weakness to alienate a rightful succession, to destroy what has been built by proud, God-fearing, and honourable men, who were among the founders of this nation."

"Good evening, gentlemen." Rowland's tone was calm, even pleasant, but in his eyes glinted the blue fury that had characterised the Sinclair men for generations. He watched silently as they departed with no further word of farewell.

Milton was right—Daniel Cartwright had sent him to war.

Chapter Three

NO MORE EULOGIES.

American editors are, as a rule, fond of blunt talk, but none of them can beat the editor of the "Purcell (Okla.) Call" in rubbing the ginger in. This is how he does it in a recent Issue:—

"The average country editor is a chump. He will submit to the abuse of some old, miserly skin-flint or Shylock in the community for years, and when death in all its merciful kindness removes the worthless old carcass to a place that has possibly been eager and yawning for years to even up his devilish score, Mr. Editor, in lauda-tory language and half-column space, will pour out his sympathy touchingly, yea, pathetically. Not so with the 'Call.' The next old reprobate that shuffles off may die with this troubled fact on his mind, that we are going to everlastingly lambaste him as soon as we have proof that his grouchy life has been snuffed out and he is on his way home. Some of you old reprobates, be you one or many, had better take due notice and come in and 'make good' with us before the last call, for there is not a drop of sentimental hypocrisy or snivelling pretence in our heart."

—*Camperdown Chronicle*, 9 May 1935

∼ᴔ∽

Edna poured coffee from the silver service just delivered to the suite. She added cream and placed the cup and saucer on the small circular table beside Rowland's chair. He looked up for the first time in hours.

Edna smiled. She was in pyjamas—Rowland's, if the monogram on the pocket had any proprietary force. Which of course it did not. The sculptress had been helping herself to the clothes of the gentlemen she lived with for years, sleeping in Rowland's pyjamas and working in Milton's shirts. Rowland glanced at his watch. It was late.

"What are you doing up?" he asked sipping the coffee, closing his eyes briefly as the hot, dark liquid soothed the weariness behind them.

Edna added sugar to her own cup and curled up in the armchair opposite him. "Is there anything I can do to help, Rowly?"

He shook his head. "I'm just trying to get through all the papers Burr left me to read."

"Can it wait till morning?"

"Probably. But I can't sleep."

"Have you tried?"

Rowland reached for the coffee pot and poured himself another cup. "This is a real mess, Ed."

"One of Danny's brothers looked old."

"That was Frank. He's Wil's age, I believe. Wil might object to you calling him old."

"So why did Danny control the Cartwright wealth?" Edna asked. "Doesn't that responsibility usually fall to the firstborn?"

Rowland drained his second coffee and placed the empty cup and saucer on top of the pile of papers he'd been reading. "Danny's father died in 1925. His estate was split, in accordance with his will, among his wife, his three sons, and one daughter—Molly. Geoffrey, Molly, and their mother all entrusted their inheritances to the steady financial hand of Frank. Frank invested it, and his own fortune in the stock market...which was all well and good till 1929."

Edna gasped. "The crash?"

Rowland nodded. "It seems the Cartwrights, aside from Danny, lost everything—probably everything and more. Danny had made his own investments, which apparently did well. Rather well, in fact. It seems Danny was very astute. He's been financing them all since, which I suppose is why they're so concerned about who'll get what."

Edna frowned. If Wilfred Sinclair were to die, she could not imagine that the contents of his will would be foremost on Rowland's mind. "Did Danny's brothers say anything about who might have killed him?" she asked tentatively.

"No. They didn't seem particularly concerned about that."

"Are you sure there's nothing I can do to help?" Edna looked at the small tower of documents Rowland had yet to read.

Rowland sighed. "Not really. It's all a bit miserable." He shook his head. "You should go to bed."

Edna nodded. But she couldn't leave him to deal with it all alone, not without at least trying to soften his sadness somehow. "How about we just talk about Danny?"

He smiled faintly. "What do you want to know, Ed?"

"I don't need to know anything, Rowly. I just thought you might like to talk about Danny."

He said nothing for a beat, and then, "Actually, I should perhaps tell you all. It might just blow up tomorrow." He exhaled. "Are Milt and Clyde asleep?"

Alarmed, Edna left her chair so that she could move to the arm of his. "Yes." She took his hand. "Why don't you tell me, Rowly? I can tell them if you don't want to go through it again."

He kissed her hand. "It's not really that awful, Ed. But it could become awkward. From what Danny's brothers said, I expect it will become awkward."

Edna waited. Though she'd known Rowland for many years, and they were the best of friends, she knew there remained things he'd never talked about.

"I met Danny when I first went up to Oxford. He'd been there for a couple of years by then." Rowland smiled faintly as he remembered. "He took me under his wing, I guess, kept me from making social mistakes that may have proved quite disastrous. The English can be particular."

This Edna knew, as she did the fact that Rowland had been young and troubled when he arrived at the English university in the midst of the years he'd spent in exile after his father's death. Daniel Cartwright's friendship had probably been timely, and valued.

"I know Danny was a little eccentric, but he was a good man, Ed, and a good friend. I was really homesick when I arrived at Oxford—I felt like Wil had sent me to England and forgotten me. I was miserable and angry and quite lost." His mouth quirked. "And then I met this loud, ridiculous American who dressed like a character from a regency novel and spoke the worst French I'd ever heard. We rubbed along famously until..." Rowland grimaced—there was no delicate way to put it—"Danny confessed he was in love with me."

"Oh." Edna was more interested than shocked. She had always assumed Daniel Cartwright had an eye for gentlemen, and consequently she did not find it surprising that a man as handsome as Rowland might have drawn his gaze. "How did you respond?"

"Disgracefully." Rowland shook his head. "Childishly. For some reason, I was terrified. I punched him."

"Oh, Rowly." She stroked the hair back from his face. "Clearly, he forgave you."

"Yes. He was very good about it. Declared he could forgive my breaking his heart but not his nose." Rowland smiled wryly. "I hadn't actually broken his nose."

"But he remained in love with you?"

"No, I don't think so. There were many chaps after that."

"He made you his executor, though."

"He had other reasons for that." Rowland exhaled. "Danny's left most of his estate to a gentleman called Otis Norcross. I expect he made me his executor to ensure the gift stood."

"Why wouldn't it stand?"

"Danny's brothers already suspect that his will does not favour them. I suspect they'll take action to defeat the bequest." Rowland rubbed his face. "That's why he couldn't trust either of them to administer his estate, I suppose."

Edna watched him, moved by his sadness.

"Do you know this Otis Norcross, Rowly? Was he at Oxford with you and Danny?"

Rowland shook his head. "If he was, we were never introduced. Mr. Burr hasn't been able to contact him as yet."

"Did Danny never mention him in his letters?"

"I'm afraid not. As such, Mr. Norcross is something of a mystery."

"It's probably not surprising."

Rowland looked up. "What do you mean?"

"Danny was murdered, Rowly. Perhaps he's scared."

Rowland groaned. "Of course." The letter. He took it

from the breast pocket of his jacket and handed it to Edna. "This is the letter Mr. Burr gave me earlier—the one that hadn't been posted. Danny wrote it not long before he died." Edna opened the folded page. She smiled as she read the opening salutation.

The first paragraphs were rambling declarations of *amitié profonde* and trust. "You are a rare creature among men, Rowland Sinclair—a man who is willing to let another man be, who does not question another's heart."

"As you can see," Rowland said, "he was drunk when he wrote it."

Edna continued to read, and her smile faded.

"But he was also convinced someone was trying to kill him," Rowland said, watching her face carefully. "He wanted to thwart them by making me his executor."

Edna frowned. "But what does he mean? Is he accusing his previous executor of trying to kill him?"

"I'm not sure, Ed." Rowland rubbed his face. "He wants to ensure that the terms of his will are observed."

"Because Otis Norcross was his lover?"

"Maybe. Probably." Rowland pointed to a paragraph. "He wants me to protect his beneficiaries."

"Which means?"

"Otis Norcross probably values his reputation. And Daniel's brothers are going to do everything they can to defeat this will."

"Can they? Defeat it, I mean?"

"I don't know. They could try to have him ruled incompetent, I guess."

"Will they succeed?"

"People have been committed for Danny's preferences, Ed."

Edna shook her head. "That's abominable."

"Yes."

Edna stopped him before he reached for a third cup of

coffee. "Rowly, you're exhausted." She took his hand and pulled him to his feet. "Go to bed. I suspect tomorrow will be a long day."

Rowland glanced back at the files he'd been reading. He hadn't taken anything in for several pages. "I have to write a eulogy," he said.

Edna smiled. "I don't think you're going to come up with anything particularly coherent now. Get some sleep, Rowly—we'll deal with tomorrow's problems tomorrow."

Rowland awoke to the sound of his companions at breakfast. He'd slept soundly, dreamlessly. For a few moments he lay in bed listening to Edna shushing Clyde and Milton with a warning that he was still asleep. He glanced at his watch and groaned. It was nearly eight.

He opened the door and stepped out into the drawing room in order to tell them that whispering was no longer necessary. He stopped, somewhat startled. The young woman who sat at the small dining table with Edna was elegant, immaculately attired in a black skirt suit. Her short dark hair was tucked beneath a pillbox hat with a short veil, and Rowland had never seen her before in his life. "Good...morning," he said, aware that he was receiving her in a robe and pyjamas.

Edna looked up from a cup of tea and smiled. "You look much better!"

"Ed made us let you sleep late." Clyde abdicated responsibility from the outset.

Edna ignored him. "This is Miss Molly Cartwright, Rowly."

The young woman offered him a gloved hand. "Danny was my big brother—my dear brother."

"My sincere condolences, Miss Cartwright." Rowland shook her hand. "I'm afraid I—"

"Oh, you mustn't be embarrassed!" she said emphatically. "I came unannounced and obscenely early. I just wanted to catch you before my brothers did."

"Why don't you go and get dressed, Rowly?" Edna suggested. "We can entertain Molly until then."

"Yes, please do," Molly urged. "I didn't mean to be such an inconvenience, and I'm having a lovely time conversing with your friends."

Rowland showered quickly, shaved, and put on the black suit which had apparently been delivered to the suite early that morning. It was well cut—a bespoke single-breasted three-piece suit, much like any he might have commissioned for himself. He was surprised and not a little impressed by the lawyer's tailors. He would possibly need them. They'd been limited with luggage on the flights, and it would be a few weeks before the trunks they'd sent by sea caught up with them. He slung the black silk tie which had been delivered with the suit around his neck, and tied his customary Windsor knot with practised speed, combing back still-damp dark hair with his fingers before he joined the gathering in the dining room.

Covered trays of codfish cakes and bacon, bowls of fresh fruit, and silver pots of coffee had been delivered in his absence. He took the seat that had been left for him between Edna and Molly Cartwright, and apologised that he'd not been up when she first arrived.

"Nonsense," Molly said. "It's frightfully common to call on a gentleman before noon. I wouldn't have done so if I wasn't in a lather that Geoffrey and Frank would get here first and scare you off."

Rowland smiled. "Your brothers stopped by last evening—"

Molly gasped. "Well, allow me to apologise, Mr. Sinclair. They've got some insane notion that Danny left everything to me!"

"There's no need to apologise, I assure you." Rowland avoided being drawn on the nature of his conversation with the brothers Cartwright. "Would it be indelicate of me to ask about Danny?"

Molly's brow arched shrewdly. "You mean about how he died...who killed him?"

Rowland was a little startled, but he didn't hesitate. It was what he'd meant. "Yes."

"Danny's body was found on the banks of the Charles River." Molly's eyes clouded. "He'd been shot—three times in the chest, once in the head."

Edna's hand covered her mouth. Clyde flinched. Rowland's eyes held steady.

"He was dressed for dinner. His pocket watch was still in his fob pocket and on its gold chain. His wallet, which contained bills which totalled forty-two dollars, was in the inside breast pocket of his jacket. And he was wearing a diamond ring."

"I see."

"I hope you do, Mr. Sinclair." Molly bit her lower lip to steady it before she continued. "My brother, one of the best men in the world, was brutally murdered, but it was not in the progress of a robbery."

"I agree."

Molly Cartwright stopped, surprised. "You do."

"It seems clear."

Molly smiled at him. Dimples accented warmth.

"Do you know of anyone who'd want to kill Danny?" Edna asked.

Molly turned as if she'd only just realised that she and Rowland weren't alone. "I've been abroad for a couple of years. I know Danny was in love, that, whoever she was, she was leading him on a merry dance. His letters were either ecstatic or heartbroken."

Milton lowered the *Boston Globe*. "The heart will break, but broken live on."

"Byron," Rowland murmured.

"Well, perhaps she..." Molly shuddered and corrected herself. "Perhaps she might know more."

"Do you know her name?"

"Danny only wrote of her as 'my beloved O'."

Milton folded the paper and handed it to Clyde. "Do you know what Danny was doing in Boston, Miss Cartwright? Rowly always said he preferred New York."

Molly nodded. "He did. Swore he'd never return after..."

Milton's eyes narrowed. "After what?"

Molly smiled brightly. "After he left."

"But why did he leave?" Milton pressed.

"To attend Oxford University." She laughed. "He wouldn't even consider another Cambridge, so it had to be Oxford. And that's where he met you, wasn't it, Mr. Sinclair?"

Rowland nodded. "It was. Though Danny had been there a couple of years before I went up."

"He wrote to me about you," Molly said warmly. "Said he was beguiled by your brutish Antipodean ways."

Rowland laughed. "That sounds like Danny, though I have no idea what he was talking about."

"He said you were a pugilist, had a phenomenal left hook."

Rowland poured more coffee. "I did box for a while."

"I'm glad Danny made you his executor so that we may all meet you at last."

"Your brothers didn't seem to be particularly pleased to make my acquaintance."

"Oh, they're being positively tiresome. You mustn't pay them any mind. They like to live under the illusion that they're in charge now."

"In charge of what?" Edna asked, helping herself to codfish cakes and bacon.

"Oh, everything. Danny was the cleverest of us, you see. He looked after everything, was in charge of everything."

Edna understood. The Sinclairs, to her observance, had a similar arrangement, with all the considerable power of the family being vested in Wilfred Sinclair. But that was not something with which Rowland was unhappy. She doubted that Geoffrey and Frank Cartwright were similarly content, especially now, when it seemed Danny had chosen an outsider over his own brothers to administer his affairs.

They finished breakfast, and as Molly Cartwright rose to take her leave, the gentlemen stood in response. "Can I ask you all to not mention my visit to my brothers? I'm sure they'd deem it improper."

"Of course," Rowland replied. "May I see you home?"

"That's very kind, Mr. Sinclair, but I have a car waiting." Molly gazed up at him. "Though you may walk me down, if you'd care to do so."

Rowland grabbed his hat from the rack by the door while Molly farewelled the others, thanking them for breakfast and their company, looking forward to their next meeting, and urging them to enjoy Boston. Rowland smiled as he recognised the natural exuberance that had been so much a part of his old friend. Danny had never said a great deal about his sister; in fact, he'd said very little about his family at all. Despite this, it seemed to Rowland that Danny's relationship with Molly had been close.

He escorted her down to the foyer of the Copley and then waited with her till the valet brought round a PD Plymouth convertible.

Molly slipped him her card. "Please don't hesitate to call if you should need anything at all."

"Thank you, Miss Cartwright."

"Molly," she insisted. "I have seen you in your pyjamas!" Her eyes were bright and mischievous. "Surely, having already allowed standards to slip so shockingly, we can throw propriety to the wind and use our Christian names?"

"I expect we can. It's been a pleasure to meet you, Molly. And again, my condolences."

She hesitated for a moment. "You'll remember that Danny was murdered, won't you, Rowly?"

"It's not something I can forget."

Chapter Four

GROWING BIGGER.

HARVARD UNIVERSITY MEN

Studies made at Harvard University of the measurements of three generations of Harvard men, including 2000 pairs of fathers and sons, and of 501 mothers and daughters in three generations of Wellesley, Vassar, Smith, and Mount Holyoke graduates, disclose a marked tendency of University men and women to grow taller, broader shouldered, narrower hipped, and heavier, says the New York correspondent of the London "Times."

The results of the studies, which were made by Mr. Gordon Bowles, of Tokyo, a graduate student in anthropology, under the auspices of the Museum of Comparative Zoology, were made public in Cambridge.

According to the report the present generation of Harvard students, whose fathers and grandfathers were Harvard men, is one of the tallest groups in the world. It averages in height 5ft. 10.1 in. and the annual Increase in stature has been at the rate of about 1 in. every 32 years over a period of 50 years. The sons are more than 8lb. heavier than were their fathers at approximately the same age.

—*Queensland Times,* 23 July 1931

∾⟨Ǝ⟩∾

"Did you tell her?" Edna whispered when Rowland returned to the suite.

"Tell her what, Ed?"

"That 'my beloved O' is Otis Norcross."

He grimaced. "I don't know that it is, not absolutely."

Edna's brow arched sceptically, but she let the matter be.

"You met Danny at Oxford, didn't you?" Milton said, pulling thoughtfully at his goatee.

"Yes."

"I don't suppose he attended Harvard as well?"

"Harvard?" Rowland shook his head. "No, he was an Oxford man through and through. To be honest, Danny could be quite pompous about its superiority." He regarded the poet curiously. "Why do you ask?"

Milton opened the paper again and directed Rowland's attention to a picture in the social pages. "Isn't that one of the blokes who came by last night?"

The photograph, taken at what was apparently the ten-year reunion of Harvard's class of 1922, did indeed include Geoffrey Cartwright. "Aren't your lot usually particular about what school tie you wear? The whole family singing the same school song and all that?"

Rowland studied the picture. Daniel Cartwright had, throughout their friendship, compared Oxford positively to Harvard many times. In fact, his opinion of the American university had been quite vitriolic. Rowland had assumed the prejudice was familial, an elite yearning for empire, despite their American independence. But perhaps it had been born of simple sibling rivalry.

"I attended a different university from my brothers," he pointed out.

"Only because Wilfred shipped you off to England to prevent you being arrested."

Rowland didn't reply. Milton spoke the truth.

"Maybe Danny was shipped off too." Clyde shrugged. "But what makes you reckon he went to Harvard first?"

"Molly Cartwright said Danny would not even consider *another* Cambridge," Milton replied. "I thought it was strange when she said it. But Harvard's across the river in a city called Cambridge, I believe. Maybe that's what she meant."

Clyde laughed. "She was talking about the rivalry between Oxford and Cambridge University, you fool."

"She said 'another.'"

"Conan Doyle has gone to your head, Isaacs!"

"Does it matter if he went to Harvard?" Edna asked as the argument began. Clyde and Milton were prone to bicker about inconsequential things.

"Danny was murdered," Milton said. "Everything matters."

❧

Rowland broached the subject of the eulogy quite awkwardly while sharing the back seat of the lead automobile with Daniel's lawyer, Oliver Burr. They were travelling in convoy to the Mount Auburn Cemetery in Cambridge, about four miles east of Boston, to bury Daniel Cartwright. The graveside service was not due to begin for another hour, but Rowland and the gentlemen of Burr, Wilkes and Mayfair had decided to arrive early in the hope that Otis Norcross might attend. They had no way of recognising the man, but Rowland hoped that by introducing themselves to arriving mourners, they might have some luck.

"I'm afraid I don't know a great deal about Danny's background," Rowland admitted. "He was at Oxford when we met and he didn't really... I'm a little concerned my eulogy might be a bit patchy."

Oliver Burr gave the matter a moment's contemplation before he said, "I regret, Mr. Sinclair, it's a little late to fully rectify that situation." He scribbled several lines in a notebook and handed the leaf to Rowland. "A few biographical details as I remember them. I'm sure you'll do Mr. Cartwright justice."

Rowland glanced at the page. Date and place of birth, education, and net worth. He doubted the place of the last item in a eulogy. Danny's age did not surprise—as much as his old friend had been coy about the subject—nor the fact that he was born in Boston, but a detail on the next line did stop Rowland short.

"Danny attended Harvard?"

"Just for a year and as a freshman—in 1920, I believe. He completed his studies at Oxford."

So Milton had been right. "He didn't ever mention that he'd studied at Harvard," Rowland said, though more to himself than Burr.

"I expect Mr. Cartwright considered himself an Oxford man." Burr shrugged. "People can be quite particular about allegiances, and there are certain people who still elevate English institutions." He frowned, clearly disapproving of such bigotry. "I'm a Yale man, myself."

A rural garden cemetery, Mount Auburn was a landscape of tranquil meadows and rolling hills. They passed through Egyptian-style gates, and left the vehicles in the cemetery parking lot before finding their way to the Cartwright family plot into which Danny was to be interred. Gentle paths wound through secluded stands of trees and past classical monuments and graves. Mid-autumn colour added a visual vibrancy to this place of rest.

Rowland turned up the collar of his overcoat against a wind which whispered of a New England winter. Though Daniel Cartwright had not been a landscape artist, he would have appreciated the natural beauty of this place—considered it a fitting backdrop for another self-portrait.

Burr directed Rowland to the open grave which had been ready to receive Cartwright. Daniel was to be buried on the far end of the family plot. The site had been chosen by his siblings, and as much as Rowland was struck by the stark separation of the location, he knew also that the selection was a matter for the Cartwrights. The position on the hillside did offer a grand panoramic view over the city of Boston.

Burr introduced him to the Episcopal priest who would conduct the burial service. Reverend Hawkins shook Rowland's hand, closing his other hand over the top.

"Very good of you to come, Mr. Sinclair. Am I to understand you hail from the Antipodes?"

"Yes, sir."

"Well, never mind. We are, all of us, sinners."

Rowland blinked. He decided not to enquire.

The reverend outlined the order of service. Rowland was a little startled by its sparseness. A couple of prayers and his eulogy. It was starkly simple for a man who had loved flourish. But he said nothing. It was not for him to tell the Cartwrights how they could commemorate their brother.

Even as he exchanged pleasantries with the minister,

Rowland noticed a man watching proceedings from the trees. He excused himself and walked in that direction. He extended his hand as he approached. "I say, are you looking for the Cartwright burial?"

The man looked uneasy. "I was just passing."

Rowland regarded him closely. The man was probably in his thirties but his hair was white and in need of a cut. His suit was relatively new, but quite dishevelled—as if he had slept in it, and his face...his face was a picture of grief and confusion. He took the hand Rowland offered.

"Rowland Sinclair. How d'you do, Mr...?"

"I do well enough, Mr. Sinclair."

Gathering that the man was not going to volunteer his name, Rowland asked, "Were you acquainted with Mr. Cartwright?"

"No, just passing. You're British?"

"No, Australian."

"Why are you here?"

Rowland was a little wrong-footed by the question. "I'm burying my friend, sir. Why are you here?"

The man shrugged, his face clouding defiantly. "What's it to you?"

"Are you by any chance, Otis Norcross?"

The man looked at him sharply and stepped back. "What do you want with Otis Norcross, Mr. Sinclair?" His eyes moved past Rowland's shoulder to the gentlemen of Burr, Mayfair and Wilkes, who waited by the open grave. He turned to go.

Rowland grabbed his arm. "Please wait..."

The swing caught him by surprise. A fist met Rowland's jaw with force enough to propel him back and allow his assailant to break free and run. The lawyers shouted as they gave half-hearted chase. Rowland took a handkerchief from his pocket and wiped the blood from his lip. He was more perplexed than injured or even outraged by the assault.

Oliver Burr reached him, panting. "By Jove! Are you all right there, Mr. Sinclair?"

"I'm quite well, Mr. Burr."

"Who was that scoundrel?"

"I'm not sure. He was a little less than receptive to my enquiries."

The lawyers who had given chase returned. It seemed their quarry had escaped into the tranquil woodlands of Mount Auburn.

"He may have been some ne'er-do-well intent on picking the pockets of mourners," Burr said, scowling.

"Possibly," Rowland agreed. "Perhaps I was too eager for him to be Otis Norcross."

Burr sighed. "It would have been rather convenient if he was."

Funeral-goers were now beginning to arrive, an elegance of society and better families in black.

"Otis Norcross may still be here," Burr said optimistically. "It's just a matter of making his acquaintance." The lawyer handed Rowland an umbrella. "I expect the weather is about to turn," he said, glancing skyward.

Rowland spotted Edna standing with Milton and Clyde on the fringe of the gathering and adjusting the latter's tie. Ties had never sat particularly well around Clyde's neck.

"Hello, Rowly." Edna smiled as he approached.

"Any luck, mate?" Clyde asked.

Rowland shook his head. "Not as yet."

"We've been milling around with Ed," Milton said quietly. "Plenty of men very keen to introduce themselves, but, at this time, no Otis Norcross."

Rowland's brow twitched. "You're using Ed as bait."

"It would have happened, regardless," Milton replied, unrepentant. "We're just paying more attention to the names of the fellows vying for her attention. Lots of Putnams, Cabots, and Lowells, but no Norcrosses."

"The Cartwrights have arrived," Edna said, directing their gazes. "I expect the hearse will be here soon."

"Have you got the eulogy sorted, Rowly?" Clyde asked somewhat tentatively. He was aware that Rowland was not one for making speeches at the best of times, and these circumstances were far from the best of times.

Rowland grimaced. "I've been trying not to think about it."

Edna took his hand. "Just talk about Daniel Cartwright, the artist," she whispered. "It's how he'd want to be remembered."

Rowland nodded. Edna was right, and he couldn't help but note she often was. The hearse pulled up.

Milton's hand gripped Rowland's shoulder. It was time to begin.

Rowland joined the Cartwright brothers, and their second cousins, George and Harvey Buchannan and Percy Hawkins, at the back of the hearse. The gathering fell silent as the vehicle's doors were opened and the oaken coffin pulled out on chrome sliders. The undertaker counted, and on three, the pallbearers heaved in unison to lift Daniel Cartwright's coffin onto their shoulders. A moment to rebalance and to counter the fact that Rowland was somewhat taller than the others, and they began their sombre path to the graveside. The coffin was placed onto the ropes that would ease it into the earth. Geoffrey and Frank took their places beside Molly as principal mourners, and Rowland remained with George Buchannan.

The minister commenced proceedings with a few words appealing to the mercy and forgiveness of the Almighty before he invited Rowland Sinclair to say his piece.

Rowland introduced himself. The silence was tense, hostile. Molly smiled and nodded encouragingly from between the stony visages of her brothers.

Rowland began by explaining how he'd first met Daniel Cartwright, how Cartwright had introduced him to life in Oxford and eventually to painting. As Edna suggested, he spoke about his friend as an artist, the self-portraits for which he was known. "Most artists turn their eyes outward, to models and landscapes, sky and sea; we try to capture beauty and power and tragedy, to create something that contributes to the understanding of the world by the world. Danny was far more ambitious, and he did something that was infinitely more difficult. He sought to understand himself, to see himself; he looked inward for answers. His paintings were honest, and curious, joyful, and compassionate; they confronted demons with acceptance and candour. They were true portraits of their subject. I cannot say what the world has lost with the passing of Daniel Cartwright, I know only that I have lost one of my truest friends."

Rowland stepped back.

"Well said," George Buchannan whispered.

Molly sobbed openly. Neither of her brothers made any move to comfort her.

Daniel Cartwright's coffin was lowered into the earth. Ashes to ashes, dust to dust, and it was done. Frank Cartwright turned and walked away, declaring silently that the service was complete.

Geoffrey hung back, and when the crowd had thinned, he stepped up to Rowland. He shook Rowland's hand, smiling. "Bravo, Sinclair! You made the fact that Danny was only interested in himself sound like a virtue. And made your relationship with him appear very milk and cookies, indeed."

Rowland held his gaze. "Again, Mr. Cartwright, my condolences for your loss."

Geoffrey opened his mouth to say more, but Molly Cartwright interrupted.

She offered Rowland her hand. "Thank you for your words,

Mr. Sinclair," she said, smiling, though her eyes still glistened with tears. "We look forward to seeing you at the house." She hooked her arm through Geoffrey's and pulled him away. Rowland watched them go, Geoffrey stiff, Molly bright.

Then Edna's arm was entwined with his. "You did well, Rowly."

"I don't know if I did, Ed. But at least it's done."

Milton slung his arm around Rowland's shoulders. "Good job, comrade—it was a tough crowd."

Rowland smiled. "I'm afraid it's not over yet. We're expected at the house."

"Whose house?" Clyde asked.

"Interesting question." Removing his hat, Rowland dragged a hand through his hair. "It was the Cartwright family home—Molly and Geoffrey Cartwright still live there, but it forms part of Danny's estate."

Clyde groaned. "Do they have any idea?"

"Frank and Geoffrey seem to have an inkling..."

"But not Molly?" Edna said.

"I don't think so." Rowland exhaled. He had no choice but to deal with the estate as Daniel wished, but he'd take no pleasure in throwing the Cartwrights out of their home. He glanced at the still-open grave, the lonely plot as far away as possible from the other Cartwrights. He wondered what had happened to cause such a deep rift, to make Daniel distrust his brothers so absolutely. He thought about Wilfred, the horns they'd locked over the years.

"Wills bring out the worst in families, mate." Clyde seemed to read his thoughts. "Any crack widens..."

"So it seems." He opened his umbrella against the strengthening drizzle and held it over Edna. "We'd better get moving before the storm begins."

Milton opened his own umbrella. "It's begun, comrade. It's begun."

Chapter Five

TRAGEDY AND COMEDY LURK IN MAN'S
FINAL PRIVILEGE, HIS WILL

ERRORS CREEP INTO MORE CAREFULLY
WRITTEN WILLS SOMETIMES, ORPHANS'
COURT IS GROUND OF INTERPRETATION

...But when a man makes a will, even if he makes a mistake, the court is bound by law to execute the will as well as the mistake. However certain highways are open if the heirs desire to make use of them...

—*Sunday News*
(Lancaster, Pennsylvania), July 7, 1929

Once, Clyde Watson Jones might have been daunted by the grandeur of the Boston mansion at which they pulled up.

He might have been unnerved by the formal elegance of the reception for mourners, the sheer number of servants who took hats and coats, opened doors, and served drink and canapes. But he had been Rowland Sinclair's friend for nearly eight years now; he lived at Woodlands House, which, if a little informal under Rowland's stewardship, was the equal of most estates in magnificence. He'd come to take the nonchalant opulence of the well-to-do in his stride, though even now he felt like a spectator.

He watched as Molly Cartwright introduced Rowland to other guests, noting the manner in which she held onto his arm for just a moment more than was necessary to guide him to the next bastion of Boston society; the way she smiled as she said his name. Like Rowland, Clyde was an artist and very observant when the picture did not include him.

Milton handed Clyde one of the drinks he'd taken from a circulating tray. "Molly Cartwright's set her cap for our Rowly," the poet murmured. "Do you think he realises?"

Clyde laughed. "I doubt it."

"Should we tell him?"

Clyde shook his head. "She might change her mind once the will is read."

Milton nodded. They had not missed the tension between Rowland and the Cartwright brothers. "Where's Ed?"

Clyde pointed to the far corner of the room where three gentlemen stood talking to the sculptress. The conversation was animated, punctuated with laughter. "Miss Cartwright introduced her to those blokes—university chums of Geoffrey Cartwright apparently."

"That would be *pals*, comrade," Milton corrected. "This is America."

Clyde shook his head. "Not this lot. For Americans, they're very British."

Milton smiled. "Like Rowly's mob, then." The refined inflection of Australia's bunyip aristocracy was something for which they often mocked Rowland Sinclair, though in him it had become less pronounced over the years.

"The lawyers have arrived," Clyde noted as Oliver Burr walked in with an argument of colleagues.

Frank and Geoffrey Cartwright broke off from their individual conversations. Frank went to greet his late brother's attorneys.

Geoffrey caught Molly's attention, and she in turn placed her hand on Rowland's sleeve and pointed out the new arrivals. Rowland nodded and excused himself to follow the Cartwrights out of the hall.

"And so it begins," Milton said. "Come on."

Clyde grabbed his shoulder. "Steady on, mate. They're not going to let us sit in."

"Let's stay close by, anyway," Milton replied. "We can just lurk in the hallway or something."

"Why?"

"In case the Cartwrights try to kill him after the will is read."

"Don't be ridic—" Clyde groaned. Milton was already on his way. Clyde swigged the last of his whisky and placed the glass on the sideboard before he followed.

The room set aside for the reading of Daniel Cartwright's will was fittingly sombre and formal. It was dominated by an elaborately carved and inlaid desk. Several chairs had been placed to face it. Oliver Burr directed Rowland to the chair behind it. The Cartwrights took the first row of seats facing the desk. The attorneys settled in the second. They were uniformly grave, except for one who smiled tentatively at Molly. She ignored him, and one of his colleagues scowled him back into legal impassivity.

Frank Cartwright snarled at Rowland to "get on with it."

Molly smiled at him.

Burr began. "The purpose of this meeting is to inform you, as Daniel Cartwright's beneficiaries, of the terms of his last will and testament. Regrettably, we have not been able to locate all Mr. Cartwright's heirs, but Mr. Sinclair, as the executor, felt that a timely reading would at least allow you some level of certainty whilst a search is conducted."

Frank folded his arms across his chest and glared at Rowland. "Jesus holy Christ! Read the goddamn will, and let's get this over with."

"Language, Frank!" Molly warned.

"You need not be so smug, dear sister. No court is going to uphold Danny putting you in charge, regardless of what you might have talked him into."

"Lady and gentlemen, please!" Burr said sharply before the argument could escalate. "Mr. Sinclair, if you wouldn't mind."

Rowland proceeded to read. "'I, Daniel Fullerton Cartwright, of The Warwick, New York City, being of sound mind, and free from duress or undue influence hereby...'" He read out the formalities, the appointment of himself as executor with almost unfettered discretionary powers to deal with the estate in whatever way necessary to make a number of gifts. Rowland read through a number of smaller legacies—to servants and associates—sentimental bequests of portraits to friends including Rowland Sinclair. And then, "'...give to my brothers, Frank Hamilton Cartwright and Geoffrey Laurence Cartwright, and my sister, Molly Charlotte Cartwright, the sum of ten thousand dollars each.'" Rowland paused for just a second before continuing. "'The remainder of my estate, I give in its entirety to Mr. Otis Norcross.'"

There were other paragraphs after that, legal clauses and so forth, but any attempt to keep reading was futile. Frank and Geoffrey exploded.

"Ten thousand dollars? Ten thousand dollars!" Geoffrey Cartwright leaned forward and slammed the desk with his fist. "He must have been out of his goddamn mind. I'll have you know, Sinclair, that we will not stand for this! Who the hell is this Norcross?"

"Mr. Norcross has not yet been located or informed that he is Danny's heir," Rowland said calmly. "A search is currently underway."

"Are you sure there's no mistake, Rowly?" Molly was crying. "Why would Danny do this to us?"

"This is his last will, Miss Cartwright, properly executed and lodged with Burr, Mayfair and Wilkes."

"This house? Our home? Does that also belong to Mr. Norcross?"

"Yes."

"My motorcar? The furniture? My jewellery?"

Burr intervened. "Any property which Mr. Cartwright personally gifted to you does not form part of the estate, but everything else, aside from the sums of ten thousand dollars he devised to each of you, is to be vested in Mr. Norcross."

Molly looked at Geoffrey, tear-streaked and in terror. "We're homeless. My God, he's made us homeless."

The young lawyer who'd dared to smile at Molly earlier, now offered her a handkerchief, and distracted, she took it.

Frank stood slowly. "Do you intend to enforce this injustice, Mr. Sinclair? Is this how you intend to use your discretion as my brother's representative?"

"This is Danny's will, Mr. Cartwright. It's what he's charged me to do."

"Then be aware that we will be challenging it." He stepped up to the desk. "I hope you are not in a hurry to get home to Australia, Mr. Sinclair, because we will give you a fight, and when my attorneys are finished, neither you nor this travesty of a document will stand!"

Burr tried to soothe the situation. Geoffrey grabbed him by the collar. Rowland left he desk to go to the lawyer's aid. The other men of Burr, Wilkes and Mayfair also stood.

Rowland pulled Geoffrey Cartwright off.

"Get out of my house!" Geoffrey bellowed. "I want you and all your thieving minions out of my house!"

Burr straightened his tie, smoothing down the collar which had just been in Geoffrey's fist. "I am afraid, sir, this is no longer your house."

Molly sobbed now. "Oh, God!"

Rowland stepped between Geoffrey and Burr and spoke quietly to the lawyer. "Surely the Cartwright family need not vacate until we find Mr. Norcross?"

"That, Mr. Sinclair, is up to you," Burr replied, not unsympathetically. "But Mr. Cartwright's will is clear. This house and all the other properties have been left to Mr. Norcross."

"Who do you think you are, Sinclair?" Geoffrey turned on Rowland now. "Who are you to decide where we live? What we own?"

"Rowly, please!" Molly said desperately. "You can't do this…"

"I am your brother's representative."

Geoffrey's upper lip curled. "Take a care then, that you don't meet a similar end," he hissed.

Rowland was aware of the rise of his own temper, but he tried to keep it in check. The sobs of Molly Cartwright reminded him that this was a financially devastating and probably terrifying change of circumstances, and he bit back his anger.

"We might take our leave and allow you to consider your position in private," Rowland said evenly. "Mr. Burr will be able to answer any questions you may have later. And you know where to reach me."

"We do." Geoffrey's voice was cold. "Now get out!"

⤜❦⤛

Clyde and Milton were waiting in the hallway when Rowland emerged with Daniel Cartwright's lawyers. Rowland spotted them, and so he shook Burr's hand and hung back to walk out with his friends.

Milton put his hand on Rowland's shoulder. "You all right, comrade?" He and Clyde had overheard the raised voices that had followed the reading. They both knew that Molly's distress would have had far more impact on Rowland than her brothers' threats.

Rowland shook his head. "Dammit, Danny, what have you done?"

"Ten thousand dollars is a lot of money, Rowly," Clyde offered. "They won't be destitute."

Rowland said nothing. He didn't want to criticise Daniel Cartwright. But giving the family home to Otis Norcross, as well as the lion's share of everything else, seemed cruel. The look of betrayal and fear on Molly Cartwright's face haunted him. Ten thousand dollars was a substantial sum, but in comparison to the Cartwright fortune, it was an afterthought, an intentional slight.

The Cartwrights stepped out into the hallway now. Molly saw Rowland and ran over to him. She grabbed his hand. "Please, Rowly, I'm begging you, I was born in this house, I've never lived anywhere else—don't do this."

"Goddamn it, Molly, stop humiliating yourself!" Geoffrey grabbed her arm roughly and yanked her away.

Rowland seized Geoffrey's arm in turn. "Let go of her."

Geoffrey tightened his grip. "This is my sister, Sinclair. She is a Cartwright. I will not have her throw herself at a lowlife fairy from some foreign backwater!"

"Geoffrey!" Frank Cartwright snapped now. "Stand down. Molly, pull yourself together!"

Slowly Geoffrey released Molly. On cue, Rowland lifted his own hand from Geoffrey's arm.

"You'll understand if we don't see you and your companions to the door, Sinclair," Frank said tightly.

Rowland glanced at Molly uncertainly. She nodded tearfully. "Good afternoon, gentlemen."

The Australians began their retreat, returning to the room in which the funeral reception was being held.

"Oh, there you are!" Edna broke away from the small cluster of men who had been vying for her attention. She regarded Rowland carefully. "Was it that awful?"

"Wretched."

Milton glanced over his shoulder as Geoffrey Cartwright returned to the reception. "We should go, Ed."

"I'd better say goodbye—"

"Just wave," Milton advised.

Edna's brow rose, but she did as he suggested despite the vocal protestations of the gentlemen who were the recipients of her hasty farewell.

The car and driver, which Oliver Burr had left for the Australians, returned them to the Copley.

Rowland loosened his tie as they entered the suite, tossing his hat and coat at the rack. The coat caught, the hat missed. Edna picked it up and placed it on an unused hook. She pulled off her gloves, slipping off her shoes before she curled up on the couch beside Rowland.

Milton opened the drinks cabinet and mixed and distributed their various preferences. Rowland leaned forward, his elbows on his knees, as he swirled the gin and tonic, distractedly.

With a little prompting, he told them what had happened.

"He left their house to someone else?" Edna said, shocked. "How could he do that?"

"It would seem Frank lost the house in the crash—he'd mortgaged it and the bank foreclosed," Rowland explained.

"Danny bought it back, for his mother. When she died, Geoffrey and Molly continued to live there, but it belongs to Danny and was passed on with his estate."

"Do you think he realised?" Edna asked.

"Realised what?"

"That the house was part of the estate."

Clyde scoffed. "How could you forget you owned a house?"

"Spoken like a true member of the proletariat," Milton replied. "Danny probably owned two dozen houses."

"It is possible," Rowland said thoughtfully, "that having come to think of the house as belonging to his mother or his siblings, Danny simply forgot to exclude it from his greater estate."

"Do you believe that's what happened?" Edna asked.

"I don't know, Ed. Danny genuinely thought someone was trying to kill him. Perhaps this will was a form of self-defence."

"What do you mean?"

"Well, if Danny's fortune was your object," Rowland said contemplatively, "you'd hardly kill him if you knew, or even suspected, that his will did not favour you."

Clyde nodded. "You've got a point."

Rowland put down his glass. "The Cartwrights are intent on challenging Danny's will, which means I'm stuck here for a while. I can't ask you all to—"

"There's no one waiting for us back home, mate," Clyde said. "Well, not for me or Milt anyway. There's always half a dozen hopeful fools waiting for Ed."

Edna rolled her eyes. "We need to find Mr. Norcross," she said, ignoring any talk of them leaving Rowland to it. "He might be able to shed light on what Danny was thinking. And who Danny thought was trying to kill him."

"Unless, of course, he did," Milton murmured.

"What?"

"I'm just saying," Milton said. "Norcross has arguably gained the most by Danny's death."

"He won't gain a brass washer if we can't find him," Rowland said.

"What happens then?" Edna asked.

Rowland sat back and recited what Burr had already explained. "After seven years, the court may be petitioned to declare him dead. In which case that part of Danny's will fails and an intestacy is created. In the event of an intestacy, his next of kin inherits."

"And his next of kin—"

"Are his siblings...unless he has a child of whom we're not yet aware."

"Seven years is a long time to wait," Milton observed.

Rowland nodded. "Which, I suspect, is why Frank plans on proving Danny was not in his right mind when he wrote the will."

"Which will mean?"

"That unless he has an older, valid will somewhere, he died intestate, and his next of kin will inherit, immediately on judgment."

"Good grief, Rowly." Clyde drained his glass. "You planning on hanging out a shingle?"

Rowland smiled. "Burr took me through all the possibilities. He thinks the best outcome would be to find Otis Norcross and then work out a settlement with the family."

Clyde glanced at Milton. "Well, let's find him, then."

Chapter Six

No Poor In Boston—125 Years Hence

The Herald Cable Service

BOSTON. Sunday.

Providing for the poor of the future, Mr M. J. Curley, Mayor of Boston, took out an insurance policy four years ago, it is disclosed. This policy, for 11,000 dollars a year (nearly £3000 Australian), is "for the relief of the needy poor of Boston." It does not become effective until 125 years after the death of Mr Curley's last surviving child. It is expected then to be worth 45,548,000 dollars—sufficient to provide 2105 families with 20 dollars a week. Mr Curley said that if two more Boston citizens would take out similar policies there would be no poor in Boston 125 years hence, and no need for welfare work.

—*Herald*, July 8, 1935

❧

The Cadillac parked in the hotel lot would probably have caught Rowland's eye simply because it was a beautiful machine, and Rowland Sinclair was partial to beautiful machines. The gleaming 452 Madame X was a 1930 model and had clearly been prized. The fact that a man stood beside it, holding a homemade sign that read "$200," made Rowland look a second time. The gentleman wore a well-cut but very worn and patched suit. His face was gaunt, his shoulders slumped and defeated as he drew on his cigarette until the last flake of tobacco was used.

"It probably doesn't run," Clyde murmured as he and Rowland gazed admiringly at the Cadillac.

The man with the sign overheard. "She's in perfect working order!" he said, affronted. "The engine's barely worn in." He opened the bonnet and stood back. "You'll find nothing out of place!"

Intrigued, they inspected the car's workings.

"He's right," Clyde said quietly. "The engine seems sound. Maybe she's stolen."

Rowland introduced himself and Clyde to the hopeful vendor.

"Aaron Leonowski," he replied, shaking their hands.

"Is this your vehicle, Mr. Leonowski?" Rowland asked.

"Yes." Perhaps he'd overheard Clyde, as he produced a bill of sale which he offered as proof of ownership.

Rowland glanced at the document. "You realise that $200 is an extremely reasonable asking price?"

"Not these days, Mr. Sinclair. I need the cash—my children need shoes and feeding. I can't afford to put gas in her anyway."

"If you don't mind me asking, Mr. Leonowski, how did you come by her?"

"I put my money down in 1929 when it looked like the party would never end." He shook his head. "I should have got rid of her years ago, but I kept hoping... Nobody had any money anyway, and there were a lot of fancy cars for sale."

"Are you from Boston, Mr. Leonowski?"

Leonowski shook his head. "Drove down from Salem. Borrowed a few bucks for gas. My father-in-law was of a mind that the folks staying here might still be able to afford a car."

"That's possibly true, sir. I expect they could afford a price that's fairer than what you're asking."

"The market is what the market is." Leonowski eyed him. "It's a good deal... I can't go any lower."

"I'm afraid we're only visiting."

"Oh." Leonowski's shoulders slumped further. He looked for a cigarette and cursed when he found his pockets empty. Clyde offered him one from the handful he'd rolled earlier.

"You know, Mr. Leonowski, I could use a car while I'm in your country, but I don't want to have to ship it back to Australia when we leave. So, if you'd be happy to take the car off my hands when we do..."

Leonowski pulled back. "I need this money, Mr. Sinclair. All of it. I can't afford to buy her back."

"I don't want you to buy her back, Mr, Leonowski. Just take her back. Unfortunately, I can't tell exactly when that will be, but if you are content to give me your word that you will come and get her when I send for you, then I'll buy your car."

Leonowski stared at him.

"With an added compensation for the inconvenience of having to collect it, naturally."

Leonowski looked back at his car. He swallowed and dragged his sleeve across his eyes.

Rowland looked at his watch. "Why don't you join us for

a drink, Mr. Leonowski? I'll arrange for your money, and then we'll drop you home to Salem."

Leonowski nodded.

They closed the bonnet, which Leonowski informed them hoarsely was a called a *hood*, and asked the hotel valet to refuel the vehicle for later use, before proceeding into Copley Plaza Dining Room and Bar.

Edna waved from a table on the Copley's famous revolving bar. Designed to resemble a carousel, the booths were set like spokes around a circular bar and completed a full revolution every hour. Rowland introduced Aaron Leonowski to Edna and Milton before he excused himself to see the hotel bursar about organising payment for the Cadillac.

He returned to see that food was arriving.

"I was starving," Edna informed him. "We ordered for you, Rowly."

Rowland smiled. He was fairly certain that Edna's state of starvation had been contrived as an excuse to feed their guest. They'd had breakfast barely two hours before, and Leonowski looked hungry.

He handed an envelope to the man. "Are you sure you wouldn't rather I arrange for that to be deposited into a bank account, Mr. Leonowski?"

"I can't say I trust banks anymore, Mr. Sinclair," Leonowski murmured, his mouth full.

"How far away is Salem?" Edna asked Rowland.

"About thirty miles, I believe." He looked to Leonowski for confirmation.

"You don't have to take me back, Mr. Sinclair; it is too much to ask. I'll find my own way."

"Look, mate," Clyde said quietly, "you don't want to be walking about with that much money on you."

"The drive will allow me to familiarise myself with your car while you're on hand to point out her idiosyncrasies,"

Rowland added. "And to be honest, I wouldn't mind getting out of Boston."

Rowland had met with Oliver Burr that morning to discuss the implications of the legal challenge Frank, Geoffrey, and Molly Cartwright had already initiated. He was not being merely polite in saying he looked forward to the drive to Salem.

They did not rush Aaron Leonowski through his meal, during which they managed to glean he had once worked in New York on the money markets. After the crash, he'd lost everything but his family, and the Cadillac, and the latter only because he couldn't sell it. In the end, Leonowski had packed his family into the motorcar and driven to his wife's people just outside Salem, where the Cadillac had been stored under sheets in the barn until his father-in-law had demanded he sell it.

"It might be a good thing you driving me back, Mr. Sinclair," he said. "The old man's not going to believe the deal we struck."

"Did you find work in Salem, Mr. Leonowski?" Edna asked.

"No…not yet. I hoped there'd be something when they were building the Coast Guard Air Station." He shrugged. "It's been a tough few years, but"—he patted the breast pocket into which he'd placed the envelope Rowland had given him, "it could be my luck's changing."

"I hope so, Mr. Leonowski." Edna stood and the gentlemen followed suit. "If we're venturing out to Salem, I had better go up and fetch my coat."

"I'll walk up with you," Rowland volunteered.

"We'll have the valet bring round the Cadillac." Clyde rolled up his sleeves, anticipating a few moments before they set off to check the engine again with satisfaction if not pleasure. He had never seen an engine the size of the Cadillac's V-16 motor.

Milton rolled his eyes. Whilst he had always enjoyed driving Rowland's motorcars, he'd never understood his friends' admiration of pistons and gears.

Rowland stepped off the carousel and offered Edna his hand. The concierge caught up with them as they made their way through the foyer.

"Mr. Sinclair." He handed Rowland an envelope. "A Miss Cartwright called to see you whilst you were out this morning."

Rowland thanked him and extracted a note written in a precise if slightly ornate hand. Molly Cartwright asked him to call on her at home that day, mentioning that her brother Geoffrey was out and not expected back till the next morning. She wished to speak to him privately.

He showed the page to Edna.

"Should you go now?" Edna asked as they let themselves into the suites.

"I'll call on Molly once we get back from Salem."

Edna disappeared into a bedroom to fetch her coat. Rowland waited by the window, his gaze on the view of the plaza, his mind on his conversation with the police that morning. A Detective O'Brien was leading the investigation into Daniel Cartwright's death but had been too busy to talk to him at that time. Burr had organised for Rowland to be briefed in the interim by one of the lesser-ranked officers dealing with the case. Murphy, a young man, spoke with a strong Irish accent. He was polite but clearly not privy to the reasoning of the detectives on the case.

The discussion had nevertheless confirmed in more detail what Molly had told them: that Daniel Cartwright had been shot four times. The first three shots had not been fatal. The fourth was fired at close range, possibly to ensure that it did in fact "finish the job." The weapon had not been found, and Danny had died where he'd fallen. Beyond that, there was nothing the officer was either permitted or willing to share. Rowland informed Murphy that his old friend had been in fear of his life.

"Well now, that's most interesting, Mr. Sinclair, as well as tragically prescient. But can I ask how you'd be aware of what Mr. Cartwright was in fear of?"

"Danny's last letter. I received it with his papers, after he died."

"Do you have it on you, sir?"

"It's back at the hotel," Rowland said, realising uncomfortably that the letter with its florid endearments would need to be handed to the police. "I'll bring it in this afternoon."

A knock at the door brought Rowland out of his reverie. He answered, expecting it to be either a chambermaid, or Milton or Clyde, impatient to get going. Instead, it was two men he'd never met before. The first greeted him with an outstretched hand. "Mr. Sinclair? Bobbie Everett, *Boston Daily Globe*. This is my colleague Johnny Maddox."

"Mr. Everett, Mr. Maddox," Rowland said carefully. "What can I do for you, gentlemen?"

"Was hoping we could have a word, Mr. Sinclair."

"About what, sir?"

Everett looked over his shoulder. "It's a matter of some sensitivity... Perhaps if we were to step inside?"

"Yes, of course, please come in." Rowland stepped back to let them through to the suite's drawing room. "I'm afraid I don't have long—I was just on my way out."

"This won't take long, Mr. Sinclair." Everett and Maddox took seats without being invited to do so. "We were hoping you might like to comment on the story we're working on."

Rowland remained standing.

"We are informed that you are about to evict Daniel Cartwright's grieving family from their ancestral home."

"Are you?"

Everett sat back and looked up at him. "Our information is that Daniel Cartwright, having led a dissolute life, agreed to consign the family's fortune in his will to a person of similar moral turpitude under the direction of a foreigner with whom he'd also had an unnatural relationship."

Everett and Maddox did not know Rowland Sinclair, and so perhaps they mistook the inscrutability of his face for calm or indifference.

"You are a rare creature among men, Rowland Sinclair," Everett said with one hand over his heart, the other against his forehead, "a man who is willing to let another man be, who does not question another's heart..."

"Get out!" Rowland snarled.

"Of course, if it turned out that Mr. Cartwright's beneficiary did not actually exist, was, say, the creation of a diseased mind, then of course one would conclude that any letters he may have written were also indicative of affliction."

"Are you trying to blackmail me, gentlemen?"

"Rowly?" Edna walked into the drawing room. "Oh...I beg your pardon."

Everett and Maddox lumbered to their feet.

Rowland opened the door. "These gentlemen were just leaving, Ed."

"I take it we're no longer welcome," Maddox said. Both men crowded Rowland as they walked past him. "We'll be in touch, Sinclair. Think about what exposure could mean. This needn't get nasty."

"Just get out."

Rowland closed the door firmly after them, and went immediately to the roll-top writing desk in the drawing room. He rifled through the papers on the desk and cursed.

"Rowly, what are you looking for?" Edna came to help him. "Who were those men?"

"They claimed to be reporters—from the *Boston Daily*

Globe...but to be honest, I doubt very much that they were from any rag." He pulled down the roll-top angrily. "I'm looking for Danny's letter to me."

"Why?"

"Because they quoted part of it at me."

Edna gasped. She'd read the letter. She understood the implications of it being in the wrong hands. "And you can't find it?"

"No, I can't." Rowland cursed. "Someone's taken it."

"When did you last see it?"

"I showed it to you late on the evening we arrived... To be honest, I don't remember seeing it since then."

"Are you sure you left it on the desk, Rowly? Who could have taken it?"

"Yes, I'm sure," Rowland said, rummaging through the desk one more time. "A dozen people have been through here...the lawyers, Molly, not to mention the hotel staff. And that's just while we were here." Rowland rubbed his face, berating himself for not thinking to secure the letter somehow. "Dammit!" He picked up the telephone and had a call put through to Oliver Burr.

Edna watched as Rowland outlined the contents of the letter to the attorney. "Part of it was written in French, but Danny was clearly concerned about his own safety." He didn't flinch as he explained the extravagant blandishments and declarations of affection it also contained. "It was in Danny's nature to be effusive, Mr. Burr, and he was by his own declaration inebriated when he wrote the letter. But a stranger reading it could well take it the wrong way."

They spoke for several minutes with Rowland reiterating the letter as closely as he could recall. By the time he hung up, Milton had arrived to find out what was keeping them.

"Nothing now," Rowland said, picking up his hat from where he'd left it on the sideboard. "Burr will call the police station and explain."

"Explain what?"

Rowland quickly told him what had transpired.

"Bloody hell!" Milton shook his head. "Someone took the letter from here?"

Rowland nodded, gathering up all the other documents and papers Burr had given him.

"What are you doing?" Milton asked.

"I'm closing the proverbial farm gate. I'll have these stowed in the hotel safe, just in case."

When they finally joined Clyde and Leonowski, Rowland apologised for the delay. He climbed in behind the wheel; Leonowski took the front passenger seat beside him and spent a few minutes familiarising Rowland with the various dials and switches. The Madame X turned over and roared to life.

"They drive on the right here," Clyde cautioned Rowland as they pulled out of the parking lot. Rowland didn't need to be reminded, and being ambidextrous, he adapted to the reversal of driving habits with ease. They fought the downtown traffic and headed north out of Boston, picking up speed and putting the Cadillac through her paces after they left the outskirts of the city. It was a mental distraction that was welcome.

It took a little less than an hour to reach Salem by coastal roads that meandered in and out of the various peninsulas, river towns, and fishing villages. The effects of the economic Depression were visible in some towns more than others.

As they drove through Court Street, Leonowski pointed out the ruins of the State House, which had burned down a few months before. "I was in town the day it happened. Never seen anything like it." He shook his head. "It felt like America was on fire, and then when the dome collapsed..." He stopped. "Gotta tell you, I thought it was an omen."

"Of what, Mr. Leonowski?" Edna asked, leaning in from the back seat.

Leonowski smiled as he turned towards the sculptress. "It was just Salem getting to me, Miss Higgins. This is a superstitious town, and I've felt cursed for years. That fire felt like a funeral pyre for the life I had—an end of all hope, an omen of nothing but ashes."

"Oh, how terrible, Mr. Leonowski. I'm sorry your circumstances looked so bleak."

"A lot of folks have it a lot worse, Miss Higgins. I was just low when the fire happened. And being in Salem—" He laughed. "It was easy to believe in curses and witches…"

They stopped to refuel the Cadillac, and Leonowski ran into the general store to purchase bacon, tobacco, talcum powder, and sweets. "The powder is for my wife, the tobacco for her father, and the sweets are for my boys and my little girl," he said as he climbed back into the Madame X.

"And the bacon?" Milton asked.

"I haven't had bacon since 1929—my youngest three have never tasted it." Leonowski directed them out of the main part of Salem to the rural outskirts—small farms with rundown buildings, bedraggled children chasing dogs and chickens in dusty yards.

"This is it," he said as they came upon a side-gabled house with a steeply pitched roof. A red door stood out against almost black walls. An old man was patching a hole in the deck of the open porch, shouting intermittently at half a dozen children who hovered around him as he worked. He stood as the Cadillac approached, his face thunderous.

"Your father-in-law?" Rowland asked as he stopped the vehicle.

Leonowski nodded.

A woman with a fair, worried face stepped out onto the porch and stopped beside the old man, wiping her hands on her pinafore apron. Leonowski alighted first; the Australians followed. The children ran to him shouting "Daddy" and spouting news about Mabel, who had apparently died while he was away. Leonowski hugged them and gave out the sweets, telling them that Mabel had been very old and not much use for anything aside from costing them money.

Milton glanced at Rowland. "Clearly times are tough."

"I'm pretty sure Mabel is some kind of animal," Rowland whispered in reply.

"We'll buy a new cow tomorrow," Leonowski announced.

He handed the talcum to the woman and kissed her. She smiled tentatively, and Leonowski introduced his new friends to Flora, his wife, and her father, Athol Barwick.

Flora apologised for her appearance. "We weren't expecting visitors."

"Forgive the intrusion, Mrs. Leonowski," Edna said. "We've not been in America long, and this seemed like a splendid opportunity to see a little bit of your country."

"You're English?" Flora asked, still a little bewildered.

"Australian."

"Oh, I see. You speak English very well."

"Why, thank you." Edna didn't miss a beat.

"Did you sell the motorcar?" Athol asked gruffly.

"In a manner of speaking—" Leonowski began.

"You were supposed to sell it! Where'd you get money for these extravagances?"

"Pa," Flora cautioned. She took her husband's hand. "There's work at Parker Brothers, Aaron. We were worried you'd not get back in time to go see Ed Parker. He asked about you particularly." She smiled sadly. "You might not have needed to sell the Caddy."

He handed her the bulging envelope Rowland had given him. "Mr. Sinclair and I came to an arrangement, Flora. It'll be all right." He looked down at his patched attire. "I can buy a proper suit before I go see Mr. Parker."

"There's no time for that, boy," Athol barked. "Go now before he finds someone else."

"But I can't go looking like this—"

"You need steady work, Aaron." Athol glowered contemptuously at his son-in-law. "Your children are thin, boy! There ain't no time for your airs and graces."

"We'll drive you back into Salem, if you like," Rowland offered.

"You've already been too kind. I can walk—"

"It's no trouble."

"I might stay and help Mr. Barwick with this porch," Clyde said, taking off his coat. He handed it to Leonowski. "You might as well wear that, mate." He loosened his tie and handed that over too. "You'll be doing me a favour if you take that as well."

"If Clyde's staying, why don't you come into town too, Mrs. Leonowski?" Edna said. "If you're not too busy, of course?"

Flora glanced nervously at her father.

"Go on," Athol said. "Keep an eye on your dang fool of a husband, and I'll watch the young'uns."

While Flora went inside to remove her apron and fetch her hat and gloves, Milton, too, decided he would stay and help fix the porch. The Leonowskis' little girl, Miriam, seemed to take a liking to the poet and invited him to come look at Mabel, who was apparently lying in state in the barn.

Chapter Seven

Burying A Cow.

A McGoldrick pleaded guilty to burying a dead animal in a public reserve, an act likely to foul the same. Harvey Innis Gale, Health Inspector of the Municipality of Wollongong, deposed that defendant killed a cow on October 15th, and buried it in Gilmore Park.

To the defendant, it was satisfactorily buried at a depth of about three feet. Defendant stated that Gilmore Park was more of a common than a park, and that one alderman had gone down and failed to find where the animal was buried, whilst another alderman had only found it after great difficulty...His Worship imposed a fine of £2 with 8/- costs, in default 14 days.

—*Illawarra Mercury*,
26 November 1926

The Parker Brothers' offices and manufacturing facility were located in Bridge Street, Salem. On the way there, Leonowski explained that the company published board and parlour games.

"They put out a new game earlier this year, and it's been very popular. I expect they've had to expand to meet demand." Flora nodded. "They've put a lot of men on the floor, but they need someone to help with the books."

Rowland pulled up at the imposing building, which fronted a complex that occupied an entire block of Bridge Street.

Flora straightened Clyde's tie around her husband's neck, her face full of tentative hope. She fussed with his collar as if she was unwilling to let him go.

"Don't worry, Flora," he said quietly. "Our luck's changing."

They got out of the Cadillac together and Rowland pointed out a teahouse a little further up the road. "We might wait for you there, Mr. Leonowski."

Leonowski shook Rowland's hand. "I don't know how to thank you, Mr. Sinclair."

"Then don't. Good luck, Mr. Leonowski."

Rowland and the ladies walked the couple of hundred yards to the teahouse and took a table. They ordered tea and journey cakes, which were apparently a specialty of the house. The latter turned out to be a type of pancake with raisins, and over these they chatted with Flora Leonowski, who, after an initial shyness, told them about the life she and Aaron had once known in New York before the crash. "We lived in Manhattan, and we entertained and were entertained. All sorts of people. Even after our eldest was born... It was exciting and breathless, and we felt like we would never grow old." She smiled nervously. "And then in just a few months, it was all gone."

"The crash?" Edna asked.

Flora nodded. "We didn't realise exactly how much we had till we lost it. Pa isn't always kind to Aaron," she added quietly, apologetically. "He doesn't see that the poor man is doing his best to provide for us. Why, I catch Aaron sneaking his food onto the children's plates and..." She stopped. "It doesn't matter now. This job won't pay like the one he had, but we'll feel rich just getting by. If it hadn't been for Pa... But maybe we'll be able to get our own place again."

"My father bullied every boy I ever stepped out with," Edna said. "He claimed he was testing their courage."

"Did any pass?" Flora said, glancing at Rowland and relaxing a little.

"Oh, no," Edna replied brightly. "One or two survived, but nobody ever passed."

Flora laughed.

Rowland watched as the sculptress gently eased Flora's embarrassment over the way in which her father had treated her husband in the presence of strangers.

Flora asked why they were in America.

"A dear friend of ours died. We came for his funeral."

"Oh, my condolences."

"Thank you."

"Had he been ill?"

"No. He died unexpectedly, I'm afraid." Rowland avoided any mention of murder lest he alarm the lady.

"Oh, dear. An accident?"

"No..."

"I'm sorry, I don't mean to be nosey."

"It's not that—"

Edna interrupted. "Danny was murdered."

Flora stared at them. "You don't mean Daniel Cartwright, do you?"

Rowland and Edna paused, startled.

"Did you know him?" Rowland asked.

"Aaron used to work for Frank Cartwright when we were in New York. That's why he went down to Boston. He thought Frank might buy the Cadillac for old-time's sake. Or maybe take him on in some capacity."

Rowland's brow rose. "I see."

"Is that where you met Aaron, Mr. Sinclair? At Mr. Cartwright's?"

"No. Mr. Leonowski was outside the Copley when we encountered him."

Flora sighed. "Pa told Aaron that Mr. Cartwright wouldn't even know who he was. That he was better off parking the Cadillac outside the Copley and hoping some high hat would give him something for her."

Rowland smiled wryly. "I'm the high hat, I suppose."

Flora laughed. "Yes." She looked directly at Rowland, her eyes misting. "Aaron told me about your arrangement, Mr. Sinclair. I can't help but think you're not a very good businessman, but I thank God for you. You see, for Aaron, that motorcar is hope. Even in the barn under a sheet." She hesitated as she searched for words. "What I mean to say is, we are beholden."

"There's no need to be, Mrs. Leonowski. The deal was fair. I'm perfectly content with my end of it."

Flora looked uneasily at the clock on the teahouse wall. "There's a toy store across the street. The children haven't had a treat in so long, and now we have a little money—I wonder if you'd mind…"

"Not at all." Edna said, sliding out her chair. "It's a splendid idea."

And so they removed to the truly tiny toy emporium on the other side of Bridge Street. Rowland waited outside because the establishment did not seem large enough to accommodate the three of them in its overcrowded aisles.

"I'll keep an eye out for Mr. Leonowski," he volunteered, taking a position outside the shop that gave him a clear view down the street to Parker Brothers, as the ladies went in. Edna, who delighted in toy stores, poked her head out periodically to show him some new wonder.

When Leonowski stepped out of the building, he spotted Rowland quite easily and walked briskly up to join them. As he approached, Flora and Edna emerged with small rag doll, a ball, a whistle, and a drum.

Leonowski glanced at the purchases. "Flora—"

"I barely spent anything, Aaron—I wasn't extravagant. But the children—"

"I must say I'm disappointed, Flora. The wife of a working man need not be so mean."

"A working man?"

Leonowski beamed. "I start tomorrow."

Flora Leonowski began to cry.

Leonowski embraced his wife with one arm and passed a box to Rowland with the other. "That's for you, Mr. Sinclair. Compliments of the company's new accounts clerk. The game that's saved Parker Brothers and, to be honest, the Leonowskis!"

Rowland looked at the printed cardboard box. A caricature waving money, a large dollar sign beneath a red banner reading "Monopoly." "Thank you. But wouldn't your children—"

Leonowski waved the idea away. "They're too young. And I don't know if I want them thinking about money and property just yet...even in a game."

Flora pulled herself together. "Pa will be so pleased," she said quietly.

They returned to the car and took the Leonowskis home, pulling up to find Athol smoking on the porch— now fixed—watching the children play with a bat fashioned out of a paling and an imaginary ball. The boy with the bat waved it in the air and shouted, "It's called cricket. The men taught us."

Rowland laughed as a younger boy bowled air at his brother and yet another child leapt for the invisible ball. "At least they won't break any windows that way."

"Where are Clyde and Milton?" Edna asked as gifts were distributed.

"They're digging a hole for Mabel," Athol replied.

"Oh, Pa!" Flora protested. "They're visitors."

"They wanted to. Helpful fellas. Sent the young'uns back with me 'cause Johnny got sad and Miriam wouldn't quit poking the carcass. There's something unnatural about that girl of yours, Flora."

Rowland took off his jacket and tossed it into the Cadillac. "I'd better see if they need any help."

"I'll come with you." Leonowski removed Clyde's jacket and rolled up his sleeves. "It might take all of us to drag poor Mabel into the hole…and she is my cow. Flora, why don't you make a pot of coffee?"

❧

Not far from the barn, Clyde and Milton had excavated a significant amount of earth. Milton tossed his shovel to Rowland. He extracted a handkerchief from his pocket and mopped his brow. "It turns out that cows require a bloody big hole."

Rowland laughed, loosened his tie, and began digging. Leonowski tried to take over from Clyde, but Clyde refused, adamant that he had not yet worked up a sweat.

As they dug, Rowland took the opportunity to ask Leonowski about Frank Cartwright. "Your wife mentioned that you hoped he might buy the Cadillac."

"I did. He talked me into ordering it when times were good, so I hoped that he might take it off my hands."

Rowland heaved another shovelful of soil out of the deepening hole. "And he refused?"

"Athol was right. He didn't remember who I was. Threatened to call the police."

"So you went to the Copley?"

"I was already at the Copley. I just put up the sign."

"But why were you at the Copley?"

"Mr. Cartwright is staying there."

Rowland stopped digging. "Why? He lives in Boston."

Leonowski shrugged.

"How did you learn he was staying at the Copley?"

"I called at the house—where he lived when he was not in New York when I worked for him—and spoke to his sister. She told me he was staying at the Copley."

"Rowly, mate," Clyde interrupted pointedly. "Is there any reason you've stopped digging?"

"Sorry." Rowland got back to work, and shortly thereafter Clyde declared the hole big enough.

"I'll fetch some ropes and we can drag Mabel over," Leonowski said.

"Fetch the car," Clyde directed. "We'll use it to drag her over."

"Whoa!" Leonowski was clearly alarmed. "It's a Cadillac not a tractor."

Clyde took the hand Milton offered him, and climbed out of the hole. "Trust me, mate. Even with four of us, dragging her over is going to be one helluva job. You don't want to do your back the day before you're due to start work."

Clyde helped an uncertain Leonowski back the Cadillac into the barn and tether Mabel to the rear bumper. Then he took over the wheel and gunned the overhead-valve, sixteen-cylinder engine. The ropes pulled taut as the Cadillac's 165 horsepower motor was applied against the weight of the deceased bovine. With Rowland and Milton signalling directions, Clyde pulled Mabel to the edge of the hole, and then all four of them worked with shovels and planks to slide the carcass in. Mabel descended into her final rest with a slightly undignified thump. Clyde crossed himself.

Milton clutched his hat over his heart and said a few words. "I weep for Mabel—she is dead! Oh, weep for Mabel! Though our tears thaw not the frost which binds so dear a head."

"I have no doubt Shelley is weeping," Rowland muttered.

They backfilled the grave and returned to the farmhouse to wash up and toast Mabel with coffee.

"We should get going too," Rowland said, glancing at his watch as the Leonowski children ran out to see Mabel's grave. He wrote Oliver Burr's details on the back of his own calling card. "If you need to get in touch with us, Mr. Leonowski, Mr. Burr should always know how to find us. In the meantime, our very best wishes for your new position."

Leonowski shook his hand. "Thank you, Mr. Sinclair. I reckon Australians could be my lucky charm."

Chapter Eight

MONOPOLY—THE GREAT PARKER
BROTHER GAME

The fascinating Real Estate game which
demands astute bargaining from the two to
nine players, and provides much of the thrill
of Real Estate with little of the risk.

Now only $2
Toys—Second Floor—Annex
Mail or phone orders filled until
10 p.m.—HUBbard 2700

—*Boston Globe*, April 12, 1935

∼◎∽

On the drive back to Boston, Rowland and Edna brought
their friends up to date with respect to Frank Cartwright's
current address.

"Why on earth would he move into a hotel?" Edna asked.

"Danny lived at the Warwick when he was in New York," Milton reminded her. "It's the kind of thing rich people do."

"I suppose there was no reason he needed to mention it." Rowland frowned. "It's just a bit of a surprise."

"If he can afford to stay at the Copley, I wonder why he's so worked up about where Danny's money goes?" Clyde mused.

"Wills aren't just about where the money goes," Milton said ominously.

Rowland agreed. His own father had disinherited him. It was an expression of fury, a paternal slap from beyond the grave which never found its mark because his brother had chosen to share his inheritance without saying a word.

"Perhaps Mr. Cartwright moved to the Copley to keep an eye on you," Edna suggested. "Perhaps he took Danny's letter."

The thought had occurred to Rowland. As a guest of the hotel, it would probably be much easier for Frank to gain access to their suite.

They arrived back in Boston just after five. Rowland grimaced as he looked at his watch. He'd expected to be back earlier. "I'll drop you all back to the Copley and go see Molly. If I'm not back by half past eight, go down to dinner without me."

"Do you want any company, mate?" Clyde asked.

Rowland shook his head. "I expect this is about the will." He rubbed his temple. "To be honest, I do feel quite sorry for Molly."

Edna nodded. "She seemed to really like you, Rowly. Perhaps if you talk to her, she can keep her brothers from turning this into something frightfully ugly."

Milton's brow rose. "Bit late for that, comrade."

Rowland pulled up in the sweeping drive, and alighted. He wondered too late if he should have thought to clean up a little before calling on Molly Cartwright. He had, after all, spent part of the afternoon burying a cow.

Rowland knocked on the door, surreptitiously rubbing a smear of mud off his waistcoat.

The door was answered by a maid, who invited him to wait in the drawing room while she informed her mistress that he was here.

Rowland looked about the room. The drawing room was smaller but no less formal than the ballroom in which the reception after the funeral had been held. A grand piano occupied the area by the window. There were several portraits on the walls, though none by or of Daniel Cartwright. As Rowland studied each piece, compared the brushwork, the palettes, and composition, he became aware of a resurgent longing to paint. He'd not picked up a brush since receiving the telegram informing him of Danny's death. It was not that he hadn't wanted to paint—working had always been a solace, and he'd needed that as he came to terms with the fact that Cartwright was gone. But there had been no time, no chance.

"Mr. Sinclair."

Rowland turned. Molly wore black. But despite its colour, the dress was no mourning weed—elegant, styled to show the wearer's figure to best effect. There was something in the way Molly held her head that reminded him of Daniel, and he realised that there was a vague resemblance at play. "Good evening, Miss Cartwright. I'm sorry I could not come earlier."

"Please don't apologise, Mr. Sinclair. I appreciate you coming at all after the scene we made at the reading." Molly stepped closer and looked up into Rowland's face. "Please say you'll forgive us."

"There's nothing to forgive. I understand that the contents

of Danny's will were…"—he struggled to find the appropriate words—"difficult to accept."

Molly's eyes filled. "Oh, we accept it. It's understanding that is impossible, Mr. Sinclair." She stepped away from him to take a framed photograph from on top of the piano. Returning, she pressed it into his hands, standing close so they could look at it together. Two young children, wearing voluminous lacy frocks, bows, and cascading curls and posing with shepherd's crooks. They looked like twins. She pointed to each in turn. "That's me and that's Danny. He's two years older, but he was small for his age. We shared everything, toys, sweets, secrets. So you see, Mr. Sinclair, my brothers and I can't understand why Danny appears to have hated us. Why he wanted to punish us. We were his family… We loved him!"

Rowland handed her his handkerchief. "I'm so sorry."

"You were his friend, Mr. Sinclair. He obviously trusted you. What did he tell you about us?"

"Not a great deal, to be honest. I was aware that there had been a rift, but he was never specific about its cause."

Molly dabbed at her eyes. "Heavens, I must look a fright."

"You look lovely," Rowland said without thinking, though he was not insincere.

Perhaps it was a kindness too much because Molly broke down completely, burying her face in his chest as she sobbed.

Rowland was a little startled, but he made no attempt to stop her. Tentatively, he placed his arms around Molly Cartwright and waited until the tears had expended.

"I'm so sorry," she said finally, pulling away. "It breaks my heart that Danny was persuaded to hate us."

"Persuaded?"

"He must have been persuaded. There must have been someone poisoning him against us."

"Who would—"

"The woman he was seeing. Or this man Norcross, who he…" Molly shook her head. "Why else would he do this to us, Mr. Sinclair? Humiliate us like this? The Cartwrights must be the laughingstock of Boston!"

"I'm sure he didn't intend to do anything of the kind," Rowland said, though he wasn't entirely sure if that was true.

"That's what Frank says." Molly's eyes brightened. "He's surmised that maybe Danny didn't know what he was doing… that he was not in his right mind."

Rowland shook his head. "That's not what I meant."

"But mightn't it be true? Why, we have no evidence that this Otis Norcross even exists."

"We haven't found him yet, but that doesn't mean he doesn't exist," Rowland said calmly. "Danny was so rarely in Boston, so perhaps Mr. Norcross lives in New York or even abroad."

Molly's face darkened. "Oh no, Mr. Sinclair. If he exists, I warrant he's in Boston, or he was when Danny died."

"What do you mean?"

"I mean anyone capable of talking a man into disinheriting his family is also capable of much worse."

"You're suggesting that Otis Norcross murdered Danny?"

"It makes sense, don't you think? Who gained the most from his death?"

Rowland said nothing for a moment, and then, "Is this why you wanted me to call by?"

Molly gasped. "Oh, heavens! I haven't even offered you a seat. I do apologise—please sit down, Mr. Sinclair."

Rowland declined a drink. Molly poured one for herself from the selection of crystal decanters on the sideboard. She sat next to him, playing nervously with the stem of a glass.

"Look, Rowly… You don't mind if I call you Rowly?"

"Not at all."

"I know you must feel we're really cold, mercenary sort of people to be squabbling over poor Danny's will—"

"I assure you, I don't."

Molly smiled at him. "Of course you do, you're just too polite to admit it." She swallowed. "Ever since our parents died, Danny looked after me. In every way. I didn't know he resented it, and now…it breaks my heart to think…"

Rowland struggled against an impulse to reassure her of her brother's affection. He didn't know what exactly Danny had been thinking and why. He knew only that, in the end, Danny wanted to give everything he had to a man named Otis Norcross, and he'd entrusted Rowland Sinclair with the responsibility of ensuring that happened.

"Rowly, I don't mind admitting that I'm scared—"

"What on earth is going on here?" Geoffrey Cartwright stalked into the drawing room. He wore a dinner suit. Rowland recognised the small leather valise he held at his side as a regalia case. Cartwright was apparently on his way to a Masonic Lodge meeting.

Molly looked at him, startled. "Geoffers! You're back early…"

"I forgot my handkerchief," he said coldly. "What the hell is this? Come to take inventory, Sinclair?"

"Don't be silly, Geoffrey," Molly said, standing. Rowland followed suit. "I invited Rowly—"

"Rowly? For God's sake, Molly, surely you're not so desperate as to throw yourself at—"

Molly slapped him. For a moment Geoffrey simply looked at his sister. Then he grabbed her arm and shook it. "Don't think I'm going to let you—"

Rowland stepped in. He placed his hand on Geoffrey Cartwright's shoulder and tightened his grip. "Let go of her, Mr. Cartwright."

"Mind your own business, Sinclair! I'm not about to let my sister behave like a common tramp!"

"That's enough!" Rowland's temper was beginning to flare now.

"For the love of God, Molly, didn't Daniel bring enough disgrace upon this family without you—"

Rowland stepped between Geoffrey and his sister. "Mr. Cartwright, there is nothing improper going on. Miss Cartwright merely wished to discuss who might have killed your brother." In desperation, and though he felt a little ridiculous resorting to such things, Rowland invoked Masonic code in the hope that brotherhood in the craft might carry some weight. "I assure you, sir, I am on the level."

Either Geoffrey Cartwright did not know his Masonic codes or he didn't care. He pointed at Molly. "You'll be sorry."

Molly's eyes widened. "Geoffers, please."

"Shut up! Sinclair, why don't you get out?"

Rowland glanced at Molly Cartwright. She looked frightened. "No, I don't believe I will."

Geoffrey turned around and swung at him. Rowland pulled back and Geoffrey Cartwright's fist flew uselessly past his jaw. Molly screamed.

Rowland grabbed Geoffrey's wrist before another punch could be thrown. He held it immobile and spoke to Molly without taking his eyes off Geoffrey. "Miss Cartwright, perhaps it would be best if you came back to the Copley with me for tonight."

Geoffrey's face suffused into a strange shade of claret. "You dare... You dare to proposition my sister in my presence, you filthy, indecent cad. Why, I'll... You hear this, Molly? Do you hear? He thinks he can just take you back to his hotel like a two-dollar harlot—"

"I believe your brother Frank is staying at the Copley," Rowland said calmly, still speaking to Molly despite her brother's remonstrations. "I can escort you to him."

Geoffrey looked distinctly shocked. Rowland could not tell if it was because he was not aware that Frank was staying at the hotel or because Rowland Sinclair knew that was the case. "Don't you dare leave this house, Molly! I forbid it!"

Molly looked at him and then back to Rowland. "Just give me a minute to pack a few things, Rowly."

When they left the house, Geoffrey Cartwright was quite apoplectic and threatening all manner of retribution for what he insisted was the seduction of his sister under his very nose. Molly was quiet. Rowland didn't press her for conversation. He wasn't sure if this was just a particularly intense sibling spat or something altogether more sinister. Geoffrey was at the least a bully.

"Rowly," Molly said suddenly, "must you take me to Frank's suite?"

"Is there somewhere else you wish to go?"

"Just about anywhere... just for a little while."

"You could join us for dinner—"

"Frank might come down. I couldn't bear another scene." She placed her hand on his arm. "Can you dance? Do men dance in Australia?"

"Yes..."

"Then, will you take me dancing?"

Not sure how he could refuse, Rowland agreed. "Yes, if you'd like."

Molly directed him to the Back Bay neighbourhood just a few blocks from the Boston Public Gardens. Three signs on the facades of the brick and concrete complex read, "DINE AND DANCE, COCOANUT GROVE AND MELODY BAR." The nightspot apparently had humble origins as a garage and warehouse, before becoming a speakeasy. The end of prohibition meant that the sale of alcohol was no longer a clandestine enterprise, and purveyed openly along with dining and dancing.

Rowland opened the passenger-side door. Molly smiled and held out her hand so he could help her alight. She had repaired the effects of tears with the help of a compact, pressed powder, and lipstick in a becoming shade of red. "Thank you, Rowly," she said. "You're an absolute peach to do this."

"I hope they'll let us in," he said, glancing down at his dark three-piece suit, with its smears of mud. "I'm not exactly dressed for dinner."

Molly rubbed a little dirt off his lapel. "What have you been doing? Never mind. You'll do."

❧

They were admitted into a dining hall decorated with a South Pacific theme. Linen-draped tables in the shade of artificial coconut trees formed a kind of shore around the main dance floor. Seaside murals on the walls were surprisingly convincing in the candlelight. The nightclub was crowded, but the maître d', who seemed to know Molly, managed to find them a table. They ordered from a menu that continued the island theme and took a turn about the dance floor while they waited for their meals to arrive. After months in Shanghai, where swing was very popular, Rowland fell easily into the steps and rhythm.

"For a tall man, you're surprising light on your feet," Molly observed. "Wherever did you learn to dance?"

"The boxing ring." Rowland took her hand as the number finished and led her through the press of couples back to the table. Drinks had been delivered in their absence—frothy rum cocktails served in pineapple-shaped receptacles, garnished with glacé cherries.

"Before your brother arrived, you said you were scared," Rowland began as they sat down.

"Did I?"

"Yes. Did you mean of Geoffrey?"

Molly paused. "Geoffrey is my brother, Mr. Sinclair. Are you afraid of your brother?"

Rowland smiled faintly as he thought of the numerous battles in which he and Wilfred had engaged over the years. "No, I'm not, though I am occasionally, and quite sensibly, wary."

Molly laughed. "I, too, am sensibly wary of my dear brothers." She sipped the frothy cocktail, her eyes fixed on his. "When I said I was scared, I meant of the situation in which I find myself. You're about to turn me out of my home, Rowly."

Rowland said nothing. There was nothing he could say to comfort her. He was powerless to do anything but enforce the terms of Cartwright's will.

"I can't tell you how galling it is that Danny did not love me as I did him, that he harboured some wish to see us humbled."

"I can't tell you what was in Danny's mind," Rowland said slowly, "but ten thousand dollars is a not an insubstantial sum. You won't—"

"Oh, yes, I could buy a little cottage somewhere and take in laundry I suppose...or marry." She shuddered.

Rowland's smile was wry. "Miss Higgins shares your sentiments on that score...about marrying, I mean. I must admit I've never heard her express any particular animosity to laundry."

Molly shook her head. "Miss Higgins has you, Rowly."

"But she doesn't need me...not for that anyway."

"She has her own fortune, then?"

"Not that I'm aware. Not yet anyway. I expect that once this Depression is over and people are buying art again, Ed's name will be spoken alongside Picasso and Rodin."

"And, in the meantime, you look after her?"

Rowland was becoming a little uncomfortable with the conversation. "Ed's my guest on this trip. I'd do anything in the world for her, but I've never thought she needed looking after."

Molly reached across the table and placed her hand on his. "Do you know what Danny once said about you, Rowly? He said you were endearingly naive."

Rowland wasn't quite sure how to reply. He was distracted from doing so by the entry of a familiar figure into the dining room. Frank Cartwright walked in with several men in dark double-breasted suits, smart hats with brims worn low over the eyes. They were shown to a large table. Several waiters rushed over to take their orders, and bottles of champagne and spirits were supplied immediately. Frank, it seemed, had not seen them.

Before Rowland could inform Molly of her brother's arrival, the band struck up Fred Astaire's hit "Cheek to Cheek" and she squealed. "I do love this song! Come on, Rowly, let's dance." Molly grabbed his hand and pulled him behind her, back to the dance floor and into quickstep. Momentarily, Rowland forgot about Frank Cartwright as he and Molly worked their way across the floor. "Cheek to Cheek" gave way to a slower, less popular number. It was possibly because so many couples had left the floor that Frank Cartwright noticed his sister in the arms of the man who stood between him and his brother's fortune.

Chapter Nine

Dancer Foran, Daughters Score Hit at Cape Club

Tom Foran and his Daughters, Mary and Bernice, are at the Gables Casino, Falmouth Heights, between engagements at the Cocoanut Grove, Boston, and are being well received at the smart Cape Cod night club.

Their unique military dance is especially popular and Mary's type of comedy is proving particularly engaging. Tom Foran is a well-known dancer both in New York and Boston. He has played with Eddie Cantor in the "Midnight Rounders" and in several Winter Garden productions by the Shuberts. His daughters have been dancing with him for the last three years.

—Boston Globe, July 27, 1935

Rowland's attention was focused on Molly, and so he did not notice Frank Cartwright rising from his table. It was not until the smile faded from Molly's face that he turned to see the eldest Cartwright.

"Mr. Cartwright. Hello."

"Sinclair. Good evening, Molly. What a surprise."

Molly pulled out of Rowland's arms. "Frank... I..."

Frank smiled. "Actually, I'm delighted to run into you. Please, why don't you both join us for a drink?"

Rowland glanced suspiciously at the table of men awaiting Frank's return. "That's very kind, but we wouldn't want to impose."

"Malarkey! This is my baby sister, Sinclair. I want to introduce her to my partners."

Rowland waited for Molly's lead.

"Sure," she said. "Just one drink."

The gentlemen who'd walked in with Frank Cartwright stood as they approached. Joseph Lombardo, Vincent Sorrentino, and Phil Messina were, as their names suggested, of Italian extraction, well dressed and fragrant with cologne. Sorrentino and Messina deferred to Lombardo, or Mr. J. L., as they called him. A little less than forty years of age, Lombardo was swarthy and handsome, diminutive in stature, yet large in presence. His eyes moved quickly, aware and assessing, and though his smile was white and broad, there was a hint of menace in his gaze.

"Mr. Sinclair," he said, looking up at the Australian, "welcome to Boston. Frankie tells me you were a good friend of his late brother."

"I was." Rowland made mental notes of Lombardo's face, the slight downward slant of his eyes, the strong, straight nose, and full, almost pouting lower lip. It was a powerful face, not so much for its features, but for the manner in which they were held.

"Tell me, Mr. Sinclair, what line of work are you in?"

"I'm an artist."

Lombardo registered surprise and then he laughed. "You hear that, fellas, he paints pictures." Sorrentino and Messina guffawed.

Rowland's eyes darkened.

"Don't you pay any attention to these clowns." Lombardo patted Rowland's shoulder. "Their mugs are too ugly to paint anyway." He ordered more champagne as they sat down.

"So what kind of business are you in, Mr. Lombardo?"

"This and that. Speculation, mainly." Lombardo smiled thinly.

Rowland glanced at Frank Cartwright, noting that he seemed unsettled.

"Frankie's come in with us on a couple of ventures."

French champagne was poured into glasses. Lombardo raised a toast to Daniel Cartwright and then to family.

"Did you know Danny?" Rowland asked Lombardo.

"I cannot say that I had that pleasure, though Frankie's spoken often of his baby brother. It's tragic that he went a little bananas at the end, but the artistic temperament, you understand—it lends itself to a certain instability." He lowered his voice to a whisper. "Everybody's got that one uncle who likes to wear petticoats."

Rowland said nothing.

"Can I ask you, Mr. Sinclair, when Danny Cartwright's estate might be settled? There are some opportunities for Frankie at this time, you understand, pending the distribution of family assets."

"I'm not sure, Mr. Lombardo." Rowland smiled pleasantly. "I can say that the estate will be distributed according to Daniel Cartwright's wishes as soon as possible."

"Ah yes, his wishes. Sometimes, Mr. Sinclair, we wish things in a moment of weakness, and we think later, 'Thank

God that I had friends who stopped me making a mistake, who prevented my making a jackass of myself.' You understand?"

Again Rowland refrained from responding.

Lombardo smiled. "I'll say no more. Frankie tells me that you were his brother's best friend. You'll do what's right."

"Our meals have arrived, Rowly," Molly said. "Perhaps we should get back to our table."

Rowland nodded thankfully and wished Frank Cartwright and his associates a good night. Lombardo shook Rowland's hand and, calling the maître d' over, insisted that the bill from Rowland Sinclair's table be added to his tab. "Next time, pal, you will join us for dinner, but tonight I will leave you to your *bella signora.*"

Sorrentino laughed and muttered to Lombardo, "*Si pigliano più mosche in una goocciola di miele che in un barile d'aceto.*"

The Italians sniggered and made no attempt to translate.

Rowland gave no sign that he'd understood every word, regardless.

He and Molly returned to dinner. She ate little; Rowland made up for her. And when she commented on the fact, he explained that he'd worked up an appetite burying a cow. He told her how he'd acquired the Cadillac.

"You dug a hole yourself?" Molly seemed appalled.

"I just helped. Clyde and Milt had dug half of it by the time we got back."

"And this man knew Frank?"

"Worked for him before the stock market crashed. Though he did say Frank didn't recognise him."

Molly sighed. "A lot of people worked for Frank. They helped him lose everything."

Rowland caught the bitterness, the resentment in her voice. "Still," he said carefully, "he must be doing all right now. He's living at the Copley."

"At least he has somewhere to live. That won't be true for

Geoffrey and me once you throw us out." She looked up at Rowland and then reached for his hand. "I'm sorry. I know it's not you. It's this lover of Danny's who persuaded him to cut us off." She stood. "I'm suddenly very tired. One more dance and then shall we go?"

The band was playing a waltz when they returned to the floor. Molly rested her cheek against his chest as they danced. Rowland did not mention the tears that dampened his lapel, holding her close to protect her from curious eyes. When the dance finished, they fetched their coats from the cloakroom and drove back to the Copley. Rowland made arrangements to check Molly Cartwright into her own suite, asking the receptionist to ensure it was discreetly distant from any rooms her brother might occupy.

He walked her to the door, and she invited him to join her for coffee, which she ordered. When the tray was delivered she asked him to pour while she "freshened up."

Rowland did so, and he had in fact finished his first cup of the brew when Molly emerged again into the small sitting room of the suite. Being an artist who painted from life, he was less alarmed than he might have been by the fact that she was naked. Rowland had seen the female form unclothed many times before, various models of every size and shape, and most of them he found beautiful, as he did Molly Cartwright. Her body seemed long and very slender, her breasts small but perfect on the slightness of her frame. He was nevertheless startled. "Molly..." he began, standing.

"Stay with me, Rowly," she said, stepping close. "There's no need for either of us to be alone tonight."

Rowland swallowed. "Molly, I'm the executor of your brother's will. It wouldn't be appropriate—"

"Danny would be delighted, Rowly. He wrote to me of

how handsome and charming you were. I suspect he always planned this."

"I'm fairly certain that's not what he meant, and I doubt very much his opinion of me would hold if I took advantage of his little sister."

"His opinion of you can't change, Rowly. Danny's dead. But I'm here, I'm alive…" She traced a finger over his lips. "And I want you to touch me, to have me."

Slowly Rowland removed his jacket, and then he placed it around Molly Cartwright's shoulders. "Molly, I'm sorry, I can't. It wouldn't be right."

She stepped back and pulled his jacket tight around her, shaking her head frantically. "Oh, God, I'm sorry. You must think I'm—" She began to sob, humiliated.

"I don't think anything other than that you are lovely and the timing is bad."

"You're just saying that because you're kind. Danny said you were kind. Damn you, Danny!" She backed further away until she was against the wall. "Please…you won't tell anybody—"

"Of course not." Rowland wanted to comfort her, but he was afraid any move to touch her would make matters worse. He tried to meet Molly's eye, which was difficult since she did not want to look at him. He felt like a cad. "Molly, I suspect that those cocktails were much more potent than we realised. By tomorrow morning, I guarantee you, I will have no recollection of this evening."

For several long trembling moments, there was silence, and then Molly raised her head. "And you won't be scared to take me dancing again? You haven't decided I'm a common tramp?"

"I don't think anything of the kind, and I'd be honoured to take you dancing."

She smiled faintly.

He retrieved his hat from the hook by the door but made no move to reclaim his jacket. "I'm going to say good-night. Are you all right, Molly?"

She nodded. "I am sorry."

"So am I."

Chapter Ten

The Week of a New Yorker
in Hollywood

WEDNESDAY: To the factory and for a confab with Bebe Daniels who is perfectly swell...and who will star in "Forty-Second Street"...and to spend the morning building the lady a new set of dialog for her pet scene...and so to luncheon on the lot...and to tootle off to the California Hospital to see how the Andrese gal is doing, being sorry for the youngster ill and alone in Hollywood... to labor some more...and...home...and the Wally fords to dinner...and to hear the story of Wally's wife which the most fascinating yarn we've ever heard...ANYWHERE... and is THAT material for a book! Ooowah!... And so to the opening of Jean Malin's "Club New Yorker"...and everybody in Hollywood, who is anybody there...albeit as far as we're concerned, pansy entertainment is pansy entertainment, no matter in what town you see it...

—*The Brooklyn Daily Eagle,*
October 3, 1932

∽ତ⌐

Clyde opened the door. "Rowly...what happened to your jacket?"

Even if the Copley had been the kind of place in which men wandered about without their jackets, Rowland was not the kind of gentleman to step out publicly in shirtsleeves. And Clyde distinctly remembered that his friend was fully dressed when he'd dropped them back at the hotel.

"I must have left it in Molly's suite. I'll collect it in the morning."

"Molly's suite? Are all the flaming Cartwrights here?"

Rowland explained the argument between Molly and Geoffrey Cartwright. He did not elaborate on the circumstances that had prompted him to remove his jacket in her suite. Clyde and Milton drew their own conclusions about his reasons, which were, in fact, along the lines of what Molly had intended. Clyde, though often reluctant to offer advice on such matters, went so far as to caution him on the precariousness of his situation in relation to Molly Cartwright, the inadvisability of an affair with one of Danny's beneficiaries.

"I'm not a fool, Clyde."

"I know, mate, but you are something of a romantic."

Rowland laughed quite convincingly. "It wasn't anything

like that. I took it off while we were having coffee and forgot to put it back on before I left. You chaps need to stop being such old Sydney town gossips."

Only Edna sensed there was something more to it, but she didn't press him.

Rowland told them about the Cocoanut Grove and Frank Cartwright, Joseph Lombardo, and his associates.

Milton whistled. "Gangsters?"

Rowland shrugged. "They could be legitimate business-men, I suppose, but I doubt it somehow."

"Why would they be interested in Danny's will?" Edna asked.

"Something about Frank's investment opportunities."

Clyde scowled. "Did they threaten you?"

"Not really... They just made it clear what they thought should happen. On the whole, they were polite."

"Manners maketh the mobster," Milton murmured. "So what are your thoughts, Rowly?"

"That we have to find Otis Norcross."

"We should go to New York," Edna suggested. "That's where Danny lived. Surely Mr. Norcross is more likely to be there."

Rowland agreed. "I'll talk to Burr tomorrow. We could probably stay at Danny's place at the Warwick. Perhaps someone there will have heard of Otis Norcross."

"Or have some idea who might have killed Daniel Cartwright," Clyde added.

❧

Rowland was still up when Edna knocked on the door, though it was well past midnight.

"You can't sleep?" she asked, noting the slim leather-bound sketchbook that usually resided in the breast pocket of whatever jacket he was wearing was in his hands. She climbed onto the bed beside him so she could look over his shoulder. "What are you working on?"

He smiled. "This is Joe Lombardo. He lends himself to oils, I think."

"Would he sit for you?"

"Maybe. But you wouldn't want to disappoint him."

Edna laughed softly and turned over the page. Molly Cartwright gazed out at her in exquisite detail. She studied the sketch thoughtfully, quietly marvelling at Rowland's gift—his ability to draw from memory with startling accuracy. "I wonder why Frank Cartwright was so motivated to introduce Molly to his business partners."

"I got the distinct impression the whole charade was more about introducing me."

"Why?" Edna curled up next to him on the bed as she often did on the couch. It was an impropriety to which Rowland was accustomed, an intimacy rather than a flirtation—natural and uninhibited, like the sculptress herself.

"To be truthful, I don't really know. The large chap, Sorrentino, said something strange as we went back to our own table—*Si pigliano più mosche in una goocciola di miele che in un barile d'aceto.* You can catch more flies with a bit of honey than a barrel of vinegar."

"Perhaps they're going to try to bribe you?"

"They didn't."

"Not yet."

Rowland shook his head. "I don't know what they think I could do. Danny's will was clear."

Edna glanced back at his book of sketches. "You remembered your notebook but not your jacket?"

Rowland flinched. It was difficult to get anything past Edna. "Molly noticed my notebook and gave it back to me before I left."

"She had your jacket?"

"I loaned it to her. I thought she might be cold."

That, Edna accepted. Rowland had always been gallant—he'd put his jacket around her shoulders many times. Still, she knew there was something he was not saying.

"Are you falling in love with Molly Cartwright, Rowly?"

"I am here as the executor of Danny's estate, Ed."

"She's very beautiful."

"She is, but she is also challenging the validity of Danny's will. That kind of involvement would be inappropriate, to say the least, and utterly irresponsible."

Edna smiled impishly. "Well, hello, Wilfred. Fancy meeting you here!"

Rowland laughed. It did sound like something his brother would say.

Edna put her head on his shoulder. "I'm not going to ask you to tell me what happened with Molly, because I know full well you're a gentleman. But you be careful."

"Molly's not dangerous, Ed."

"Not physically perhaps. But she's scared and hurt and the sister of your old friend. And you do have an alarming history of proposing to women in need of rescue."

He smiled, unoffended. "To be fair, I only actually asked one of those women to marry me; the others just assumed." He glanced down at her face. She'd closed her eyes, her cheek pressed gently against his chest. Rowland wondered if she could hear his heart, surely she'd notice the way it raced, pounded. "You could put a stop to it all by marrying me yourself," he said softly.

Drowsily, Edna murmured. "Wouldn't that be funny?"

Rowland could tell by her breathing that she wasn't really conscious. "It'd be grand," he said.

Rowland let the sculptress be while he ruminated on the question of Otis Norcross. Could Molly be right? Had Daniel

Cartwright's heir murdered him? To Rowland's knowledge, Danny had often chosen badly, become devoted to men not able or inclined to return his feelings. Rowland thought about his own reaction years ago to Danny's declaration of passion and undying love. Perhaps Otis Norcross had also been surprised. Perhaps he, too, had reacted violently, but more extremely. Danny particularly admired men who were brooding and brutish—he'd thought Rowland Sinclair so once, and perhaps he had been. Rowland remembered that his friend had been delighted by his interest in art but disappointed when he'd given up pugilism to pursue it.

"I don't see why it has to be one or the other, Rowly," he'd complained.

"Because," Rowland had tried to explain, "I'm not angry anymore. I just don't want to fight so much."

"But occasionally…"

"Occasional boxers are more likely to get killed. Honestly, Danny, I don't belong in the ring anymore."

In the end, Danny had accepted it, as he'd accepted the fact that Rowland was not homosexual. "If you can't be my lover, *mon ami*, at least you're not competition." His friendship had thereafter been platonic and steadfast, and he'd looked for what he insisted calling *l'amour* elsewhere.

But that had been Oxford. Rowland was aware that Danny was much more circumspect about his preferences in America, taking the posture of an eccentric aesthete. His wealth protected him from conclusions if not speculation.

God, he missed him. Rowland did, however, remain puzzled by the manner in which the will had dealt with Danny's siblings—particularly Molly. It seemed cruel, and the man he'd known had not been cruel.

Edna stirred, rubbing her face against him like a cat before she opened her eyes. She felt for his hand and checked the time on his watch.

"Heavens, it's two in the morning…have I been asleep that long?"

"About an hour and a half."

She smiled, stretching. "I'm sorry, Rowly. I'll get out of your bed now. I dreamt you asked me to marry you."

"I dreamt you said yes."

Edna laughed. "And you didn't wake up screaming? I guess we're engaged then!"

Rowland laughed too. He didn't mention that the dream had little to do with sleep.

~~~✑~~~

Detective Matthew O'Brien looked up from his paperwork at the tall Australian who was about to take up his valuable time. He assessed him quickly: shoes, suit, hat. Low-heeled, single-toned, brogued Oxfords, polished that morning—modern but not flashy. A three-piece suit with a single-breasted jacket, well cut and probably expensive; the tie sported a double Windsor knot. Of course you could tell the most about a man by his hat. This fellow's hat was a variation of the fedora that he'd not seen before. Dark brown felt, a sufficient but not excessive brim, the crown was not as high as the fedoras sported by local mobsters, and it was pinched on both sides to form a distinct crease in the front—the hat of a man who knew when to remove it. The band was plaited leather, no embellishments, and the edge of the brim was finished with leather binding—O'Brien had definitely not seen that before. Could be foreign.

"Detective O'Brien? Rowland Sinclair. How d'you do?"

Definitely foreign. British. O'Brien hoisted his bulk from the chair and shook the man's hand.

"Mr. Sinclair. What can I do for you?" The detective pointed at the empty chair in front of his desk.

Rowland removed his hat as he sat down, and explained

his interest in the murder of Daniel Cartwright. "I spoke to an Officer Murphy a couple of days ago, who was able to appraise me of the basic facts. As Mr. Cartwright's executor, and more importantly his friend, I was wondering if there was anything more you could tell me about his murder."

O'Brien's chin pressed into the cushion of his jowls as he considered the request—polite and unemotional. Emotional civilians got in the way of investigations. Murphy had said something about Sinclair, and Oliver Burr had called to insist he be seen by an officer of rank. Bloody lawyers! Sinclair was a Protestant name, of course, but Cartwright had been a pansy, after all. Though Sinclair didn't seem like a pansy. It didn't matter, he supposed. According to Father O'Malley, the Protestants were all going to Hell anyway, and better a pansy than a Freemason. There was a special more hellish Hell for Freemasons. O'Brien rummaged for the file.

"Mr. Cartwright's body was found on the ground floor of the Weld Boathouse." He drew Rowland's attention to a map of the area. "Just about there. The boathouse is on the Charles River, of course, and homes Harvard's freshman rowing team."

"And he'd been shot?"

"Four times. Three shots to the stomach and chest area and the final shot to the head. The head shot killed him, but judging from the volume of blood and the smearing, he was alive for a few minutes before it was delivered." O'Brien pulled out a couple of photographs taken at the crime scene.

Rowland forced himself to look at them, to not flinch as he did so. General pictures of the scene. A large room—hanging sculls and oars. The body lying in what seemed an impossible amount of blood. Danny had been dressed formally in a dinner suit.

"He was wearing scarlet lipstick," O'Brien said, watching Rowland's face carefully. "Though that's a fact that the family have asked us not to release to the general public for obvious reasons."

Rowland frowned. "Surely that must tell you something, Detective O'Brien?"

"It tells me plenty, son, but to exactly what were you referring?"

"Danny was not in the habit of wearing lipstick, scarlet or any other shade! It must have been—"

"I take it you're from England, Mr. Sinclair?" O'Brien's chin compressed his jowls once again.

"No, sir. I'm an Australian."

The chin leapt out from its fleshy pillow, and O'Brien's lips pursed in surprise. "Well, I must say you speak English rather well."

"Thank you." Rowland chose to avoid a conversation about geography. He assumed O'Brien was confusing Australia with Austria. "I did meet Mr. Cartwright when we were studying in England."

"And you generally reside...?"

"In Sydney...Australia."

"And Mr. Cartwright lives here," O'Brien boomed triumphantly. "My point is, son, how could you possibly be sure what his habit was? There were many young men led astray by the Pansy Craze, you know. Saw Jean Malin perform myself, and I must say it was an excellent night's entertainment, but it did turn the heads of some fellas."

Rowland said nothing. As clumsily as O'Brien put it, the detective was correct. He could not swear that Daniel Cartwright had not formed the habit of stepping out wearing scarlet lipstick, however much he doubted it.

"The bullets?" he asked, finally.

"From a .45."

"Do you have any suspects, Detective?"

"Rather too many, Mr. Sinclair. A man that wealthy...

We looked at the family, of course. And we are searching for Otis Norcross, who Mr. Burr has just informed us is the principal beneficiary of Mr. Cartwright's will. I hope I can rely on you to let us know if he contacts you."

"Certainly."

"Of course, it was in all likelihood a robbery of opportunity."

"Miss Cartwright tells me Daniel wasn't robbed."

O'Brien shrugged. "Perhaps the villain was startled somehow, or perhaps there was some valuable in Mr. Cartwright's possession of which we are not aware—a chance encounter with a robber is not something we can rule out."

"Daniel was in fear of his life. His last letter—"

O'Brien shuffled through the file again. "That'd be the letter that was stolen from your hotel?"

"Yes." Rowland waited for the detective to find the relevant report.

O'Brien scanned the page. "Just prior to an attempt to extort you by Messrs Everett and Maddox, who claimed to be reporters and who seemed to have knowledge that it contained compromising material."

"No... Well, yes...but the letter didn't contain anything actually compromising. Danny was just prone to flamboyant turns of phrase, which I expect they hoped I would find embarrassing if made public."

"And would you?"

"Yes, but not enough to abdicate my duty as Daniel Cartwright's executor."

"I see." O'Brien began to feel a little sorry for the Australian. From what Burr had told him, Rowland Sinclair had not been a beneficiary of Daniel Cartwright's will. It seemed he would gain nothing and lose a great deal.

"Do you have any idea what Mr. Cartwright was doing in the Weld Boathouse that evening, Detective?"

"Our investigations establish there was a reunion of his Harvard class, I believe, but he wouldn't have been invited to that."

"Why not?"

"Because he was expelled." O'Brien's brows rose, reassessing now. "You didn't know that, did you, son?"

"No. Danny didn't mention it—nor did the family."

"Understandable, I suppose."

"Do you know why he was expelled?"

O'Brien's eyes narrowed. "A few boys were expelled for reasons that were not made public except to say the transgression was nothing to do with academia, gambling, drink, or what would be characterised as natural sexual impropriety."

"I see." Rowland got up to leave. "Thank you for your candour, Detective. You will let me know if there are any developments? You can reach me via Oliver Burr."

O'Brien shook Rowland's hand. "Rest assured, Mr. Sinclair, in Boston, murder is murder, regardless of who the victim is."

Chapter Eleven

If U.S.A. Has Dictator

What will Happen?
Sinclair Lewis Answers with
Powerful Pen in His New Novel,
"It Can't Happen Here"
—An Imaginative Picture of American
Life Under Fascist Tyranny.

By Prof. W.T. Allison

Sinclair Lewis has been studying very carefully the recent trend of events in the United States and has written a novel that will peal like a fire-alarm bell throughout the sorely troubled country which has always been fond of fancying itself as the real home of liberty. The very title of this new novel, "It Can't Happen Here" (Doubleday, Doran and Gundy, Toronto) wans in inspiration. As a stimulus to curiosity it ought to be of prodigious assistance in selling the latest story by the most popular writer on this continent.

Well what is "it"? This may be stated in one word, Fascism. What would be likely to happen in the United States if a dictator more merciless than Mussolini and more unscrupulous than Hitler seized the supreme power and proceeded to wipe out freedom of the press, popular government, trial by jury and other safeguards of democracy?

—*The Winnipeg Tribune*
(Winnipeg, Manitoba, Canada),
16 November 1935

Edna's wave caught Rowland's attention from across Copley Square. The sky was that peculiar greenish shade of grey that promised snow, and it was certainly cold enough. Edna's cheeks had been rose-pinched by the cold and her eyes sparkled. Milton had taken plummeting temperatures as an opportunity to proudly don the bright orange overcoat that the rest of them considered an eyesore, and Clyde looked a little miserable.

"What have you done to Clyde?" Rowland asked as he reached them.

"He's just being a baby about the cold," Edna replied. "You'd never tell he was mountain-born and bred."

Rowland smiled. Clyde hailed from the small town of Batlow in the foothills of the Australia's Snowy Mountains, and yet he suffered more than any of them from the cold.

"I've become soft living in Sydney," Clyde admitted. "Not to mention that I have to appear in public with a man dressed like a carrot."

Milton rolled his eyes. "Save us all from provincial taste."

"What's that?" Rowland asked, noticing the book in Milton's hand. He liked to keep an eye on the poet's reading material, just so he'd know who Milton was likely to steal from next.

Milton handed him the volume, not poetry but a novel: *It Couldn't Happen Here.* "The latest by your Nobel-winning cousin—according to the bookstore proprietor, it's a bestseller."

Rowland laughed. At some point in the distant past, his brother had mentioned within Milton's hearing that a branch of the Sinclair family had settled in Minnesota, a fact the poet now used to claim the American Nobel Laureate, Sinclair Lewis, as Rowland's cousin. There was a similar rumour, from what was most likely a similar source, that Milton Isaacs was the grandson of Australia's current governor-general.

"Is it any good?" Rowland asked.

"I'll let you know."

Edna turned her face up towards Rowland's. Her hair had begun to form gentle ringlets around her face in the damp. "Did you find out anything?"

"Rather a lot, actually."

"Shall we find somewhere out of the blizzard to talk about this?" Clyde asked as the first flakes began to flutter down.

"It's snowing!" Edna said, beaming. "Look!" She caught a soft flake on the dark wool of her coat sleeve.

Rowland turned up the collar of his own overcoat and laughed at her delight. Edna Higgins had the capacity to find joy in little things, to notice tiny transient wonders in a way that never failed to shake him out of brooding. "As much as I hate to contribute to Clyde's softness, we probably should get out of the weather." They were in the middle of the square, between the Trinity Church and the Copley Plaza Hotel. "Church or bar?"

"Why would you even need to ask?" Milton shook his

head and began striding back to the Copley, leading the way to the Carousel Bar, which they were already coming to know well. Even this early, it was crowded and lively. Regardless, they managed to claim a table near the rotating bar and ordered hot drinks while Rowland recounted his conversation with O'Brien.

"Danny was expelled from Harvard?" Edna said. "For what?"

"Deviancy, apparently. It explains why he was at Oxford and perhaps why he never mentioned it."

"Oh, poor Danny." Edna shuddered.

"The Weld Boathouse is on the other side of the Charles River, on university grounds—not far from Harvard Yard. It houses their rowing team." Rowland tried hard not to see the crime scene photographs in his mind's eye as he spoke. "Danny was dressed formally for dinner. Apparently the reunion dinner of what would have been his graduating class was taking place that evening, but Danny hadn't been invited."

"Perhaps a separate function," Clyde suggested, "or maybe he was meeting someone who lived in one of the residential colleges."

"Who hasn't come forward," Milton added darkly. "I don't suppose Danny intended to crash the reunion...emerge like the Phantom of the Opera to proclaim injustice."

Rowland smiled faintly. "I don't know. Danny didn't ever tell me about Harvard, so I don't know if the expulsion still rankled enough for him to do something like that. I'm almost certain he wouldn't embarrass his family like that."

"Like you were certain he wouldn't disinherit them?" Milton asked.

Rowland conceded. Perhaps he did not know Daniel Cartwright as well as he'd thought.

"Could it be," Milton asked, "that Danny's falling out with his family is to do with the expulsion? It would explain why even Molly didn't mention that he'd attended Harvard and why he left the bulk of his fortune to Otis Norcross."

"Did the police talk to whoever drove Danny out there?" Clyde asked. The other side of the Charles was walking distance by Australian standards, but Daniel Cartwright had maintained a vocal and fervent opposition to any form of exercise in the weeks that they had stayed with him.

"The police haven't been able to work out who drove him there," Rowland replied.

"Danny was afraid of flying!" Edna said suddenly.

"Yes." Rowland turned to the sculptress, wondering where her thoughts were heading.

"Well, he wouldn't have flown down from New York. He must have driven, unless he caught a train…"

"No. Danny detested trains too," Rowland murmured. "He would have brought his own motorcar and driver. Ed, you're brilliant!"

"So what's happened to his car and chauffeur?" Clyde asked.

"Perhaps the chauffeur took the vehicle back to New York," Rowland replied. "I'll enquire of Burr about Danny's New York staff. I'm not sure if they've been let go yet, but even if they have, we'll find them."

Rowland telephoned Oliver Burr from the reception desk.

"Now that the will has been read, we can terminate their employments," Burr replied, misinterpreting the reason for Rowland's query.

"Wouldn't it be wiser to wait until Otis Norcross is found?" Rowland suggested hastily. "He might wish to keep them on."

"That's your decision to make, Mr. Sinclair."

"Then let's retain them for the time being," Rowland said, relieved. "I might go up to New York and talk to Danny's staff. See if any one of them has heard of Otis Norcross."

"The staff? Oh yes, excellent idea, Mr. Sinclair, though I could send one of the associates—"

"Thank you, no, Mr. Burr. I'm quite looking forward to a change of scenery right now—provided, of course, that there's nothing to keep me in Boston for the next couple of days."

"Nothing as important as finding Otis Norcross. Go with my blessing, Mr. Sinclair."

And so it was settled. Clyde inspected the engine of the Madame X to ensure she was ready for the two-hundred-and-fifty-mile drive to New York. Rowland helped for a while, but when it became clear that he was in the way, he left Clyde to it, and returned to the suite. He wrote to his brother explaining why they had not yet embarked for home.

"I assure you, Wil, I do not delay by any contrivance on my own part. I would make tracks for Sydney tomorrow if I could do so knowing I had done my best by Danny. I don't pretend to understand the choices Danny made, but it appears to be my lot to protect them. He trusted me to do that, and I cannot let him down. I hope that by the time you receive this, Danny's missing heir and his murderer will have been found and we will be on our way home.

"Until then, I must continue to rely on my nephews to keep Lenin from feeling too abandoned. Before we left Singapore, Milt received a letter from Mother informing him that she was cruising with Aunt Millie, so I trust she is weathering our absence well…"

Rowland finished the letter with his sincere and fond regards to his brother's family. He hoped the missive would placate Wilfred, whose irate telegram demanding to know what the hell he was doing in America had reached him at the Copley the day before. Rowland had considered explaining the situation in full, appraising Wilfred of the lawsuit, the Cartwrights' threats to ruin him, but he decided against it. There was not a lot that even a man of Wilfred Sinclair's power and influence could do to help him here.

He wrote a second letter, a message to Molly Cartwright informing her that he was sojourning to New York for a couple of days. There was no reason to let her know, and yet, considering the events of the night before, it seemed impolite and callous to just disappear. He was leaving the note for her at the reception desk when the lady herself appeared.

"Rowly," she said, casting her eyes down shyly. "I've had your jacket cleaned and pressed."

"Thank you. That's very thoughtful."

"They'll have it by tonight, if you'd—"

"I'm afraid I'm going to be out of town for a couple of days. In fact, I was just leaving you a note."

She took the envelope from his hand and read the contents there and then. "Oh. Is this because of what I—"

"No, Molly. Not at all."

She placed her hand lightly on Rowland's sleeve. "I told Frank to drop the challenge, but he won't hear of it. He won't let me pull out either. I know that sounds weak, but Frank and Geoffrey—"

"Please don't give it a thought, Molly. If we can actually locate Otis Norcross, then a case based on the contention that he doesn't exist will go away." He frowned. She seemed fragile today. "Will you be all right?"

She nodded. "Can I stay here?"

"Yes, of course. I've already informed the hotel." The cost of Molly Cartwright's room was being billed to Rowland personally, as opposed to the estate, and so he felt no conflict. "Are your brothers aware you're here?"

She shook her head. "Geoffrey will assume I spent the night in your bed."

"Would you like me to speak to him?"

"God, no!"

"Would you like to come with us to New York?"

Molly's eyes softened. She tilted her head to one side and smiled. "You really don't know how to go to war, do you, Rowly? You don't ask the enemy to go on holiday with you."

"You're not the enemy, and you can rest assured we're not on holiday."

"Even so." She reached up and gently kissed his cheek. "You go see if you can find this man, but promise me you'll be careful, Rowly. The fiend could well have killed my brother for his fortune."

Chapter Twelve

Rabbi Wise Warns Father
Coughlin

SAYS CONTINUED ATTACKS ON JEWISH BANKERS WILL DEEPLY WRONG JEWISH PEOPLE

Appeal Made To Priest

Detroit Cleric Asked to Reconsider
Statements Ascribed To Him Last Sunday

[By the Associated Press]

New York, March 24—Questioning whether
the Rev. Charles E. Coughlin "desires to make
himself responsible for a terrible anti-Semitic or
anti-Jewish outbreak in America" Rabbi Stephen
S. Wise appealed today to the Detroit priest to
reconsider statements ascribed to him last Sunday.

The Rabbi, addressing the free synagogue at Carnegie Hall, declared Father Coughlin had said in effect, "though he has not used the name Jew," that a group of Jewish bankers were chiefly responsible for the nation's economic woes.

WILL HURT JEWISH PEOPLE

"Father Coughlin," he said, in a broadcast, "I need not remind you, a priest of your church, of the commandment which bids men to refrain from bearing false witness against their neighbors..."

HOW NAZIS BEGAN ATTACK

Discussing anti-Jewish movements, the Rabbi remarked that "Naziism began its assault upon Jews by iterating ten thousand times directly and indirect that Jewish bankers were destroying the German Nation."

"And now," he said at another point, "we come upon a new horror of mendacity and calumny in the publication of pamphlets by certain groups in America which hold Jews responsible for the murder of the Lindbergh baby, in connection with so-called synagogue and ritual purposes, and exonerate the convicted murderer."

—*The Baltimore Sun*
(Baltimore, Maryland), March 25, 1935

It had been a little over three years since they'd enjoyed the hospitality of Daniel Cartwright at The Warwick in midtown Manhattan. Oliver Burr had called ahead to make sure Rowland Sinclair and his party would be admitted to the deceased's apartment. They rode the brass-doored elevator from the quietly opulent foyer to the thirty-first floor in sombre reflection, knowing they would not be met by the eccentric Francophile who had so enthusiastically and warmly welcomed them to New York on their last visit. The door to the apartment was opened by a stern-faced man in black tie and tails—Daniel Cartwright's valet.

"Mr. Sinclair," he said immediately. "A pleasure to see you again." There was, however, nothing aside from his words to indicate he felt anything akin to pleasure, then or possibly ever.

"Mr Bradford. Hello." Rowland shook the valet's hand. "I wonder if you remember—"

"Mr. Watson Jones, Mr. Isaacs, and Miss Higgins. Please come in. I expect you've had a long journey."

Daniel Cartwright's drawing room was unchanged: a lavish formal room with expansive arched windows that looked down onto Sixth Avenue. The wood panelling was painted white against dark red walls upon which were hung a series of elaborately framed portraits.

Rowland was struck by the strangeness of walking into a room in which more than a dozen likenesses of Daniel Cartwright were hung. Each seemed to capture some different part of their subject more absolutely than the others. Over the mantel was the piece Rowland had painted on their last visit—an artist at work on a self-portrait, peering at his own reflection while trying to capture it on his canvas. The composition was made up of three renderings of its subject. Danny had discarded a Picasso in order to hang it, so taken had he been with the depiction. The painting startled

Rowland now more than the others. It had been the last time he and Danny had painted together, and in each brushstroke had been conversation and camaraderie, Danny's absurd French, and a common love of paint.

Edna wiped her eyes, overcome for a moment by the presence of their late friend in this place.

"Would you care for a refreshment, sir?" Bradford broke the silence.

"Yes, thank you, Mr. Bradford." Rowland tipped the porters who brought in their bags.

"I'll just be a minute, sir, if you'd care to help yourselves from the bar." Bradford motioned towards the massive brass and Bakelite globe which housed the drinks cabinet. Milton did the honours, mixing drinks from the various bottles and decanters.

Bradford returned with tiered trays of finger sandwiches and pastries, which he set down before turning to return to the kitchen.

"Please don't go, Mr. Bradford," Edna said. "We'd like to talk to you."

"Would you like a drink, Mr. Bradford?" Milton asked. "Why don't you join us? We should drink to Danny."

Bradford seemed startled. Milton handed him a glass of scotch. "You look like a whisky man. Am I right, Mr. Bradford?"

"You are, Mr. Isaacs. You are." He raised his glass. "To Mr. Cartwright. May God rest his soul."

The Australians responded in kind.

"Mr. Bradford, do you know of an Otis Norcross?" Rowland asked. "Has he ever visited here?"

"Not to my knowledge, sir."

"Had Mr. Cartwright ever mentioned an Otis Norcross?"

"Not to my recollection."

Rowland sat back, deflated. He'd been sure that if anyone knew it would be Bradford.

"Perhaps he was someone Mr. Cartwright met on his summer vacations," the valet ventured.

"His summer vacations?"

"Oh, yes. For the last three years, Mr. Cartwright has set out on motoring holidays."

Rowland sat forward, surprised. "Do you know where he went, Mr. Bradford?"

"No, sir."

"Do you know what Danny did on these vacations?"

"I was led to understand that it was fishing."

"Really?" The scepticism was plain on Rowland's face. In his experience Daniel Cartwright detested being out of doors.

"I've prepared rooms for you all." Bradford put down his empty whisky glass, signalling the end to the appalling familiarity to which he had for a moment succumbed. "Mr. Cartwright's room is as he left it. I expected the family might come to go through it, but they haven't."

Edna looked at the valet compassionately, seeing through his gruffness to real grief. "We can pack up Danny's room, if that helps, Mr. Bradford." She placed her hand gently on his sleeve. "We are very sorry for your loss."

"Mr. Cartwright was my employer, nothing more."

"Even so, Mr. Bradford, I'm sure he was a good and kind employer."

Bradford seemed about to protest, and then suddenly his eyes softened. "Aye, he was that."

"Did Mr. Cartwright still have a chauffeur on staff?" Rowland asked.

Bradford nodded. "Billy. Miss Davies has borrowed him."

"Does she still have the penthouse here?" They'd met Marion Davies, the actress and mistress of media tycoon William Randolph Hearst, on their last visit to New York, when she'd invited Daniel Cartwright's Australian guests to one of her famous parties. Davies had been gracious and warm.

Rowland stood. "Do you mind if I use the telephone, Mr. Bradford?"

"I was Mr. Cartwright's valet, sir—I'm not his widow. I have no right to mind or not mind."

"Yes, right," Rowland said awkwardly. "The telephone still in the study?"

"Yes, sir."

Rowland left his friends with Bradford and slipped into the Regency-inspired study. He sat down at the ostentatious gilt desk with its fussy claw-foot legs and called reception, asking to be patched through to the penthouse. He gave his name and qualified himself with the fact that he was an old friend of Daniel Cartwright and asked to speak to Miss Davies.

When she came to the phone, he reminded her who he was.

"Of course! Poor Danny's Australians. I remember you well. How is that gorgeous young actress who Archie Leech was so taken with?"

"Ed? She's well." Rowland recalled some American actor called Archibald Leech pursuing Edna while they were in New York. "She and Mr. Isaacs and Mr. Watson Jones have accompanied me once again."

"Oh, Mr. Sinclair, I miss Daniel very much, you know."

"As do I, Miss Davies. I'm actually trying to track down Danny's chauffeur, who I believe is driving for you at the moment."

"Billy? I'm afraid he's driving my niece today. Patty's home from school, you see."

"Perhaps if you could ask him to come see me when he gets back?"

"Most certainly. Where are you?"

"We're all staying in Danny's apartment."

"Oh, my! Really. Well, then you must come to dinner tonight. I'll instruct the cook to make something especially delicious, and Patty will so enjoy meeting Australians. You simply must come, Mr. Sinclair."

"We'd be delighted, Miss Davies."

"In that case, I shall be sure to send Billy down to you as soon as he gets back."

～❧～

Rowland was still getting dressed when Bradford came into the bedroom to inform him Cartwright's chauffeur was at the door.

"Ask him to come in, Mr. Bradford," Rowland said, affixing his cuff links to the cuffs of his dress shirt. He grabbed the bow tie from the bureau and turned up his starched collar to tie it. "I won't be a minute."

"Do you require any assistance with your tie, sir..." Bradford trailed off as Rowland secured the perfect knot with expert speed.

"None at all, Mr. Bradford." He pulled on his dinner jacket, finger-combed his hair, and stepped out into the anteroom.

The chauffeur was young and bespectacled.

Rowland put out his hand. "Rowland Sinclair, Mr.—"

"Collins. William Collins, sir." He shook Rowland's hand. "Miss Davies said you wanted to see me."

"I do, indeed. I have a few questions I need to ask you."

Collins looked a little alarmed. "Are you with the police, sir?"

"No. Mr. Cartwright was my friend. I'm just trying to find out what happened to him."

Collins continued to regard him warily.

"Did you drive Mr. Cartwright to Boston a couple of months ago, Mr. Collins?"

"Yessir."

Rowland exhaled. Finally, something. "Did you drive for him *in* Boston?"

"Yessir."

"On the night Mr. Cartwright died, did you drive him to the Harvard campus?"

A pause. "Yessir, I did."

"Did you wait for him?"

"No, sir. He told me to go straight home."

"He was dressed for dinner—do you know what he was doing out there?"

"He was meeting a gentleman who was working at the university, sir. They planned to go to dinner."

"Do you know who the gentleman was?"

Collins shook his head. "He was an artist, like Mr. Cartwright."

"Can I ask how you know that, Mr. Collins?"

"Mr. Cartwright was excited, talking French a lot, and he had a present for the gentleman. A paintbrush."

Rowland frowned. "Do you know where he died, Mr. Collins?"

"Yessir, in the boathouse."

"Do you know what he could have been doing there?"

"We were early when I dropped him off at Harvard Square just outside Harvard Yard. He said he would take a stroll. He said he was feeling nostalgic."

"Did the Boston police never question you, Mr. Collins?"

"No, sir. I wasn't sure what to do, so I contacted Mr. Bradford and brought the Buick back to New York."

"Just one more thing, Mr. Collins. Did you drive Mr. Cartwright when he went on his summer vacations?"

"No, sir. Mr. Cartwright always insisted on driving the Buick himself then."

Rowland was surprised to hear this. He hadn't known his friend could drive a motorcar. One last shot. "I don't suppose you've ever heard Mr. Cartwright mention an Otis Norcross?"

Collins swallowed. "Otis? Maybe, sir."

"What do you mean, Mr. Collins?"

"There was a painting." Collins led Rowland to the drawing room and pointed out a small portrait. Daniel Cartwright's face. The technique was hesitant, a little unskilled, but the likeness was excellent and the depiction tender. It was not signed. "I came in to collect him one day. He was looking at this and I thought I heard him say, 'Oh, Otis.'" Collins shook his head. "When he saw I was there, he shouted at me, which was strange and not like Mr. Cartwright. He appeared to have been crying."

For a moment Rowland said nothing as he grappled with what the chauffeur had revealed. "Thank you, Mr. Collins, you've been very helpful."

Collins hesitated. "Mr. Sinclair, sir, if I could ask... I need this job and—"

"I'm hoping that when we find Mr. Norcross, he will retain Mr. Cartwright's staff."

"And if you don't find him, Mr. Sinclair?"

"I will see you right, Mr. Collins. You have my word."

The darkness of Edna's gown set off the creaminess of her skin, and its cut showed her curves to full effect. Her hair, which she'd allowed to grow quite long in the last year, was caught in a beaded net at the base of her neck, and her only jewellery was a silver locket delicately embellished with seed pearls. She adjusted her long gloves as she walked into the drawing room. Rowland stared at her, intoxicated by her presence.

She noticed his gaze and laughed. "Has it been that long since we dressed up?"

Rowland shrugged. "You do look pretty, Ed."

"Why, thank you." Her eyes sparkled. "It'll be lovely to see Marion and WR again. I can't believe it's been three years."

"I wonder if we've changed."

Edna sighed. "I'm not sure if we have. But the world has changed."

He looked at her, sensing a certain disquiet. "Has something happened?"

She took his hand and glanced at his watch. "There's a radio in my room—I turned it on when I was dressing." She pulled him after her into the guest room that Bradford had allocated her. "Close the door," she said.

Once Rowland had done so, she turned on the chrome-grilled Philco radiogram. It was tuned to a national broadcast, a political address criticising Roosevelt's New Deal, and the grasping greed of Jewish bankers, which the broadcaster claimed was preventing monetary reform and pushing the working man towards socialism.

Rowland turned off the radiogram.

"Who is this chap, Ed? I didn't catch—"

"He's a priest!" Edna said angrily. "A man of the cloth. Father Coughlin—he has a weekly radio show, apparently."

"How many people are going to tune in to a priest, Ed?" It was an attempt to comfort the sculptress rather than the fact he was unconcerned. "Church once a week is all most people can take."

"Would he have a radio show if they didn't?"

A knock at the door. "Miss Higgins, is there anything I can get you, madam? Mr. Isaacs and Mr. Watson Jones are ready to leave. I presume Mr. Sinclair is somewhere about the place..."

Rowland grinned. "Well, what do you know—old Bradford is concerned about your virtue."

Edna shushed him and opened the door.

"Rowly was just helping me with the clasp of my necklace," she said, grabbing a silk shawl from the back of a bedroom chair.

Bradford looked Rowland up and down. The old valet remained steadfast by the door, scowling, until Rowland had walked out of the lady's bedroom.

Chapter Thirteen

Orson Welles and Bride Visit Here on Friday

Mr. and Mrs. Orson Welles, who have played with Katherine Cornell in "Romeo and Juliet," this past winter in New York, are visiting in Chicago and at Wheaton with the Leo Nickolsons, the parents of Mrs. Welles (Virginia Nicholson). It is rumoured that both will have parts in a play to be produced in Chicago in the near future.

Orson and Virginia, who were members of the Todd Theatre Festival company, of last summer, playing in "Trilby," "Hamlet," and "Tsar Paul," have many friends here, who wish them success.

Their romance began here on the campus at Todd School, and their wedding took place last December in New York where they have been living.

Mr. and Mrs. Welles were guests of the Roger Hills on Friday, and enjoyed being at

Todd, where the young actor spent many of
his early boyhood years.

—*The Daily Sentinel*
(Woodstock, Illinois), April 29, 1935

∽◎∾

The Australians were not the only guests of Marion Davies
that night. It was difficult to tell whether the party had
been organised before or after her invitation to Rowland
Sinclair had been issued. Marion had many friends, and
most of them were available for one of her dinner parties
at short notice.

When the penthouse door was opened, the party was in
full swing. A five-piece band played the ballroom while guests
mingled throughout. The Australians were announced by the
servant who took them to the hostess. Marion Davies glittered under the weight of her jewellery. William Randolph
Hearst was a more reserved presence, a darker backdrop to
Marion's luminescence, but perhaps he was more noticeable
for that fact. He stood by the baby grand piano with a clearly
excited teenage girl.

Marion greeted them all warmly, effusively, and reminded
the much older Hearst of "Danny's divine Australians." She
introduced her niece, Miss Patricia Van Cleve. "Now one of
you handsome gentlemen must dance with Patty, so I can
talk shop with Eddie—"

Hearst interrupted. "I wouldn't mind having a word with
Mr. Sinclair."

Clyde looked decidedly anxious until Milton stepped up
and offered Patricia his hand. "Miss Van Cleve, if you would
do me the honour?"

She took his hand enthusiastically. "Of course, Mr. Isaacs. Do tell me all about Australia!"

Milton led her onto the dance floor, reciting Paterson's verse as if he were composing it on the run.

Rowland followed Hearst into the vast study, the walls of which were hung with Marion Davies film posters, mounted, framed, and lit with individual sconces. A collection of Greek vases was displayed on marble plinths. In the centre of the room was a circular bar. The barman mixed cocktails at its centre.

"A martini, Mr. Sinclair?" Hearst asked.

"Thank you."

The barman obliged, and when the martinis had been prepared and set before them, he left the room. Hearst motioned towards the barstool beside his and invited Rowland to take a seat. "Word has it you have upset the Cartwrights, Mr. Sinclair."

"It was never my intention, Mr. Hearst. But it does seem to be the way it's panned out."

"Well, the Cartwrights are not Brahmins, at least... You'd know it if you'd upset the Brahmins."

Rowland said nothing. He vaguely understood the Brahmins were Boston's traditional social elite. But he had trouble following even Australia's social delineations without trying to grasp the more complicated caste system of the Americans.

"The problem with Frank not being a Brahmin is that he is not restrained by their virtuous pretensions." Hearst removed the olive from his martini. "He will fight dirty."

"I see."

"Marion was very fond of Daniel Cartwright, Mr. Sinclair, and so you may rely on the fact that Hearst papers will not publish any muck that may be raked against you. I can't speak for the *Boston Globe*, of course."

Rowland frowned. "Have your papers been approached, sir?"

"Yes."

"With what muck, exactly?"

"Revelations about your relationship with Daniel Cartwright. In fact they claim to possess a rather damning letter."

Rowland exhaled. "Right." So they intended to see through their threat. "I shall make it a priority to speak to Mr. Burr...see if there is not something he can do legally. Thank you for the warning, Mr. Hearst."

"I wish you luck, Mr. Sinclair. I've dealt with Frank Cartwright before. I'm afraid a couple of salacious tabloid articles may be the least of your problems."

Rowland drained his martini. "I'll certainly watch my back, sir."

Before they returned to the party, Hearst took Rowland to a formal reception room which was not being used for that evening's event to show the artist his latest acquisitions: a Van Dyck, a Vouet, and George Washington's snuff box.

"Danny used to give me his opinion, from time to time. He identified a forgery for me once."

They discussed the paintings for a while, and once Hearst was satisfied that the latest additions to his collection had been sufficiently admired, they rejoined the other guests. It seemed that several more people had arrived in the meantime. The penthouse was crowded with starlets and moguls and media. The band had picked up tempo, and the dancing was in earnest.

Rowland found Clyde by the buffet holding a square-faced dog with a short nose and large, upright ears, who was far too big to be comfortably held. Rowland rubbed the hound's ears, wordlessly, raising a single brow in enquiry.

"Some woman asked me to hold her dog while she danced," Clyde replied.

"And you agreed?"

"It was either that or dance. This is the lesser of evils."

"Does it have a name?" The dog licked Rowland's hand. He didn't pull away—he'd always liked dogs.

"She calls the poor bloody creature Smoochy."

Rowland winced. "Which one is she?" he asked, surveying the dancers.

Clyde pointed out a young woman in a black-and-white ensemble that resembled the markings of her dog. Rowland noticed Edna on the dance floor near her in the arms of an older man. "Who's the chap dancing with Ed?"

"Some bloke called Kennedy—Joe, I think. He owns movie studios, apparently. Marion introduced him to Ed." Clyde's brow furrowed. "He seems pretty taken with her."

"He wouldn't be the first man."

"He's under the illusion she's an actress. Said something about having just the film for her."

If he was not standing in the penthouse of Marion Davies and William Randolph Hearst, Rowland might have disregarded the claim as a ludicrous attempt to seduce the sculptress, but in this circle it was possible that Kennedy was, in fact, the proprietor of a studio. Of course, that didn't mean he wasn't trying to impress Edna.

"If you don't need my assistance with Smoochy here, I might cut in."

"Go," Clyde said without hesitation. For some reason he couldn't put his finger on, he didn't like Kennedy.

"Rowly!" Edna took her hand from Kennedy's shoulder to reach for Rowland. "There you are! I was wondering what Mr. Hearst had done with you... This is Mr. Joseph Kennedy."

"Mr. Kennedy. How d'you do? Rowland Sinclair."

Kennedy met his eye. "Mr. Sinclair. You're not going to ask me if you can cut in, are you?"

"Yes, I am."

"And what if I say no?"

Edna laughed. "You can't say no. It's not done."

Kennedy smiled, rather too broadly. "You can't blame a man for wanting to keep you to himself."

Edna moved directly and determinedly into Rowland's arms. Rowland almost felt sorry for Kennedy, who wasn't to know how much his attempt at flattery would irk Edna Higgins. She would not be kept anywhere by any man. The band was playing a swing, and Rowland and Edna stepped into the rhythm.

The beat was too quick to allow them to sensibly hold a conversation, and so it was not until the next number, a jazz waltz, that she asked about his conversation with William Randolph Hearst.

"What does he mean that the articles will be the least of your problems?" Edna said uneasily after Rowland had filled her in.

"I suspect that's just hyperbole, Ed." Rowland led into a turn. "He just means that Frank is not going to be easy to deal with." He changed the subject, telling Edna what he'd learned from William Collins.

"He was crying?" The sculptress pressed her cheek against his lapel. "Oh, poor Danny. Do you think Otis Norcross broke his heart?"

"I don't know." Rowland glanced down at Edna. "Perhaps Norcross was just someone Danny could not have, for one reason or another."

"Wouldn't that break his heart?"

"Only if there was no hope. Danny was an optimist."

The band stopped playing and an announcement was made that the dinner was served. Guests were invited to find their seats at the long dining table, which had been set for the purpose. Rowland found himself seated beside their hostess. Edna was on the other end of the table between Kennedy and a chubby young man with a deep baritone voice, who Marion whispered was a radio actor. Milton sat between Marion and the young Miss Van Cleve, who it seemed had taken a particular liking to the poet. Milton, for his part, seemed quite at home in conversation with the fifteen-year-old. Clyde seemed to have finally relinquished the dog and was deep in conversation to one of the follies girls who'd attended as both guests and entertainment.

A series of courses began, a feast of immense proportion and exquisite presentation. Lobsters, various roast meats, salmon, caviar, served with wine and champagne.

"Joe's quite smitten with Edna," Marion observed.

Rowland thought her smile triumphant, slightly excited. He said nothing.

"He owns a studio, you know. Catching his eye could make Edna's career." She stared at him. "Oh, shoot. Are you and Edna—? I didn't realise. When she stepped out with Archie Leech, I thought..."

"Ed has not been spoken for," Rowland said carefully.

Marion stopped, relieved. "Well, thank goodness! Joe could do a lot for Edna." She looked over at the sculptress, who was fielding the attentions of both men beside her. "Joe could make her a star. Edna really is quite extraordinarily beautiful...and," she added wistfully, "she's still so young."

Milton snorted. "Ed's not *that* young!" He glanced dubiously in the direction of Kennedy. "If he's after a pretty little thing to mould, he might be disappointed."

"Oh, no—Edna could be anything she wanted!"

"I think what Milt means," Rowland said quietly, "is that, though Ed is capable of being anything she wants, it will only be what *she* wants."

"But who wouldn't want to be a star?" Patricia Van Cleve piped in.

Marion glanced at her niece fondly. "Your turn will come, darling. Your turn will come."

A couple of courses into the meal, the band struck up again and the long table became a kind of buffet to which guests would return in between sets. Marion introduced Rowland and Milton to various quite beautiful young women. Rowland suspected she was making sure they did not interfere with Edna's chance. Neither were likely to do so—not because they believed that Joseph Kennedy was the potential patron that Marion believed him to be, but because they knew Edna Higgins. Marion also dragged the young radio actor away from Edna and Kennedy and introduced him to the Australian men, before leaving to attend to her other guests.

Orson Welles appeared noticeably disgruntled to have been taken from Edna's company. "We must all make way for another rich man to acquire a woman he can fashion into a star, I suppose," he said resentfully. "After all, how better to demonstrate your power than to elevate a woman devoid of talent into public acclaim?" Welles glanced back at Edna. "It's a pity. Miss Higgins has a life about her, a wit, that is about to be crushed under Kennedy's need to prove that he can acquire the shiniest toy."

Rowland's lips quirked. "I wouldn't be too concerned, Mr. Welles."

A little concerned that Patricia was becoming enamoured with him, Milton attempted to encourage her towards someone her own age. There were a few adolescents amongst the guests who Patricia invariably deemed "too childish" or "a bore."

"What about him?" Milton asked, pointing to a boy who stood awkwardly by the window with his gaze fixed rather ambitiously on Edna. "Thick hair, good teeth, a little skinny, but he'll probably fill out."

"John Kennedy? No way!"

"Kennedy?" Rowland overheard the name.

"Yes. He's a real Abercrombie—thinks his father's going to be president!"

"Sorry, I thought you said his name was Kennedy?"

"It is. His old man is Joe Kennedy." She rolled her eyes. "All the Kennedy boys think they're the cat's pyjamas!"

"There's more of them?"

"He's the only one here, but there's half a dozen at least." Patricia lowered her voice.

"And Mrs. Kennedy?" Milton prompted.

"At home with another baby, I expect," Welles said maliciously. "Nothing like a good Catholic wife."

"Hearst has one of those, too, I believe," Milton whispered to Rowland. "I guess Marion doesn't find that a problem." They cast their eyes towards Edna and the elder Kennedy on the dance floor, just as the sculptress stopped dancing and shoved her partner furiously back.

"She might just have found out about Mrs. Kennedy," Rowland murmured, excusing himself as Joseph Kennedy tried to pull her back.

Edna shook Kennedy off and met Rowly on the edge of the dance floor. "Dance with me, Rowly, so I don't have to speak to that beastly man!"

Chapter Fourteen

JOSEPH KENNEDY IS SEEN AS
POWER IN FILM WORLD

BOSTON BANKER IS PROBABLY MOST DYNAMIC
AND INFLUENTIAL PERSONALITY IN MOTION
PICTURE INDUSTRY TODAY, MISS PARSON
SAYS—TRACES HIS RISE

By Louella O. Parsons

Los Angeles, Cal., July 14.—Who is this
Joseph Kennedy, the unseen force that
stalks through Hollywood, striking uncertainty to the hearts of thousands of film
people? Who is this dynamic power whose
very name is sufficient to start a discussion
and whose deeds are being as much marvelled as any of the picturesque exploits of

Andrew Carnegie in the days when he rode
to fame as a steel baron?

—*The Star Press*
(Muncie, Indiana), July 15, 1928

~~⁐~~

Rowland took the sculptress into his arms and manoeuvred
away from Kennedy, even as the businessman tried to reach
them. "Are you all right, Ed?"

"Yes. Just angry. What an appalling man! I was trying to
be polite for Marion's sake, but when he..." She bit her lip,
her eyes welling.

Rowland's jaw hardened. "What did he do? If he—"

Edna stopped him. "It was nothing like that, Rowly. Well,
it was, but that's not why I am so wild with him."

"Then?"

"We were talking about Germany. He said the Nazis'
dislike of kikes was well founded."

"Kikes?"

"He means the Jews, Rowly. He said Mr. Hitler's only
mistake is the loud clamour with which he is going about his
purpose of ridding Germany of them." She exhaled. "That's
when I pushed him." Edna shook her head. "He couldn't comprehend what he'd said to upset me—surely I wasn't a sheenie."

Rowland held her close. He directed her attention to
John Kennedy, who was now talking to Milton and Patricia.
"That's his son."

"Well, hopefully he hasn't poisoned the poor boy!" She
looked up at him. "I thought that America might be different."

"I don't believe it is, Ed. In fact, I fear some things might
be worse over here."

They were distracted then by excitement at the door as latecomers were admitted. A celebratory group had arrived with glasses of champagne in hand. Among them a man, with a young woman on each arm, whose arrival caused a gasping stir.

Their hostess moved to greet him. "Errol, darling! You made it after all."

"I couldn't resist when you said you had Australians on board." Errol Flynn kissed Marion's cheek and then, looking right past her, boomed, "Sailor! And Rowly—it's you!" He sidestepped Marion and leapt over to them.

Edna laughed as Errol lifted her off her feet with an embrace. He shook Rowland's hand vigorously. "Back from the dead, mate! Gosh, you're a sight for sore eyes! Blow me down, the whole crew is here!"

Milton and Clyde took their turns to shake Errol Flynn's hand. They were not unaware that, since they'd last seen him, Flynn's star had risen to something of a zenith. He was now the American film industry's most popular leading man, and if they had considered that acting was art, they might have been more impressed. Even so, the elevation did not appear to have changed him particularly. He was still garrulous and friendly and prone to absurd maritime references. He seemed happy to see them and told wildly exaggerated accounts of the charity motor race that he and Rowland Sinclair won, despite the fact that Rowland had died in the effort.

Rowland let him go—he'd become accustomed to, even fond of Flynn's theatrical flair, and he couldn't remember the actual accident in any case to contradict the actor's version. He relied instead on the fact that he was standing there, and not dead, to give Flynn's current audience some small pause.

The party became more raucous as the hours of champagne took effect. Patricia Van Cleve was duly sent to bed by her aunt, and Milton joined the drinking with notably less inhibition. Smoochy's owner convinced Clyde to accompany her as she walked the hound. Clyde accepted the invitation with only a vague display of panic.

Milton laughed at him. "Go on, comrade, it's not as if she's expecting you to dance. As I always say, gather ye rosebuds while ye may!"

Clyde glanced at Rowland.

"Herrick," he said, confirming that what Milton "always said" was stolen.

Clyde seemed to find that comforting and fell into step with the lady and her dog.

Edna divided her time between Rowland, Milton, and Errol Flynn. She and Flynn had conducted a brief affair the previous year in the lead-up to the Maroubra Invitational. The mutual infatuation had been fleeting, as many of Edna's infatuations were. The sculptress had always been careful to love only men she could leave.

Joseph Kennedy watched her intently from a distance but made no further attempt to approach her.

Eventually, in the early hours of the morning, the Australians thanked their hosts and made their way down to Daniel Cartwright's apartment. Clyde was waiting for them with the dog. He looked bewildered.

Despite the hour, Bradford brought them tea and honey, which apparently Daniel Cartwright had insisted upon after a night out. He paid no attention to the dog asleep on Clyde's lap. When the valet had retired, they asked their questions.

"She gave me the dog," Clyde said. "To remember her by."

"Is she dying?"

"No...she's going to London."

"Clyde, darling," Edna said gently. "What in heaven's name are we going to do with a dog?"

"I know." He swallowed. "We went for a drive, and then we stopped and we..." Clyde's face was crimson. "I was still speechless when she dropped me back, and so when she gave me the dog..."

Milton started to laugh. "Looks like she sold you a pup, comrade! Must have really wanted to get rid of the dog."

"What was her name?" Rowland asked more kindly.

"Jean." Clyde groaned. "She didn't tell me her surname."

"We can ask Marion, I expect," Edna said. "She probably didn't realise we don't live here, and since the dog seems to like you so much..." She reached over and squeezed Clyde's hand. "We'll sort it out tomorrow."

Milton agreed. "Perhaps she gives away her dog every time she's had a little too much to drink."

Rowland woke late the next morning. He turned over drowsily, deciding that it was not yet late enough. It was only the sound of Edna's voice that dragged him from his bed. He pulled on his robe as he stepped out into the hallway and made his way to the drawing room.

"Ed?"

Edna was still in her pyjamas, her arms folded across her chest. The room was filled with roses.

"I don't want them, Mr. Bradford."

"Good morning." Rowland regarded the roses, bemused. "Who sent these?" Edna often received flowers, but this amount was quite absurd.

"The card says Joe Kennedy," Edna said coldly.

Clyde and Milton were now up, though unhappy with the fact. The dog Clyde had acquired the night before sniffed the flowers.

"I presume these are for Ed," Milton said.

"Kennedy," Rowland replied.

"Can you find out where he's staying and send them back, Mr. Bradford?" Edna asked.

"Steady on, Ed," Milton cautioned. "Kennedy's married. You might be lobbing a stick of dynamite sending them back."

"Well, what do I do?" Edna asked, frustrated. She had no wish to participate in Kennedy's deception, but neither did she wish to be cruel.

"Ignore him," Milton advised. "We won't be in New York long, and he'll find some young starlet to distract him soon enough."

Bradford cleared his throat. "And the flowers?"

Edna paused. "Have them taken up to Marion. Tell her that I am sure they were delivered here by mistake and that, in any case, they make me sneeze."

"She'll know—" Clyde began.

"And she'll let him know." Edna was firm. "Marion means well, but it's better that she stops this."

The dog crouched with its hind haunches up, its entire back half wagging. Short sharp barks.

"I suspect Smoochy wants to play," Edna observed, bending to pat the creature.

"We can't call the poor bloody thing Smoochy," Milton muttered. "That's embarrassing for all concerned."

Sometime during their morning ablutions and breakfast, it was decided, primarily by Milton, that the dog would hereafter be known as Windrip, after the American president in Sinclair Lewis's satirical novel, which the poet now claimed was prophecy rather than fiction. The dog seemed indifferent to the change in title, which would, after all, only apply until they could return him. While Bradford was taking the twelve dozen roses up to the penthouse, Rowland told Milton and Clyde what Daniel Cartwright's chauffeur had told him the evening before.

They examined the painting more closely.

"A talented amateur," Clyde said.

Rowland concurred. Edna took the portrait from the wall and turned it over in search of some clue. There was nothing.

Bradford returned and reported to Edna. "I'm afraid Miss Davies had stepped out with Miss Van Cleve. I left your message and the flowers with Mr. Hearst."

"Was he cross?"

"He laughed. Quite a lot."

"Mr. Bradford," Rowland asked, trying not to smile obviously, "do you recall when Danny acquired this piece?"

"I can't say I do, sir. Mr. Cartwright was always quite taken with it."

"So what now, Rowly?" Clyde asked.

Rowland drummed his fingers on the arm of his chair, his eyes still fixed on the painting. Was Otis Norcross the artist? Why had Daniel Cartwright left so little information about his heir? Perhaps Norcross was married, like Kennedy and Hearst, even Welles, though the fact did not seem to make those gentlemen particularly circumspect.

Bradford returned the painting to its place on the wall, adjusting it until it was perfectly straight. Rowland wondered if the manservant understood about his old employer. The flash of prudishness he and Edna had seen the evening before did make him wonder.

"Let's take Windrip to the park," he said in the end.

The idea was met with enthusiasm, and coats, gloves, and hats gathered against the brittle chill of the mid-morning. Bradford produced a lead for Windrip. "Mr. Cartwright had a beagle for a time."

"Really?" Rowland secured the lead to Windrip's collar. Daniel Cartwright had never mentioned a dog in his letters.

"The beagle resided here for only a short time," Bradford said gravely. "It was unsuited to this address."

"Oh. What happened to it?" Edna asked.

"I believe Mr. Cartwright gave it away."

"That seems to be something of a tradition," Milton observed.

Bradford scowled.

They took the elevator down to street level and stepped out into Sixth Avenue, becoming engulfed in the scale and life of the city. Country-raised Clyde looked straight up to orient himself with a glimpse of the sky. On this day it was grey. Rowland grabbed Clyde's shoulder and steered him away from the lamp post.

"Thanks, mate." Clyde laughed when he realised where he'd been headed. "That would be an embarrassing way to break my nose."

"Happy to be of service."

They made their way up Sixth Avenue to find Central Park, the vast parklands which made up the centre of Manhattan between the Upper East and West sides. The autumn was advanced enough that most of the trees were naked, and yet every now and then, a late stayer surprised them with a show of gold or russet. Milton began to sing Billie Holiday's "Autumn in New York," which they'd first heard in the swing clubs of Shanghai just months before. The poet had a good voice, and so they did not immediately threaten him into silence—it was a nice change from random proclamations of stolen poetry.

"Things have improved," Clyde noted. He painted in Central Park when they were last in New York. Back then the park had been a refuge for thousands of desperate homeless men who'd clustered there in tents and rough-built shelters. The shanty towns seemed to have disappeared now.

Rowland nodded. The grip of the Depression did seem to have loosened—here at least. Perhaps the state-sponsored public works of Roosevelt's radical New Deal were having some effect.

As they walked by the lake, they talked more freely of Daniel Cartwright's life and death and the mayhem that had been left in its wake, returning to the easy uncensored honesty to which they'd become accustomed when they were just themselves.

"Perhaps we should find out where Danny went on these motoring holidays of his," Rowland said. "It could be that he was meeting Norcross."

"That could be anywhere, and Norcross might have been coming from somewhere else to meet him too," Clyde cautioned.

"I know, but—"

"I'm not saying we shouldn't try, Rowly," Clyde bent to untangle Windrip's paw from the lead, "but let's not go off half-cocked. We've only just got to New York, and we don't know if Danny's vacations were anything to do with Otis Norcross."

Milton agreed. "We should try to find out where that painting came from." He turned to Rowland. "Did Danny have painting chums, Rowly?"

"Painting chums?"

"You know...that painting circle thing you people do."

Rowland regarded him, bemused. "I really don't know what you're talking about, Milt. You're describing a coven."

Milton sighed. "When you were at the Sydney Art School, there'd be a bunch of you painting the same thing..."

"Those were classes, Milt." Rowland shook his head. "Sometimes painters will share a studio or a model to defray costs, but Danny wasn't really in that position. He never painted anything but himself, for one thing."

"What are you thinking, Milt?" Edna asked.

Milton shrugged. "Danny lived here; he must have known

other artists. People who might recognise that painting of him."

"You're right."

Milton pointed at Rowland as a thought occurred. "Rowly, where do you keep those items that are most important to you, the things you want to see every day?"

"Most important to me?"

"Don't get existential on me: photos, mementos, journals."

Edna answered for him. "They're in your studio," she said, thinking of the photographs on the mantle, in the once-elegant and immaculate drawing room of Woodlands House, and the drawings done by Rowland's nephews which were hung beside the painting by Picasso that Daniel Cartwright had given him, as well as years of sketchbooks, the small sculptures she'd made for him at various times, even the glowering portrait of his father by McInnes. In the bureau, the letters his brothers had sent him from the front during the Great War, odds and ends which had stories that Rowland had not yet volunteered. She laughed. "You'd park your car in there if you could."

Rowland nodded. "Ed's right. Most things end up in my studio." And he saw Milton's meaning. "We should look through the contents of Danny's studio while we're here."

"It's locked," Milton said. "I tried."

"I wonder if Mr. Bradford locked it before or after we arrived," Clyde murmured.

Rowland did not respond. He, too, realised that Bradford did not trust them—that while the servant was probably not lying to them, he was not readily volunteering information either. It might be simply that he was a good valet; it might be that he was hiding something.

As they walked further into the park, there seemed to be more people doing likewise. They were approaching the Heckscher Playground when they first heard bleating. It was an unexpected sound in the middle of New York.

"Is that a sheep?" Rowland asked, perplexed.

"Shame on you, Rowly." Clyde tilted his head towards the sound. "The Sinclairs are supposed to be pastoralists! That's a goat."

The gathering came into view then. A banner for the Brewers, Board of Trade, a makeshift stage with ramps, and what seemed a herd of goats waiting to trot across it. Clyde picked up Windrip, lest he be inclined to give chase, and Edna pressed into the crowd, intrigued. She returned for them after a few minutes' investigation.

"It's a beauty contest for goats," she said merrily. "They're choosing a mascot for a beer company." She pointed out a beast with shiny spiral horns and a luxuriant beard. "That's the defending champion—Pretzels."

"Who would have thought so many New Yorkers kept goats?" Milton sounded quite envious.

They watched until Pretzels was once again awarded the title of "Mr. Manhattan" to a divided crowd, some of whom were vocally in favour of a challenger named Lincoln.

Clyde spoke quietly to Rowland while Edna and Milton were arguing over whether Lincoln was robbed. "Have you noticed the two blokes standing by the tree over there?"

Rowland glanced briefly in that direction. Two men—one large, his companion wiry—both well dressed in double-breasted pinstripes and gleaming patent leather shoes. "I have now. What about them?"

"They were outside the Warwick when we first stepped out."

"You think they're following us?"

Clyde shrugged. "They may just be goat lovers, I suppose."

Chapter Fifteen

GOAT BEAUTY DISAPPEARS

New York, Feb. 24 (U.P)—Pretzels, which is the goat whose picture in saloon windows heralds the advent of spring each year as surely as the first robin, has disappeared. He walked out of the stable in suburban Hastings and strolled into limbo yesterday just as the Brewers' Board of Trade was pepping up its publicity staff to push the type of spring beer that uses Pretzels' picture as a trade mark. Cynics said he probably would be back in time for the brewers' annual goat beauty contest in Central Park, which he has won for two years.

—*Republican and Herald*
(Pottsville, Pennsylvania), February 24, 1936

Rowland and Clyde both kept watch for the two gentlemen trailing them as the caprine beauty pageant concluded and they left the playground. For a time, the pair seemed to vanish, only to reappear as they reached the zoo in the southeast corner of the park. The men came no closer than about forty or fifty feet, but made no other effort to be inconspicuous.

"I might go have a word with them," Rowland said.

"What?"

"I'll just ask them their business." Rowland shrugged. "We've seen them, they know we've seen them. Surely, carrying on as if we haven't is absurd."

Clyde glanced over his shoulder. Milton and Edna were absorbed at the wolf enclosure. "Fair enough, let's go."

The men watched the Australians approach without reaction. The smaller man lit a cigarette and drew on it with his eyes closed, savouring the sensation and the taste of the smoke, exhaling finally into the crisp air.

"Gentlemen." Rowland nodded. "Is there by any chance something we can do for you?"

"Not we. Just you, Mr. Sinclair."

"You have me at a disadvantage, gentlemen."

"Indeed, we do, Mr. Sinclair. But who we is or isn't don't amount to much."

"Is there any reason you're following us?"

"Who says we are? Of course, if we were, it would only be that we were worried about you—New York can be a dangerous place. You'd be much better off in Boston, making sure that your dead pal's family got what was theirs."

Rowland's face was unreadable. "I take it you work for Frank Cartwright."

The small man looked at his companion and laughed. "Now why would we work for Frankie? Thanks to you, he ain't got squat."

"Gentlemen, I think you misunderstand my role as Daniel

Cartwright's executor. There is nothing I can do about who he selected to inherit his fortune. In fact, there's nothing anyone can do about that."

"We'll see, Mr. Sinclair." The man discarded the remains of his cigarette and crushed it under heel. "Go back to Boston and tell them hotshot briefs that this geezer, Norcross, don't exist. Help your dead friend to look after his family. If he'd done that in the first place, he might be with us today." His eyes refocused behind Rowland, and he smiled and nodded. "That's one red-hot tomato you got there, Mr. Sinclair. Now if I had a dame that ginchy, I'd have better things to do than chase imaginary men."

Rowland glanced back and saw that Edna and Clyde had spotted them. His jaw hardened. "Gentlemen, I'd advise you to go back to whoever your employer is and let him know that I cannot change the terms of Daniel Cartwright's will, and that following me around like hungry strays is simply a waste of your time. Good day, gentlemen."

For a moment the four men stared at each other, and then, without further word, the Australians turned and walked away.

"I don't know if you just poked an ants' nest, mate," Clyde whispered as they joined Edna and Milton.

"Who was that?" Edna asked, as she hooked her arm through Rowland's.

"They didn't issue calling cards, but I gather they are associated with Frank Cartwright somehow." Rowland shook his head, exasperated. "I might ask Oliver Burr to try and make Danny's idiot brothers understand that I cannot rewrite his will."

"They're not really asking you to do that, Rowly, just to agree that Otis Norcross doesn't exist," Clyde pointed out.

"Well, Rowly can't do that either," Edna said firmly.

Milton looked back at the men. "We outnumber the

mongrels right now, Rowly. Shall we go over and ask them to back off a little more explicitly?"

"Don't be an idiot, Milt," Clyde said sharply. "Nothing's going to be helped by brawling in the streets!"

Rowland agreed with Clyde, though not enthusiastically. "We might just have to put up with them for the moment. They're not doing anything apart from following us around."

"I'm famished!" Edna declared. "Let them follow us to lunch."

They lunched at The Plaza because it was not far from where they stood and Edna was hungry. Indeed, now that she'd raised the subject, they realised it was nearly three o'clock and a repast would be welcome. Rowland paid the concierge to take charge of Windrip while they were in the Persian Room.

They were seated for a late luncheon in the oval-ceilinged restaurant, whose motif was echoed in the massive murals on its high walls. The room was vast and, at this time, relatively empty, though there were a few tables of patrons enjoying a late meal or early cocktails. They ignored the two men who took stools at the bar while they ate, though they did not speak of Daniel Cartwright or his heirs, discussing instead what they were going to do with Windrip.

Even so, it was uncomfortable to know they were being monitored.

And so they returned directly to the Warwick, rather than spend the rest of the afternoon in the city.

Not wishing to disturb Bradford unnecessarily, Rowland unlocked the door without knocking. If it hadn't been for the murmur of voices, they might have assumed the drawing room was on fire for the amount of smoke opening the door pulled into the vestibule. Rowland moved to investigate and came upon what appeared to be a meeting—mostly men, though there were one or two women, of various races clustered around ashtrays listening to a man making some kind of speech. Bradford was taking notes. He stood, alarmed, as Rowland walked in. "Mr. Sinclair..."

Milton poked his head in now. His gaze went straight to the man who had been speaking. "Earl! What the hell are you doing here?" He looked around. "Cripes, is this a Party meeting? Mind if Clyde and I sit in? What were you saying—go on, comrade, do carry on."

Bradford looked at Rowland.

Rowland shrugged. "Ed and I might leave you to it. Do you have the key to Danny's studio, Mr. Bradford?"

The manservant looked for just a moment as if he might refuse.

The man Milton had addressed as "Earl" cleared his throat. Milton and Clyde found seats and sat down.

Bradford exhaled and removed a key from his fob chain and handed it to Rowland.

A few moments later, Edna shut the studio door and leaned back against it. Her eyes were bright. "Mr. Bradford is a Communist!" she said. "How very interesting. Do you think Danny knew?"

"He never mentioned it," Rowland replied, looking around the expansive studio, which was made to seem even larger by the triage of gilt-framed mirrors, ten feet high and six wide, which adorned the far wall and had facilitated Cartwright's obsession with self-portraiture. Massive drying cupboards and open shelves bearing all manner of equipment—paints and pigments, brushes, palette knives, canvases, jars of turpentine—lined the other walls. In the space between were several studio easels.

Rowland removed the dust sheet that covered the stretched canvas on the easel closest to the mirrors. He stood back silently as he looked at the half-finished piece in oil. Daniel Cartwright's last work. Another self-portrait but unlike the jaunty flattering pieces that adorned the drawing room. The composition was dominated by the artist's face, a study of pain. The eyes, Danny's eyes, reflected a kind of desperate agony, and his hands were twisted and clenched against his forehead. Rowland swore. This was his friend's best work and his worst.

"Oh, my God—Ed...I'm sorry," he said remembering she was in the room.

Edna could not have cared less about Rowland's shocked profanity but the painting itself broke her heart. She wrapped her arms around him, unable to take her eyes away from Cartwright's rendering of grief.

Rowland held her, struggling with the realisation that Daniel Cartwright had been in such profound pain. "God, Danny, why didn't you tell me? I would have come. Whatever it was, we could have..."

Edna took a deep breath and slipped her hand into Rowland's and pulled him away. "Come on, Rowly."

"Where—"

"Just to the kitchen. We'll come back."

"Why?"

"For tea, and a moment. You need a moment."

He allowed her to lead him to Bradford's kitchen, a part of the apartment into which they'd never before ventured. It was neat, immaculately clean. The canisters were all labelled and so it did not take Edna long to find a pot and tea leaves.

"You make a pot," she directed gently. "I'll find cups."

Rowland did as he was told. He lit the stove and put the kettle on to boil. Edna had taught him how to warm the pot and measure the leaves in Shanghai when they found themselves without servants for a time. The process was strangely comforting. No doubt that was the reason Edna asked him to do it again now.

"I'm all right, Ed," he assured her when they sat down at

the kitchen table. "Danny always seemed so content, almost smug, about life. It's hard to..." He shook his head. "I just wish he'd asked me for help."

Edna let the pot draw, turned it three times for luck and poured. "Was Danny prone to melancholia?"

"Not that I'm aware. I certainly didn't see it at Oxford." He winced. "But I was young, preoccupied. Perhaps I was just too selfish to see it."

"Oh, darling." Edna fixed her gaze on his. "You are occasionally distracted, sometimes naive, but never indifferent. There was a lot my mother hid. And things she disguised so that we did not understand, until she killed herself. If there was something you didn't see, it was because Danny didn't want you to see it, and as much as you wish you could have helped him, we are all entitled to keep some part of ourselves unseen."

Rowland reached for the sculptress's hand. He knew, of course, that Edna's beautiful, talented mother had taken her own life. That before she'd died, Marguerite Higgins had raised her daughter to never belong to a man, to enjoy love, but to distrust it. "Promise me, Ed, if you ever need something from me, you'll just ask. Even years from now when we're old, even if we haven't seen each other for years, whatever it is, you'll ask...because I don't trust myself to know, and I would give you anything and everything."

Edna faltered, overwhelmed for the moment by the impulsive sincerity of what he asked. "Oh, Rowly."

"Promise me, Ed."

"I promise. Really." She smiled. "Whatever the consequences, I'll turn to you."

"Consequences?"

"Your wife and six children. They might be put out when I demand you drop everything and help me hide a body."

Rowland shrugged. "They'll just have to understand."

A cheer from the drawing room. A bark from Windrip, who had apparently joined the Party.

"What do you think they're talking about?" Edna said as the jubilation rose in volume.

"The Communists? Revolution. Either that or they're drinking."

Milton's voice above the rest, leading the meeting in the "Internationale."

Rowland smiled. "Definitely drinking."

Chapter Sixteen

LINDY HOPPER ACES
WELCOME TO DANCE TEST

...Don't fail to register NOW, you Harlem lads and lasses! The News has a registration office at the Savoy Ballroom, 140th St. and Lennox Ave., the famous Harlem dancing center where the Lindy Hop was originated, where you can enter and obtain all information about the contest. Since some imaginative couple (their names are lost to history) first did the Lindy Hop on the Savoy Floor eight years ago, the fame of this dance has spread all over the world, and now scores of tourists flock to the Savoy nightly to see it done.

—*Daily News*
(New York, New York), July 14, 1935

Rowland and Edna remained in the kitchen for a time, staying away from the meeting being conducted at volume in the drawing room. Neither were members of the Party, though Clyde and Milton had long been involved with the Australian chapter. They drank tea and talked of New York and Joseph Kennedy and Father Coughlin. They pored over the crisp, uncreased copy of the *New York Times* which Bradford had left on the table, orienting themselves with news of the city. The social pages reported on Marion Davies' soiree, with pictures of Errol Flynn and Joseph Kennedy.

"Oh, my lord!" Edna held the paper up. "It's Clyde and Windrip!"

"So it is." Rowland laughed. "Milt won't let him forget this."

"Poor Windrip," Edna said frowning. "Imagine being passed from person to person, like a cricket ball."

Rowland thought about pointing out that the object of the noble game of cricket was not actually to pass the ball from person to person, but he decided against it. He understood what the sculptress meant. "Come on," he said, standing. "We should probably get back to the studio."

When the Communists finally dispersed, Clyde and Bradford were a little merry. Milton, who was a singularly talented drinker, showed no effects of intoxication at all. Emboldened by socialist fervour, Bradford declared that he was feeling slightly queasy and left his current oppressors to fend for themselves while he retired to bed.

And so it was just Milton and Clyde who found Rowland and Edna in Cartwright's studio. Windrip followed them in, skittering across the polished floor before growling at himself in the large mirrors. In his mildly compromised state, Clyde, too, found the mirrors confronting.

"Come across anything yet?" Milton asked, surveying the neatly stacked piles of boxes and sketchbooks through which Rowland and Edna had already been.

"Look, a flyer for a dance competition at the Savoy Ballroom." Edna handed him the bill.

"Was Danny a dancer?" Milton directed the question at Rowland.

"Yes. He was pretty good, from what I recollect. Of course, in those days it was the Charleston." Rowland moved a stack of boxes from one of the upper shelves and set them on the floor where the others could reach them. "But I presume he kept up with modern dances."

"We should go," Milton said, studying the flyer. "I do enjoy a good dance competition."

Clyde groaned.

Edna decided to check on Bradford, lest the old valet was really unwell or required a cup of tea or some other remedy.

"Rowly." Clyde sat cross-legged in front of the flat boxes Rowland had taken down from a high shelf. It helped the room to stop spinning. "This box has your name on it."

"Really?" Rowland was up a library ladder handing items down to Milton. "What's in it?"

Clyde removed the lid. "Jesus, Mary, and Joseph!"

"All three of them?" Milton murmured. "That box must be bigger than it looks."

The box contained at least fifty individual sheets of cartridge of various sizes: some crisp and white, others yellowed with age. Each bore a sketch, in pencil or charcoal, quick watercolours or more detailed pieces in pen and ink. "They're you," Clyde said. "Every single one!"

Rowland stepped down as Clyde began to display the pages across the floor. Sketches of a younger him, boxing, training, reading, asleep. More recent drawings of Rowland before an easel.

"This is here," Milton said, recognising the studio in the background. "It must have been when we were here in '32."

Rowland was dumbfounded.

"Who—" Clyde began.

"Danny," Rowland said quietly. The pictures were unsigned but he recognised his friend's hand in the sketches and the situations. It could only have been Daniel Cartwright.

"I thought he only painted himself."

Rowland frowned. "I did too."

"You didn't know?"

"No."

"Don't you find this disturbing, Rowly?" Clyde asked.

Rowland paused. Clearly Clyde found it so. "Considering what's in my own notebook, it would be decidedly hypocritical of me to find it disturbing."

"Even so."

Edna returned. She gasped, crouching beside Clyde to look closely at the drawings he'd spread out before him. "Why, these are beautiful. Did Danny draw them?"

"Yes." Clyde turned to Rowland. "Why wouldn't he tell you?"

"Because Rowly's not a model," Edna said, picking up a pen and ink of a young man reading a letter, a faintly discernible smile on his lips. But in his eyes, the artist had captured a kind of confused sadness despite the smile. "If he'd known what Danny was doing, we'd be looking at fifty drawings of Rowly's poker face, which"—she smiled—"though handsome, would not make a particularly interesting portrait." She leafed through the pile that Clyde had not yet spread out, laughing occasionally as if she were looking at old photographs.

Milton opened one of the other boxes. "Maybe he drew other people. Perhaps there's a drawing of Otis Norcross."

The box contained letters from various people, bundled randomly. "Someone's going to have to read these," Clyde said, grimacing. "He must have kept every letter he was ever sent."

Milton opened another box. "What the hell is this?"

Rowland peered over the poet's shoulder and laughed. "For Pete's sake! It's Lygon's bear."

"What?"

Hugh Lygon had been at Oxford with Rowland and Daniel Cartwright. The son of the 7th Earl of Beauchamp had moved with an aesthetic, eccentric set among whom carrying children's toys was not considered odd. Rowland had first met Lygon in the ring.

He pulled the large teddy bear out of the box. "Lygon would sit this thing in his corner."

"Whatever for?" Edna asked.

"Word had it, he was trying to unsettle his opponent. To be honest, it was pretty unsettling." He shook his head, chuckling. "When I fought Lygon, the bear disappeared. There was all sorts of teeth-gnashing and uproar, but neither the culprit nor the bear was ever found."

"So this is Hugh Lygon's bear?" Edna took the bear from Rowland delightedly.

"One and the same."

"And Danny never told you?"

"No." Rowland climbed back up the ladder and checked the shelves one last time. "But in the greater scheme of things, the fate of Lygon's toy bear is probably trivial."

"Rowly." Clyde had taken over inspecting the drawings. "Is this a bad likeness, or is this not you?" He held up a pencil sketch. The man in the drawing bore a resemblance to Rowland, but the lips were fuller, the jawline softer.

"No, that's not Rowly," Edna said. "Danny was too talented an artist for these to be mistakes."

"Are there any others?" Rowland asked.

"No," Clyde replied confidently. "The rest are definitely you."

"So then who is this?" Rowland said, studying the sketch.

The drawing, like all the others, was unsigned. He turned the cartridge over. A tiny notation in the corner. A date: *19 July 1935, NC.*

"Norcross!" Edna exclaimed.

"Got to say," Milton said admiringly, "it was a brilliant place to hide that sketch. Clearly, Otis Norcross looks enough like Rowly that most people would assume it was just an inaccurate drawing of him and not think to turn it over."

"We don't know that this is Otis Norcross," Rowland cautioned.

"It's a reasonable guess, Rowly." Milton took the drawing from Clyde. "Until a few minutes ago, we thought Danny only ever painted himself. And then we find a cache of... well, you." Milton continued cautiously, "Danny appointed you his executor. He knew people would go through his studio, you included. But anybody else would assume this was just another picture of you. He left this for you, mate—so you'd know who you're looking for."

"But why, Milt? Why wouldn't he just write down Norcross's address?"

"I truly don't know. Danny seems to have been a planner of Machiavellian proportions. He may be dead, but you can feel his hand on everything. Perhaps he wanted to make sure that you found Otis Norcross first. If he'd written down his address, other people would have found him before we were even in the country." Milton regarded Rowland sternly. "And before you tell me I'm being melodramatic, comrade, remember, someone murdered Danny."

~ↀ

It was Edna who decided they would go to the Savoy that evening. A distraction from discoveries they'd made in Danny's studio. As much as the collection of drawings was interesting, she knew Rowland's mind was still on Daniel Cartwright's last self-portrait and the anguish it confessed.

"We found the flyer for the dance competition among Danny's possessions," she argued. "Perhaps he left that for Rowly, too. Perhaps we'll find Otis Norcross at the Savoy—he could work there."

"More likely he owns it," Milton murmured. But it did not take much to persuade the poet. Milton was an excellent dancer and rarely gave up the chance to demonstrate that fact.

Rowland, of course, had never been able to refuse Edna.

Only Clyde, who loathed dancing, put up a fight. "You go," he insisted. "I'll stop here. To be honest, being in Danny's studio makes me want to work."

That, Rowland understood. He had the same impulse himself, a pull to paper and line. He hadn't done anything more than the odd sketch in his notebook since he'd received the news that Daniel Cartwright was dead, and the thought of working offered a kind of release.

"We can't take Windrip to the Savoy, in any case," Clyde added, rubbing the dog's head. "And I'm not game to wake Bradford simply to ask him to keep an eye on my dog."

Milton snorted. "No, I wouldn't do that either."

Edna tried to persuade Clyde to change his mind, but to no avail. "I understand, Ed, that there will be occasions on which I cannot avoid dancing, but please don't deny me the satisfaction of avoiding the excruciating practice when I can."

"Leave him alone, Ed!" Milton came to Clyde's aid. "Aren't two men enough for you?"

Edna gave in and left them to it, while she changed into something more suitable for dancing at the Savoy. Milton, too, refined his attire, changing his burgundy cravat for one of green silk. Rowland stayed as he was, helping Clyde find materials and equipment while they waited.

"You don't think Danny would mind, do you?" Clyde asked as they set up an easel.

"I think he'd be delighted." Rowland smiled. "You might hear him blithering on. Danny's the only artist I ever knew who needed to talk while he painted. It was relentless."

Clyde laughed. "I remember. After a while it was like having the radio switched on." Clyde placed a clean canvas on the easel and stood back to anticipate the evening. "Leave through one of the trade entrances," he advised. "Those jokers from the park might still be watching the hotel."

Rowland nodded. "That's not a bad idea—we could catch a taxi."

"Be careful, Rowly. Frank Cartwright strikes me as a desperate man."

Chapter Seventeen

A Day in New York

By Paul Harrison

Black Reds

Your night-blooming correspondent strolled
Lennox Avenue the other evening and listened
to some of the spellbinders and was discomfited
no little on two occasions by being pointed out
for the inspection of large audiences as a hinkty,
slumming white man and one of the united
enemies of the African people. I also watched
collections being taken up of the defense of
beleaguer Ethiopia. Since the country several
times has refused to cash contributions for its
defense, it is only fair to assume that torch-
waving speakers pocket the proceeds.

Later I mention all this to a night-club manager, who exploded in wrath against "red agi-
tators who been gettin' themselves rich all over
Harlem jes' by yellin' a bunch of lies." Mostly

they're "foreign" colered people, he said—West
Indians and such. And one of these days "the
decent folks is gonta chase 'em so far they never
can come back."

—*Arizona Daily Star*
(Tucson, Arizona), August 24, 1935

～ⓔ～

The Savoy Ballroom encroached upon an entire block of the
Harlem neighbourhood of Manhattan between 140th and
141st Streets. There were already lines outside to get in when
the Australians arrived. When they finally were admitted, it
was clear that the notion of finding the man drawn by Danny
Cartwright in the crowded ten-thousand-square-foot ballroom
was ludicrous. There were thousands of people in the elegant
hall. Mirrored walls added to the sea of people. Crystal chandeliers sparkled above a sprung, layered wood dance floor. A
double bandstand against one wall housed two bands, playing
in tandem so the music was continuous. The clientele was
mixed, but mainly black—for unlike many ballrooms and clubs
in New York, the Savoy had no colour bar. The atmosphere
was charged, exhilarating, and within seconds they were swept
onto the dance floor. Beautiful hostesses demonstrated steps.
One took Milton in hand, and soon she was showing the poet
how to execute some of the more acrobatic moves for which
Lindy Hop dancers were becoming famous. Rowland and Edna
watched the professional dancers known as Whitey's Lindy
Hoppers in the corner reserved for the most virtuosic before
joining the dancing themselves on a different part of the floor.

"They're amazing, aren't they?" Edna said, laughing as
she and Rowland tried to duplicate some of the steps.

"Smashing!" Rowland lifted Edna into a swing, a little surprised by the momentum of the move. "Warn me if you're going to try anything particularly acrobatic. I'd hate to drop you."

"Don't you dare!"

"I wasn't saying I'd do it on purpose!"

The crowd cheered as a young vocalist, Miss Ella Fitzgerald, crooned "Stompin' at the Savoy." Rowland knew Benny Goodman's instrumental recording, which had climbed the charts the year before, but Miss Fitzgerald's voice added a sultry, almost hypnotic dimension to the tune, and he abandoned the open stance of the Lindy Hop to take Edna in his arms. In time, other men cut in, and Rowland took a succession of women onto the floor. Many taught him new steps. Dancing was primary here, over conversation or other social niceties or divisions, and by the time he returned to the table they'd managed to secure, Rowland realised that he had thought of nothing but Lindy Hopping for hours. He wondered how often Daniel Cartwright had come to the Savoy Ballroom. Had it assuaged the sadness that was evident in that final self-portrait?

He took the notebook from his inside breast pocket and sketched as he waited for Edna and Milton to flag, capturing the energy and the movement of the dancers in quick, clean lines as he thought about how he might reproduce the almost hysterical, exuberant atmosphere on canvas.

Edna spotted him at the table and brought over her current partner. Rowland stood and shook hands with the gentleman, who Edna introduced as Leon Otis. The sculptress's hair had escaped the neat coif in which it had started the evening and now framed her face like a cloud at sunset. Rowland thought it suited her, beautiful and slightly wild. Edna tried to tame the locks back into a hairnet while she explained that she hadn't anticipated being upside-down when she'd dressed her hair. Otis, a professional Lindy Hopper who apparently had only a couple of months ago won the Harvest Moon Ball, laughed and explained that the inversion had been more the result of a slip than intention. He stayed chatting for a few minutes before kissing Edna's hand and returning to the professional corner.

Edna reached across the table and rubbed Rowland's arm. "You look better."

He smiled. "Better?"

"You know what I mean."

"I do. This was an excellent idea, Ed."

"Perhaps that's why Danny left the flyer in his studio."

Rowland regarded her, amused. "You think Danny wanted us to go dancing?"

"I think Danny loved you and knew what he was asking of you. He didn't want it to become too much."

He said nothing at first. It was possible. That Daniel Cartwright had been infatuated with him had been obvious in the sketches. Of course, he hadn't realised that Cartwright's feelings had lasted much beyond that first ill-fated declaration of love.

"Most of those drawings were made at Oxford—he couldn't possibly have still felt that way."

"Does it bother you?" Edna asked. "That he loved you?"

"To be truthful, it bothers me if it made him miserable... that last portrait bothers me."

"Oh, Rowly, you're not blaming yourself for that?"

He met her gaze. "No, I'm not. Danny knew who I was. I just wish he'd been able to tell me things were so bad. I might have been able to help, somehow."

"He might have told you if he hadn't been killed. Or perhaps he didn't finish that portrait, Rowly, because he didn't feel that way anymore. We all have moments of passing wretchedness."

Rowland nodded. Daniel Cartwright's artistic practice was about self-examination. He was curious about every moment as it was reflected in himself. The portrait could well have been the painting of a moment. Rowland hoped so.

"If Danny was still in love with you, perhaps Otis Norcross wasn't his lover, after all," Edna mused.

"That doesn't always follow, Ed." Rowland thought of the women he had loved in the past eight years while being in love with Edna. "But you're right. There may be some other reason he left his fortune to Norcross."

Milton flopped into the chair beside Rowland, mopping the perspiration from his brow with a handkerchief. "I'm done!" He glanced out at the dancers, sighing as Leon executed a perfect backflip mid-step. "Rowly, I fear we may be old."

Rowland laughed. "Well, perhaps we'd better leave the Savoy to the young folk and go home before arthritis sets in."

Milton nodded. "It's time to fold, I think."

The ballroom's concierge hailed a cab, and they returned to midtown Manhattan and the Warwick.

Rowland noticed the police car in front of the hotel's entrance but, initially, he didn't think too much of it. It was in the hotel's foyer that the manager signalled him for a word.

"Mr. Sinclair, just so you know, the police are still with Mr. Watson Jones."

"Clyde? Why?"

"To take his statement, sir."

"About what?"

"The incident. On behalf of the Warwick—" Rowland, Edna, and Milton were already making their way to the elevator. "Perhaps it would be best if Mr. Watson Jones was to explain…"

The elevator seemed to take an age to reach the thirty-first floor. There were two police officers waiting to take it down when the doors opened. Rowland introduced himself to Officers O'Hara and Rourke.

"Mr. Sinclair. We'd like to have a word with you."

The policemen followed the Australians back into Daniel Cartwright's apartment. Bradford was up, standing by the chaise on which Clyde was stretched out.

"Oh, my God, Clyde!" Edna gasped.

He put his hand up to calm her from beneath various ice packs. His shirt was completely bloody, one eye was swollen nearly shut. "It's not as bad as it looks."

"What the hell happened?" Milton asked.

"I went out to walk Windrip...just in front of the hotel." Clyde winced as he sat up. "Those mongrels from the park jumped me. Told me to take a message to you, Rowly."

O'Hara turned to Rowland. "Mr. Watson Jones claims that he was attacked by two men who had been following you since earlier in the day, seeking to intimidate you in a dispute of a deceased estate."

Rowland nodded, for a moment too furious to speak.

"Do you know who the men were, Mr. Sinclair?"

"I'm afraid not. I suspect they work for Mr. Frank Cartwright or his dubious associates—Lombardo, Sorrentino, and...Messina, I think. Has anyone called a doctor?"

The names clearly meant something to the policemen. They glanced at each other.

"The hotel doctor has been and gone," Bradford said haughtily. "Mr. Watson Jones refused to go to the hospital."

"Clyde—"

"I'm all right, Rowly. Just a tad tender."

"But neither of the gentlemen following you was any of these three?" O'Hara pressed.

"No."

"Did they say they were working for J. L. Lombardo?"

"No—but it seems likely."

"You'd better hope not, Mr. Sinclair. Mr. Lombardo is not a man you want to cross, and Sorrentino is vicious. If they'd attacked Mr. Watson Jones themselves, you'd be calling funeral directors, not doctors."

"I see."

"I'm afraid that, without names, it might be difficult to identify the men involved."

"If you'd just give me a minute, Officers." Rowland extracted his notebook and drew quickly from memory. He tore one page out and handed it to O'Hara before beginning on the second. "Saints preserve us! That's Joe Costello."

A second portrait was recognised as "that guy Brown." Both men, it seemed, were known petty thugs.

"We'll pick them up, see if Mr. Watson Jones can identify them."

It wasn't till the officers had left that Edna asked, "Where's Windrip?"

"He went with them," Clyde said.

"They stole him?"

"No. Bloody mongrel turned on me. One of them whistled, and next thing I know, Windrip is trying to rip out my throat. And then they called off the dog and started laying into me themselves. If it hadn't been for Bradford—"

"Mr. Bradford was there?"

"Yes..." Clyde seemed a little confused now.

"I saw you leave, sir," Bradford said. "And I realised you must have been walking the dog. And I thought about how appalled Mr. Cartwright would be to know I was allowing his guests to walk their own dogs, and so I went after you."

"And you frightened them away?" Rowland was obviously sceptical. Bradford was an old man and quite small.

"He had a gun," Clyde said.

"I always carry a gun outside the Warwick, sir," Bradford explained calmly. "This is New York, after all."

"I see." Rowland turned to the manservant. "We are very grateful to you, Mr. Bradford."

Bradford nodded. "I shall see about some supper, sir. I expect you're all hungry."

Milton poured Clyde a drink, while Edna disappeared to run him a hot bath.

"I'm so sorry, mate," Rowland said as Clyde spluttered over the whisky.

"'Struth, Rowly, this isn't your fault. I'm the bloody fool who—I should have known."

"How could you possibly have known?"

"Jean—the woman who gave me that flaming mutt, she asked a lot of questions about you, Rowly. I thought she fancied you. And then, when she gave me a break, I told myself... Well, I don't know what I told myself, but I forgot that it was you she was interested in. And then she gave me a dog." He drained the glass. "I should have known it wasn't right, but she kinda dazzled me."

Rowland loosened his tie and rubbed the back of his neck. "You think she planted the dog with us?"

"It turned as soon as that bloke whistled. One minute it was friendly, next minute it was savage. And while I was trying to fight it off, they jumped me."

Milton swore. Rowland agreed. Using a dog seemed below the belt.

"And all this to send Rowly a message?" Milton asked.

Clyde squinted at them through the eye that was not black and swollen. "When they were kicking me, they asked about Otis Norcross—said we wouldn't be doing him a favour by finding him."

Chapter Eighteen

Getting Married on Nothing

By Kathleen Norris

...If you haven't imagination and originality enough to use you own judgment about your own affairs, don't marry on a small income...

In 1885 you had to put cobwebs—filthy germy cobwebs, on delicate little cut fingers. Then it was peroxide, which bubble agreeably at least. Then only wicked mothers used peroxide and good mothers used iodine. And now iodine is as bad as cobwebs, or worse, for it spreads the infection and we're all for mercurochrome!...

—*The Nebraska State Journal*
(Lincoln, Nebraska), July 19, 1931

Rowland stood alone in the studio. The apartment, probably the entire building, was asleep. Why he'd chosen to brood here, he wasn't sure. Removing the dust sheet from the canvas on the easel, he looked at it again, trying to forget that it was Daniel Cartwright so that he could see what the artist had been attempting to paint. He employed a technique that Daniel had taught him. "Name the painting, Rowly, then you'll know if it's saying what you want it to say."

Rowland stood back and studied the portrait, the anguished figure—but it was more than that. There was a kind of shock etched into Cartwright's features. It wasn't simple melancholia or hurt or disappointment. There was an anger in the way the hands were clenched. It came to him then: betrayal. This was a painting of betrayal. The more he studied it, the more certain he became.

So who had betrayed Daniel Cartwright? Was it Otis Norcross? But if that was the case, for what reason could he possibly be Cartwright's heir? It didn't make sense. Rowland walked away from the easel. He had no doubt that Daniel had meant for him to see this painting, to know that he'd been betrayed. Was it a reference to his siblings? Could that be why he'd effectively disinherited them?

Rowland collected the box of letters from the shelf and took it into the drawing room. He switched on a single lamp by an armchair opposite the mysterious unsigned portrait. Opening the box he began to sort its contents into piles. There were several in his own hand, written over the years. A number from Molly, sent from Paris, London, Berlin, and Boston. One or two from Frank and Geoffrey. He struggled against his aversion to reading the correspondence. It was appallingly bad form, but Rowland needed to find Otis Norcross, and he wanted to know who had killed his friend. Still, he found the invasion of privacy awkward and distasteful. He read the letters from Frank and Geoffrey first. Both were brief and curt.

Molly's letters were full of news and gossip, the occasional poetic plea for funds, couched in affection and accompanied by amusing stories of social disaster that necessitated the financial help for which she asked. Rowland read them carefully, though he felt like the worst kind of cad doing so. There seemed a real warmth to Molly's letters, a playfulness. She chided her brother about the "bores" to whom he'd introduced her, the various Cabots and Lowells, "and then, when finally you bring me a pretty man with a modicum of wit, he turns out to be impervious to my charms. Really, Danny, you'll have to do better! I am your sister, after all." And then a later letter. "I have not heard from him in months. Perhaps that's why I think of him still. The heart is a contrarian beast."

Rowland wondered fleetingly if she was talking of the pretty man or one of the bores, and then turned his mind away immediately. Who Molly fancied or had fancied was none of his business.

Then there was a note on cartridge. *"My dear Danny. My paintings are sordid and colourless without you. When will you come? N."*

Rowland sat forward, examining the fragment in the light. There was a smear of viridian in the corner, and the edge was ragged as if the cartridge had been torn from the larger sheet. The message was written with an artist's pencil, and the line curved to fit on the fragment of paper. Whether it was a dedication on a painting or whether the artist had scribbled the note on whatever came to hand, he could not tell.

"Rowly?" Milton came into the drawing room. "Are you still up? It'll be sunrise in a couple of hours."

Rowland grimaced. "Did I wake you? Sorry. Couldn't sleep so I thought I'd go through these."

Milton poured two balloons of brandy and set one before Rowland. "Did you find anything?"

Rowland handed him the cartridge.

"You're thinking *N* is for Norcross."

"Danny kept it."

Milton glanced at the multiple stacks. "He seems to have kept everything, mate."

"Still—"

"You're right." Milton turned the fragment over. "Is there an envelope?"

Rowland shook his head. "No, Danny didn't keep any envelopes. There's no clue as to who sent that note...if it was sent."

"What do you mean?"

"You'll note, it's a torn-off corner of drawing cartridge. It may have just been passed to him."

Milton glanced again at the note. "So this tells us just about nothing."

Rowland frowned. "It's on drawing cartridge. So Norcross was probably an artist, which adds weight to the probability that he painted that." He pointed to the unsigned painting of Daniel Cartwright.

"That's true. So we look for Norcross in Daniel's artistic circles?"

"Yes, I expect so." Rowland pulled out a letter that had caught his eye earlier, from a John Lavalle. It thanked Daniel Cartwright for his condolences on the death of Lavalle's daughters and mother, and went on to say he looked forward to seeing Daniel when he was in town. "I wonder if Lavalle was the person Danny was meeting for dinner when he was killed."

Milton regarded him thoughtfully. "Well, we can't do that till morning, so why don't you get some sleep, Rowly?"

Rowland nodded, though he made no move to do so.

"Clyde's all right," Milton said.

"Thanks to Bradford. What if he hadn't gone after him?"

"I dunno, comrade. It might have been ugly. But Bradford did go after him."

"But what about the next time, Milt? They said it was a warning."

"So now we're warned—we'll be careful." Milton sat back.

"I think it's time to go home, Milt."

Milton looked at him, startled. "You're going to pull out of being Danny's executor? Is that even something one can do?"

"No, that's not what I meant. You, Clyde, and Ed should go home. I'll come as soon as I've sorted this out."

Milton sighed. "We're not going to do that, comrade." His dark eyes were steady on Rowland's. "Tell me, mate, why are you so angry with Daniel Cartwright?"

"I'm not—"

"Yes, you are. You're sad, and you miss him, but there's part of you that's angry with him. Why exactly?"

At first Rowland said nothing. If he was angry, he didn't know it. And when he said it, it was almost a surprise to him. "Because he waited till it was too late. Because he didn't ask me for help when he was alive."

"Well then, don't make the same mistake...or"—Milton shrugged—"make it. We're not going to leave when you need our help, whether or not you ask for it. Clyde's taken a kicking before; so have I—and for much less worthwhile reasons."

"Ed—"

"Ed should definitely go back to Sydney and wait for us. Learn to knit, so she can send us socks and admiration." The poet grinned. "You tell her."

Rowland smiled. "You're quite happy to abandon me to my fate there, I see."

"Mate, friendship will only go so far." He yawned. "If you want to try and tell Edna Higgins what to do, there ain't nobody who can protect you."

∽◎∾

They remained in the apartment the next day because Clyde was in no condition to venture out and they were unwilling to leave him alone, even with Bradford and his gun. The doctor Bradford had summoned the evening before returned early in the morning to check the dog bite wounds in particular. Clyde assured the physician that Windrip had not been foaming at the mouth or exhibiting any other signs of rabies. The lacerations were cleaned and coated in generous amounts of bright red mercurochrome antiseptic and redressed to ward off infection. The swelling around Clyde's eye was less pronounced, though the area had taken on some spectacular hues of blue and black, as had his rib cage, which had also taken a pounding. In some respects, he resembled his own painter's palette.

Even so, he limped back into the studio to resume his painting. Rowland joined him, using his drawings from the Savoy to paint Lindy Hoppers in loose dripping lines of dilute gauche. Painting movement more than form, bright and energetic.

Edna sat in the window sketching the Manhattan skyline for a sculpture series based on cities. Her sketches were engineering diagrams as much as anything else. The actual sculpture would have to wait until she was back in the converted tack shed that served as her studio in the grounds of Woodlands House. But she had, over the past months, been collecting her impressions of her beloved hometown of Sydney, as well as Shanghai, Singapore, and now New York. Back home she had drawings of London, Munich, and Paris. Details as well as broad strokes, she bent the straight edges of the buildings to capture the spirit and movement of each city.

Rowland peered over her shoulder, and she stopped

drawing to explain what she hoped to create with bronze and steel.

"Will it actually fit in the tack shed?" Rowland asked.

"I can do it in segments," Edna replied, turning to the drawing to show him where the sculpture would come apart. "I'll have to find someone to commission it, of course, but I think it might work."

Rowland nodded. The scale of the piece was ambitious, but he could see how Edna's vision might be manifested. He'd commission it himself if she would allow it, which of course she would not.

Clyde stood back from his easel, carefully regarding the composition on his canvas. Daniel Cartwright's easel, the shape of the canvas defined under the drape of the drop sheet. Its position in the middle of an empty studio had a still and haunting quality. It was a visual requiem to the artist.

For a while Rowland said nothing, startled by the sense of finality Clyde had imbued into the painting of a draped easel. "That's excellent, old boy. Truly excellent."

"I started it last night," Clyde said, shifting painfully. "I didn't want to not finish it, but now I think I need a drink."

"Oh, for goodness sake!" Edna put down her sketch while Rowland offered Clyde a shoulder. "You should be in bed."

But Clyde would not have that, preferring to watch Rowland work. To that end, Rowland moved an armchair into the studio and set it behind his easel so that Clyde could be as comfortable as possible. He was accustomed to having his friends watching him work from time to time. Clyde would offer occasional advice, Milton would read, and Edna often fell asleep. He chose a canvas from the stack already stretched onto frames, and hesitated. The subject of Clyde's painting was still in the centre of the room.

Edna stepped between Rowland and Daniel Cartwright's easel. "Would you like me to sit for you, Rowly?"

"Oh…yes," he replied, realising how long it had been since Edna had sat for him. How much he'd like to lose himself in painting her.

"How would you like me?"

Rowland considered it for a moment. "Can you lean against the mirror?"

"I won't be a moment." Edna moved to the door of the studio. "I'll get undressed and come back. Then you can pose me." Edna was a life model, Rowland a life artist—she didn't need to ask to know that was how he wanted to paint her.

By the time she returned, Rowland had adjusted the lighting, turned up the heating in the studio, and prepared a canvas. Edna slipped off her robe and waited for Rowland to tell her how he wished her to stand. She flinched as her bare shoulder made contact with the cold surface of the mirror.

Rowland apologised for the discomfort.

"As long as you don't want me to stand on one leg," she said, smiling. Edna relaxed against the mirror as he asked. Already, she had an idea of what he wanted to paint, and so she adjusted the angle of her body so that her reflection would be visible from where he stood. Edna turned her head to look directly at Rowland without being asked. For all the time she had known and modelled for him, Rowland Sinclair had asked his subjects to look directly at him, even in those early days when he could not look at a naked model without blushing.

He stood back, framing the composition with his hands. "Bring your hair forward, Ed, so I can see the line of your shoulder in the mirror."

Edna twisted her dark auburn tresses into a thick coil and pulled it forward. "Like this?"

"Yes, that's perfect." Rowland paused to take her in. "You're perfect," he added quietly.

Rowland began, blocking out her figure in sepia and

pushing the paint into shapes. The reflection, he under-painted in blues. He worked quickly at this stage, to establish the basic composition, form, and shadow.

Clyde watched Rowland paint and read out headlines and stories from the *New York Times*. Edna chatted to Clyde without moving her head. Entirely absorbed in what he was doing, Rowland barely heard them.

He established the bones of the painting, and then he tossed Edna her robe. "Thank you, Ed. Relax for a bit. Would you like a drink?"

Edna slipped on the robe and came round the easel to see what he'd been doing, and for a time they discussed it. Rowland had always valued the sculptress's opinion—she was more than just his model. For her part, Edna liked the way Rowland painted her.

Milton poked his head into the studio. The poet had glanced at Rowland in his shirtsleeves, Edna in her robe. "You'd better both get dressed. We have visitors."

Chapter Nineteen

REEL LIFE IN HOLLYWOOD

'Queen Kelly' is Shelved and Gloria Swanson Retrenches—Lili Damita's Suitors

Rumors are rife in Hollywood as to what is to become of Gloria Swanson and her latest disaster "Queen Kelly." The liveliest rumor has it that after spending 8 months and $750,000 on the lavish production, both written and directed by Erich von Stroheim, the picture is to be "re-" everything—re-written, directed, cut—with even Gloria left out and a new leading lady supplied for Walter Byron.

Last week, the picture was to be permanently shelved, so rumor had it, as Gloria Swanson took the train East for a conference with her financial backer, Joseph P. Kennedy. Running these rumors down at Pathe Studio, of which Mr. Kennedy is head with title of "special adviser," I find that no definite decision will be reached until the return of Miss

Swanson. It was strongly intimated, however,
that Paul Stein is rewriting "Queen Kelly" as
a 100 per cent talkie deleting all the censorable
von Stroheim touches.

—*Hartford Courant*
(Hartford, Connecticut), May 12, 1929

Rowland unrolled his shirtsleeves and refastened his cuff
links, irritated by the interruption.

"Who is it?" he asked while Edna slipped out to put on
some actual clothes.

"Marion and that bloke, Kennedy."

Rowland tried to shake off his mood. Marion Davies had
always been kind to them, and it would be an opportunity
to ask her about the guest who had given Clyde a dog. He
strode into the drawing room ahead of Clyde and Milton and
greeted their guests graciously.

Kennedy looked him up and down, noting the smears of
colour on his waistcoat.

"Oh, Mr. Watson Jones!" Marion exclaimed on seeing
Clyde. "I heard you'd been mugged. Oh, you poor man."

Clyde assured her he was all right and shook hands with
Kennedy.

"Lying in till midday?" Marion said, laughing. "I told
you, Joe, the girl's star material."

While they were waiting, Rowland asked Marion about
the woman with the dog at her party. "We were wondering
if you might know how we could reach her."

"You know," Marion said, frowning, "I don't believe I
got her name. I assume she arrived with one of the other

guests. To be honest, I'm not fond of dogs, so I kept my distance."

Edna arrived, attired in the slim skirt and blouse with which she'd started the day, though her hair was still loose, a red-gold reminder of how she'd looked against the mirror. The gentlemen stood. Edna embraced Marion and shook hands with Kennedy, who presented her with a black velvet box. "Something to mark this occasion," he said.

"I'm sorry, Mr. Kennedy," Edna asked, nonplussed. "What occasion do you mean?"

"Joe has decided to get back into the movie-making business," Marion said excitedly.

"To put it bluntly, Miss Higgins," Kennedy said, "I'd like to do for you what I did for Gloria Swanson. I'd like to make you a star."

There was just a hint of a smile on Edna's lips when she replied. "Thank you, Mr. Kennedy, but I don't think so."

Kennedy's eyes flickered. "Perhaps you should open your gift."

"Go on, Edna," Marion effused. "I've been dying to see what it is."

"I really don't think—"

"Just open it," Kennedy said, smiling broadly.

Edna handed the box back to him. Clearly frustrated, Kennedy opened the box to reveal the diamond necklace inside.

Marion gasped. "Oh, it's magnificent. Edna, you lucky girl!"

Edna blinked. "Thank you for the kind thought, Mr. Kennedy, but that's not something I can accept."

"Nonsense. This is just a taste of what's to come!"

"No, it isn't, Mr. Kennedy. As soon as Rowly's business here is concluded, we'll be going home to Sydney."

"I see." Kennedy stood. "Perhaps we should be going. Marion!"

Marion Davies looked shocked, even frightened.

"Mr. Sinclair, would you care to accompany us back up to Marion's place?" Kennedy left the velvet box on the table. "I'd like a word."

Rowland agreed for the sake of Marion Davies. It was only a couple of floors.

"Please don't forget your gift, Mr. Kennedy," Edna said firmly. "As I said, I cannot accept it."

"Keep it for a while," Kennedy said. "Try it on. It may grow on you."

"I assure you, it will not. Please take it."

Kennedy's jaw hardened a little, and he slipped the box into his pocket.

~⊙~

Joseph Kennedy waited until they'd all stepped out of the elevator at the penthouse before he spoke again. "Marion, if you'd excuse us, Sinclair and I need to have a frank conversation, man to man."

"I'll go see what WR and Patty are up to."

Once she'd gone, Kennedy's manner hardened further. He turned to Rowland angrily. "Right, Sinclair, what will it take?"

"I beg your pardon."

"I want Edna Higgins. She clearly defers to you."

Rowland laughed. "Ed defers to no one. She's given you her answer."

Kennedy exploded. Rowland was almost amused by the foul-mouthed vitriol. Then Kennedy paused, almost visibly reining in the profanity of his temper. "I am not asking you to give her up entirely. We all understand how these arrangements work. She will have plenty of time to keep you happy, but you don't want to deny her the opportunity of being managed by me. And you don't want to make an enemy of me, Sinclair."

"Mr. Kennedy, if it were really up to me, I'd simply deck you for what you just said." Rowland spoke calmly, though his eyes glinted dangerously. "But it's not, and Miss Higgins has already told you she's not interested in your management or your flowers or your diamonds. I'd leave it at that if I were you, because I don't particularly care what enemies I make, and I will not tolerate you insulting Miss Higgins again."

The exchange might have deteriorated further if Hearst had not appeared. "Rowland!" he said, smiling broadly. "Are you going to join us for lunch?"

Rowland declined politely and, without another word to Kennedy, returned to the thirty-first floor, where he walked in on Bradford serving luncheon and recounting a cautionary tale of Gloria Swanson like an ancient, tail-coated mariner.

"...and while Mr. Kennedy made a fortune, Miss Swanson was left with *Queen Kelly*, a film that defied all notions of decency and good taste, as well as millions of dollars in debt."

Edna smiled at the valet. "Please don't worry, Mr. Bradford. I have no interest in Mr. Kennedy's proposition, though I am now quite eager to see *Queen Kelly*. Is it showing anywhere?"

"I shall make enquiries, Miss Higgins. I'm pleased to hear you have no time for Mr. Kennedy. He has somewhat sordid a reputation. Connections with the Irish gangs—he became very rich very quickly."

"We all have reputations, Mr. Bradford." Edna unfolded her napkin, amused by Bradford's obvious concern for hers as well the litany of accusations and gossip he was levelling at Kennedy. "But I have neither the time nor the inclination to be made a star."

"Very good, Miss Higgins."

"So what exactly did Kennedy want, Rowly?" Milton asked as Rowland opened the telegram he'd just picked up from the silver tray on the sideboard.

"In a word: Ed," Rowland replied while reading.

"You told him to sod off?"

"Ed told him to sod off; I merely concurred."

"Forget about Joseph Kennedy," Edna interrupted. "Marion didn't know Clyde's Jean."

"If you knew Marion Davies was having a party, I suppose it wouldn't be that difficult to just come along." Milton pulled at his perfectly groomed goatee. "Prohibition is over—it's not as if there was a list at the door or a password."

Rowland sat down. "There were a lot of people in attendance, and I presume the Warwick staff were aware—it wouldn't have taken much for these chaps Costello and Brown to send in a female associate."

"Or perhaps Jean was just a woman with excellent taste in men and terrible taste in dogs," Edna said, reaching over to rub Clyde's hand.

Clyde laughed. "You really are a brick, Ed, but even I don't believe that!" He helped himself to new potatoes. "Gotta admit it was clever. You have to take a dog out every now and then. Even if there had been two of us with him, Windrip turning would have put us on the back foot." He shook his head. "Poor bloody mutt."

"You feel sorry for the dog?" Milton said, looking his friend up and down pointedly. "I gotta tell you, comrade, the dog won that fight."

Clyde frowned. "I have an idea what you have to do to a dog to make it savage on command. Anyone who can do that..." He shuddered. "These blokes aren't playing, Rowly."

Rowland nodded. "We might head back to Boston tomorrow."

"We're not giving up?" Clyde protested immediately. "Rowly, we can't—"

"We aren't. We're just going to look elsewhere for Mr. Norcross. I think we found out all we can in New York."

"You think he's in Boston?"

"I don't know." Rowland held up the telegram. "It's from Burr. I need to go back to deal with Frank's petition to have Danny declared incompetent. I expect it's just a couple of signatures, but it might not be a bad idea to get out of New York while Costello and Brown, not to mention Windrip, are still at large, and—" He frowned. "I wouldn't mind checking that Molly's all right."

"You think she might be in danger? Why?"

"Not danger exactly. But I am concerned that the brothers might read some kind of betrayal into the fact that I took her dancing."

"Though your presence at the Cocoanut Grove turned out to be convenient for Frank," Milton pointed out.

"Even so."

"Rowly's right," Edna said. "Molly's in the middle of this, and her brothers are bullies. We should go back to Boston, at least for now."

"As long as he doesn't panic and propose," Milton muttered.

"We need to find out who it was that Danny was supposed to dine with the night he was killed," Clyde added, reaching out to clout the poet on Rowland's behalf. "It seems strange that he or she has not come forward."

"Unless the meeting was not just about dinner," Milton observed. "In which case, he'd be a fool to come forward."

And so it was agreed that they would quit New York the following day. For the rest of that day, however, Rowland and Edna returned to Daniel Cartwright's studio and he finished his portrait of the sculptress. The time behind the easel was, for Rowland, clarifying. He had always thought best with a paintbrush in his hand, and there was something about the drawing of Otis Norcross they'd found the previous day. The likeness itself was of little use when they did not know where Norcross was.

Clyde and Milton came in to see the finished painting. Milton swore his appreciation, slapping Rowland's back in congratulations.

Clyde was more quietly taken by the cleverness of the composition. By leaning Edna against the mirror, Rowland had painted her from both sides, but this was not a clichéd painting of woman considering her reflection. Rowland's subject was indifferent to what the mirror held. Her back was to it, her eyes fixed on the artist. The placement of her hair exposed the elegant line of her shoulder in the reflection. The colour of red-gum honey, the tresses were warm against her fair skin and curled around the curve of her breast. It was almost overwhelming in its allure, and in every brushstroke, Clyde could see that the artist worshipped his model. Deep in the mirror's image, the shadowy form of the easel and artist. It was the closest Rowland had ever come to self-portrait. "Rowly...mate..." was all he said.

Edna smiled as she looked at the portrait. "When this is all over, you must shut out the world and paint," she said.

"Are you saying I need to practise?" he asked, cleaning his brushes.

"I'm saying you need to paint." She looked at him fondly. "You are breathtakingly talented, my darling, but easily distracted."

He laughed. "I've hardly been chasing butterflies, Ed."

"You haven't exhibited anything in over a year."

"The invitations to exhibit in Australia have been a bit thin on the ground," he said ruefully.

Edna's face softened. Rowland's reputation as an artist had taken rather a battering after his last exhibition, which had ended in something of a riot. As much as he was philosophical about the consequences, she knew he felt the professional exile. "I expect that America has a lot of galleries. And they probably have no idea that you're a dangerous subversive radical."

Clyde folded his arms. "She's right, you know, mate. You shouldn't just sit back and accept that you're not going to exhibit again."

Rowland studied his painting. He was happy with the way it had turned out. There had been a time when painting was more important than anything. "I promise you, Clyde, I haven't accepted it."

Chapter Twenty

At the Vose Galleries

One of the most delightful exhibits of the season opened yesterday at the Vose Galleries with the preview of Mr John Lavalle's notable group of portraits. Mrs Lavalle, whose portrait is one of this collection, wore simple distinctive black with huge creamy gardenias as she received yesterday with Mr Lavalle, and others there yesterday whose portraits afforded interesting studies were Mrs George H. Lyman Jr in hunters green velvet with cleaver blouse of matching lame and little peaked hat of velvet, Mrs Basil Gavin in stunning coat of black moire caracul, Miss Natalie Folsom in fetching black with sparkling twin slips of frosty leaves, and Mrs Henry G. Nickerson (Laetitia Orlandini) who attended with Mr. Nickerson...

—*Boston Globe*,
November 19, 1935

~⊙~

Rowland took the boxes of drawings and the letters as well as the unsigned portrait, promising Bradford that they would be returned to the studio in time. The old valet was vigilant in the guardianship of his late master's home and unhappy that the contents of the studio in particular were being disturbed. Rowland tried to explain.

"Finding Otis Norcross is my only hope of honouring Danny's wishes." Rowland broached the bequest made in favour of Bradford himself. "You know that Danny left you a considerable sum, Mr. Bradford?"

"I do, sir. And when I can hand his home to his heir, I will retire. But until then, I have my duty."

"Thank you, Mr. Bradford. And thank you again for your intervention in aid of Mr. Watson Jones. I am in your debt."

Bradford studied him, as if he were still deciding. "In the last months, Mr. Cartwright was not himself. He trusted no one, not even me. You be careful, Mr. Sinclair."

Rowland's painting and Clyde's were still wet, and so, with Bradford's indulgence, they left them in the studio.

Clyde rang the NYPD and informed Officer O'Hara that they intended to leave town. He left the details of the Copley Plaza Hotel. O'Hara informed him that Costello and Brown had not yet been apprehended, but that he would be in touch if and when progress was made.

All in all they were a little glad to leave New York behind them.

When they arrived at the Copley, Rowland enquired about Molly Cartwright at the reception. The concierge patched a call to her suite and informed him that Miss Cartwright was out.

Leaving Edna to take a still battle-weary Clyde up to

their own suites, Rowland and Milton left for the offices of Burr, Mayfair and Wilkes. Oliver Burr welcomed them straight into his office and apprised Rowland of the latest legal machinations in the dispute over Daniel Cartwright's estate, as well as the search for Norcross.

"We've conducted an extensive search for anyone named Otis Norcross. The Norcrosses are a prominent Boston family, though there are obviously Norcrosses elsewhere. Otis is also a popular name among the Norcrosses, it being the name of their most illustrious ancestor, who was once mayor of Boston. Some of the Otis Norcrosses are numbers I, II, and so forth, but Mr. Cartwright did not indicate if that was the case here. And there are a number of Otis Norcrosses currently residing in Boston."

"Well, how on earth are we going to find out which one he met?"

"That, sir, is up to you and Mr. Cartwright's executor. We will, of course, assist you by trying to find an Otis Norcross with whom he was friendly or associated, but the determination of whether an Otis Norcross is Mr. Cartwright's intended beneficiary is a determination he had left in your hands."

"Capital!" Rowland said exasperated. What the devil could Danny have been thinking? "Have you found an Otis Norcross amongst Danny's friends and acquaintances?"

"One. There was an Otis Norcross born here in Boston in 1900, who was in Daniel Cartwright's class at Harvard."

Rowland sat forward. "Well, that's excellent. Is he still in Boston, Mr. Burr? Why hasn't he come forward—does he not know that he is the primary beneficiary of Danny's will?"

"He is still in Boston, Mr. Sinclair, in a manner of speaking. Otis Norcross is interred at Mount Auburn. He died of influenza in 1933."

"So Danny didn't know that he'd died?" Rowland asked.

"Mr. Cartwright attended the funeral."

Rowland sat back. "Do you mean to tell me, Mr. Burr, that Danny intentionally left his estate to a dead man?"

"Unless we can find another Otis Norcross who Mr. Cartwright might have known, that would appear to be the case."

For a moment Rowland said nothing as he struggled for some way to explain his friend's actions. "So what does this mean, Mr. Burr?"

"Well, it does add credence to the family's contention that Mr. Cartwright was not of sound mind when he wrote this will. We will, of course, continue our efforts to find a living beneficiary, or at least one who was alive at the time the will was made, but, failing that, it is my recommendation that we enter into negotiations with the family to concede an intestacy."

Rowland exhaled. "I see."

"I'm sorry, Mr. Sinclair, but I cannot see any other reasonable course of action."

"No, you're right." Rowland dragged a hand through his hair. Had Danny lost his mind? He couldn't believe that. "But we should expend every effort to find a living beneficiary if one exists. I'll pay the expenses of the search personally so that it is not a burden on the estate, but I do want you to do everything possible, Mr. Burr."

"Certainly, sir."

"In the meantime, let us concede nothing about Daniel Cartwright's competency. Can we hold the family's claims at bay until we have had time to either find Otis Norcross or satisfy ourselves that he does not exist?"

Burr made some notes. "Of course. I'll ask the court for an adjournment. We should be able to buy a few weeks at least."

"What are you looking for?" Edna dealt hands to Clyde and Milton as Rowland rummaged through the box of letters they had brought back from the Warwick.

"A letter from John Lavalle. I was hoping it might have a return address."

"Why?"

Rowland explained his discussion with Burr.

"Otis Norcross is dead?" Clyde asked and signalled for another card.

"*One* Otis Norcross is dead… He may not be Danny's Otis Norcross." Rowland found the letter.

"What do you think, Rowly?" Edna asked, folding her hand.

Rowland sat down. "I don't know, Ed. Bradford said Danny was becoming paranoid. Maybe…but I have to be sure. And, regardless of whether or not his will stands, someone murdered him."

"So what has Lavalle got to do with it?" Clyde asked.

"Perhaps it was Lavalle who Danny was appointed to meet the night he was killed." Rowland looked down at the letter in his hand and groaned. There was no address noted on the page. "I'll have to get Burr to try and find him."

"Maybe not." Clyde picked up a copy of the *Boston Daily Globe* and handed it to Rowland. "Second page. Bottom right-hand corner. Lavalle's holding an exhibition at the Vose Gallery. They could probably tell you where to find him."

Rowland opened the paper and read the article. An exhibition featuring the portraits of the renowned painter John Lavalle. "I'll drop in tomorrow and leave a message for him." He stood and retrieved his hat from the hook by the door.

"Where are you going now?" Milton asked, his eyes focused on his cards.

"I thought I might call on the Norcrosses."

"What Norcrosses?"

"Otis's parents—he wasn't married."

"Why?"

"To ask how well their son knew Daniel Cartwright. Perhaps attending the funeral was a just a social obligation." Rowland had attended funerals for that same reason. "If he didn't really know the deceased, it's likely that we are looking for a different Otis Norcross."

"I'll come with you." Edna left the card table and pulled on her gloves. "I have a terrible hand anyway."

Rowland waited for the sculptress to affix her hat, while Milton protested the "cowardly retreat."

The Norcross residence in Back Bay was no more humble than that of the Cartwrights. Rowland had called ahead to make an appointment, and so they were admitted into a formal parlour and invited to take a seat on the Victorian settee while they waited.

Mrs. Norcross swept into the room just moments later. Rowland and Edna both stood. Their hostess was a woman of advanced age and quite regal bearing. She invited them to sit again and rang for tea.

"I understand you were a friend of the late Mr. Daniel Cartwright, Mr. Sinclair."

"I was, Mrs. Norcross. And I am the executor of his estate."

"Yes, I had heard that. If you don't mind me saying, it's scandalous. Poor, poor Molly."

"You and Molly are acquainted?"

"If God had not taken Otis so suddenly, I had hoped she might be my daughter-in-law someday."

"Molly was engaged to Otis?" Edna asked.

"Not formally, no. But it would have been an excellent match—they were very well suited."

Rowland sipped his tea. "Are you aware, Mrs. Norcross, if Otis knew Daniel Cartwright well?"

"Well, of course he did, Mr. Sinclair. This is Boston. All the good families are acquainted. He escorted Molly to Otis's funeral, I believe. Of course, there were so many mourners—Otis was a well-loved young man—that I was unable to talk to everyone."

"Our condolences, Mrs. Norcross," Edna said. "We didn't know Otis, but we are sorry for your loss."

"Thank you, my dear. We bear what the Lord asks of us. Otis was a devastating loss…but the influenza, you know."

Edna glanced about the room, her eyes settling on a framed portrait of a gentleman with Victorian sideburns and a luxuriant moustache. "Is that a picture of Otis?" she asked.

Mrs. Norcross smiled. "Oh no, my dear! That's my husband, Mr. Norcross. He will be very flattered by your mistake!" She sighed. "I'm afraid there are no pictures of Otis. I cannot bear to see him."

Edna nodded sympathetically.

"Can I ask, Mr. Sinclair, why you wish to know about Otis?"

"There was a bequest to an Otis Norcross in Mr. Cartwright's will," Rowland said, surprised that Mrs. Norcross seemed unaware. "We're trying to establish which Otis Norcross."

"Well, I'm afraid the Good Lord took Otis nearly two and a half years ago. And even if he hadn't, I'm not sure that Otis's acquaintance with Mr. Cartwright warranted such a remembrance."

꩜

Rowland grabbed the blanket from the parcel shelf of the Madame X and placed it around Edna. The decision to drive out to Mount Auburn graveyard had been made on impulse. The temperature was dropping rapidly, and the air was damp, but they did not need a fine day to visit Daniel Cartwright's grave.

The cemetery was cloaked in cold quiet as they walked towards the Cartwright plot. It was still too early for the headstone to have been laid, and so they stood before the simple cross that marked the new grave to pay their respects. A paintbrush had been placed before the cross, a remembrance from someone who cared that Daniel Cartwright had been an artist.

Rowland sighed. "What the hell is it you want me to do, Danny?"

Edna slipped her hand into his and, after a time, they headed back. On the way, they passed the Norcross plot and Otis Norcross's monumental headstone.

"Do you think it's odd that Mrs. Norcross has no pictures of Otis?"

"People react unexpectedly to grief," Rowland said, thinking of his own mother, who refused to accept her middle son's death, becoming determined that Rowland was his late brother and accepting no evidence to the contrary. "I was going to show her Danny's drawing until she said she could not bear to see him."

"We can ask Molly if it's Otis, I suppose." Edna frowned. "Did she ever mention to you that she knew Otis Norcross?"

"No, she didn't."

"Does that not strike you as peculiar, Rowly?"

"It does. But perhaps she just assumed it was another Otis Norcross. Perhaps it's a particularly common name in Boston." Noticing that Edna was shivering, he removed his overcoat and placed it around her shoulders. "She said from the beginning that Norcross didn't exist. Perhaps that's what she meant."

"She also said she thought he killed Danny—"

"If he existed. I presume she meant if we found another Otis Norcross."

Edna pulled his coat tighter, wrinkling her nose against the numbing cold. "Still, if the dead Otis Norcross was her beau, then it's strange she wouldn't have just said so when the will was read." She bit her lip thoughtfully. "What happens if it's shown that Danny's Otis Norcross is the dead Otis Norcross?"

"If that were the case, then the residual clause would come into effect."

"And what's a residual clause?"

"It's basically an 'anything left' clause. It operates only if one of the beneficiaries is not able to take their share—in this case, because he's dead. In Danny's will, the residual was in favour of a small private gallery in a place called Manchester by the Sea. I presume they must have shown Danny's paintings."

"Do they know?"

"The lawyers sent them a letter, I believe, but it's a residual clause. It will only have any effect if the gift to Otis Norcross fails."

"So the Cartwrights won't benefit by the fact that Danny left most of his estate to a dead man."

"Except that Danny knew that Otis Norcross was dead when he made the will. So if it can be shown that the dead Otis Norcross was the man he intended, you would have to question his competency and the whole will could be struck out, in which case his next of kin inherit."

"So why wouldn't the Cartwrights just tell you about Otis Norcross from the beginning? Molly stepped out with him, she went to his funeral, she had to know he was dead."

Rowland shrugged. "I really don't know, Ed. Perhaps it was the shock. Molly was distraught. Or perhaps they just didn't know what it would mean and wanted to get their own legal advice first. I wouldn't even know what a residual was if Oliver Burr hadn't taken me through everything so meticulously." It was clear by his expression that the education had not been one he particularly enjoyed.

Edna laughed. "You're right."

Chapter Twenty-One

4 DEAD AS FIRE RAZES LAVALLE HOME AT BOSTON

CRIPPLED MOTHER OF ARTIST, 70, BURNED IN BED—CHILD DIES

7 OTHERS INJURED

BLAZE TRAPS OCCUPANTS IN UPPER FLOORS OF 4-STORY HOUSE

(By Associated Press)

Boston, May 7—Four persons, including the mother and 14-year-old daughter of John LaValle, internationally known portrait painter, were burned to death or killed in leaps as fire swept the artist's home today. Seven other persons were injured.

Artist Absent

The fire occurred in the absence of the
socially prominent artist and his second wife,
the former Virginia Wilson of Cincinnati,
daughter of Robert Wilson, tobacco-trade
multi-millionaire.

—*The Record*
(Hackensack, New Jersey), May 7, 1935

∿◕∿

Rowland and Edna returned to the hotel but, as it was still
light, decided to call in at the Vose Fine Art Gallery before
heading back up to the suites. They stepped out on foot.
The gallery was in Copley Square, so they had only to cross
the plaza to Boylston Street. Established in the prosperity of
the twenties, the building was four storeys high, and exhibited both American artists and those from abroad. Paintings
placed in every window declared the business of Vose to all
who passed.

Rowland and Edna were greeted by a young man, no more
than twenty-five, who introduced himself as S. Morton Vose
II. Despite the loftiness of his name, Vose himself was per-
sonable and courteous. Rowland enquired after the Lavalle
exhibition, and Vose took them up to the room in which the
portraits were being displayed.

Though it was not their primary purpose, they viewed the
exhibition with interest. Lavalle's style was distinctive and
his portraits, of wealthy Bostonians in the main, traditional
in composition and soft in line. His paintings of children had
a particular vibrance.

Vose explained that the artist, a great-grandson of the Argentinian dictator, Juan de Lavalle, was quite a well-known name in fine art circles and a familiar figure in Boston generally. His voice became a little hushed as he told them of the fire earlier that year that had consumed Lavalle's house and studio and taken the lives of his mother and two of his young daughters.

"Oh, how horrible," Edna gasped. "The poor man."

Vose nodded. "Mr. Lavalle has thrown himself into his work. Of course many of these portraits were finished before the fire and are hung for exhibition purposes only. We do have a number of works which are available for purchase."

Vose showed them a number of landscapes, as well as several paintings of biplanes in dogfights. "Mr. Lavalle was a bomber pilot during the Great War," Vose explained, noticing Rowland's interest in the aircraft.

Rowland purchased two paintings of battling biplanes, before he mentioned that he would like to get in touch with John Lavalle. "Perhaps if I was to leave a note for him?"

"I'd be happy to pass on a message, Mr. Sinclair, but if you'd care to wait half an hour or so, Mr. Lavalle is due to come in at six o'clock. I'm sure he'd be delighted to meet you."

And so Rowland and Edna waited, spending the time viewing the gallery's other pieces, while Vose wrapped and packed their purchases. The young art dealer seemed very gratified, even relieved by the sale, though neither painting had been particularly expensive. Rowland presumed that, despite the extraordinary size of the gallery, selling art was not an easy exercise in the current financial climate. Though they had seen signs of recovery, he expected it would be a while before Americans were confident enough to buy art again.

Vose enquired about their business in Boston.

"We came for the funeral of an old friend," Rowland said. "Perhaps you were acquainted? Daniel Cartwright?"

"Oh, yes, Mr. Cartwright was a client. He bought quite a few pieces about six months ago. He had an excellent eye. I was very sorry to hear of his passing."

"The paintings he bought—what were they?"

Vose checked his ledger and listed several names. Rowland knew one or two.

"It was quite an eclectic selection," Vose commented. "Landscapes, abstract, still life."

"Did he have them shipped to New York?" Rowland asked.

"No. He had me cut the canvases from their stretchers and send them to him at the Copley Plaza Hotel."

"He was staying there?"

"I believe so."

John Lavalle arrived at the Vose Gallery just after six that evening. A handsome man, his Argentinian heritage was evident in dark features. Rowland sketched him mentally—high forehead, strong narrow nose, a sense of purpose about the set of his mouth. Vose introduced Rowland Sinclair and Edna Higgins.

"Mr. Sinclair, how d'you do? Miss Higgins, a pleasure to make your acquaintance."

"Mr. Sinclair has purchased two of your paintings, Mr. Lavalle." Vose clearly assumed Rowland wished to speak to Lavalle on a matter of art.

"Can I commend you on your excellent taste, Mr. Sinclair?"

Rowland laughed. "Could I possibly impose on a moment of your time, Mr. Lavalle?"

"Certainly, Mr. Sinclair. What can I do for you?"

"Were you acquainted with the late Mr. Daniel Cartwright?"

Lavalle's eyes widened. "Why, yes. For many years."

"The night Danny was killed, he was to meet a friend for dinner. Might that person have been you, Mr. Lavalle?"

Lavalle studied him for a moment. "It might have been, if Daniel had kept the appointment. But I'm afraid he did not."

"Where were you to meet?"

"The Waldorf Lunch in Harvard Square—the students quite like it. I was on the campus that week painting the dean's portrait." Lavalle shrugged. "It was convenient to me, and so Danny kindly agreed to dine there."

Rowland's brow rose. The Waldorf Lunch was a casual eatery where the meals were fast and inexpensive. "Danny was wearing a dinner suit. Wouldn't that have been a little overdressed for the Waldorf Lunch?"

"Yes. If he had arrived, he might have looked somewhat out of place."

"But he didn't arrive?"

"He didn't—I was put out, to be honest. It seemed a poor way to treat a friend. It was not till later that I learned what happened."

"You didn't speak to the police?"

"They didn't speak to me. And there didn't seem to be any point. There was nothing I could tell them." He sighed. "I did speak to Frank Cartwright before I returned to New York—I assume he passed it on to the authorities and the missed appointment was of no interest."

Rowland regarded the artist carefully. "Was it you or Danny who made the appointment for dinner, Mr. Lavalle?"

"Oh, that was Daniel. He did not come to Boston often."

"Do you know what he was doing here?"

"He wrote that he was trying to get a friend released."

"Released? From prison?"

Lavalle shrugged. "Daniel was excitable in his choice of phrase. I assumed he meant from an unfortunate association. He was aware, after all, what ruin such associations could bring."

"You mean Danny's expulsion from Harvard?"

"Yes. I graduated in 1918, but I was still in Boston. It was, at the time, an unspeakable scandal." He shook his head. "Young men facing lifelong ruin. Daniel, of course, had the means to seek letters abroad, but not all were so able."

Rowland's eyes narrowed as a thought occurred. "Did anyone resent Danny for being able to put it behind him?"

"I wouldn't know, Mr. Sinclair." Lavalle's brows furrowed. "I expect I should have spoken to the police, that I should have been more concerned about the death of my dear friend...but after...It's been a difficult time, Mr. Sinclair."

"Forgive me, Mr. Lavalle, I didn't mean to imply—"

"No, Mr. Sinclair, it is my own conscience that troubles me on that account."

"Mr. Lavalle," Edna said gently, "please accept our deepest condolences."

Lavalle turned to the sculptress and smiled sadly. "Daniel was with me in New York when I first got the news. He was a very good friend to me then. I'm sorry if I was not able to be the same in return."

❧

There were only a few people in the square as they crossed it. Bostonians were ending the day or beginning the evening. It was cold and dark, and so they were brisk in the crossing to the warmth of the hotel foyer.

They were barely through the door when a young man intercepted them. "Good evening, Mr. Sinclair. Alexander Smythe of Burr, Mayfair and Wilkes." He handed Rowland a letter of introduction, embossed with the firm's letterhead and signed by Oliver Burr. "Mr. Burr sent me to find you. I'm afraid he needs to see you immediately."

Rowland checked his watch. "At this time?"

"I'm afraid so, sir. There is some information that has

come to light with respect to Daniel Cartwright's estate, about which he would like to speak with you immediately. He directed me to wait for you and ensure you got the message as soon as you returned."

"I'll just walk Miss Higgins up—"

"If you don't mind, sir, Mr. Burr is quite anxious that you don't delay. Perhaps if I was to see Miss Higgins to her suite."

"Don't be absurd," Edna said. "I'm quite capable of taking the elevator by myself without legal representation. You go see Mr. Burr, Rowly. Maybe he's found Otis Norcross."

There was a black Chevrolet and chauffeur waiting outside the Copley. Smythe opened the rear passenger door for Rowland, and then took the seat beside the driver. Just a block away from the square, the Chevrolet pulled over, and before Rowland could ask why, the rear doors were opened and two men got in on either side of him. He'd seen them before, in Central Park. Costello had a gun, a fact he made clear by shoving the barrel into Rowland's ribs. The man who'd called himself Alexander Smythe turned around and grinned. "Don't panic, Mr. Sinclair. We'd just like a word."

Rowland didn't move. "What do you want?"

"We'd like you to stop messing around, Mr. Sinclair. To admit that your pansy friend was bananas and allow the court to distribute his assets to his next of kin, as is only right. We'd like you to stop sticking your foreign nose in the affairs of others and move on. If you do that, nobody gets hurt."

"I see."

"This little confab is just by way of making you realise that we can reach you or any of your friends whenever we want to. You won't see us coming, Sinclair."

Rowland thought of Smythe's offer to see Edna to the suite in his stead. He felt sick.

"Now, killing you would just mean more delays, but you should know that your friends are surplus to the process."

Rowland flared. "If you—"

Brown punched him in the ribs before he could move, and then again several times. It was more than just a fist. Even in the confines of the Chevrolet's back seat, the blows were brutal in their impact. It was Smythe who called a stop to it.

"Put your knuckles away, you boob! He ain't no use to us dead!"

Brown pulled back reluctantly and removed the brass knuckles.

For a moment Rowland thought he might continue with his fist, but instead, he patted Rowland's cheek. "No harm done. See, his face is still pretty."

Smythe continued. "Contrary to popular opinion, Mr. Sinclair, we get no pleasure from violence."

Costello and Brown laughed. Smythe glared at them. "We particularly don't get any pleasure from hurting women. I mean, there are so many more ways you can hurt a woman, but we don't like doing that."

Rowland's blood ran cold now. He stared at Smythe.

That smile again. Mirthless. Ruthless.

"I'm glad we got your attention, Sinclair." He told the driver to pull over, and Costello and Brown dragged Rowland out of the Chevrolet. Costello took his pocketbook.

Smythe pointed. "The Copley is about five blocks that way. Do the right thing, Sinclair."

Despite the damage done by Brown's knuckleduster, Rowland did not wait for the Chevrolet to leave before he began to run. Neither pain nor the surprised and censorious glances of the pedestrians he bolted past slowed Rowland in any way.

The elevator attendant looked a little alarmed when

Rowland ran in and panted the floor, but he pressed the relevant buttons.

"Rowly!" It was Milton who responded to the pounding on the door. "What the hell—"

"Is Ed here?"

"Ed? She was with you..."

Chapter Twenty-Two

GLOVES

GLOVES can tell an amazing lot about a woman. The average woman, who spends much of her day life in black, nine times out of ten chooses black or beige gloves. But she who seeks to avoid mediocre results and who accordingly keeps her eyes open to new influences will affect immaculate white doeskin gloves with her all-black costumes. It's slightly more trouble, but ever so much more elegant and a great chic at the moment among some of the smartest women seen about town.

—*Inverell Times*, 27 May 1935

⟲❧⟳

Clyde called Oliver Burr and the police while Rowland and Milton returned to the foyer to search for Edna and speak to the manager. The staff were consulted, but no one recalled seeing the sculptress. There was no sign of her in the foyer or the restaurant or the bar. Edna Higgins, it seemed, had disappeared.

Rowland went through the events of that day with Detective O'Brien, who had been called in on his request and, probably more effectively, on Oliver Burr's.

"Could Miss Higgins have run into a friend after you left her and stepped out with these men?" O'Brien asked.

Rowland shook his head. "Edna would never have just left—not without letting Clyde and Milt, at least, know."

"Right, we'll put out an alert." O'Brien looked grave.

"Frank Cartwright is behind this," Rowland said, pacing.

"He's been in his suite all evening, Mr. Sinclair, but I will be speaking to him further." O'Brien sighed. "You wouldn't be considering approaching Mr. Cartwright yourself, would you, Mr. Sinclair? That would not be a good idea. Leave this with the proper authorities."

"You don't understand, Detective. God knows what they might do to her—"

"I do understand, Mr. Sinclair. Too well, I'm afraid. We are doing everything we can. The best thing you can do is go back to your suite and stay there."

"What—why?"

"If Miss Higgins has been abducted, her abductors may make a ransom demand. They need to be able to reach you."

Rowland looked blankly at him, terrified now and becoming more so with every moment. Smythe's words: "…so many more ways you can hurt a woman…"

Milton's hand on his shoulder. "Come on, comrade."

O'Brien shook his head. "Have a doctor look at him," he advised Milton. "Brass knuckles are no joke."

A police officer was sent up to the suite with them, in case the kidnappers called or perhaps just to ensure Rowland stayed put. Milton poured Rowland a large glass of gin in lieu of the medical attention O'Brien recommended and which Rowland categorically refused.

"There's nothing broken, Milt."

Milton didn't argue. He set the glass down before Rowly. "Take the edge off with this for now."

"What happened?" Clyde asked. "What the hell's happened to Ed?"

Rowland clenched his hands in his hair and swore. Milton explained. Clyde sat down, shocked. "They took her from the foyer?"

Milton nodded. A knock on the suite's door, and Murphy, the young police officer, answered. He admitted Oliver Burr, who walked in and sat opposite Rowland.

"Mr. Sinclair, I cannot tell you how sorry I am about Miss Higgins." The lawyer shook his head. "Please consider the resources of Burr, Mayfair and Wilkes at your disposal."

"I take it you did not send for me this evening."

"No, sir. I did not."

"Can you find her, Mr. Burr?" Rowland rubbed his face, trying to think straight. "Is there something you can do to find her?"

Burr spoke calmly. "The police are already searching every known haunt of these men, Costello and Brown, as well as those of J. L. Lombardo. I've spoken to Mayor Mansfield personally to ensure every effort is expended." He met Rowland's eyes. "It is my hope that they took Miss Higgins simply to demonstrate that they could, that this is just an act of intimidation."

"Regardless of how they did it, Mr. Burr, how do I get her back?" Rowland stood, unable to stay still. "I'll resign as Danny's executor, we'll go home—"

Clyde grabbed Rowland by the shoulders. He spoke firmly, recognising panic, defying his own by trying to stem Rowland's. "Mate, let's just wait till they tell us what they want."

"Did they have time to come back to the Copley to grab Ed after they threw you out of the motorcar, Rowly?" Milton asked.

"No. I don't think so. Ed should have been back at the suite by then anyway. She had just to ride up in the elevator."

"Think, Rowly. Did you see her get into the elevator before you left with this bastard Smythe?"

"No, she didn't."

Milton turned to the officer. "Murphy, you go down and find the elevator driver who was on duty. If Ed rode up to this floor, he'll remember—she's not the kind of woman you forget. If she did ride up, find out if there was anyone else in the elevator and if they got out on her floor."

For a moment Murphy hesitated. "I'm not sure I should—"

"For God's sake, man, go!" Milton snapped. "We don't need protection!"

"Come along, Officer Murphy," Oliver Burr said, opening the door. "Shall we speak to Detective O'Brien about Mr. Isaacs's suggestion? I believe it's a good one."

They'd been gone only moments when Milton moved to follow them.

"I'm going to talk to the parking valets and bellhops. Maybe one of them saw her get into a motorcar."

"I'll come—"

"No, Rowly. Stay here in case someone calls."

Rowland cursed as Milton shut the door. He felt powerless. Clyde's hand braced his shoulder.

"Rowly, sit down. You look like hell."

"God, Clyde, what have I done?"

"This isn't your doing, mate."

"I should have seen her to the suite—what did I think I was doing? Danny left his estate to a dead man...of course he was bloody crazy! Why didn't I just let it be?"

"Because Danny was your friend. Rowly, come on. They'll

drive Ed around for a while, like they did you, and let her go somewhere in the city." Clyde didn't really believe what he was saying, but he wanted Rowland to believe it, for the time being at least.

"Clyde, if they've hurt her—"

"We will find her, Rowly. Now sit down before you collapse."

Rowland winced as he lowered himself onto the couch. Clyde noticed the faint bloodstains on Rowland's shirt where his waistcoat had fallen open. "Bloody hell, Rowly, have you been stabbed?"

Rowland looked down. "No. Brown was wearing knuckle-dusters." He lifted his shirt gingerly to reveal the bloody bruising to his abdomen. "It's just broken the skin in a couple of places."

Clyde grimaced. "We should get you cleaned up a little before Ed gets back." He went to the drinks cabinet and used the Copley's aged Scotch to soak a handkerchief. "Hold still. You're lucky they didn't accidently kill you, mate. I've known knuckledusters to break a man's breastbone."

Rowland flinched as the alcohol made contact. "There wasn't really enough room to swing properly in the car, and Smythe called him off. Apparently, they didn't want to kill me."

"Why?" Clyde asked. "Wouldn't killing you remove the one person standing between Danny's fortune and his blasted brothers?"

"Perhaps." Rowland refastened the buttons. "But Danny apparently stipulated that if I was unable or unwilling to act as his executor, then everything was to go to Yale."

"University?"

"Yes. It was one last shot at Harvard, I guess."

"It was also an attempt to protect you, Rowly. Flamin' oath! He must have realised."

Rowland closed his eyes. "I should have realised that, as much as it protected me, it put you all in danger."

Clyde shook his head. "Do you think it would have made a scrap of difference, Rowly? Do you think any of us would have gone home and left you to it? Particularly Ed."

Rowland's face was rigid. "If anything happens to her—"

A knock at the door. Rowland rose to his feet and answered it quickly, hopefully. For a moment he didn't register who he was looking at. "Molly..."

She threw her arms around him. "Oh, Rowly, I just got back and heard. I'm so sorry."

He pulled back from her embrace. "Do you know where she is, Molly?"

"No, of course not!"

"Are you sure? Has Frank mentioned anything, has he done anything that might—"

"Rowly, you're frightening me!"

Clyde intervened. "Rowly, mate." He turned to Molly. "I'm sorry. We're all just—"

"—worried. I know." She looked back at Rowland, and fought back the tears. "If I could do anything, I would. If I knew anything, I would tell you. I'm so sorry. Oh, Rowly, I couldn't bear it if you hated me." She was crying without inhibition now. Rowland let her sob into his chest.

"Molly, look, I apologise. I'm not thinking properly." He took the handkerchief from his breast pocket and handed it to her. He glanced at Clyde. "I'll walk you back to your room."

Clyde nodded. "Go. I'll stay near the phone."

Molly chattered nervously as they caught the elevator down to the floor on which her suite was located. She'd gotten out of Boston for a couple of days, she didn't know why, but with him in New York, she didn't feel safe, she was sorry about Edna, but perhaps she'd just run into someone and gone dancing; it had been known to happen.

Rowland wasn't really listening. When they arrived at her suite, she gave him the room key. "I know this is silly, but would you look inside please? With everything that's happened I'm a little frightened."

"Of course." Rowland took the key and opened the door. He switched on the lights and checked the sitting room.

"Would you have a look around the bedroom, too, before you go, please?"

Rowland did so.

"You must think I'm a dreadful goose," Molly said as he gave that too the all clear.

"Given what's happened I should have insisted on doing so without you asking."

"Will you stay? Just a little while until my heart stops pounding?"

Rowland hesitated. "I really have to get back, Molly."

"I could distract you."

If Rowland had been in a better frame of mind, he might have recognised that Molly Cartwright was trying once again to seduce him, and he would have answered with more thought. As it was, he simply said, "I don't think you could."

Molly started to cry once again. "Rowly, please don't go. I'm scared."

A knock at the suite's door. Rowland answered immediately in the hope it was Clyde or Milton with news.

"Of course!" Geoffrey Cartwright glowered at him. "I should have known you'd be here."

Rowland stared back blankly, entirely disinterested in Geoffrey's salacious accusations.

"Geoffers! What are you doing here?" Molly did not seem pleased to see her brother.

"Frank said someone tried to abduct you. I came to check on you."

"How did Frank—?"

"Did someone try to abduct you, Molly?"

She glanced at Rowland, and then she nodded. "Someone's been following me, and today a man tried to seize me—"

"What?" Rowland stared at her, startled. "Where?"

"Just outside the hotel."

"Why didn't you tell me, Molly?" Rowland demanded.

"What business is it of yours, Sinclair?" Geoffrey returned.

Confused and tearful, Molly looked from Rowland to Geoffrey. "I intended to, and then I heard about poor Edna, and I didn't want to bother you…anyone, with what could be nothing. Finding Edna is the most important thing."

"This man who tried to grab you, what did he look like?" Rowland pressed.

"Heavens, Rowly, I've no idea—it happened so quickly. I was so scared. He grabbed my arm and started to pull me towards a cab. I fought, slipped out of his grasp, and ran into the hotel."

"Right," he said, "we'd better go down and tell Detective O'Brien."

"No!" Molly recoiled. "He's busy trying to find Edna."

"Look here, Sinclair," Geoffrey snarled, "just who do you think you are ordering my sister about like some common housemaid?"

Rowland ignored him.

"He's not the only man in the New York Police Department, Molly, and knowing someone tried to abduct you as well might just help them find Edna." He stepped towards the door. "Molly, please."

"Molly, I forbid you to go with him," Geoffrey said quietly.

She stared at Rowland for a beat. "Yes, of course, if you think it will help."

~⌖~

Milton was in the manager's office with O'Brien when Rowland came in with Molly. The Australians stepped outside into the hall while the detective questioned Molly about the incident. They leant against the wall, shoulder to shoulder.

"Why would they try to snatch Molly?" Milton asked.

"I don't know. Maybe they're trying to pressure Frank as well."

"Would taking Molly do that?"

"She's his sister, Milt."

Milton snorted. "Look, Rowly, nobody saw Edna leave the hotel. There are always bellhops and parking valets at the front of the hotel, and no one saw her leave, by herself or with anyone else."

"What are you saying, Milt?"

"Could she still be here?"

"In the hotel?"

"It's a big place, comrade. Who knows who's occupying these rooms?" Milton grabbed Rowland's arm as he started to move. "We can't just knock on doors, Rowly."

"I don't see why not."

"I've spoken to O'Brien. Apparently, the fact that no one saw Ed leave is not sufficient cause to warrant a police search of each room, particularly when you're dealing with the kind of people who stay at the Copley. And the hotel is adamant that we do not disturb their guests."

"I wasn't planning on waiting for the police—"

"Steady on, comrade. How long do you think it would be before O'Brien was arresting us?"

"Milt, we can't just—"

"Of course not." The poet's eyes glittered fiercely. "We can't let Ed be in the hands of those mongrels a second longer than necessary. But we won't find her by going off half-cocked either. If we're going to go knocking on doors, we've got to make sure the good residents of the Copley don't start complaining about the invasion of their privacy before we find Ed."

"So what do you suggest?"

Milton peered into the office. O'Brien was still talking to Molly Cartwright. "Molly's in safe hands." He put his arm around Rowland's shoulders. "First we go back to the suite and find gloves."

Chapter Twenty-Three

News About This Fall's Fur Coat Silhouettes and Style Details

By Athena Robbins

A preview of the fur coats we will buy and wear this fall and winter makes a truly exciting fashion story. Many unusual new developments in fur coat styling have been achieved by the famous couturiers for the coming season. And you may not see them in all their newness and luxurious beauty at your favourite furriers.

—*Green Bay Press-Gazette*
(Green Bay, Wisconsin), September 12, 1935

Back in the suite, Milton explained his plan, such as it was.

"We each take a pair of gloves, knock on a door claiming

we are looking for the owner of the said gloves, the mysterious young lady having left them at the Carousel Bar. While the door is open, we'll have a chance to glance inside the room. People may think we're excessively gallant, but they're unlikely to be so outraged as to make a complaint."

"And what if they don't open the door?"

"If nobody answers, then we look through the keyhole, we call out, and we listen at the door. Ed will respond somehow if she hears us."

If she can respond, Rowland thought. But he was ready to storm every room by force, so this seemed at least a strategy.

"Change your shirt, comrade," Milton said as he went into Edna's bedroom in search of gloves. "The bloodstains may alarm people."

"Hold your horses a bit," Clyde said. "What do we do if we find her? These bastards are hardly going to exchange Ed for a pair of gloves."

Milton thought for a moment. "We work the same floor, so we're all within shouting distance. And if there is any sign of Ed, we raise hell. Three of us should stand a chance."

Rowland pulled his jacket back over a fresh shirt and tie. It was a ridiculous plan, but they were desperate.

"What about the telephone?" Clyde asked.

Milton swore. He had not considered that.

Rowland made a quick decision then to trust Oliver Burr. He telephoned through to the lawyer's home and explained what they planned to do. "Mr. Burr, would you mind coming here to be by the telephone in case the kidnappers call, so that the three of us can conduct this search?"

Burr sighed. "You are fortunate, Mr. Sinclair, that I have a daughter Miss Higgins's age. I'll be there in ten minutes, and at least I shall be on hand if you do get yourselves arrested."

And so, ten minutes later, they began knocking politely

on each door with a story and enquiry about the owner of lost gloves.

Edna had always taken care to wear beautiful gloves. Though he loved her strong, art-scarred hands as he loved the rest of her, Rowland had commissioned the best George and Pitt Street glovers to make pieces specifically for the sculptress. Consequently, they were able to carry the kind of gloves that one would imagine the owner would be anxious to get back. Naturally there were many people cross to have been roused from their beds at that time of night, but the fact that they were young men, and clearly foreigners, made the gesture seem romantic and forgivable even at that time of night. It was a slow but steady process. The Copley boasted nearly three hundred rooms on seven floors. About half the rooms were empty because the economic times had brutally culled the hotel's usual clientele, but even those rooms had to be checked. As the next day dawned, rousing guests on pretext was a little easier, but it became more difficult to avoid the Copley's staff, who were delivering trays and cleaning rooms. Of course, some rooms were dispensed with by that very fact.

It was perhaps because they were walking the hallways that they heard the chambermaids discussing the supply closet on the fifth floor that could not be opened because a substance of some sort had been poured into the lock. The matter would require the attendance of a locksmith, and in the meantime, beds could not be made.

They didn't wait for the elevator, running down from the sixth floor. There were two chambermaids arguing with a more senior staff member about how the rooms could be possibly made up when they couldn't access fresh sheets and pillowcases. He was all but accusing them of having interfered with the lock to avoid work.

"Perhaps we can help," Rowland interrupted. "A couple of shoulders and we could force the door."

"I couldn't ask you to do that, sir. The locksmith will be here in a few minutes, and the problem will be resolved."

"Oh, no, I insist," Rowland said, pushing past him to the door.

"He is, in fact, insisting," Milton said before the man could protest.

He and Clyde placed their shoulders alongside Rowland's and, indifferent to unhealed bruises, they charged the door while one of the chambermaids ran for help and the other implored them to desist.

On the third attempt, the door gave way and flew in. Rowland found the light cord and pulled the switch.

The three of them blocked the view of those outside, so they alone saw the sculptress. Bound and gagged and naked. She stared at them with wide terrified eyes, her lashes clumped with tears. She was bruised, the print of a large hand livid on her thigh. Her head had been roughly shorn, her glorious copper tresses now only hacked stubble.

Rowland removed the gag while Clyde cut the bonds and Milton barked at the staff to fetch the police and a doctor. With the gag removed, Edna sobbed audibly. Rowland took off his jacket and wrapped her in it. He picked her up, holding her close, relieved and devastated. Clyde and Milton, too, were beyond words, beyond anger.

"I'm going to take Ed back to our suite," Rowland told Milton.

The poet nodded, pale. "I'll wait for O'Brien. Get her out of here."

They took the stairs to avoid other guests. Clyde stayed close in case Rowland flagged, but he did not, carrying the sculptress as if she were a small broken bird. And she clung to him as if he were the last floating thing on a black ocean, as if she would never let go.

Oliver Burr opened the door. He barely paused to assess

what he saw, making way and picking up the telephone to call for the immediate delivery of tea, as Rowland took Edna into her bedroom.

Clyde fetched her robe. "Sweetheart," he said gently as she held on to Rowland. "A doctor will be here soon and the police. They'll want to talk to you."

For a while she just cried.

Clyde left the room to tell both the doctor and the police that they had to wait.

In time, Edna pulled back and exchanged Rowland's jacket for the robe. "Don't go," she whispered.

"I won't." He didn't add *ever*, but he felt it.

She was shivering so he pulled back the bedcovers and huddled her beneath them before he signalled Clyde through the open door. The doctor came in first with the tea that Burr had ordered. He asked Rowland to leave, but seeing that the suggestion seemed to distress his patient, he did not insist upon it. Rowland stared out the window while the physician examined the sculptress, treating and bandaging wrists and ankles rubbed raw by the bonds.

"I'm going to prescribe a sedative, Miss Higgins, for you to take after you've spoken to the police."

Edna nodded vaguely. She hadn't said a word throughout the examination.

He left the powder beside a glass of water on the bedside table.

O'Brien and Burr came in. Edna didn't need a lawyer, of course, but Rowland was glad. At that moment, neither he nor Milton nor Clyde were in the best frame of mind to think rationally, and he'd come to trust Oliver Burr. The lawyer kept O'Brien from pushing too hard or too quickly with his questions, while still allowing the statement to be taken.

Slowly, Edna recounted what had happened in a voice that was hoarse and halting. A woman had approached her in the foyer with a fur coat and a claim that it had been left in the Carousel Bar by Molly Cartwright. "She said the concierge had pointed me out and mentioned we were acquainted." The sculptress had volunteered to return the fur and, knowing the location of Molly's suite, had ridden the elevator to the fifth floor. Rowland was not oblivious to the irony that a similar ploy had been used to capture the sculptress as to find her. As Edna walked down the hallway, she passed the supply room. The door had been opened and she was dragged inside by three men. They'd gagged her and, under gunpoint, they'd stripped and bound her, and then cut her hair off with a knife. When that was done, they'd tied her up and left her in the darkness, barely able to breathe, let alone make a sound.

Through all of this, Rowland, Milton, and Clyde were silent in their grief and rage.

Detective O'Brien cleared his throat and asked the sculptress if she'd been molested.

For a moment the question seemed to hang in the air.

Edna shook her head, breaking down again. "No, Detective O'Brien. I was subjected to nothing more than what I've already described. But for hours I lay there wondering if they would come back for that purpose."

"Can you describe these men, Miss Higgins?"

Edna did the best she could. They'd threatened to cut her eyes out if she did not close them, so all she had were glimpses. But two of them had accents that were not American.

"Italian?" O'Brien asked, nodding knowingly.

"No," she said definitely. "Irish."

"Are you sure?"

"Yes."

"Does that mean something?" Rowland asked.

O'Brien frowned. "Irish sounds like the Gustin Gang. But they barely exist anymore. Most of them were murdered one way or another on the orders of Giuseppe Lombardo, of the Patriarca family."

"Lombardo—who's in business with Frank Cartwright?"

"So you mentioned." O'Brien took a cigarette from his pocket and lit it. "But can't see the Italians and the Irish joining forces."

Rowland glanced at Edna. "Are we finished here, Detective?"

"Nearly. Can I ask how you fine gentlemen knew where to find Miss Higgins?"

Milton told him.

O'Brien may have had more to say had their efforts not yielded results, however indirectly. Instead, he contented himself with glaring at the poet, before he informed them he'd be leaving two officers outside their suite, in case of further trouble. He took his leave and, after dismissing their thanks, so, too, did Oliver Burr.

Milton and Clyde walked them to the door while Rowland stayed with Edna. He pulled a chair up beside her bed, within reach.

She ran her hand over her scalp, cringing as she felt the stubble. She bit her lip before it could start trembling again. "I think I'll have a shower. It might warm me up."

"I'll see if I can turn up the heating," Rowland said, standing. He was desperate to do something for her.

Edna struggled to smile. "Have them send up some food," she said. "I'm famished and you all look exhausted. You should eat...and sleep."

"Whatever you want, Ed. I'll have them send up everything on the menu—"

"Bacon and eggs will be fine."

Chapter Twenty-Four

WOMEN SCARE MORE EASILY THAN
MEN BUT THAT IS SIGN OF STRENGTH

By Marjorie Van de Water

...Using a day-by-day record of how his subjects felt and acted in the real thrilling situations
of life, not the fictitious or synthetic scares of
the laboratory, Dr. Stratton has made an anal-
ysis disclosing what factors are associated with
fear and anger.

Sex is one of these factors.

"The frequent opinion that women are
more emotional than men is supported." He
said, in reporting some of his conclusions in
the *American Journal of Psychology*. "There is also
support for the particular opinion that women
are more timid than men.

"The opinion, however that women are
less inclined to anger, that women are more
placid in situations which arouse men to wrath
appears quite unsupported."

Is this greater tendency of women to fly off the handle, to become angry, or to tremble with fright over some disturbing incident, indicative of her general weakness? Dr. Stratton disagrees with some psychologists by declaring that it is not. Rather it is the sign of strength.

A display of emotion is not necessarily a signal of failure to meet a situation: emotion may be a means of meeting an emergency more adequately. Fear and anger are connected with the invigorating not only of the muscular system, but also of the powers of thought, or impulse and of desire.

—*The Winnipeg Tribune*
(Winnipeg, Manitoba, Canada), 5 January 1935

∾⟨℘⟩∾

Exhaustion had its benefits.

Initially, the Australian men maintained a vigil while Edna, assisted by a sedative, slept. They didn't talk about what had happened; they didn't talk at all, simply sat in a kind of mutual horror and grief and fury. Exhaustion stepped in after a couple of hours to allow them an unconscious respite. Rowland had fallen asleep in the chair beside Edna's bed. It was late afternoon when finally he stirred, feeling stiff and battered. He woke Milton to take his place before he showered and shaved, returning looking much more like himself.

"She's still asleep," Milton said quietly. He exhaled. "What are we going to do, Rowly?"

"We're going home."

"Can you do that? What will happen to Danny's estate?"

"I don't care. Clyde was bad enough, but when I think about what they did to Ed—"

"How dare you!" Edna's voice. Trembling. The sculptress sat up, her eyes blazing as she turned on Rowland. "Don't you dare use me as an excuse to let Danny down!"

"Ed..."

"Do you think I'm not angry? Do you think I'm not furious? How dare you!"

"I didn't—"

"I will not go home! I will not let them get away with this!" Edna was crying now. "How dare you think that I would! How dare you, Rowly!"

Milton intervened to help Rowland. "Ed, sweetheart, you've got to understand how scared we were."

But the sculptress would not be deterred. "No matter what happens to you, you don't stop! Nothing will make you compromise your principles...except me, apparently. Well, what about my principles you, you—?"

"Jesus, Mary, and Joseph! What the dickens is going on here?" Clyde was awake now. He stumbled into the hallway, bleary-eyed.

"Ed's shouting at Rowly," Milton replied as Edna continued to berate Rowland, even as she broke down completely.

"At Rowly?" Clyde was surprised. "That's a turn-up for the books." In his experience, the sculptress very rarely had cause to shout at Rowland. Milton—yes, but not Rowland.

Rowland moved to the bed and wrapped his arms around Edna, though she fought him. "I'm sorry, Ed. God, I'm sorry. We'll do whatever you want to do, but I can't help wanting to protect you. I couldn't bear it if—"

"This is not about what you can bear!" she said, pushing him away.

Clyde stepped in because it did not seem to be getting any better, and Edna seemed least angry with him. "Rowly, why don't you order some tea?" He signalled that both Rowland and Milton should leave.

"Come on, comrade." Milton draped an arm around Rowland's shoulders. "We might check if the working stiffs stationed outside the door want anything."

"But—"

"Let Clyde speak to her."

And so Rowland and the poet left the sculptress's room, the former bewildered, the latter sympathetic.

"Don't take it to heart, mate," Milton advised. "It might take Ed a while to be herself again. The bastards hacked off her hair with a knife and left her naked in a cupboard. It was designed to humiliate her and you."

"I don't feel humiliated, Milt, just...so angry. And scared. I've put you all in danger."

Milton shrugged. "And Danny put you in danger. Some friendships are dangerous."

Milton opened the front door. He introduced himself and Rowland to the officers, and asked if they would like a refreshment. The response was enthusiastic, and Rowland called down to order tea and cakes from the restaurant.

He replaced the receiver and glanced at the short hallway that led to Edna's room. "Do you think—"

"Clyde will let us know when it's safe." Milton raised a decanter enquiringly.

Rowland declined and the poet poured himself a glass of Scotch. "Ed doesn't want to leave, Rowly, so it looks like we're going to see this through."

"It may all be over soon, anyway. Otis Norcross is probably dead."

"Oh, yes—you and Ed went to see Mrs. Norcross. Did you find anything?"

Rowland recounted their conversation with Norcross's grieving mother and their visit to the cemetery.

"She had no photographs of him? Not one?"

"No."

"So we still can't be certain that Danny's sketch is of Norcross."

"We could ask Molly, I suppose."

Milton's lips pursed. "Oh, yes, Molly. Sounds like she had a close call yesterday."

"Yes… Oh, dammit!" Rowland cursed as he realised the implication of Edna's account of what happened.

"What?"

Rowland moved for the phone. "The woman who gave Ed the fur, who sent her past that bloody supply closet, she must have known the location of Molly's suite. That's how they trapped Ed."

Milton swore as it dawned on him why Rowland was alarmed.

There was no answer at Molly's suite.

"You took her dancing," Milton reminded him. "These bastards might assume—"

"I'm just going down to the fifth floor—"

"I'll come with you."

"No—I'll be fine. You stay and look after Ed."

Milton was firm. "Clyde's here and there are two policemen outside. Your back needs watching more than Ed's."

"What's wrong?" Edna demanded, when he stuck his head into her room to inform them that he and Rowland were stepping out for a couple of minutes.

"Nothing, as far as we know," Milton replied. "We just thought we should check on Molly."

"Why?"

"They must have known returning the coat would take you past the supply closet." Milton chose not to mention that someone had tried to kidnap Molly, too—there was no point upsetting Edna unnecessarily. "And because she was worried about you."

They used the fire stairs to descend two floors to the fifth. The supply closet in which the sculptress had been held was closed, a police officer posted outside. Rowland knocked on the door of Molly's suite.

"I say, Molly, it's Rowland Sinclair."

He was relieved when she responded. "Rowly, just a minute." She opened the door in a bathrobe and seemed a little flustered to see Milton beside Rowland. "Come in, please. I'll just throw something on."

"We could just wait here—" Rowland began.

"Don't be absurd, Rowly. You'll do my reputation more harm by loitering outside my door!"

And so they waited in the sitting room while Molly got dressed. Rowland was impatient, anxious to return to Edna, even if she was livid with him. Molly eventually came out to greet them, beaming. "I hear Edna's been found! How absolutely wonderful! You must be so relieved."

"She has," Milton replied. "And we are."

"You must forgive me for the fuss I made yesterday, and while you were so worried about Edna."

"Not at all," Rowland said. "It's what we've come to speak with you about, actually." He took the seat to which she directed him. "Molly, the men who took Edna knew where your suite was."

Molly gasped.

He continued. "I don't think you're safe here anymore."

"But surely—"

"We've got to find somewhere else for you to live until these men are apprehended, Molly."

"Well, I could just go home, though I suppose I will only be able to stay there until you find Danny's Mr. Norcross."

"You didn't mention that you knew Otis Norcross," Milton interrupted.

"I knew an Otis Norcross; actually I've known three. It's not an unusual name. One died in the war, one died three or four years ago, and I have neither seen nor heard from the other since 1920. None of them could have killed Danny."

"I beg your pardon." Milton was confused.

"Molly believes that Otis Norcross persuaded Danny to change his will and then killed him," Rowland explained.

Milton stroked his goatee thoughtfully. "I suppose that's possible."

"Well, who else would kill Danny?"

Rowland reached inside his jacket and extracted Daniel Cartwright's pencil sketch. "Do you recognise this man, Molly?"

Molly was wrong-footed, visibly startled. "Misery me…" She licked her lips. "This looks a bit like you, Rowly," she said in the end. She held it up next to his face. "It's not very good, but it's probably meant to be you."

Another knock. Repeated. Insistent. And from outside, "Molly—open the door! It's Frank and Geoffrey."

Rowland and Milton stood. Rowland slid the sketch back inside his jacket.

Molly admitted her brothers. They swaggered in. Their expressions darkened and they ignored Molly when they saw the gentlemen in her sitting room.

Geoffrey spoke first. "So, Sinclair, come to collect another payment for your suite?"

"For pity's sake, man, you're talking about your sister!" Rowland said, disgusted.

"Shut up, Geoff," Frank snapped. He met Rowland's gaze. "Miss Higgins has been found."

"She has."

"Unharmed?"

"Not entirely."

"You made some pretty slanderous accusations yesterday, Mr. Sinclair."

"If I offended you, I apologise, Mr. Cartwright. I just wanted to find Miss Higgins."

"Mr. Sinclair and Mr. Isaacs are worried that I may no longer be safe here," Molly said nervously.

"Sick of paying your hotel bill, more likely," Geoffrey sneered.

"Be quiet, Geoffers," Molly said irritably. "It's not as if you've ever paid your own bills." She turned to Rowland and smiled. "But I have been imposing on your generosity for too long, Rowly. I've decided I'm going to take a little vacation. I have friends with a love country cottage somewhere near Rockport. I might go stay with them for a while."

"What friends? Where exactly?" Frank demanded.

"I'm not going to tell you, Frank."

"Why not?"

"Because Rowly will be less worried for my safety if you and your business associates don't know where I am."

Rowland said nothing. It was true.

Frank swore. "That's stupid, Molly."

"I don't think you're trying to kidnap me, darling," Molly said soothingly, rubbing her brother's arm. "But this way, you and Rowly can carry on squabbling, and nobody need be concerned about me."

"For Christ's sake, Molly, you're impossible!" Frank made for the door, beckoning Geoffrey to follow. "Do whatever the hell you want—you always do!"

Silence after the door slammed.

"Would you like me to drive you to your friends' cottage?" Rowland asked.

Molly smiled. "I can't very well refuse to tell Frank

where I'm staying and then tell you. That would be disloyal. Whatever else we Cartwrights may be, we are loyal."

Rowland smiled. "But how will you—"

"I still have my car, unless you've decided that, too, is part of Danny's estate. I'll drive myself tomorrow morning."

"I'm so sorry about all this, Molly."

"So am I, Rowly." She looked at them both with moist eyes. "I had hoped we'd all be such friends. Danny would have liked that."

Rowland and Milton returned to their own suite to find an elegant repast had been delivered with the compliments of the Copley and the management's regrets that one of their guests had been abducted in the hotel. There were also flowers for Edna, from the hotel; Burr, Mayfair and Wilkes; and Frank Cartwright.

"Guilt?" Milton suggested quietly as he and Rowland glanced at the last card.

Edna seemed in better spirits. By silent agreement, nobody mentioned the shouting. And Rowland did not raise going home. After dinner, or whatever a meal taken at five in the afternoon by people who had not eaten since breakfast might be called, Milton distributed concoctions he claimed were cocktails, and they discussed what they knew and what they didn't.

"O'Brien's sent one of the officers from outside our suite to keep an eye on Molly's," Rowland said. He shook his head. "She didn't seem to recognise this portrait as Otis Norcross."

"She was lying." Milton was blunt. "She recognised him. I don't know if he's the dead Norcross or not, but she recognised him."

"I thought so, too," Rowland said, studying the sketch.

He turned over the cartridge paper and looked again at the inscription on the back: *19 July 1935, NC.* "The sketch is dated two years after Norcross—the one whose funeral Danny attended at least—died. Maybe it's not him, or anyone named Norcross. What else could NC mean?"

"He's noted a date," Edna said quietly. "Perhaps NC is a location?"

"As in North Carolina?" Rowland asked.

"Perhaps that's where he went on his vacations."

Rowland's inhaled sharply. "God, you're right. That could be what it means." He was still a little tentative when he met Edna's eyes. She smiled. A flag of truce.

"So perhaps we need to search for Norcross, or whoever this is, there." There were the beginnings of excitement in Milton's voice.

"North Carolina is a big place," Clyde warned. "That's like saying we have to search in Queensland."

"Danny couldn't have gone on vacation for months without contacting anybody," Milton said.

"He didn't trust his family, and Bradford didn't seem to have any idea where he went," Clyde argued.

"A fortune the size of Danny's rarely carries on by itself," Milton speculated. "He couldn't have disappeared for months without sending the occasional instruction to a minion of some sort."

Rowland followed now. "Burr. Danny may have contacted Burr while he was on vacation." He stood and made the call immediately.

"Mr. Burr, do you recall if Danny ever called or wrote to you from North Carolina."

"Why, yes, Mr. Sinclair. Mr. Cartwright was always travelling somewhere. I believe I sent him some documents to an address in North Carolina...a hotel, I believe. Let me look through my files and get back to you."

They waited for Burr to call back. When finally he did, it was with puzzled apology. "Last summer we posted some urgent documents to Mr. Cartwright, as per his instructions to the Grove Park Inn, in Asheville, North Carolina. The peculiar thing is, and I am embarrassed to say that this fact slipped my mind until I checked the file after you mentioned North Carolina, Mr. Cartwright had us send the documents in care of Mr. Rowland Sinclair."

Chapter Twenty-Five

Platinum Blond Now "Has Been"
Hairdresser Says

KANSAS CITY (AP)—M. Paul Richard—to whom every little curl has a meaning all its own—says the platinum blond is passé.

In her place M. Richard, president of the Coiffure Guild of New York, says the auburns, the venetians and the rich browns are appearing.

"The hair is to be brushed again and again," he said, "to regain its natural gloss and color."

Heavy-browed, solemn and sporting a bit of a mustache, the French hair dressing expert is in town to address hair dressers and beauty shop operators.

This theme is a cry for more active scissors, with a very soft pedal on the razor and the clippers. The thought of the latter pains him.

"Use such instruments on men and horses,"

he advised. "But never use them in cutting a woman's hair... Leave the hair long enough to give curls a softness and the head its natural beauty."

—*The Post-Star*
(Glen Falls, New York), March 8, 1935

⚬

Milton laughed. "We've gone down the rabbit hole now. Danny found himself another Rowland Sinclair!"

"Don't be daft." Rowland sat down. "He was obviously staying at this Grove Park Inn incognito. He just borrowed my name."

"And left a trail for you," Edna said quietly.

Rowland nodded. "Possibly."

"So what do we do?" Clyde asked.

"It's obvious," Edna said firmly. "We follow the trail."

And so it was decided that they would quit Boston for Asheville, North Carolina. For a while they argued over how exactly to get there. Rowland was confident that they could drive there fairly comfortably in two days. "If we leave tomorrow morning, we'll get to Washington by day's end. We can overnight there and drive to Asheville the next day." He persuaded his companions that nine hundred miles were better travelled in the Madame X than by train.

Rowland contacted the reception desk and informed the concierge that they were taking a trip and could be contacted through Oliver Burr of Burr, Mayfair and Wilkes. "No, we won't be checking out of the Copley. We shouldn't be gone too long."

Then he called Burr back and asked him to arrange

accommodation in Washington and at the Grove Park Inn for the four of them. He informed the lawyer of their plans. Burr was in favour of the scheme. All things considered, he was no longer comfortable with them staying at the Copley. Milton raised a glass as Rowland put down the receiver. "Well, I suppose the only thing to do is to drink to finding Otis Norcross."

～◎～

Having spent the previous night walking the halls of the Copley, and the morning sleeping in a chair, Rowland was relieved to lie flat. Sleep was elusive, however. That morning he'd been ready to abandon Daniel Cartwright and his perplexing legacies and go home. He still was, if truth be told. The knowledge of what happened to Edna, the thought of what might have happened to her, filled him with fury and fear in equal measure, regardless of how calm and indifferent she seemed to want him to be. She'd been strange with him that evening, quiet and distant. He wondered if she could really hate him for caring too much, for letting down his guard and forgetting that she was not his. Had he ruined everything?

"Rowly?" A whisper in the darkness, and for a moment he wondered if he was still awake.

She sat on the end of his bed. "Rowly, wake up." He could hear tears in her voice.

He sat up. "Ed, what's wrong?" He cursed silently as the question left his lips before he could pull it back.

"I'm sorry, Rowly. I'm sorry I was angry with you. That I shouted at you. I was just so…" She shook her head, unable to find the words.

"Sweetheart, if you need to shout at me—go ahead. I can take it."

She climbed in next to him, pulling the covers up under

her chin and resting her cheek against his shoulder. "I think you scared me, Rowly, because for an instant I wanted to run home. I wanted you to protect me, to decide for me, and I could see me collapsing, disappearing into a frightened, protected person I didn't recognise."

"I was wrong," he said. "It was because I was scared, Ed."

"I know, Rowly, but I'm in no more danger than you or Clyde or Milt. I am no more fragile."

Fleetingly Rowland heard Smythe's words: *There are so many more ways you can hurt a woman.* "These men are animals, Ed."

"I know." She smiled. "But I am as entitled to do stupid things on principle as you are."

"Of course. But, Ed, if you change your mind, just tell me and we'll go home."

Edna said nothing for a while, just sat with her head leaning against his shoulder, and then she reached over and turned on the small lamp beside the bed.

She moved so that she was facing him, pulling nervously at a ragged curl that survived the close hacking of her hair. "Is it horribly ugly, Rowly?" she asked quietly.

He gazed at her. "It's unusual, Ed, but you're still the most beautiful creature I've ever seen. Sometimes when I look at you I forget to breathe."

She began to cry again. "How could I care so much about hair, Rowly? It will grow back. But I feel like I've lost something, like they've taken something."

He put his arms around her. "What can I do?"

"Can you give me one night without consequences? One night without changing anything?"

"I'm not sure I follow."

"I want to lie with you, Rowly. To be your lover. I want the last hands that touched me not to be their hands. I need to feel something other than anger and fear and humiliation…

But I want to do that without hurting you, without changing anything."

"You want me to take advantage of you?"

"Dammit, Rowly, I know my own mind. My own heart. I'm worried about taking advantage of *you*, and I don't want to do that." She paused, her eyes deep in his. "I just want to feel joy and passion and desire, with someone who won't judge me for wanting it or require promises in return."

Rowland could feel his heart pounding. "One night, and then you want to pretend it didn't happen?" he asked, still trying to understand what she was asking.

She smiled and pressed her hand to his cheek. "Yes, in a way. We'll always know we were something more than the best of friends for one night, but we will still be the best of friends when this is over. I promise you, Rowly, I will expect nothing more than what we were before." Her face became unsure. "But if you cannot just love me for one night, if the thought appalls you, or you just don't want to—"

He kissed her then, so gently she barely felt the pressure of his lips on hers, though every part of her seemed to reach for him in response. "I want to," he said.

Slowly, Edna removed his shirt, kissing his chest as she worked her way down. She stopped when she came to the damage left by the brass knuckles. "My God, Rowly, what happened?"

"I can't remember," he murmured. "In fact, I'm not sure I can remember my name."

She laughed softly. "You're shaking." She traced the line of his jaw. "Rowly, you're not nervous, are you? Not of me?"

"I'm not nervous," Rowland said, trying to slow the over-whelming intensity of his feelings. God, he'd wanted her for so long.

He asked permission before he unbuttoned her shirt. She

nodded, touched by the fact that even now he asked, that even now, he did not expect. She was accustomed to Rowland Sinclair's gaze, the unwavering focus of his dark blue eyes, but it had always been from a distance before.

Rowland undressed his muse, taking his time, savouring the process, the privilege of her trust. Edna was his model, the subject of his best work as an artist, his dreams as a man. He'd spent a good part of his career painting her from life, but never before had he removed her clothes himself. Never before had he touched the curves that so suited the sweep of his brush or tasted the skin he'd rendered on canvas.

He explored her with a kind of wonder, though he knew her body, understood how every arc began and ended. He kissed the graceful line of her neck, the undersides of the breasts he'd shadowed with burnt umber, the nipples which had called for a rose in his palette, and in the end, it was she who was shaking.

Edna gasped as his hand slid along her inner thigh. Once again he asked permission, and she laughed at his manners because they reminded her who her lover was, and it delighted her. She climbed on top of him and allowed him to enter her body as she had entered his soul years ago.

They became lost in each other, every feeling heightened by the other's response, every pleasure deepened, until it was complete and perfect.

And then when they lay in a tangle of arms and legs and beating hearts, he began again, rousing her from a languid descent. "You said one night, not one time, right?"

She smiled. "That was our bargain, I believe."

It was just before dawn when she kissed him goodbye. The darkness had lightened a little. "Thank you, Rowly," she said as she stroked his dark hair back from his forehead.

"Did it help?" he asked. He wanted desperately to pull

her back, to beg her to stay, to tell her he adored her, that he wanted to spend his life making love to her and the world be damned. But he remembered his promise, what she had asked and what he'd said he could give.

"Yes, I think so. What happened seems longer ago, further away now. I feel stronger and"—her eyes were bright with emotion— "and a little embarrassed that I asked this of you."

He tensed. "Do you regret it?"

"No. Never. But it was a lot to ask. You never would have asked it of me." She inhaled, swallowing a sudden surge of uncertainty. "I wish sometimes, Rowly, that you and I could be happy to let the world be unchanged, to become lazy and indifferent in love, but those are not the stars under which we were born."

He wanted to tell her that she was wrong, or that he would rearrange the stars if that's what it took, but he knew that would terrify her anew. "You can ask anything of me, Ed. Anything. Always."

She embraced him and held on for a while. "I'm going back to my own bed now before Clyde and Milt wake up."

He let her go.

Chapter Twenty-Six

N<small>AZIS</small> P<small>ROTEST</small> N. Y. I<small>NCIDENTS</small>

G<small>ERMAN</small> P<small>RESS</small> A<small>VERS</small> A<small>POLOGY IS</small>
D<small>UE</small> B<small>ERLIN</small>

New York Communists Strip Flag from Liner
Bremen

By The Associated Press

...a Communist demonstration at the sailing of
the crack liner *Bremen* Friday night in which the
German flag was defiled. German newspapers
demanded diplomatic amends.

While seven of the demonstrators were
arraigned in New York and two more, suffer-
ing from bullet wounds, were arrested in hospitals, a state department official in Washington
expressed regret at the incident.

Senate leaders at the same time forecast
that a resolution to investigate the Reich's
treatment of Jews and Catholics would be

pigeonholed as a result of state department opposition.

—*Casper Star-Tribune*
(Casper, Wyoming), July 28, 1935

❧

"Hurry up, Ed! It's nearly seven o'clock." Clyde folded his arms impatiently. "Is she still cross with you?" he asked Rowland suspiciously. The sculptress did not usually take so long to get ready, and Rowland had been quiet and distracted that morning.

"I don't think so." Rowland looked up from the paper. "We made it up last night, before we went to bed."

"Glad to hear it." Clyde was genuinely so.

Edna emerged, an embroidered silk scarf wrapped around her head and tied in a knot beneath one ear, covering everything but the one copper curl that had survived the hacking of her hair. It gave her an exotic, rakish air, and highlighted that her face was exquisite. Rowland stood as she came into the room. He was conscious of not looking at her like anything had changed, like he had held her naked in his arms just hours ago, but then she had always taken his breath.

"Good morning, Rowly."

"Hello, Ed. You look pretty."

She smiled. "None of my hats could hide the...well, you know..."

Milton stared at the headpiece. "Is that my cravat, you thieving harpy?"

Edna nodded sheepishly.

"I have a green one that would look smashing, too, but stay away from the red one. It'll make you look like a pirate."

Rowland fetched Edna's suitcase. They didn't summon a porter, intent on leaving as quietly as possible. They might, in fact, have done that if Molly Cartwright had not also decided to make an early start. She left her car and walked over to them, embracing Edna tearfully.

"Oh, God, look what they've done to you—I can't tell you how happy I was when they told me you'd been found."

Edna was warm in response. "I'm perfectly well, Molly. You mustn't worry."

Molly smiled wistfully. "Well, you have not one but three handsome men to rescue you. You might be the luckiest girl in the world."

Milton put his arm around Edna. "You're too kind, Miss Cartwright. But it's not necessary... Rowly and Clyde both know they're a little on the homely side. They've come to terms with it."

Edna shoved the poet and turned back to Molly, who looked confused. "Milton thinks he's funny—you must try to ignore him."

Molly laughed uncertainly. "Oh, I see." She glanced at the bags Rowland was loading into the trunk.

"We thought we might get out of Boston and see the sights for a couple of days," Edna explained. "I'm glad you're getting away, too. We'll all sleep easier knowing you're safe."

"Oh, I'll be fine," Molly said. For a brief, careless moment she watched Rowland as he pulled on his driving gloves, her face softening. He seemed to sense her gaze, and he looked up and smiled. She waved in return.

They were on the road to Washington before eight thirty. Rowland drove till they reached Philadelphia where, in the late afternoon, they stopped for a meal. Clyde took over the wheel of the Madame X, and Rowland climbed in next to Edna. For a while they played poker on the back seat with Milton leaning over the front. That ended in outrage when Milton realised that Edna could see his hand in the rearview mirror, and the card game was abandoned. Instead, Edna and Milton began to read through the collection of letters they'd found in Daniel Cartwright's New York studio.

Rowland sat back and sketched Edna as she perused the letters. He hoped that in time he would be able to sit beside her without being preoccupied with the previous night, but he knew that today was not that day. Today, she lingered on the edge of every thought. So he allowed the sculptress and the poet to get on with the business of searching the letters for anything he might have missed, and he drew.

"Rowly, this letter from Molly..." Edna leaned into him so he could read over her shoulder. "The pretty man she mentions—I don't suppose she could mean Otis Norcross?"

Rowland frowned. "Why do you say that?"

"Well, Otis's mother seemed to think that Molly might have been her daughter-in-law."

"She says here that the gentleman in question was impervious to her charms."

"Well, there might have been a reason for that which had nothing to do with Molly."

Milton waved the letter he was reading. "In this letter she complains about not having heard from him... She all but admits to being in love with him."

"Let's not read too much into a couple of lines," Rowland cautioned.

"It would explain why she didn't want to admit to knowing Otis Norcross," Milton said. "Or recognising Danny's sketch. It might be embarrassing—especially if he'd jilted her for her brother."

Rowland shook his head. "It's all possible." It seemed

more and more like Daniel Cartwright had intentionally left his fortune to a dead man.

"Maybe the will was some type of poetic gesture," Milton suggested. "A way of declaring his love to the world, knowing it would invalidate his will and leave his estate to be divided among his next of kin."

Edna picked up the thread. "Maybe, because Molly was in love with Otis Norcross, perhaps even engaged to him, Danny couldn't say anything while he was still alive. Maybe he just wanted the world to know."

As much as the notion was ludicrous, Rowland could not deny that his old friend would have loved the theatricality of the grand declaration, the tragic drama of it all. But would he have put Rowland in danger to achieve it?

"Perhaps he did not realise that things would get this bad," Edna said softly.

Rowland sighed and rubbed the back of his neck. "To be honest, I think it's reasonably clear that Otis Norcross is dead. I truly cannot tell you what Danny might have been thinking. If I could talk to him right now, I suspect I'd just punch him again for being so flaming cryptic... But maybe if we could find out what he was doing in Asheville, it might at least give us a clue as to who might have killed him."

⌖

Clyde pulled the Madame X into the parking lot of Hay-Adams House. He allowed his companions to continue sleeping for a few minutes while the motor cooled. They'd all dropped off sometime in the last couple of hours. Clyde glanced over his shoulder at Edna and Rowland. The sculptress had fallen asleep on Rowland's chest. His arm was around her. That in itself was not unusual. Edna had never observed tactile boundaries when it came to the men she lived with. She'd used them all as pillows at one time or another. But on this occasion Clyde's artistic eye noticed a subtle change. In sleep, Edna's arm had slipped under Rowland's jacket. She was holding onto him rather than just sleeping on him. There was an intimacy that he hadn't noticed before. Perhaps it was to do with the trauma she'd suffered in that supply closet, but something had changed.

Clyde woke Rowland first. "Rowly, mate, we're here."

Rowland opened his eyes and glanced down at Edna. Clyde saw the longing in that unguarded moment.

Milton stretched and looked back. "Ed! Wake up and get off Rowly. You have the poor man pinned."

They checked into a couple of adjoining suites with views of the White House. Too travel-weary to be bothered getting dressed for dinner, they took supper in the suite and braved the cold to step out of the French doors onto the balcony to gaze across Lafayette Square to the home of the American president.

Perhaps it was the vista that adjusted their focus, but for a while they left the preoccupations of the last weeks to discuss, with growing disquiet, the state of the world: the disturbing cooperation between the Germans and the Japanese that they'd witnessed in Shanghai, the Nuremberg laws which had just stripped German Jews of citizenship, the re-emergence of the Communists in China under Mao, the non-aggression pact between Mussolini and the French. They spoke of the poverty they'd seen in New Jersey and Philadelphia, the depth of the Depression in America, and the unfathomable sympathy men like Lindbergh, Ford, and Kennedy seemed to have for the Fascists. Milton and Clyde told them of the Friends of New Germany, the American branch of the Nazi Party, about whose activities the Communists they'd met in New York were concerned.

Milton commended Sinclair Lewis's novel, its predictions

for the following year's election. "Your cousin, Harry, is doing his bit to warn the masses, Rowly."

"Let's hope the masses pay more attention to writers than they do artists," Rowland replied ruefully.

Milton sighed. "If *It Can't Happen Here* is anything to go by, they won't."

"It's like everybody's lost their minds," Edna said, using Rowland as a shield against the cutting wind.

Milton shook his head. "Fascism offers easy answers. It tells people that they are not to blame and that the situation can be fixed if only the Jews or the Negroes or the Chinese or the Communists would stop being who they are." He took off his scarf and wrapped it around Edna's neck, which no longer had an auburn mane to protect it from the cold. "It takes energy to resist easy answers, and people are tired. Struggling makes people tired. Perhaps we see things the way we do because, thanks to Rowly, we don't have to struggle."

"I think you underestimate the working man, mate." Clyde kept the faith. "The blokes we met in New York aren't tired. They aren't backing down, no matter how much the government wants them to be polite to Hitler."

"I hope so, comrade, I hope so. But it's a lot to ask of people who are struggling to feed their children." He dragged his hand down his face wearily. "How do I ask them to care about Jews in Europe when they're dealing with colour bans and lunatics in white sheets..."

"I guess that's why it's all the more important that we do what we can," Rowland said quietly. He'd struggled with the question himself. How did one prioritise persecution and discrimination?

None of them were oblivious to the plights of other peoples, the injustice and prejudice and segregation which were inherent to every nation, including Australia—especially

Australia—but the expansionism of the Nazis seemed a particular and growing threat not just against the Jews but humanity itself.

"The Nazis have not just taken over Germany," Milton said bitterly. "They have their greedy Fascist eyes on the entire world."

The Australians set out from Hay-Adams House early, determined to reach Asheville well before sundown. They resisted the temptation to divert and explore the mountains and lakes en route, though the beauty of the landscape was mesmerising. Milton drove the Cadillac until they were well into Virginia. Rowland took over at Roanoke, where they stopped briefly to eat and stretch their legs. Edna pointed out that the Grandin Theatre in the city's main boulevard was screening *Captain Blood* starring Errol Flynn, and for a moment, they contemplated stopping and passing a couple of hours at the Spanish-styled movie palace. But practicality won the day, and they climbed back into the Madame X for the last leg of the journey.

Despite their best intention, a wrong turn meant that it was just on dusk when they reached the Grove Park Inn in Asheville. The building's undulating clay tile roof reflected the colours of the setting from atop a stone construction which seemed to have emerged from the mountain rock itself. Rowland had not expected that Daniel Cartwright would stay anywhere less than grand, but he, too, was impressed by the spectacle of the inn.

They checked in at a reception desk in the expansive lobby, known as the Great Hall, which boasted enormous granite fireplaces and a sweeping porch that afforded breath-catching views of the Blue Ridge Mountains. Though only a couple of decades old, there was something almost medieval about the building, with its gargantuan walls and stonework throughout. The concierge at the Copley had booked four adjoining rooms, to which they retired to shower and change for dinner on the terrace.

Rowland, Clyde, and Milton waited in the hallway outside Edna's room for her to finish dressing.

"What could possibly be taking her so bloody long?" Clyde grumbled as the minutes passed.

"Her hair," Milton replied.

"Oh." Clyde winced, ashamed of his impatience now. "Poor kid. It's a shame it's not the twenties. You couldn't see a woman's hair under the hats they were wearing then—they might all have been bald."

"It's all a bit new to poor Ed," Milton said, leaning back against the wall. "She's never had to give a thought to what she looked like before. She was beautiful without trying."

"She still is," Rowland murmured.

The door opened and Edna presented in a black gown and long gloves. Her head was swathed in an elegant black turban embellished with a feather-shaped brooch of silver marquisate.

"What do you think?" she said anxiously.

"Crikey, Ed, you look like a film star," Clyde said, swallowing.

"Where did you get the turban?" Milton looked closely and a little suspiciously at her headwear.

"I modified one of my slips," she replied. "Can you tell?" She turned around so they could see the back.

"No. Not at all." Rowland offered her his arm.

"Can you make me one?" Milton did not attempt to hide his admiration.

The restaurant on the Sunset Terrace was, by virtue of its location, open to the cold mountain air, but they were seated close to an open fire. And over dinner they discussed what they would do next.

"I'll speak to the manager in the morning and see if he remembers Danny...or Rowland Sinclair, rather," Rowland said.

"This place seems to be a health spa of sorts," Milton said, recalling the flyers they'd been handed about the activities and services on offer. "I wonder if Danny checked himself in to recover."

Rowland thought of the anguished self-portrait in the New York studio. "It's possible."

A gentleman was seated alone at the table immediately beside theirs. Fair-haired, perhaps forty, he was dressed elegantly and smoked continuously. He cleared his throat suddenly, stood, and stepped over to their table. At close quarters he smelled of beer. "I do hope you will forgive the intrusion, but I couldn't help but overhear you mention Rowland Sinclair. The gentleman is a very dear friend of mine. I had hoped to meet him here."

Rowland glanced at his companions. Was their search to be resolved so conveniently?

Edna smiled, excited.

The gentlemen stood. Rowland offered his hand. "Rowland Sinclair, Mr. Norcross. How d'you do?"

"You're not Rowland Sinclair!" The man looked at them askance now. "And who the dickens is Norcross?"

"You're not Otis Norcross?"

"No. I'm F. Scott Fitzgerald."

Chapter Twenty-Seven

Youth of Today is Skeptical F. Scott Fitzgerald Thinks

Confident Is Lost in Grownups, He Believes

Asheville, N.C.—Idealism no longer is an outstanding characteristic of the young generation, in the opinion of F. Scott Fitzgerald, writer for a decade concerning the younger generation. Fitzgerald has been on a vacation of several weeks in Asheville. Fitzgerald believes that the present generation of young folk has lost confidence in grown-ups unusually early.

He adds: "Young people of today have a negative philosophy which they obtained from their elders. They are not long idealists. Too much has happened. Most generations grow up surrounded by strong walls of idealism, but the expression 'Oh yeah!' comes closer to expressing the feelings of the young people of today than any other two words. They are

like all mankind, essentially spiritual, but they
haven't found leadership that they can honestly
accept..."

—*Star-Gazette*
(Elmira, New York), August 15, 1935

~⊙~

"Fitzgerald? The author?" Milton asked.

"The same."

"Oh."

Perhaps Fitzgerald was not used to being greeted with such
disappointment, because he became quite irate. "Why are
you passing yourself off as Rowland Sinclair?" he demanded.

"I am Rowland Sinclair," Rowland said. "The gentleman you knew as Rowland Sinclair was the late Daniel
Cartwright—"

"Late? Are you trying to tell me that Rowland Sinclair
is dead?"

"Daniel Cartwright is dead. I'm very much alive. It seems
Mr. Cartwright borrowed my name on occasion." Rowland
noticed that they were attracting the gaze of other diners.
"Won't you join us, Mr. Fitzgerald, and we can clear up any
confusion as to who is who?"

Fitzgerald glanced at Edna, who was still seated. He
smiled slightly. "Well, thank you. I wouldn't mind some
company this evening."

And so the introductions were resumed and they took
their seats. They all knew the name F. Scott Fitzgerald,
of course. One of the most acclaimed writers of the previous decade, his name was mentioned alongside the likes of
Hemingway and Wolfe, though the economic stringencies of

the current decade had seen the popularity of stories about the lives of the thoughtless rich wane significantly.

If Scott had ever been the epitome of post-war optimism and style, he was no longer. His hands trembled now and his face twitched involuntarily with the ravages of chronic alcoholism. Though lucid, he was drunk. He ordered gin, claiming it was his first of the day, and indeed it might have been. He was beating his dependency on gin, he explained, by consuming nothing stronger than beer until dinner. So determined was he in his commitment to beat his addiction that he'd drunk no less than thirty-four glasses of beer that day.

Rowland asked him about Daniel Cartwright before the gin took effect.

"Oh, yes, he was here with me through the summer. Interesting fellow. Artist." He sipped his gin, closing his eyes as the liquor hit its mark. "Of course, the best art is produced in times of riches, but Zelda seems content to paint in this age of despair."

"Zelda?"

"My beloved wife. She's currently residing just across the valley at the Highland Hospital."

"Oh, is she unwell, Mr. Fitzgerald?" Edna asked gently.

"Nowadays, Zelda prefers the company of William the Conqueror, Mary Stuart, and Jesus Christ. And they all live at Highlands, apparently. I have been relegated to being my wife's great reality, an agent whose only purpose is to make the world tangible for her. And to that end, I pay the hospital."

Edna looked at the others, bewildered.

Milton tried to make sense of it. "Is the Highland Hospital some kind of psychiatric institution?"

"The best that money can buy, as befits the first American flapper."

"Mrs. Fitzgerald is an artist?" Rowland asked, trying to decipher Fitzgerald's erratic discourse.

"And a dancer, occasionally a mother, I suppose, a broken muse… Christ! She fancies herself a novelist now, too, despite evidence to the contrary." Resentment and glee showed in the roll of his eyes. "*Save Me the Waltz* came out three years ago to the indifference it deserved…plagiaristic, third-rate rubbish."

"Did Daniel Cartwright—Rowland Sinclair, as you knew him—know your wife, sir?" Milton pressed.

"Of course. He was giving her some sort of painting classes."

"Here?"

"No, no. At the hospital. They don't allow the inmates to leave the asylum. That wouldn't do."

They ordered meals. Fitzgerald ordered more gin, and as he became progressively more intoxicated, so too did his invectives about Zelda and her impact on his career increase in volume and bitterness.

By evening's end, Rowland and Milton were obliged to help him to his room. "She was the most beautiful woman I'd ever seen," Fitzgerald said as they helped him remove his jacket and shoes. "The most beautiful woman anyone had ever seen… Isabelle, Rosalind, Daisy… She was all of them, but we were creatures of prosperity, Catherine wheels burning bright and fast. We're lost now. Expended. We have only the compulsion to burn on to our own destruction, weak sparks destined to be dark."

The Australians heaved F. Scott Fitzgerald onto the bed, and he thanked them with slurred warmth. He asked Milton to fetch the bottle from the top drawer of the lowboy on the opposite wall.

Milton paused sadly as they walked past the typewriter on the desk by the window. "Have you read *The Beautiful and Damned*, Rowly?"

"Yes." He'd been seventeen when Fitzgerald's second novel was released. But he remembered it.

"Meeting him now, you have to wonder if Fitzgerald's ever read it."

They gathered in Edna's room that evening. Rowland arrived last.

"What's wrong, Rowly?" Edna asked when he came in. He looked troubled.

He handed her the torn piece of cartridge, the note they'd all assumed had been written by Norcross. "The signature. I thought it was an *N*. It could be a *Z*."

"For Zelda?"

"If Danny was giving her classes, the unsigned painting may be her work."

Clyde groaned as any connection between Asheville and Otis Norcross evaporated. He sighed. "I don't suppose Zelda Fitzgerald is Danny's mystery lover? Perhaps his preferences changed. Maybe her husband found out—"

"You're suggesting F. Scott Fitzgerald shot Danny?" Rowland asked, smiling.

"I promise you, comrade," Milton laughed, "Fitzgerald is no longer capable of holding, let alone firing, a gun."

"It's tragic, isn't it?" Edna said wistfully. "When mama first started drinking, I loved it. It made her happy and it was the most wonderful sound to hear her laugh. And then, after a while, she stopped laughing altogether."

Milton nodded and slipped his arm around the sculptress. "I remember." He and Edna had known each other since childhood. There was very little they did not know about each other.

"So what do we do?" Clyde asked.

"We should go see Zelda Fitzgerald," Edna said. "She might not realise Danny is dead. At the very least someone should tell her."

Milton agreed. "Even if we're on the wrong track to find Otis Norcross, Zelda might be able to shed some light on why Danny came here, and perhaps who might have killed him."

~~~

Before breakfast the next morning, Rowland telephoned the Highland Hospital, gave his name, and sought an appointment with Zelda Fitzgerald. He was a little surprised when the request was accepted and he was able to arrange to see her that morning. He expected that gaining an audience would be more difficult.

They didn't see Fitzgerald at breakfast, and so they were just themselves, something to which none of them objected. Edna wore a cloche today, rather than a scarf. The headgear was a little old-fashioned, but in the current stringencies, there were many who found themselves unable to keep up with the latest season's style, so it was not something that attracted particular note.

Rowland thought she looked a little pale.

"I didn't sleep well," she said when he enquired. She smiled. "All this fresh mountain air seems to be giving me nightmares."

"You should have woken me, Ed."

"Everybody has nightmares occasionally, Rowly."

"I know. But..." He stopped. "Let me help. I could read to you from *Paradise Lost*...or hold your hand till you fall asleep."

Edna laughed. She'd forgotten she'd told him that *Paradise Lost* rendered her unconscious or that her father had held her hand till she fell asleep for a whole year after her mother died, in order to keep the nightmares at bay. At the time she'd confided it, he'd been the one struggling with sleeplessness and nightmares. It touched her that Rowland remembered that small passing conversation.

She didn't tell him that she wasn't sure she could fall asleep holding his hand anymore, not while the memory of [1] his lover was so fresh.

"I'm all right, Rowly," she said, determinedly keeping her mind from wandering towards him. "But thank you."

They took the note scribbled on the piece of cartridge and the sketch, as well as the unsigned painting, with them. En route, Edna insisted they stop to buy flowers and chocolates and a basket of fruit.

The Highland Hospital, on Montford Avenue, looked more like a university than a sanatorium. Its landscaped grounds hosted a variety of buildings of different architectural styles. The hospital's reputation had been built on progressive care, a commitment to the notion that mental ills could be arrested or cured and patients returned to society. It offered programs for mental disorders and addictions that were based on exercise, diet, and occupational therapy. For the well-to-do, it afforded hope, and perhaps the first-class nature of the facilities went a long way to alleviate the guilt associated with having a loved one committed.

On the grounds, patients hiked, played tennis and ball games, participated in archery and art classes under the supervision of staff members. It seemed the hospital's strategy was to distract the patient from disordered thinking. More conventional therapies, medication, and hydrotherapy were also administered, but less visibly.

Milton raised his brow in the direction of the archers. "It seems a little risky to arm the inmates, don't you think?"

Edna shushed him.

The administration building was a fine example of the American Arts and Crafts style, a central octagonal bay window and a wide wrap around porch. There were grander buildings on the hospital campus, but Rumbough House inspired images of white picket prosperity, home and hearth and health. It was on this porch that they met Zelda Fitzgerald. Slight and fair, she carried herself with a dancer's grace. She wore her hair in a bob, parted on the side and crimped. Her famous beauty had waned, faded by years and possibly the same addictions that plagued her husband. Rowland introduced himself and his companions.

"Why, isn't that funny! I knew a gentleman called Rowland Sinclair." Her accent was soft, Southern. She regarded Rowland pensively. "Did you bring a book for me to sign?"

Rowland shook his head. He wished he'd thought to purchase her novel before he came.

"Of course...it's out of print now. You wouldn't be able to find it anywhere." She sat forward in her wicker armchair. "Scott was so angry with me when he saw it. You see, it was his material."

"His material?" Edna asked.

"Oh, yes. I didn't know, you see, that he wanted that part of our lives for *Tender Is the Night*. I rewrote it, naturally, but perhaps the material that belonged to Scott was the best parts of our lives."

Clyde showed Zelda the unsigned portrait. "Is that the gentleman you knew as Rowland Sinclair, Mrs. Fitzgerald?"

Zelda took the painting in her hands. "Oh, yes, dear Rowland." She looked at them. "What are you doing with John's painting?" She whispered now. "Did he give it to you? Do you know where he is?"

"John?"

Zelda glanced about them furtively. The nurse supervising the verandah visits was preoccupied with urging a singularly uncommunicative young man to talk to his visiting parents. "John Smith. He escaped."

Chapter Twenty-Eight

FASCINATION OF WRITING FOR STAGE
AFFECTS MANY

Inmates of Mental Asylums
Regularly Submit Manuscripts

(Copyright 1935 by the North America
Newspaper Alliance Inc.)

NEW YORK—It is impossible to gauge accurately, but there are something in the neighbourhood of 2,000 scripts wandering dismally from manager's office to manager's office in the Times Square district. Two thousand bulky manuscripts, all burning masterpieces, born in hope, living in faith, dying on charity...

This frenzy for production on Broadway has found victims in the oddest corners. For years Brock Pemberton has received script after script from the inmate of an insane asylum. The poor fellow wrote incoherently and at great length. His scripts were beautifully and neatly bound. He seems to have given up. Nothing has been heard from him in the last month.

—*Calgary Herald*
(Calgary, Alberta, Canada), 22 July 1935

∾⦿∾

Rowland showed Zelda Fitzgerald the sketch they'd found in Daniel Cartwright's studio. "Is this John Smith, Mrs. Fitzgerald?"

"Why, yes." She held the sketch up and considered it thoughtfully. "Well, it was before the treatment. His hair is white now, and he's thinner. He holds his jaw differently—like it's always clenched."

"You mentioned he escaped, Mrs. Fitzgerald," Milton prodded. "When exactly was that?"

"About two months ago. We were walking—we must, you know, because the demons in our minds are confined by exhaustion. John is much better at walking than I am... He liked hiking and woodsy things. I called him Robin Hood sometimes." Her eyes became dreamy. Zelda shook her head quickly, and the motion seemed to reattach her to the present. "They took a group of about a dozen of us hiking near Bent Creek. One moment he was there, and then he was gone." She waved at no one in particular and gasped, "Run, Johnny, run!"

"Do they have any idea where he is?" Rowland felt a cautious surge of excitement.

"If they did, they would have brought him back. Johnny was a top-floor patient—he'll never be going home." She giggled. "He's probably made a home with the tramps who live in the forest. Rowland Sinclair and his merry men."

"Is he dangerous?" Edna asked.

"I thought he was sweet...shy...but you never can tell." She pointed to one of the nurses, a motherly woman in a pristine uniform. "Nurse Hammond used to be a patient here—her parents had her committed after she set fire to their house the third time. Killed three people and a dog."

They tried not to look too obviously.

"How well did John Smith know Dan—I mean Rowland... the other one?" Milton asked.

"Oh, they were great pals. Johnny would cry like a baby when he left."

"Mrs. Fitzgerald, do you know what disorder John Smith suffered?"

"Like the rest of us, I expect he was mad."

They remained talking with Zelda Fitzgerald for a time. She spoke of the past, the burning love that she and Fitzgerald had shared. "We built a fire of our love, and for a time it was so bright the world watched in awe, and then we used it to burn each other to ashes." She looked at Edna and laughed. "Now we steal art and life and hope from one another and take pride only in the genius of our cruelty."

Rowland glanced at Edna. She looked shaken.

Zelda shook off the reflection and asked if they would like to see her studio. "I exhibited last year, you know. Some people were very kind."

Rowland excused himself, leaving his friends to accompany Zelda to view her work.

"I'm going to see what I can find out about John Smith," he told Clyde and Milton quietly.

"I'll go with Rowly," Edna volunteered.

Milton nodded agreement. He'd noted how shaken Edna had been by Zelda's account of her marriage. He wondered if the sculptress was thinking about her own parents, the madness and depression that had been her mother's end. Or was it something else about the tragedy of the Fitzgeralds that so disturbed her?

Rowland and Edna went back into Rumbough House, and Zelda led Clyde and Milton away. Rowland asked to the see the physician in charge—a Dr. Adams—and enquired of the man about a patient named John Smith who had escaped a couple of months before.

Adams frowned, perplexed. "Escaped? There has been no escape. I assure you, Mr. Sinclair, all our patients are present and accounted for."

"Mrs. Fitzgerald is convinced that a patient named John Smith escaped in early October."

"Mrs. Fitzgerald?" Adams' face relaxed. "Oh, I see what has happened. John Smith is a delusion, Mr. Sinclair."

"I beg your pardon?"

"He is a delusion. Mrs. Fitzgerald is prone to hallucinations and delusions. I'm afraid there is no patient named John Smith at Highland Hospital. I expect Mrs. Fitzgerald is manifesting her own desire for release in this fantasy of a fellow patient who escaped."

"She says that he bolted while a group of patients were hiking near some place called Bent Creek," Rowland countered the denial with details.

Adams nodded sadly. "We do take patients hiking at Bent Creek, though not Mrs. Fitzgerald anymore. The forest seems to make her regress—hallucinations about Robin Hood."

Rowland persisted. "Perhaps she's mistaken as to the name. The man I'm talking about may have taken instruction in painting from a man calling himself Rowland Sinclair, who instructed some of your patients in painting."

Adams went to his desk and checked a ledger. "There was a gentleman called Sinclair who would give Mrs. Fitzgerald private classes from time to time—arranged by her husband,

I believe. But he saw no other patient. That would have been highly improper."

Rowland took Daniel Cartwright's sketch from inside his jacket. "Do you recognise this man at all, Dr. Adams?"

Adams looked at the drawing and shrugged. "No, I don't, Mr. Sinclair. He certainly doesn't look like any of our patients."

For a moment Rowland said nothing. And then he thanked Adams for his assistance. "There appears to have been some misunderstanding."

Adams smiled. "It is an understandable mistake, Mr. Sinclair. Mrs. Fitzgerald is very charming. It is easy to forget that she suffers from a significant disorder of the mind."

"We won't detain you any longer," Rowland said, shaking the psychiatrist's hand. He offered Edna his arm and they left Rumbough House to find Milton and Clyde.

"You don't believe him, do you?" Edna whispered, as they made their way down the verandah steps.

"Not for a single moment," Rowland replied. "But insisting might have had ramifications for Zelda Fitzgerald."

"So what now?"

"Well…he's not here. But we know that he was."

"And that means—"

"That Danny didn't leave his estate to a dead man. That he wasn't insane, and there is some purpose to all this."

By the time they found Milton and Clyde, a nurse had arrived to find Zelda Fitzgerald and remind her that she was due at the hospital farm. Zelda pouted, reluctant to leave the studio and her discussion with Clyde on watercolour technique. But the nurse was firm. Work on the farm was part of her physiotherapy and not to be avoided.

And so they took their leave of the first American flapper, thanking her for her time.

"Remember me to Johnny," she whispered into Rowland's ear. "Tell him for me that I hope he made it home."

～❧～

In the Cadillac on the way back to Grove Park Inn, Rowland and Edna recounted what they'd been told by the hospital psychiatrist.

"What do you think is going on, Rowly?" Clyde asked.

"I don't think Zelda Fitzgerald is hallucinating."

"So why would this chap Adams deny that John Smith was a patient?"

"Another man that nobody wants to exist?" Edna said thoughtfully.

"What do you mean, Ed?"

"Well, Otis Norcross is dead; John Smith never was." The sculptress leaned forward and rested her elbows on the backrest of the front seat. "It seems that every time we think we might have found Danny's heir, it becomes impossible."

Clyde shook his head. "If John Smith is Otis Norcross, then who the hell is buried at the Mount Auburn cemetery? Why do his parents believe he's dead?"

"Perhaps they know he's not," Rowland said thoughtfully. "Perhaps it's something to do with why he was committed to Highland Hospital."

"So what do we do now?" Clyde said exasperated. "Assuming Zelda Fitzgerald didn't imagine John Smith, he could be anywhere."

"Zelda said she hoped he made it home," Edna said. "Maybe that's where he was going."

"Boston?"

Edna shrugged. "Maybe."

"How the devil would he have got to Boston?" Milton shifted the gears of the Madame X as they began the climb up Sunset Mountain. "From what Zelda said, he would have had to run with nothing but what he was wearing."

"Perhaps he had help," Rowland said.

"Danny?"

"Possibly." Rowland tapped his fingers on the armrest pensively. He glanced up at the inn, which now loomed before them, to the rooms overlooking the entrance. "Or perhaps he had a friend help him out."

"You don't mean Fitzgerald?"

"Well, it seems it was Fitzgerald who arranged for Danny to give his wife painting lessons. Perhaps Fitzgerald returned the favour."

Milton shook his head. "I don't know, Rowly. F. Scott Fitzgerald doesn't seem capable of much at the moment."

"He may have more sober moments than we saw last night. Maybe his beer cure keeps him vaguely lucid through the day."

Milton parked the Madame X. "We could ask him, I suppose. At least he won't lie."

"Why do you think that?" Clyde asked.

"In my experience, comrade, drunks only ever deceive themselves. About everything else they are unnecessarily honest."

～❦～

F. Scott Fitzgerald was sitting at his typewriter when Rowland and Milton tapped on his door. The page in the carriage was as yet blank, and the writer was instead staring out the window. He summoned them in and told them to sit down without moving his eyes.

"What's going on?" Milton asked.

"New arrivals," Fitzgerald said, picking up a set of binoculars and peering through them. "I can see everyone who walks up the driveway to check in. It's why I request these rooms."

Rowland and Milton exchanged a glance. Did Fitzgerald fear some kind of attack? Could he be keeping a lookout for Smith or Norcross, or perhaps whoever it was who killed Daniel Cartwright?

"Why do you want to see who walks up?" Rowland asked.

"I like to know if there are any pretty women checking in." He put the binoculars down and sighed. "I'm afraid today's offering is quite uninspiring. I might join you gentlemen and Miss Higgins for dinner again tonight."

Rowland nodded. "We'd be pleased to have your company, sir."

"Good, good."

"Before we leave you to get back to work, would you mind if I asked you a couple of questions about the gentleman you knew as Rowland Sinclair?"

Fitzgerald sat back. "Rowland. Oh, yes. You said he was dead, didn't you? How did he die?"

"He was murdered."

"Oh. Christ. What a terrible business."

Rowland agreed. "Did you arrange for Rowland to give your wife painting lessons?"

"My wife? Oh, Zelda. Yes, I did, though I don't know why I bothered—she probably has conversations with Rembrandt and da Vinci these days."

"Whose idea was this arrangement, Mr. Fitzgerald? Yours or his?"

Fitzgerald reached for a bottle stashed behind his typewriter and, after offering his guests a drink, poured himself a glass of beer. "I do believe it was his. He'd met Zelda when he was visiting a friend of his, and came to me with the notion."

"Did you pay him, Mr. Fitzgerald?"

"I rather think that's a matter between him and me."

Rowland pressed on. "Did you perhaps do him a favour to return the kindness?"

"Jesus Hopping Christ! What are you trying to ask me?"

"Did you help a Mr. John Smith escape Highland Hospital?"

"No. He escaped on his own. I merely drove him to the railway station and bought him a ticket."

"A ticket where, Mr. Fitzgerald?"

"I believe it was Boston."

Chapter Twenty-Nine

"Yes, that's it. A return passage to Boston." Whilst Fitzgerald made a show of trying to remember, he was clearly enjoying the reveal.

"Return? He came back?"

"I have no idea whether he came back. I do know he went and that he wanted a return passage."

"It was Smith who wanted the round ticket?" Rowland clarified, frowning.

"Yes, he was adamant. Seemed quite frightened of Boston, to be honest." Fitzgerald shrugged. "I knew Sinclair would be good for it, so I bought him what he wanted."

"How did you know when and where to be waiting for John Smith?" Milton asked.

"Sinclair arranged that before he returned to Boston the previous week—wanted to make sure he was there to meet Smith on the other end, I expect. Before he went, he gave me a map, so I knew where to wait and agreed on a date."

"A date, not a time?"

"I picked Smith up after dark a couple of days after he absconded from the hike, once the police had given up looking for him." Fitzgerald rummaged through his desk and pulled out a road map. He pointed out the cross marked on the edge of the National Forest.

Rowland's eyes narrowed. "So what did he do for two days in the forest?"

Fitzgerald considered the question whilst sipping his beer. "He wasn't in the forest. There are a few houses here... huts, really. They've been abandoned for years. Apparently, Sinclair owns them." Fitzgerald pointed to a place several miles from the cross. "That's where they were hiking."

"How did he—?"

"He said he ran." Fitzgerald drained his glass and refilled it. "He waited until they were a couple of hours down the trail before he absconded, so by the time the authorities had been informed and a search party organised, he had about five or six hours' head start. The thing with the program at Highland Hospital is the inmates end up very physically fit." The writer gazed at the blank page on his typewriter thoughtfully. "It was one helluva story."

Rowland's eyes were bright, focused. Finally, something other than a dead end. "Do you know why Mr. Cartwright arranged this escape, Mr. Fitzgerald?"

"He seemed to be of the opinion that Mr. Smith was in danger." Fitzgerald took out a silver cigarette case as Rowland slipped the map into his pocket.

"From whom?"

Fitzgerald lit a cigarette and savoured a drag before he answered. "No idea. Bit of an odd fellow, Sinclair-Cartwright. May have been more sensible to admit him to Highland than to break Smith out." He exhaled a cloud of smoke. "Cartwright—as you call him—was very upset about the treatment, if I recall. Perhaps Smith was scheduled for more treatment." His face clouded just momentarily. "Cartwright swore me to secrecy, of course, but since he's dead, I suppose it doesn't matter anymore." Fitzgerald tensed as he noticed something in the periphery of his vision. He picked up the binoculars. "Finally, a woman capable of furnishing the pleasantries of life."

Rowland had no interest whatsoever in Fitzgerald's selection, until the writer added, "I'll have to get rid of the dog, of course."

Fitzgerald protested as Milton stood to look out the window. Milton borrowed the binoculars and focused on the young woman tripping up the driveway, leading a dog, and four men.

Milton swore and handed the binoculars to Rowland.

Clyde's Jean, Costello, Brown, and two other thugs. Rowland thanked Fitzgerald as he and Milton walked out.

They ran back to their rooms. Rowland went straight to Edna's door, while Milton tried to find Clyde. There was no answer when he knocked, but Edna's door had been left unlocked. Rowland went in. "Ed?" The room was empty. He cursed, picking up the phone.

"Rowly?" Edna opened the door and came in. She looked at his face. "Oh, my God, what's wrong?"

"Where were you? I thought—"

"Clyde's room. I just ducked in to get a book." Her face softened. "Rowly, darling, what's wrong?"

"Costello and some others are here. They've just arrived."

"And you thought—"

"I don't know what I thought."

Clyde and Milton came in now. Milton closed and locked the door.

"We're assuming these clowns and their bloody dog have come looking for us, I suppose?" Milton said.

"I think that's a fairly safe bet," Clyde said.

"We'd better leave." Rowland thought quickly. Costello's men were probably in the lobby. It was unlikely they would get past them unnoticed. "They're probably trying to get our room numbers out of the front desk staff now."

"So why don't we just ring the reception and tell them that Costello and Brown are wanted in New York and Boston, and suggest they call the police?" Edna said calmly.

Rowland considered it. "We have nothing to lose, I expect. They clearly already know we're here." He picked up the receiver, called through to the reception and asked to speak to the hotel's manager. Rowland explained that he had recognised two of the gentlemen who had just walked into the Grove Park Inn with a lady and her dog, and the men had assaulted him in Boston and Mr. Clyde Watson Jones in New York and were consequently wanted in both cities.

The manager seemed confused. "I'm afraid there are no

guests at the reception desk, Mr. Sinclair. If you'd just hold the line... Nobody's checked in for at least a couple of hours. Are you sure you aren't mistaken, Mr. Sinclair?"

"I saw them come in, as did Mr. Isaacs and Mr. Fitzgerald."

"And did they recognise these gentlemen?"

"No, just me, but they saw them."

"Perhaps if you were to make a report at the police station..."

"They are in your hotel."

"I'm afraid I can't see them, sir. Perhaps they decided against coming in."

"Or they've bypassed the lobby and are somewhere in the hotel." Rowland's voice became harder, more authoritative. Edna thought he sounded like Wilfred.

"I'll contact the sheriff, sir. Perhaps he'll send an officer."

"Yes, thank you." Rowland hung up, unwilling to waste any more time. "That was spectacularly unuseful," he said, exasperated.

"We'd better get out of here, Rowly." Milton looked out the window.

Clyde nodded. "Milt and I will pack and bring our suitcases, yours too, Rowly. You stay with Ed and lock the door after us. Then we'll work out how we're going to get past them."

By the time Clyde and Milton returned, Rowland was helping Edna close her case, which was bulging with hasty packing. The moments had given them all time to think.

"They can't have surrounded the hotel," Clyde said. "And they don't know that you've seen them arrive. So maybe the most sensible thing is just to leave quietly."

Rowland agreed. "It's a big hotel and they haven't had time to familiarise themselves with it. If we leave via the back porch, we might slip past them."

"And if we don't slip past them?"

Milton glanced at Edna and his dark eyes glittered fiercely. "Well, this time it's not four against one."

Rowland picked up the telephone.

"Who are you calling?" Clyde asked.

"Burr—I thought we should let him know what's going on."

Milton shook his head. "Hold your horses, Rowly. Do we know that we can trust him?"

"What?" Rowland said surprised. "You think—"

"I've got to wonder how these clowns knew we were here."

"He's a lawyer. He's Danny's lawyer."

"Exactly." Milton pulled at his goatee. "Didn't Costello and his mates use Burr's name to get you away from Ed? And as far as I can tell, he's the only person who knew we were going to Asheville."

Rowland was unconvinced. "Why would Oliver Burr do this? He's not a beneficiary, and he's Danny's attorney."

"He said he was a Yale man, didn't he?" Milton said. "Remember that clause in Danny's will which kicks in if you die or refuse to continue... Dammit! If Ed hadn't stopped us packing up and going home, his alma mater would have got everything."

Rowland cursed and replaced the receiver. Everything Milton said was true. But he'd liked Oliver Burr, trusted him. God, had Burr seen how much Edna meant to him? Had that, in itself, placed her in particular danger?

"So we leave," Milton said. "When we get back to Boston, Rowly can sack Burr, Mayfair and Wilkes."

"We still haven't found Otis Norcross or John Smith," Edna said.

"Fitzgerald bought him a ticket to Boston," Milton said.

"A return ticket," Rowland reminded him.

"Why would he return?"

"If he murdered Danny, he might," Clyde offered.

"What? Why—"

"He was in an insane asylum, Rowly. Who knows what

for—perhaps he's dangerous," Clyde said. "If Smith is Otis Norcross from Boston, his family thinks he's dead, and Danny was the only one who knew he was alive. For all we know, Danny had him committed. Maybe Norcross turned on him."

Milton picked up on Clyde's reasoning. "That makes sense. Everybody is looking for him in Boston. And if he is a homicidal maniac, he might just have returned here after he got even with Danny, in order to settle a few more scores."

"Now you're writing a novel," Rowland muttered.

"Look," Clyde intervened. "We haven't got time to argue about this now. Let's get out of here, and then we can decide what to do."

"Bearing in mind that if Burr has betrayed us," Milton warned, "Costello and his goons might know which rooms we're in."

Rowland turned on the radio to create the illusion that the room was inhabited. The voice of Father Coughlin, whose broadcast had so angered Edna in New York, greeted them over the airwaves. If they were ever inclined to listen, it was not now.

They closed and locked the door behind them, taking the fire exit rather than the elevator down to the ground floor. They avoided the Great Hall as much as they could, making their way instead towards the back porch and the car lot behind the Grove Park Inn. They might have slipped out entirely unnoticed had it not been for Windrip.

The hound came tearing out of the hotel, barking joyfully. Within moments the dog's mistress had followed him out of the hotel and shouted. The Australians ran, hampered by their luggage, but even so, they reached the car before Costello and his compatriots emerged from the hotel. A whistle, and Windrip snarled and attacked.

"Get into the car!" Clyde shouted as he fended the dog off with a suitcase.

Rowland jumped in behind the wheel and turned over

the engine. Clyde got in last, abandoning Edna's suitcase in desperation.

"Get down," Rowland said as he saw in the distance that Brown had produced a gun. Costello deflected his colleague's arm before he could fire, and the two began shouting at each other. Rowland didn't waste the moment, pulling out of the lot and hurtling the Madame X down Sunset Mountain.

They were on the road back to Washington when Edna asked, "You don't think we led them to Otis Norcross, do you?"

"We haven't found Otis Norcross," Milton said.

"No, but I wonder if we're close." She removed the cloche and smoothed the ragged remains of her hair. "Whether or not he killed Danny, he is likely to have fled back here when Danny was murdered…or perhaps they always planned he would return here. After all, Danny left a trail for you, Rowly, a trail which led to Asheville."

"Costello stopped Brown from shooting," Clyde noted. "Perhaps they don't want you dead."

"If I die or abdicate, Frank, Geoffrey, and Molly get nothing at all," Rowland noted. He was much more comfortable with the idea that Oliver Burr had nothing to do with the thugs who had turned up at the hotel, that they'd been despatched by the Cartwright brothers.

"So, we can't leave," Edna said.

"Of course we can," Clyde replied.

"We've led these men to Otis Norcross or John Smith or whoever he is," she said urgently. "It won't be hard to retrace our steps to the hospital and Zelda. It's all in the visitor's book—that's if they haven't just been following us all along. She might tell them what she told us." The sculptress's eyes were fierce. "We can't just leave the poor man to it!"

Rowland slowed the Madame X and pulled over. "Ed's right. We've got to find Norcross before they do."

"So where the hell do we look?" Milton said. "He could be flaming anywhere."

Rowland drew Fitzgerald's map from his pocket. "Let's start here. He hid here once—perhaps he went back."

Chapter Thirty

TREAT INSANITY WITH CHEMICALS

Lawrence Professor Outlines
Progress of Recent Experiments

The success of recent experiments in the chemical treatment of insanity was outlined by Dr. Herbert L. Davis, assistant professor of chemistry at Lawrence college, at the first meeting of the General science club at the college Wednesday evening…

Experiments in the effects of anesthetics, launched at Cornell University in 1929, revealed that a result of anesthetics was a temporary coagulation of the brain and nerve cells and also that many persons who submitted to anesthetics went through a period of high excitement during the time the anesthetic was taking effect or wearing off, corresponding to a type of insanity.

In one type of insanity, it was found, the brain particles were too closely clustered

together and in another type too widely dispersed. Chemical treatment to remedy those
conditions was provided for 46 patients in New
York state and 90 percent of the cases yielded
to treatment. The treatment, he said, did not
necessarily strike at the cause of the abnormal
condition but provided temporary relief.

—*The Post Crescent*
(Appleton, Wisconsin), January 17, 1935

∿❧∿

Rowland took a route that kept them as far from built-up
areas and Grove Park as possible. It was consequently twilight
when they approached the boarded and derelict cabins on the
edge of the forest. As far as hideouts went, Rowland could
see its strengths. The settlement had clearly been abandoned
many years before and amounted to only four crumbling
huts in the shadow of the trees. It was isolated and hidden
from the main road, and unless you knew it was there, you
were unlikely to find it. The proximity of the trees provided
a further retreat in the case of discovery. There was no smoke
from any of the chimneys, no sign of life at all.

Rowland pulled the Madame X in beside one of the cabins. He turned up the collar of his jacket as he climbed out
of the Cadillac. They walked around the buildings looking
for any indication of recent inhabitation. Clyde checked the
boards, testing for one that was loose or hinged.

"This is...rustic," Rowland murmured, running his eyes
dubiously over the dilapidated buildings.

"I promise you, Rowly," Clyde replied, "they'd be a darn
sight more comfortable than sleeping in the open."

"Mr. Smith," Edna called. "We're friends of Daniel Cartwright. We've come to help you." Her voice echoed slightly.

"Did you hear that?" Milton said quietly.

Rowland nodded. A step in the undergrowth. "He's in the forest."

"Do we wait for him to come out?"

Rowland looked around at the vast Appalachian forest. "If he disappears, we haven't a chance of finding him in there."

"Right then, let's go."

They broke into a run. Rowland reached the tree line first. Autumn leaf fall had opened up the forest canopy in places, and it was only that which allowed the fading light to penetrate through the spruce understorey trees. Rowland watched for any sign of movement, any trace of John Smith, or Otis Norcross, as he was now sure the man was. He took a chance and called Norcross's name. "Mr. Norcross! We'd just like to—"

A hiss.

At first Rowland only registered that something had hit him in the shoulder, so hard that if he had not been standing against a tree, he might have been bowled over. And then he couldn't move away from the tree. He could feel what had happened, but it was not until he saw the arrow's shaft that the pain seemed to become real and intensify.

"What the devil!" Milton caught up with him now. Another hiss and a shot embedded in the tree above Rowland's head.

Milton swore. "Rowly, get down!"

Yet another missile thudded into a nearby tree.

"I can't," Rowland gasped. "I'm pinned to this bloody tree."

"Rowly! Milt!" Clyde's voice.

"Stay back!" Milton shouted as he tried to pull the arrow out of the tree.

"Holy mother of God—" Clyde was there now.

"Ed..." Rowland was starting to feel light-headed now. They had to keep her away.

"Rowly, I'm here." Edna's hand was on his cheek. "Get him down," she said desperately to Milton and Clyde. "Do something!"

Another arrow narrowly missed Milton, who turned around and swore at the unseen assassin.

Edna tried. "Please, just let us get Rowly down, and we'll go."

Clyde inspected the arrow which had passed through Rowland's shoulder and into the trunk. He tried to dislodge it from the tree, succeeding only in making Rowland swear despite the presence of Edna.

The arrows appeared to have paused, but for how long was anybody's guess.

"Righto, Rowly," Clyde said grimly. "We're going to have to pull you off the arrow."

"Just do it." Rowland's instinct was to struggle against the pin, to pull away from the tree but any attempt to that effect was both excruciating and useless.

"Hold still, mate." Clyde took out a pocketknife and scored the shaft, then, gripping it on either side of the score, he snapped the thin wooden rod to remove the fletching.

Rowland swore again. "Bloody hell, Clyde!"

"Sorry, mate." Clyde instructed Milton to place his shoulder under Rowland's. "On the count of three, we're going to pull him forward and up... Rowly, this is going to hurt, but once it's done, it's done, and we can get you out of here."

Rowland nodded, unable to speak now. Clyde slipped off his belt. "Bite down on this, and if you feel like you're going to faint, don't fight it."

Rowland clenched the doubled leather between his teeth.

"One. Two. Three—"

Milton and Clyde pulled him forward slowly, effectively dragging the broken arrow through his shoulder and leaving it embedded in the tree. Rowland's knees gave way. They sat him on the forest floor and tried to stem the bleeding from both sides with handkerchiefs. Edna spoke gently into his ear, trying to keep him calm while Clyde and Milton dealt with the blood.

"We need to get him back to the car." Milton kept an eye on the trees a few yards away. To have the momentum to impale Rowland, the arrow would have had to come from very nearby. The shooter could well have picked them all off by now. He stood, his arms outstretched. "Look, mate, listen to the way we talk. Danny must have told you about his Australian friend. This is Rowland Sinclair, the real one. Danny sent him to help you."

"Give it up, Milt," Clyde said applying pressure to the wound. He was angry now. "The bastard probably killed Danny."

"No!" The exclamation was so close by that, despite everything, it startled them.

In the fading light, Rowland could barely see the man who stepped into sight with an arrow cocked and aimed in an archer's bow. White-haired and drawn, he looked little like Daniel Cartwright's sketch of a young man in his prime, but Rowland recognised him. The ragged man who'd fled the funeral.

"I didn't kill Danny," he said. "I loved him. God, I couldn't kill anyone."

They all had enough good sense not to point out the irony of such a claim in the current circumstances.

Instead, Edna said softly, "Rowly could bleed to death if we don't get him to a doctor. Please."

The man lowered the bow. "Take him into the house. I can help him."

After a moment to decide that they didn't really have any other choice, Clyde and Milton got Rowland onto his feet and half supported, half dragged him out of the trees.

The wretched archer took them into one of the houses via a boarded hole in the wall. Milton went in first so that he could help Rowland from within the house. "Ed, go back to the car and get everything you can find in the drinks cabinet…and open our suitcases and grab our shirts."

By the time she returned, her arms full of alcohol and shirts, they had manoeuvred Rowland through the hole in the wall and land him on floor. A lantern had been lit, and they could see the inside of the cabin. It was unexpectedly clean and tidy. Blankets had been folded and piled neatly on a mattress near the fireplace, beside which was wood and kindling stacked in a triangular pile. There were books on the mantel.

"Roll him onto his side." There were tears streaming down the archer's gaunt face but otherwise he seemed calm. He handed Milton a hunting knife. "Cut away his clothes so we can see what we're dealing with."

Milton took the knife, wondering if they should just get Rowland into the Cadillac and drive like hell for a hospital. But the sun had now set and the roads were untarred—in the light they had been mere trails; in the dark they'd be less. Milton moved Rowland onto his uninjured shoulder and set about cutting away his jacket and shirt. Edna knelt beside him and held Rowland's head in her lap. Rowland was quiet, but he seemed reasonably lucid, all things considered.

The man instructed Milton to rip up the shirts for bandages and then turned to Clyde. "Could you start the fire, please? I only light it after dark when the smoke can't be seen. We should try to keep him warm."

Edna pulled one of the blankets over Rowland. She'd removed her cloche. Their strange host's eyes lingered upon the stubbled copper remains on her head only briefly, before he gave his full attention to Rowland's wound. There was a barrel of water in the corner of the room, and he ladled some of its contents into an enamel basin and then used the icy water to wash away as much blood from the surface of the wounds as possible. The bleeding had slowed, which he claimed was a good sign.

No longer covered by blood, the swastika-shaped burn on Rowland's chest was visible. Edna placed her hand over it as she held him.

The archer opened the bottle of single malt. "This'll burn," he warned before pouring the alcohol over both the entry and exit wounds. Rowland gasped as his shoulder seemed to catch on fire. It was all he could do to suppress the impulse to protect himself by lashing out. Instead, he pressed his face against Edna's stomach to keep from crying out.

"Hang on, darling, it's nearly over," Edna whispered into his ear. The faint scent of her rose perfume penetrated the pain and smell of whisky, and he fixed on that and the cool press of her cheek against his.

The man continued till the bottle was nearly empty, and then, folding a couple of the strips Milton had torn from their shirts into a dressing, he soaked them with the remaining whisky and applied them to each of the holes in Rowland's flesh, directing Milton and Edna to hold them in place while he bound the area with the makeshift bandages. Through all of this, he wept silently. If Rowland had not been somewhat distracted by his own condition, he would have found it alarming.

With the bleeding finally stemmed, they moved him onto the mattress and covered him with blankets while he caught his breath.

"Are you Otis Norcross?" Clyde asked as he tried to boil water over the fire.

"Yes. I was." Norcross showed him where best to place the pot.

"Good," Rowland said weakly. "We've...been looking for you."

Edna shushed him. "Just rest, Rowly." He was hot to touch. She tried to cool him with soaked cloth.

Clyde picked up a bottle of gin. "This might help." He helped Rowland to sit up and held the bottle to his lips.

Rowland swallowed and spluttered. He was starting to focus again, so he didn't take more than the one swig. Being injured was bad enough; he wasn't going to be much use drunk as well—however much drunk was tempting at the moment. He had not forgotten that Costello and his thugs were in Asheville. Still, the gin did take off the edge.

"It's my duty to inform you, Mr. Norcross," he said haltingly and with some effort, "that you are the primary beneficiary of Daniel Cartwright's estate."

If the news was something which gratified Norcross in any way, he showed no sign of that fact. Rowland noticed for the first time the broken teeth and bruises left by restraints on the American's thin wrists. Norcross looked at them all balefully and swallowed. "I should like you to know that I didn't mean to injure you, Mr. Sinclair, only to frighten you off. I'm normally a very good shot, but you moved."

"Entirely my fault then," Rowland said curtly, wincing as he moved back to lean against the wall. "I apologise."

Norcross panicked. "I didn't mean it. I didn't! You don't understand—they'll send me away again—"

"Rowly was just kidding, Mr. Norcross," Edna said.

"Yes, comrade." Milton glanced at Edna and laughed. "You wouldn't be the first person to accidentally shoot Rowly."

Edna glared at the poet. It had been more than three years now since she'd shot Rowland Sinclair, but it was not an incident about which she liked to be reminded.

"I never used to be like this before the treatment," Norcross said, wiping his face angrily.

"I assure you, Mr. Norcross," Rowland said, suddenly drowsy, "I'm not inclined to hold this against you."

"Why does everyone think you're dead, Mr. Norcross?" Milton asked.

Norcross was watching Rowland. "I suppose I am, in a way." He took the water off the flames and made tea. "They were never going to let me come home."

"Who?"

"My family...my father mainly." He poured tea into a cup, added sugar from one of the canisters on the mantel, and pressed the handle into Rowland's hand. "I'm afraid there's only one cup, but please drink, Mr. Sinclair—you've lost a fair bit of blood... Father found out about Danny. There were no more chances, he said. I was ungodly, an abomination. He would see I did not take the Norcross name to hell with me."

"They committed you because of Danny?" Rowland tried to concentrate on what Norcross was saying. "Can they do that? You're a grown man, for God's sake."

Norcross shrugged. "They did. I didn't know that they'd buried me until later."

Impulsively, Edna reached forward and touched his arm. "You poor man. You must have been terrified."

Milton sighed. "I think you mean outraged, Ed," he corrected. "Men don't get terrified."

Edna called the poet an idiot as she placed her hand around Rowland's on the cup and guided it to his lips.

Norcross looked a little confused but continued with his story. "Danny found me. I don't know how, but he did. But we had to be careful because if anyone ever found out—" He described the measures they'd taken to hide the purpose of Daniel Cartwright's visits to Highland Hospital, aided by the fact that, to the Norcrosses, he was more than dead, and to the doctors, he was just another broken and incurable deviant. Norcross took the empty cup from Rowland and filled it for Edna. "Danny taught painting at Highland, and for most of the summer we saw each other every day. He'd return to Boston periodically to try talk to my parents, to convince them that I should be released, but they wouldn't even hear him. And then the doctors decided to try chemical treatments...and for a while after that I couldn't remember who Danny was, I couldn't remember who I was."

Clyde shook his head. "Dear God."

"But Danny kept coming. He brought me back."

Edna took the empty cup back to the teapot and filled it for Norcross. Milton and Clyde seemed happy with the bottle of gin. "He must have loved you very much, Mr. Norcross."

Norcross's tears flowed freely again, but he smiled through them. "He was unshakable." He rummaged in a sack and produced a tin of dehydrated strips of meat, which he instructed Rowland to eat. For a while Norcross watched as Rowland made an effort to comply. "I'll make some soup," he decided. "That might be easier for you to get down."

"Why exactly did you escape when you did?" Rowland asked, trying to take Norcross's mind from catering.

"Something happened—I'm not sure what—and Danny said we couldn't wait, that they would never release me. Luckily, we had prepared. He'd already bought these huts. He stocked them with food and water, and he arranged for Mr. Fitzgerald. I took the train to Boston." Norcross began to shake now. "When I got there, Danny wasn't at the station. It was a couple of days before I realised he was dead."

"You were at the funeral," Rowland said, gritting his teeth as he tried to shift position.

Norcross checked the dressings to ensure they hadn't come loose. "Yes. I'm sorry I punched you. I panicked. Danny told me not to trust anybody, you see, and I suppose I was always a little jealous of you…because of Danny…and I was so angry that he was dead." He trailed off, looking around in case he'd said too much.

"So you knew who Rowly was when you impaled him to a tree?" Milton asked suspiciously.

"I didn't mean to hit him, just to fend him off." Norcross hesitated. "And I'd convinced myself that Mr. Sinclair had killed Danny."

"We were in Singapore when Danny died," Clyde informed him, but not harshly.

"I didn't know that. I am sorry. I just didn't know who to trust. I was living in the parks, moving and hiding all the time in case anyone recognised me. Though, of course, why would they?" He touched his face, clearly aware of how it had been ravaged. "After the funeral, I came back. I thought I'd be safe here."

"We need to talk about what we're going to do," Clyde said firmly. "We'll need to get Rowland to a doctor as soon as it's light—I'm not entirely happy about leaving it till then, to be honest. He could be dead by morning, for all we know."

Rowland's eyes were closed, but he smiled. "Such a ray of sunshine, Clyde old man!" He opened his eyes and looked at his friend. "I'm all right, I think. I can move my arm and hand—it hurts, but I can move it—which probably means Mr. Norcross's arrow missed anything vital. I'm not expecting a good night's sleep, but I can hang on till morning."

"I can give you something to help you sleep." Norcross rummaged in another sack and pulled out an envelope. He placed the envelope into Rowland's good hand. "A couple of those and you'll sleep like a baby."

Rowland stared at the envelope.

"It's my medication," Norcross said enthusiastically. "I stopped taking it months ago when I started remembering.

I don't know why I kept it, why I brought it with me... But it will help you sleep."

"Thank you." Rowland slipped the envelope into the pocket of his trousers since his jacket was in tatters. He had no intention of taking them, but he was not going to give the pills back either. Not while Norcross was handing out tea and cooking soup.

Chapter Thirty-One

Sugar As Healing Agent

One of the most remarkable discoveries of the war was that of the use of powdered sugar as a dressing for wounds. The Samaritan in the Bible used oil and wine for dressing the wounds of the injured man. In Spain sherry has been recognized as a capital antiseptic for wounds when iodine is not handy. A more recent discovery is that cod-liver oil has an amazing effect on raw wounds, sores and especially burns. The result is rapid healing without the necessity of skin grafting. The discovery was made by the German Professor Lohr. Soap, too, is a most useful dressing where other materials are not available. The inventor of linoleum also made a germ killer. It is now well known that oxidised linseed oil with which linoleum is manufactured destroys millions of typhoid and other germs. Linoleum is not recommended for the floors of hospitals, churches

and schools because of this germ killing quality which is attributed to it.

—*St. Joseph News-Press/Gazette*
(St. Joseph, Missouri), June 23, 1935

❧

By morning, Rowland vaguely regretted his decision to refuse the pills. He had slept only when exhaustion had overwhelmed pain, and that had not been often or for long enough. And so, by the time new light first broke, Rowland was less likely, or even able, to dismiss Clyde's concerns about infection and inevitable death. Otis Norcross also gave up trying to dissuade them from leaving what he'd clearly come to regard as the only safe place.

"You'll have to come with us," Milton told Norcross. "We found you; Costello and his gang are bound to do so too. Fitzgerald is a storyteller and this is one helluva story—I wouldn't be surprised if he's sent the manuscript in already."

Norcross shook his head.

"Look, mate," Clyde said. "We need to get Rowly to a doctor. But we're not going to let anything happen to you either. Once Rowly has settled the estate on you, there will be no point in anybody trying to kill you."

Norcross's eyes widened. "They're trying to kill me? Who's trying to kill me?"

Clyde exhaled, exasperated. "The people who think they are more entitled to Danny's estate than you are. Why else are you hiding?"

"From the hospital. I can't go back—they'll force me to take the drugs again..."

"We haven't got time for this," Milton said as he helped Clyde get Rowland to his feet.

Edna intervened. "Please, Mr. Norcross."

Norcross began to rock.

"Drive to Charlotte," Rowland said. "We'll find a doctor there."

"Rowly, that's nearly three hours' drive," Clyde said.

"We can't stop in Asheville," Rowland said slowly, forcing out the words. "Charlotte will be safer for all of us."

"Would you help me gather up the blankets, Mr. Norcross?" Edna decided not to give the man an option. She understood he was scared, but she had held Rowland's hand through the night, soothed the fevers, felt him tense with every slight movement, and she knew he was in agony.

Whether he was persuaded or whether it was that life in the asylum had conditioned him to allow decisions to be made for him, Norcross complied. They lay Rowland down on the back seat, with his head on Edna's lap and wrapped in blankets to protect him from the cold and the shudder of the car as it moved.

Norcross crouched on the floor of the Cadillac, where he would not be seen. Milton had suggested the precaution, both to make Norcross feel safer and to give Rowland more room. It was probably not a comfortable way to travel, but for the moment it would do.

By not sparing the Madame X, Clyde managed to cut the journey to about two and a half hours. Charlotte was a much larger city than Asheville, and that fact alone comforted them with perceived anonymity. He pulled the vehicle into the first hospital they passed, and he and Milton took Rowland in. Edna waited in the car with Norcross, who could not be induced to enter a hospital for any reason.

The nurses seemed shocked to see them.

Milton explained that there had been an archery accident, which they had treated with whisky and makeshift dressings. The sister directed them to St. Peter's Hospital on Seventh.

"We can pay," Milton said, thinking that might be the problem.

"This is a black hospital, Mr..."

"Isaacs. Couldn't you just help him? Please. We're not from here, and we're afraid we may have delayed too long already."

The nurse glanced at Rowland. The bandages had loosened and his shoulder had started bleeding again with all the movement, coating dried blood with new crimson. "I'll have someone see him, but then you'll have to go to St. Peter's."

Dr. Lennon was a young man. He seemed rather impressed with the wound but not daunted. "The shoulder's not a good place to be injured, usually you lose some function, if not the arm entirely, but this" —he moved his head to inspect the exit wound— "is in as good a place as you could hope for. Above the collarbone and down through the fleshy part of the upper back... Shot from an elevation, I'd say. It hasn't hit any bone and the shaft was clearly fairly narrow. Amazing it didn't go all the way through."

"It was stopped by a tree," Clyde admitted.

"That would explain it."

He turned to Clyde and Milton. "When you removed the arrow, gentlemen, was it intact?"

"I snapped off the fletching and pulled it through.... Actually, we left the arrow where it was and moved Rowly."

"Did it snap cleanly? Could there possibly be a splinter left in there?"

"I was careful to score it first." Clyde rubbed his head trying to picture the shaft which, as far as he knew, was still in the tree. "I'm pretty sure there weren't any splinters. Do you think there might be? He hasn't got blood poisoning has he, doctor?"

"You cleaned the wound with whisky?"

"An entire bottle of single malt," Milton said.

Lennon nodded gravely. "It doesn't seem to be infected, but it might have been better just to let him drink it."

"He's in a lot of pain," Clyde said doubtfully.

"That would be because someone shot an arrow through his shoulder."

Rowland smiled now, despite everything. "I guess that could have something to do with it."

"We'll clean the wound again with a more conventional antiseptic, and then dress it properly."

"Thank you," Rowland said, relieved that this wasn't going to be more complicated.

Milton and Clyde were invited to wait outside while Lennon and a nurse cleaned Rowland up and dealt with the wound.

"You don't see many arrow injuries these days," Lennon said curiously. "How did this happen?"

"My fault entirely," Rowland replied. "I moved into the path of the arrow."

"Are you sure?"

"Yes. It was an accident."

"You seem to have had a couple of unusual injuries." Lennon's gaze stopped on the swastika-shaped scar. "Cigarette burns."

"Yes."

"Quite a few." He observed the scar more closely. "How long have you been burning yourself?"

"For God's sake, I didn't do this!" Rowland said mortified. "Why would I...why would anybody—"

Lennon shrugged. "Folks do unusual things, Mr. Sinclair."

"I didn't do this."

"The gentlemen who brought you in—"

"They're not responsible for it either." Rowland tried to explain. "I was in Germany a couple of years ago. I crossed the wrong people. This was one of the consequences."

It was difficult to tell whether Lennon recognised the swastika as the emblem of the Nazis, or whether he believed Rowland's account of how he came by the scar. The physician returned his attention to the arrow wound. "You'll need to have the dressing changed at least once a day. Keep it dry, as immobile as possible, and clean." He regarded Rowland dubiously. "If you don't mind my saying, Mr. Sinclair, you and your companions look like you might have slept in the wilderness last night. I would not recommend that again."

"No. Neither would I, Dr. Lennon. It was rather uncomfortable."

"St. Peter's would probably admit you."

"I don't think that's necessary. I fully intend to sleep in a bed tonight."

"Very well. If you should experience any significant elevation of pain, fever, or swelling, you should go into St. Peter's immediately."

~~∽§∾~~

The Blue Mountain Inn, where the Australians and Otis Norcross checked in, was in the centre of Charlotte—just a couple of blocks from the city square. It was not a first-class establishment of the kind to which Rowland Sinclair was accustomed, but it was clean and conveniently located, and its manager did not baulk sufficiently at the state of them to claim there were no vacancies.

Milton described a series of mostly concocted misfortunes which had led to their current appearance, and Rowland provided whatever additional financial persuasion was necessary. Indeed, the proprietor, a Harry Whitmont, became very accommodating. He put them in his best rooms, which, though far from opulent, had adjoining bathrooms and were perfectly comfortable.

Moved by Milton's account of how they had been set upon on the road by bandits who'd stabbed Rowland and stolen much of their luggage, he organised a nearby gentlemen's boutique and his wife's dressmaker to attend their rooms with the necessities. On Rowland's request, he also arranged for a barber, and though they would probably miss lunch, which was served from twelve to one, Whitmont promised that his wife, who he assured them was the best cook in North Carolina, would accommodate them regardless.

The direction to keep his wound dry at all costs made bathing awkward and slow, but Rowland was not a man accustomed to his current level of dishevelment, and so he persevered. By the time he'd managed to wash and shave, fresh shirts had been delivered to the suite he was sharing with Milton. Clyde and Norcross were in the other suite and Edna in a room on her own. There didn't seem to be many other guests in the Blue Mountain.

Milton helped him ease the shirt on. Whilst Dr. Lennon had impressed the importance of moving his arm as little as possible, he had not bound it in a manner that precluded sleeves. Consequently, with a little help, Rowland could still pull on a shirt and jacket.

"Slip your hand into your waistcoat," Milton advised. "That way you won't move it accidentally. And you'll look just like Napoleon Bonaparte."

Rowland dismissed the suggestion. He had no desire to look like Napoleon Bonaparte, and he was still in enough pain to remind him sufficiently not to move his arm.

Despite Mrs. Whitmont's offer to send their meals up to

their rooms on trays, they ate together in the hotel's dining room so that they could decide what to do next. It being an hour after lunch and a couple of hours before dinner service, the dining room was empty and so, essentially, private.

Edna came down in a long-sleeved town dress. Appalled by her roughly shorn scalp, the dressmaker had summoned a milliner, who had provided the sculptress with several embellished skullcaps which admirably and stylishly disguised the loss of her hair. The one she'd chosen to wear this day was white and featured a spray of partially stripped feathers on one side. Rowland marvelled that, after everything that had happened, she could emerge looking so exquisite. Milton told her she looked like a chicken.

A half hour with the barber had transformed Otis Norcross. His wild white hair had been cut in a manner that was more distinguished, and he was shaved and dressed in a suit, which, while not bespoke or perfectly cut, transformed him from a fugitive to a gentleman. He still did not look entirely like Daniel's sketch, but there was now a distinct resemblance to the man in the drawing.

It was possibly because they had all missed several meals that they were able to do justice to the sheer volume of food with which Mrs. Whitmont laid the table. For a while they just ate, trying to bury memories of beef jerky soup with eggs and cornbread and a large variety of deep-fried morsels.

Edna watched Rowland, concerned that they were treating his injury too trivially. But he was obviously hungry, and she reasoned that the seriously ill rarely had an appetite. He caught her gaze and smiled. "I'm well, Ed. Really."

They spoke about heading for Boston immediately, but Edna would not hear of it.

"There's no reason to believe anyone will find us here," she said quietly. "Rowly is supposed to be on bedrest."

"I can rest in the car," Rowland said. "I can't drive anyway."

"I think Ed's right," Clyde said. "You look like hell, and tomorrow is soon enough. Costello and his clowns will have assumed we headed straight for Boston. This way we make sure we don't accidentally catch up with them. Our immediate problem is what we are going to do with Otis here until you've sacked Burr, Mayfair and Wilkes and settled the estate."

"Wait a minute," Norcross interrupted. "Why has Danny's will caused all this fuss?"

Rowland explained then the contents of Daniel Cartwright's will—the comparatively small bequests to his siblings, the major devolvement to Otis Norcross, and the codicils and stipulations which required Rowland Sinclair and only Rowland Sinclair to administer the will.

"Danny did that? Why would he do that?"

"Because he wanted you to inherit his estate," Rowland replied.

"But his family. Molly… That's cruel. Danny wasn't cruel."

Rowland recalled having similar thoughts, being surprised that his late friend had not at least made more generous provision for his sister. "He must have had his reasons."

"Can I refuse it? Give it back to his family?"

Rowland shrugged. "I expect you can. We'll have to talk to the lawyers."

"The lawyers you want to fire," Norcross clarified. "Why do you want to fire them?"

Rowland groaned. How had this become so complicated?

Milton explained their suspicions. "Oliver Burr was the only one who knew where we were going. Costello and his thugs arrived at the hotel at which he booked our accommodation. And they used his name to lure Rowly away from Edna at the Copley."

Norcross moved his eyes to Edna. "I wondered what had happened to you."

Rowland began to intervene, to divert the conversation, but Edna stopped him. "It's all right. He deserves to know what he's walking into. He may want to run like the devil." She told Otis Norcross what had happened to her.

"So these were the same people who followed you to the Grove Park Inn?"

"No, actually." Edna frowned as she shook her head, because the fact still perplexed her. "The men who took me and cut my hair had Irish accents. I'm sure."

"I'm so sorry," Norcross said. "For everything you've been through because of me. You must all hate me. I wouldn't blame you—"

"We don't hate you, Mr. Norcross," Edna said. "This is not your fault."

Norcross swallowed. "Do you think Danny was murdered because of this will?"

"I don't know," Rowland replied. "Look, Mr. Norcross"—he lowered his voice—"had Danny taken to wearing lipstick?"

"Lipstick?"

"Makeup."

"Yes, I know what it is. I was just surprised by the question. Why would he wear lipstick?"

"He was wearing red lipstick when he died."

Norcross sat back. "Well, surely that's some sort of clue, because I promise you Danny would not have been walking around with lipstick on, red or otherwise!"

"I can't think of any reason why anyone would apply lipstick to his body unless it was to humiliate him after death," Rowland said, troubled.

"Or to send a warning," Milton added. "Perhaps the killer was trying to send a warning to Otis in some perverse way."

Otis Norcross's face clouded. "Who do you think did this? Who do you think killed Danny?"

"I honestly have no idea," Rowland replied, choosing not to mention that he had until very recently wondered if Otis Norcross himself was the murderer. He inhaled sharply as he moved his left arm without thinking and the wound to his shoulder made itself known. "Do you know Daniel's brothers very well?"

"Too well, in some respects."

"What do you mean?"

"Danny and I met at Harvard." Norcross scanned the room to ensure that no one else had stepped into earshot or lurked at the door. When satisfied that he would not be overheard, he described Harvard in 1920, the excitement of college life, the passions of young men, his friendship with a fellow student called Daniel Cartwright. The love he described seemed so pure, so natural, that even Clyde, who was the most traditional of them, did not question it. Norcross told them of another student, Cyril Wilcox, who had taken his own life and the consequent investigations conducted by the dean and Harvard's president. The secret courts selected by President Lowell and held to determine guilt behind closed doors, the expulsions that resulted. He described the letters sent to every other institution of higher learning in America to ensure the guilty parties would be excluded from all of them.

"Our families were devastated, of course. Some pleaded for leniency, others sided with the dean."

"And Danny's family?"

"His parents were livid. Molly was abroad, and I don't know that she's ever officially been told."

"His brothers?"

Norcross paused. He rubbed his mouth. "Frank was shocked and outraged and ashamed. Geoffrey was not shocked." Otis Norcross's upper lip trembled. "Danny and I weren't named by any of our fellow students. Geoffrey

Cartwright spoke to Dean Greenough. It was Geoffrey who exposed his brother."

Chapter Thirty-Two

LOYALTY

What a fine thing is Loyalty—to a business organization, Loyalty to friends, Loyalty to home, Loyalty to country and, finest of all, Loyalty to church and to God.

May Loyalty Day and Loyalty Month cause us all to give practical evidence of our Loyalty to the highest and best things of human life.

City Bank & Trust Co.
ROANOKE ALABAMA
(Deposits up to $5,000 Insured by FDIC)

—The Roanoke Leader
(Roanoke, Alabama), October 2, 1935

~⊙~

There was silence for a while as they absorbed Otis Norcross's revelation.

"You're sure of this?" Rowland asked eventually, unable to comprehend such fraternal betrayal.

"Yes."

"What did Danny do?"

"I'm not sure he knew. I never told him."

"Why?"

"When it all came out, Danny and I weren't allowed to see each other, and then I was angry with him."

"With Danny?" Edna asked.

Norcross nodded. "He went to Oxford, escaped the disgrace, left it all behind. I didn't have the means to do that... so he left me behind too. I had to stay with the disgrace, with my mother's tears and my father's revulsion. I never got a degree. My parents told everyone that I was sick, that I'd left Harvard because of illness. One of my uncles got me a job working for a druggist in Rockport—he'd had a son of a similar inclination who'd taken his own life and somehow that made him more understanding than most—and I got on with it. I made a funny kind of half-life there."

"So when did you and Danny—"

"About ten years later, when he returned to Boston. We didn't talk about Harvard and the past, and for a while we were just friends. We went to parties, he introduced me to girls, we saw the latest shows. I didn't tell him about Geoffrey then because there didn't seem any point in hurting him. And then we were in love again." Norcross wiped a tear from his face. "A happy year, and we were found out again. I was committed to Highland Hospital in the dead of the night, and you know the rest."

"How were you found out? Was it Geoffrey?"

Norcross shook his head. "I don't know. We were so careful."

"Maybe that's what Danny meant about trusting no one," Milton said thoughtfully. "Maybe he found out about Geoffrey."

Rowland's eyes hardened as he thought about Geoffrey Cartwright, who treated Molly abominably and seemed to have no feeling but contempt for Danny, and who was hostile from the first, and violent. Geoffrey had always seemed to play second fiddle to Frank, but perhaps he'd always had his own more deadly agenda.

Mrs. Whitmont came into the dining room and asked if she could get them anything else at all. They thanked her sincerely for accommodating their late arrival, and Milton, in his way, complimented the meal in such lavish terms that the good lady blushed profusely.

"Don't worry, Mr. Norcross," Rowland said as they made their way up to their rooms. "We'll figure out a way to make sure that you'll be safe."

"Who I am is illegal, Mr. Sinclair. I'm not sure I'll ever be safe."

∽✑〜

Though Edna had her own room, she stayed in Rowland and Milton's suite. She and Milton took turns sleeping and kept an eye on Rowland lest any signs of infection develop. Milton had insisted on a couple of stiff drinks as a pain alleviant for both Rowland and himself.

"I know the arrow was in *your* shoulder, comrade," he said as he poured medicinal measures of gin. "But it was tough to watch." He shuddered.

So Rowland slept, rousing occasionally to check for Edna, to reassure himself that they were still in the eye of the storm into which Daniel Cartwright had sent them. Edna ordered dinner on a tray and sat with him while Milton went to the dining room with Clyde and Norcross.

"You look much better," she said, inspecting the bandages. Spots of blood about the size of Australian pennies had formed where the arrow had entered and exited his shoulder but nowhere else. The dark circles under his eyes were gone, and whilst he did still seem stiff and sore, the pain appeared to have settled and none of the signs of infection for which Dr. Lennon had asked them to watch had presented.

"I'm fine, Ed, stop worrying about me."

"Very well," she said, smiling. "I no longer care a wit." She poured him a cup of tea from the pot on the burgeoning tray. "What are we going to do with Mr. Norcross when we get back to Boston?"

Rowland frowned. "I don't know that we can risk taking him back to Boston. We may have to hide him somewhere for a while until I can retain new lawyers and make sure his parents can't have the poor chap committed again."

"How are we going to ensure that, Rowly?"

"I really don't know, Ed. That's why we need lawyers."

"Would the fact that he's now a very wealthy man help?" Edna asked.

"I'm afraid, if anything, it makes him more vulnerable. If he's declared incompetent, then his relatives will have control of his fortune."

"Oh, Rowly, this is awful. No wonder poor Danny was in such despair."

"We'll work something out, Ed," Rowland assured her, though he had no idea what. "Even if we have to take Norcross back to Australia with us, to keep him out of their reach."

~◎~

By morning Rowland had an idea about where they might hide Norcross. He broached the subject while Norcross was changing his dressings, something the American did quite expertly when he had conventional bandages and antiseptics at hand.

"You mentioned a druggist for whom you worked in Rockport..."

"Mr. Harrison? Yes—he taught me to dress wounds. Sometimes people would come into the shop who couldn't afford to see a doctor. He was a very kind man."

"Is he still there? In Rockport?"

"I don't know." Norcross grimaced. "I haven't seen him since I was sent to Highland Hospital. I expect he thinks I'm dead."

"Do you remember where he lived, where the shop was?"

"Yes, of course."

"And he knew the real reason you left Harvard?"

"Yes. It's why he wanted to help me. In memory of his boy, Jack."

"Do you think, if we told him everything, he might help us?"

"I don't know...this is a lot more than a job."

"It is," Rowland admitted. "Helping us could be dangerous."

"We could try," Norcross said. "Mr. Harrison was a thoroughly decent man. He was good to me when I thought the world had ended."

Before they left Charlotte, Rowland telephoned Oliver Burr. The lawyer sounded relieved. "Mr. Sinclair! I have been trying to reach you at the Grove Park Inn, but they had no idea where you were. I was about to send a search party."

"Someone already sent a search party, Mr. Burr." Rowland told him about the arrival of Costello and his associates.

"Oh, Christ! I trust you are somewhere safe now, Mr. Sinclair."

"We are, but you'll understand if I keep our location to myself."

"Why, you don't think I—"

"I don't know, Mr. Burr, but you were the only person

who knew where we were going, where we'd be staying. As you can imagine, I am reluctant to continue with Burr, Mayfair and Wilkes."

Silence for a moment. Then, "Look, Mr. Sinclair, I really wouldn't advise changing legal firms at this point in the proceedings."

"I don't know that I have any other choice."

"Let me look into how this could have happened, Mr. Sinclair, and let's talk when you return to Boston—you are returning, are you not?"

"Yes, I am."

"Then give me a chance to prove our bona fides, and if you remain unsatisfied, I will of course hand over the file to a firm of your choosing."

"Very well, Mr. Burr." Part of Rowland hoped that Burr would be able to prove his innocence in this regard. He had trusted the lawyer as, it seemed, had Daniel Cartwright, and it was galling as well as inconvenient to think that trust had been misplaced.

They took a different route back towards Boston, stopping in Philadelphia and Falmouth rather than Washington D.C., and even then, choosing humbler hotels than they otherwise might have. The further Norcross got from Asheville, the more stable he seemed to become. By the time they got into Massachusetts, it was difficult to believe he had been the wild, desperate fugitive who had shot Rowland with an archery set stolen from the mental asylum to which he'd been forcibly committed.

He recounted amusing anecdotes of the various film stars who had come to the hospital to be treated for "exhaustion," and talked about the work and rest programs which kept patients occupied and productive. In quieter moments he spoke of darker memories of freezing hydrotherapy and even more bitterly of chemical treatments which induced terror and seizures. "It was like being possessed," he said. "I bit down so hard my teeth shattered, and afterwards I couldn't talk or remember or fight...which I suppose was the purpose."

Edna, sitting between Rowland and Norcross, took his hand in both of hers. She could feel it shaking. "We promise you, Mr. Norcross, we will not let you be returned to Highland or any other mental hospital."

Norcross shook his head. "I'm not sure you'll be able to stop it, Miss Higgins. My parents buried me so that they could consign me to Highland indefinitely. They are determined that I not exist, one way or another."

"Well, you do exist," the sculptress said fiercely. "And we're going to make sure you're safe."

"We're passing through Salem," Milton announced. "Do you want to call on the Leonowskis?"

Rowland shook his head. "Let's make sure we don't drag them into this inadvertently."

Clyde agreed. They'd found Otis Norcross, but this was not over. Costello and his associates were still at large, as were the men who'd abducted and assaulted Edna. Frank and Geoffrey Cartwright were waging legal warfare—at the least. They had no idea who had killed Daniel Cartwright, and they didn't even know if they could trust Burr.

They arrived in Rockport late in the afternoon. The snow was several inches thick, but the road had been cleared. The druggist's shop was closed, but Norcross directed Milton to park the Cadillac around the back of the store, where Harrison had lived when he'd given a disgraced student a job.

A narrow iron staircase led to the residence above the shop. The Australians stood back as Norcross knocked on the door.

The door was opened almost immediately by an elderly man with a pipe. "Can I help you?"

"Mr. Harrison. It's me. Otis Norcross. I used to—"

Harrison stepped back and took the pipe out of his mouth. "Otis Norcross is dead. I was at his funeral."

"It's me, Mr. Harrison. I don't know what my parents buried, but it wasn't me. I've been away."

Harrison moved towards him and looked closely at his face. "Where do I keep the strychnine?"

Norcross's face fell. "I can't remember, Mr. Harrison. The treatment. I lost a lot. But I do recall you used to keep a flask of whisky in the till."

"Everybody keeps whisky in the till," he muttered. He looked out at the Australians standing behind Norcross. Edna was shivering.

"Who are these people.?"

"They helped me escape."

"Escape what?"

"The hospital."

Harrison sighed. "You'd better come in. The lady is cold."

Inside, Harrison's residence was cluttered. A portrait of a young man, fair and fine-featured, hung over the mantel. The Australians were drawn to the fire that burned brightly in a large brick hearth. Rowland moved to allow Edna to warm her hands near the flames. It was significantly colder here than in North Carolina or Boston.

There weren't enough chairs to accommodate them all, so Clyde, Milton, and Rowland stood while Edna sat beside Norcross on the couch. Harrison offered sherry and then sat down in the armchair and relit his pipe.

"So, Otis. Tell me why I paid good money to take flowers to your funeral only to find that you are not dead."

Norcross explained everything—what had happened to him, Daniel Cartwright, his escape from Highland, F. Scott Fitzgerald, the murder, and his survival in the forests of Asheville until he shot Rowland Sinclair with bow and arrow.

Rowland would probably have preferred he not be quite so forthcoming until they knew whether or not they could trust Harrison, but it seemed that once he began, Norcross could not stop. The story rushed out like a confession.

"I see," Harrison said when he was done. "Otis, are you sure you're not mad?"

"No madder than you, old man."

Harrison smiled. "Well, that'd be good enough for me."

Rowland told the old druggist about their encounters with Lombardo, Costello, and Brown and the abduction of Edna at the Copley, because he thought it only fair to tell the man what he might be getting into.

"So the Italian mob took her?" Harrison shook his head in disgust.

"I'm sure they were Irish," Edna said.

Harrison frowned. "Sounds like the Gustins. They used to run Boston, but their leaders are dead—murdered by the Italians." He shrugged. "Perhaps they're trying to retake their old territory. They'd never work with Lombardo."

"Splendid," Rowland muttered. "We're caught in the middle of a gang war."

"You do seem to have found a bit of hot water," Harrison agreed. "How can I help you?"

"We need to find someplace to stay within driving distance of Boston where we won't be noticed, just until we can figure out how to settle Danny's estate while keeping Mr. Norcross safe."

Harrison looked them up and down. "It seems to me that it's not just Otis's safety you should be worrying about."

"No, sir, but all the rest of it is about the estate Danny left Mr. Norcross. Once that's settled, there'll be no point in harming him or us."

Harrison tapped his pipe and puffed. "You can't stay here."

Chapter Thirty-Three

On the North Shore Calendar

Rockport already is planning for its annual ball for the artists' colony, which is to be held in August. Mrs Harrison Cady is chairman of the committee and she proposes to make the occasion more elaborate than ever. All through July and August the art colony of Rockport will put over an active social program which will include tours of studios and Saturday night dances for the artists and their friends.

—*Boston Globe*,
July 22, 1935

~⊗~

Norcross sucked in his breath. "Oh, of course."

"Half of Rockport files through here—it wouldn't be much of a hiding place."

"I understand, sir."

"But I have an idea." Harrison stood. "I look after a place on Bearskin Neck for a friend of mine. Fancies himself a painter—uses it in summer, and I keep an eye on it in winter. It's empty now, of course. There's no one staying on the Neck 'cept lobstermen and fishermen this time of year. It's colder than a banker's heart!"

Harrison squeezed between Milton and Clyde in the Cadillac and directed them down the street to Artist's Row on Bearskin Neck, a narrow peninsula that jutted out from the town centre into Rockport Harbour. Artist's Row itself ran along the edge of the water and was a street of sail lofts and fishermen's shacks, which were apparently rented to artists in the summer. In the winter they stood against the elements and were often empty but for an occasional actual fisherman. "The painters come for the light and stay on the Row because it's cheap, I expect. But even they are not mad or drunk enough to come of a winter."

He pointed out a red shack on the end of the wharf, which aside from its colour was like many others on the harbour. "That there is the Motive, famous now. Has turned up in hundreds of paintings as an accent or something."

Rowland laughed. If he were a landscape artist, he probably would have used the shack for precisely that purpose. It protruded into the harbour and upstaged the surrounding weathered grey buildings. Edna delighted in the Motive, its proportions and position. It anchored the composition. Milton reminded her it was a shed and not a sculpture.

They pulled up beside a sail loft towards the end of Artist's Row. The loft was a little dilapidated, but it was water- and windtight. Harrison lit a hurricane lamp just inside the door and bustled them in. The building included a large ground-floor room with a sleeping loft full of bunks. A rudimentary bathroom contained a tin bath and a shower. A fuel combustion stove with a few pots hanging above it and a rack of plates and cups were the extent of the kitchen.

"There're linens in that chest for the beds and plenty of blankets," Harrison said as he helped Clyde get a fire going in the brick fireplace. There was a large stack of firewood by the hearth and, Harrison assured them, there was more in the lean-to outside the back door. "Light the stove as well," he said, pointing out the pipework. "It warms the water for your baths."

It took them an hour or so to warm the loft to a point where it didn't hurt to breathe.

"Make sure you don't let the fire go out overnight, or it'll be a pretty miserable awakening," Harrison warned. "The fishermen here tend to get jolly fed up with the summer folk, so they're not likely to pay you any mind."

"Thank you, Mr. Harrison. I can't tell you how much we appreciate this," Rowland said.

Harrison placed his hand on Norcross's shoulder and pressed it warmly. "I should have known there was something afoot when Otis disappeared with nary a word. I should have known." He said goodnight then, promising to return in the morning once they'd had a chance to settle in. Clyde drove him back and returned with a massive box of items which it seemed had been harvested from Harrison's own larder—pies, a ham, eggs, bacon, chocolate, coffee, fruit cake, cream, and a bottle of port, as well as more blankets and fresh dressings for Rowland's shoulder.

The loft was by then warming slightly, and they were able to remove their gloves and overcoats.

Norcross and Milton had moved the loft's old settee and one easy chair in front of the fire and dragged over the trunks as extra seating so they could all huddle in the immediate radiance of the flames and make a picnic of dinner.

"Tomorrow, I'll drive to Boston, and retain another law

firm," Rowland said, helping himself to ham and washing it down with port in a tin cup. "I'll tell Burr to send them the files, and I'll get them to prepare whatever documents are necessary to settle Danny's estate on Mr. Norcross here. I'll also brief them to defend Mr. Norcross against attempts to recommit or arrest him."

"Arrest him?"

"For Danny's murder," Rowland said, choosing to leave unmentioned the indecency laws under which Norcross might also be charged. "We know you didn't kill him, Otis, but the police will probably consider you a suspect because—"

"I had a motive," Norcross finished. "Because of the will."

"I'm afraid so."

"I'd better go with you," Clyde said. "I'm not sure you should be driving just yet."

"My shoulder's good enough to drive."

"Not in this weather, Rowly. And remember, Burr has just to get rid of you for his alma mater to inherit Danny's entire estate."

Rowland screwed up his face. "You know, in the light of day, I can't see Oliver Burr killing a man for the sake of the old school tie."

Clyde agreed. "Yeah—I thought he was fair dinkum, too, Rowly, and I can't imagine anyone getting that worked up about the University of Sydney, but then Americans seem more attached to their colleges...and Burr was the only one who knew where we were."

"Talk to Mr. Burr before you retain another firm." Edna, having removed that day's hat, rubbed the rough stubble on her head. "He was very kind after you found me in that supply closet, and maybe there's another explanation."

Rowland put his arm around her as she curled up on the old settee beside him. "I'm beginning to wonder if the men who abducted Ed really were Lombardo's people."

"Costello and Brown got you away from Ed—"

"Actually, it was a chap called Alexander Smythe who convinced me to get into the car. And the only reason he didn't walk Ed to her door was because she would not hear of it." He thought of something then, a question they hadn't asked. "Ed, the woman who gave you the fur coat for Molly, was she Clyde's Jean? The woman with the dog at Marion's who was with Costello and Brown in Asheville."

Edna answered definitely and without hesitation. "No. The woman who asked me to return the coat to Molly had black hair and green eyes. She was smaller than Jean. I saw Jean at the party; I would have recognised her."

"So I wonder," Rowland said thoughtfully, "if the two things had nothing to do with each other."

Milton frowned. "Which would mean the bastards who took Ed had nothing to do with Lombardo and Frank?"

"Which may be why they attempted to snatch Molly as well."

"But who else would have any reason to abduct either of them?"

"Geoffrey? Given what Mr. Norcross has told us about his expulsion from Harvard, perhaps Geoffrey's resentment ran deeper than we realised. And he was convinced I was having some kind of affair with his sister. Molly seemed afraid of him—that's why I moved her into the Copley."

"Danny was very fond of Molly," Norcross said quietly. "He cared what she thought of him—it's why he kept what he was from her, never took her into his confidence about me."

Rowland nodded. "She assumed that Danny was in love with a woman in the beginning."

Edna sighed. "What a mess we make when we have to deny part of ourselves."

Rowland tightened his arm around her. Since her abduction had been raised, she'd been shaking—so slightly that only he could perceive the tremor in her body. Rowland struggled to appear unmoved against an internal, unspoken surge of rage and love, of desperation to protect, and of longing only intensified by that one night. The conflict was consuming and confusing, and yet he had given Edna his word that they would go on unchanged.

"Rowly?" Clyde was speaking to him.

"Sorry... What were you saying?"

"Just that if it snows tonight, we might have to shovel the car out in the morning."

Rowland nodded. "It should be easier than burying a cow."

As Clyde had predicted, it snowed overnight, but not heavily, and the roads were still traversable. They found shovels in the lean-to where the extra wood was stacked and cleared the driveway and the sidewalk in front of the loft. Rowland and Clyde decided to drive to Boston that morning. It was only forty-odd miles away, though the weather would probably add at least an hour to the journey.

With his eye on Milton, Clyde impressed the importance of keeping a low profile.

Edna laughed. "It's as if you suspect we'll run for office and go dancing in your absence, Clyde."

Milton raised his brow. "Actually, we could probably recruit a few party members from the ranks of the fishermen."

While Milton and Clyde argued, Edna dug around in the Cadillac until she found the game Leonowski had given them. "The three of us will stay put till you get back. We'll see if this *Monopoly* deserves all the fuss being made of it." She met Clyde's eye. "You and Rowly will be careful, won't you?"

"I'm a cautious man, Ed," Clyde replied. "Do not be fooled by the company I keep."

Milton snorted and, taking the box from Edna, returned to the relative warmth of the loft. Edna tried to persuade Rowland and Clyde to drink coffee to ward off the cold before they left.

"Ed, there are towns and villages all along the way; we won't ever be far from one, and the Cadillac has a heater. We're driving to Boston, not joining Mawson in Antarctica."

"Yes, I know. I'm sorry."

Clyde looked at her. "Ed, if you don't feel safe here, we can find somewhere else, or do this differently."

"Don't be silly!" Edna pulled her wool felt cap down over her ears. "Nobody knows we're here. It's you and Rowly I'm worried about. If they realise that we've found Mr. Norcross, they'll be angry."

"Sadly, Ed, we still have no idea who 'they' are."

"Which makes it all the more dangerous. There was no murder weapon found. So whoever shot Danny still has a gun."

Rowland walked the sculptress back into the loft, while Clyde warmed up the car. "Ed, if anything was to happen to me, you know to wire Wil immediately, don't you?"

"Oh, Rowly, that's not what I—"

"I know, but promise me you'll just wire Wil. He's not—"

"Like Danny's brothers? Yes, I know. And I promise... But, Rowly, you're not to allow anything to happen to you, do you understand?"

He smiled. "I do."

～◌◌～

Clyde took the wheel. The roads were treacherous, but he had learned to drive on snow-covered mountain roads in the Australian High Country. Still, it was slow if steady going. For a while they didn't talk, keeping their eyes on the road and continuing in easy silence.

Then Clyde spoke. "You know, mate, it's not Frank or Geoffrey or their hired thugs that pose the greatest threat to Norcross. It's his parents. As long as they're around, he could be sent back to Highland Hospital or some other nuthouse."

Rowland smiled faintly. "You're not suggesting we do away with them, are you, old man?"

"Of course not. I'm just not sure we can make this right for Norcross."

Rowland flexed the hand of his left arm, testing the limits of comfortable movement. "We have to, Clyde. The poor chap has already been to hell."

"I want to, Rowly. I'm just not sure there is a way. You, me, Milt, Ed—we could all be committed by our families. Milt probably should be. But, mate, even Danny with all his plans and his money couldn't get Norcross out of Highland legally."

"But he did get him out."

"Yes. I'm just saying that we may also have to resort to helping Norcross bolt."

Rowland groaned. Clyde spoke sense; he nearly always did.

"What's happened here?" Clyde slowed down and pulled over behind a steaming, overheated Ford. A gentleman climbed out of the Ford and approached the passenger side. Rowland opened his door.

"Good morning," Clyde called.

"Not so much," the man replied, glancing back at his stationary vehicle. "She seems to have blown something. I was just getting ready to walk into town."

"We'd be happy to take you in," Rowland said. "It'd be a cold walk."

"Much obliged, Mr...."

"Sinclair." Rowland introduced Clyde, who offered to have a look at the Ford.

The stranded motorist shook their hands. "Larry Vincent. Thank you for the offer, Mr. Jones, but Jesus Hopping Christ! It's colder than a witch's tit out here, and I figure there's not much you could do for her." He climbed into the back seat. "I'm not abandoning her, mind—I'd hate you gentlemen to think I was the kind of fella to just discard an automobile on the road to Manchester, but it is cold and I think she just needs to cool down… So what say we leave her here to contemplate her behaviour for a while?"

"Certainly," Rowland said, mildly amused. They were only a couple of miles from Manchester.

So they pulled onto the road again with a passenger.

"Are you from Manchester, Mr. Vincent?" Clyde asked.

"No, no… I'm from Boston. I have a cottage in Manchester. I come out here from time to time, to get away from it all. And what about you boys? You're clearly not from here."

"We're just passing through," Rowland replied vaguely.

"Well, it's a magnificent spot in the summer! Surely you've heard folks talk of the Singing Beach—well worth a look," Vincent boomed. "Of course, this isn't beach weather— Christ, it ain't—but at least let me buy you a drink for your trouble."

The remaining miles to Manchester were travelled to the sound of Vincent's friendly, enthusiastic monologue and appeals to the messiah. The American, it seemed, was the president of a beer company. They both stepped out of the Cadillac to shake his hand when they dropped him off in the seaside hamlet of Manchester.

Vincent handed them a card. "When you boys come back this way, call me and let me thank you properly."

It was only as they were climbing back into the motorcar that Clyde noticed the couple in the window at the Central Street Café, the restaurant across the road.

"Rowly, isn't that Molly Cartwright?"

Chapter Thirty-Four

Here and There

The "insanity defense" in murder cases generally arouses a cynical smile, these days. Aside from the fact that unscrupulous lawyers have too often perverted it to improper ends, one big trouble with it is that our legal definition of insanity is faulty. In most states a man is legally sane, and responsible for his acts, if he can distinguish right from wrong. What we need to realize is that emotional instability can be worse than intellectual instability. A man perfectly able to tell right from wrong can nevertheless be swept off his feet by an emotional storm he cannot control.

—*Fitchburg Sentinel*
(Fitchburg, Massachusetts), February 28, 1935

At that moment Molly Cartwright looked up, and they watched her notice them. She seemed startled at first, speaking to her companion before she waved. Rowland sighed. He'd forgotten that she was going to stay with friends near Rockport. Now that she'd seen them, they couldn't not stop. She emerged from the restaurant, smiling broadly.

"What are we going to tell her we're doing here, Rowly?"

"I have no idea."

"She's crossing the road," Clyde warned.

"We'd better get out and say hello."

"Rowly!" Molly beamed, dimples and warmth from a cocoon of mink. "And Clyde! Whatever are you boys doing here?"

"We just thought we'd come out for a drive," Rowland said. "Clyde's scouting landscapes to paint, and we were told about the seaside villages."

She looked at them sceptically. "You're going to paint… in the snow?"

"We're Australian," Clyde said. "We're a little tougher than American artists."

Molly blinked. And then as realisation dawned that Clyde was joking, she laughed.

"Well, even the most rugged painters must eat breakfast, and that place over there"—she pointed back at the Central Street Café—"serves the most delicious fried clam plate."

"You were just there," Rowland said. "Haven't you already had breakfast?"

"I stopped for a cup of tea. My appetite is intact."

"And the gentleman you were with? We wouldn't want to interrupt—"

"Adam?" She laughed. "He's a local. Manchester is a friendly town—everyone knows one another. Adam stopped to chat when I was drinking my tea."

"He's gone," Rowland observed.

Molly smiled mischievously up at him. "If I didn't know any better, Rowly, I'd think you were jealous."

Rowland found himself unsure how to respond. He glanced at Clyde.

Clyde grimaced. "You know what, Rowly? I'm hungry. We have time to have breakfast before we get back to Boston."

"Of course you do!" Molly hooked one arm through Rowland's and the other through Clyde's, and allowed them to escort her across the road. "I'm driving to Boston myself today. Perhaps I could come with you."

She took them to the table that she had not long vacated. If the waitress thought Molly's return odd, she did not say.

"So you must catch me up on everything since we last met." Molly removed her coat and hung it on the back of her chair. "It's been simply ages. How is Edna?"

"She's well," Rowland replied.

"I'm glad. I'm so sorry she had to go through that... Tell me"—Molly looked from Rowland to Clyde and then back—"did you find Otis Norcross?"

"I gather you were engaged to him," Rowland said.

"I was betrothed to *an* Otis Norcross." She bit her lip. "I don't talk about it because it's still painful. Surely you understand that. Otis died long ago. He couldn't be who Danny meant...unless..." She pulled back.

"Unless?" Rowland prompted.

"Otis and I were engaged to be married. Perhaps Danny wrote his will before Otis died, perhaps he left his fortune to Otis as a way of taking care of me." Her eyes welled. "Oh, God, that's what it must have been. Danny didn't hate me, he didn't abandon me...he just neglected to change his will."

Rowland glanced at Clyde, wrong-footed by Molly's conclusions about her brother's intentions and unsure of how to tell her that Daniel's will had been made long after Otis Norcross was supposed to have died.

"Had your engagement been announced?" Clyde asked carefully.

Molly fumbled for a handkerchief. Rowland handed her his.

"Thank you, Rowly. No, poor darling Otis died a couple of days before the banns were read." She wiped her eyes. "Otis was the love of my life. Danny knew that—I think he gave Otis the courage to ask for my hand...and then I lost Otis and... I don't know how I would have got through that time without Danny. He was my rock."

"Why do you think Danny would leave his fortune to Otis Norcross and not to you directly?" Rowland asked gently.

"To protect me from Frank and Geoffrey, I expect. If the money wasn't strictly speaking mine, they couldn't ask me for it." Her face shone. "Danny was providing for me and protecting me at the same time! Oh, Rowly, I can't tell you what this means to me. In a way, the will made me believe I'd lost both of them. You've given me back my brother's love."

Rowland struggled with what he knew...what he thought he knew. He didn't want to lie to Molly, but how could he tell her Otis Norcross was alive without revealing the rest of it?

"If you'll excuse me for a minute, gentlemen." Molly rose from the table. "I might just powder my nose."

"What do you think, Rowly?" Clyde asked as soon as she was out of earshot. "Norcross didn't mention he was engaged to Danny's sister!"

"The banns hadn't been read, so they weren't officially, but it fits with what his mother said about hoping Molly would be her daughter-in-law."

"Jesus, Mary, and Joseph, could he be playing us all?"

"Bloody hell! We've left him with Milt and Ed."

"Let's not panic, Rowly." Clyde tried to remain calm. "He's not armed, and Milt won't let anything happen to Ed. Not to mention that the engagement could simply have been one of the memories lost as an aftereffect of the drugs they gave him."

"I know. But we should go back."

They were standing when Molly returned. Rowland had already taken care of the cheque.

"What's the matter?" Molly asked, alarmed by the sudden tension in their manners.

"We've just realised we should get back quickly."

"To Boston? Could I come with you? The company would be—"

"I'm afraid there are a couple of things we need to look into before we go to Boston, Molly. In fact we might not get back to Boston today," Rowland replied. "I'm sorry."

"But where will you stay?"

"We'll find somewhere."

"Well then, promise you'll come get me tomorrow. I'll meet you here at ten o'clock."

"I don't know…"

"Please, Rowly." Molly licked her lips nervously. "I know it sounds silly, but I don't want to go back to Boston on my own."

Anxious to be on their way, Rowland relented. "Yes, of course. Would you like us to see you back to—"

She smiled. "No. The friends I'm staying with are just a couple of buildings away in the gallery. I'll go with them."

Rowland tipped his hat.

"And thank you, Rowly," she said in a way that made him feel like a heel for being so eager to get away.

They wasted no time turning the Cadillac around to return the way they had come. Neither spoke, both struggling with the possibility that they had made a terrible mistake, and going over every moment for signs they'd missed. The road had become less treacherous since they'd traversed it that morning, and so they made good time through Gloucester and back to Rockport and Artist's Row.

The street was quiet except for the odd car of tourists come to view the red fish shack, and a few lobstermen setting out. Clyde pulled the motorcar into the yard behind the loft. Rowly was out of the car before the engine was turned off. As he reached the door, he heard Edna cry, "No!"

He pounded on the door. "Ed!"

Clyde caught up with him and began pounding too.

Milton opened the door. The poet regarded them, surprised. "What the dickens are you blokes doing back...and where's the fire?"

Rowland stared into the loft. The board game was set up on a trunk in front of the fire, Edna kneeling on a pillow next to it, Norcross in the armchair looking startled. "Um...I thought Ed was..."

Milton pulled a face. "She just shrieked because she's losing. She hasn't figured out a way to cheat yet."

"I was not. You're not allowed to buy everything!"

"I am if I land on the property!"

"You're behaving like a...a *capitalist*!"

Milton inhaled, affronted. "Now that's uncalled for."

"What are you doing back?" Edna asked Rowland and Clyde. "You couldn't possibly have got to Boston and back already."

Rowland, if truth be told, felt a little ridiculous now. "We ran into Molly," he said, watching Norcross's reaction. He definitely seemed to react to her name.

"What do you mean *ran into*?" Edna asked, alarmed.

"Sorry—I didn't mean with the car. I forgot that she was staying around here... We saw her in Manchester."

"So why did you come back?"

"She said something which we wanted to clarify with Mr. Norcross before we spoke to the lawyers."

Norcross looked up sharply. Rowland sat on the second trunk so that he was between Norcross and Edna. "Molly seems to be under the impression that you and she were engaged to be married, Mr. Norcross."

"Are you asking me if we were?"

"Yes, I guess I am."

Norcross looked wounded. "Oh. No, we weren't."

"Then why—"

Norcross swallowed. "I think she might have hoped..."

"Why?" Edna asked. "Why would she have hoped?"

Norcross's shoulders slumped a little. "Danny introduced me to Molly; he wanted us to be friends. We didn't realise—"

"That she was falling in love with you?" Edna said gently.

"When we realised she saw me as more than a pal, it was too late. Danny told me to stop returning her letters and calls and she would get over it. By then she'd met my mother and... It was a mess. I tried to tell her that I didn't... I couldn't... but Molly can be single-minded."

"Did she suspect—?"

"Never. Danny could not bear her thinking he'd betrayed her."

"So when she says you were engaged, she's lying?"

"Not lying exactly. I think she really thought we would get married eventually...that she would convince me."

"Your mother seemed to think—"

"My mother's always suspected about me... So when she met Molly, she welcomed her to the family before she could get away. And then after they'd consigned me to the hospital, I suppose telling people that Molly might have been her daughter-in-law ensured there'd be no rumours."

Rowland rubbed his jaw. It was plausible, believable even. Molly was difficult to deter—he could see her refusing to be rebuffed.

"Mr. Sinclair," Norcross ventured tentatively, "you didn't think that I could be a danger to Miss Higgins or Mr. Isaacs, did you?"

"Of course not," Rowland lied. "We just wanted to establish the facts before we briefed an attorney. Molly seems to think Danny leaving his estate to you is proof positive that you were his sister's intended."

Clyde folded his arms as he looked down at the Monopoly board. "I presume that you have met Frank and Geoffrey as well?"

Norcross shook his head. "I met Geoffrey at Harvard, but Danny never introduced me to Frank. We were careful. We rarely met in Boston."

"Where did you meet?"

"Different places. Washington, D.C., Manchester—"

"Manchester?"

"There's a little gallery there that used to buy Danny's work." Norcross smiled. "In return he bought more paintings than he sold."

Rowland nodded, remembering the gallery mentioned in the residual clause of Daniel Cartwright's will. "Weren't people curious about you?" he asked. The Daniel Cartwright he knew had stood out in a crowd.

"They might have been," Norcross said, "but they didn't ask. People round here are fairly reserved. They tend to ignore you until you've been around for few years at least."

"I see," Rowland said, frowning. Molly clearly found the town more welcoming. Had Danny and Otis been ostracised, or had the gentleman with Molly—the one she'd called Adam—been more than a friendly local? Rowland could not escape the sense that he was familiar.

"It's irrelevant whether Otis met Frank Cartwright personally," Milton pointed out, returning them to the earlier point. "Frank and Geoffrey have the same interests as far as Danny's will is concerned. Surely we can assume that if one Cartwright knows something, then they all do."

"I don't know that Molly is working with her brothers," Rowland said. "They certainly bully her into cooperating with their legal actions, but I don't think she's actually working with them."

Milton's brow rose sceptically, but he said nothing. In the poet's experience, Rowland Sinclair laboured under an absurd, gallant need to give women the benefit of the doubt. He cracked his knuckles. "Well, if you're quite satisfied that Norcross is not murdering Ed and me, I'd better get back to bankrupting them."

Chapter Thirty-Five

THE WOMEN WHO POISON
THEMSELVES

Kathleen Norris Says:

There is a poison that thousands of women keep on tap and take regularly. It is the poison called jealousy. And jealousy and insanity are first cousins.

Our social scheme today permits the man to feel himself acting quite honourably when he leaves the woman of whom he has grown tired and goes to the new love; and his discarded wife is only setting herself against the current when she protests.

Nine times out of ten the smarter thing, the thing that makes for happiness in the end, is NOT to let him go...

—Dayton Daily News
(Dayton, Ohio), 11 August 1935

~∽

"What do you suppose those blokes in the Chevy are waiting for?" Clyde murmured as he stacked firewood into the crook of Rowland's good arm. They'd left the others to finish the board game while they brought in more fuel. The black Chevrolet was parked diagonally across the road from the loft. The man behind the wheel was reading the paper. The passenger was smoking.

Rowland glanced at the road in either direction. "There's a chap walking down from the post office—maybe they're waiting for him."

Clyde looked in the direction Rowland indicated. He relaxed. "I think we're both getting a bit jumpy. I had myself convinced we'd come back to a bloodbath."

Rowland's smile was wry. "I nearly broke down the door to save Ed from losing a board game."

"So what do you think—about Molly and Norcross?"

"I don't know," Rowland said. "Something's not right. That chap Molly was with... I'm sure I've seen him before somewhere. I just can't remember where."

Clyde frowned. They'd only seen him for a fleeting moment and from a distance. But Rowland was good with faces.

"Do you believe Norcross?" Clyde asked.

"About Molly? Yes." Rowland leaned against the post of the woodshed, while Clyde filled his own arms with logs. "Do you remember Molly's letters to Danny? The pretty man who wasn't interested in her initially. I suspect that may have been our friend, Norcross. Of course the idea that Danny favoured Norcross in the will as a way of keeping his sister's inheritance out of the clutches of her brothers is nonsense. In fact, I doubt even Molly believes it."

"So, is it a brave face, or a deceitful one?"

"I honestly don't know...unless..." Rowland's eyes narrowed. He didn't finish his sentence, turning and running into the loft. "Ed!"

He dropped the firewood into a basket by the hearth as the sculptress looked up from the game, her hands full of toy money. "Rowly, what's wrong?"

"Ed, the coat you were taking to Molly when you were dragged into the supply closet—it wasn't there when we found you. What happened to it?"

"I don't know." She looked at him uneasily. "I expect they took it with them."

"What kind of fur was it?"

Edna shrugged. "Polar bear? You know I don't like fur, Rowly. It was white. They must have stolen it from Molly."

"Why?"

"Her name was embroidered on a tag inside the collar. That's why I didn't think to be suspicious."

"Dammit!"

"Rowly, what's wrong?"

"She was wearing that coat today."

Edna put down the toy money. She was a little pale, but remained calm, reasoned. "Rowly, darling, she might have bought another one after the first was stolen. Or she may have had two white furs in the first place. I have two almost identical navy anoraks."

He shook his head. "I knew I'd seen the man she was with before. He was at the will reading. He works for Burr, Mayfair and Wilkes."

"So what are you saying, Rowly?" Milton asked.

"I'm not sure. Frank and Geoffrey always said Otis Norcross didn't exist; they're challenging Danny's competency but not Molly. From the first day we met her, she pushed the idea that Otis Norcross killed Danny."

"Until today," Clyde walked in and deposited more fire-wood into the basket, "when Molly decided that Danny left his money to his sister's intended husband and then neglected to update his will when the poor bloke died."

"That was just to divert us from that fact that she didn't mention she ever knew an Otis Norcross," Rowland said.

"So what about this bloke from Burr, Mayfair and Wilkes?" Milton asked. "Is Molly working with Danny's lawyers?"

"She's working with at least one."

Milton left the game and paced, pulling at his beard as he always did when thinking. "Rowly, hypothetically, what would happen if Mr. Norcross had killed Danny—in terms of his estate, I mean?"

"Well, Mr. Norcross wouldn't be allowed to inherit. The residual clause would take effect and a gallery in Manchester that used to show Danny's work would get everything that was left to Otis."

"So Molly wouldn't benefit?"

"I can't see how. There couldn't be a pecuniary self-interest behind her insistence that Danny's heir killed him."

Milton stared hard at Norcross as if he were trying to read the answer in the American's features. "What if she knew he was alive? What if this is about revenge?"

"If she knew he was alive, she's waited a long time to do something about it," Edna said quietly.

"Rowly, mate." Clyde beckoned from the boarded windows at the front of the building. He was peering through the slats of wood that were nailed across the frame. Rowland joined him. Milton, Edna, and Norcross also moved to the windows.

Rowland cursed. The Chevrolet had been joined by a Ford and a PD Plymouth convertible.

Edna gasped and pulled away from the window. She was shaking.

"Ed?" Afraid she might faint, Rowland grabbed her around the waist.

"The men in the closest black car... Oh, Rowly, they're the men from the Copley."

"Are they just?" Milton said hotly. "We wouldn't mind having a word with those bastards."

"The Plymouth is Molly's car," Rowland said, his arm still around Edna.

She was steadier now. "I'm all right," she said firmly.

"That Ford belongs to our friend from the road...Larry Vincent," Clyde said. "He's brought friends."

"How many are we looking at?" Milton asked.

"Half a dozen men plus Molly," Clyde reported. "We have to decide quickly. Are we going to try to run or batten down and defend?"

"We've got nothing to defend with, Clyde." Rowland thought quickly. "I'll go out the front and speak to them. You and Milt take Ed and Norcross out the back."

"No." Edna shook her head vigorously. "They'll kill you."

"I'm the only one they can't kill if they don't want Danny's entire estate to go to Yale."

"I'll go with Rowly," Milton said. "They'll be immediately suspicious if he comes out on his own. Clyde—if you can't get Norcross and Ed away, hide them. Ed, don't argue—there's no time." The poet looked at her. "We can't ever let those men touch you again."

Clyde nodded and grabbed the fire iron from the stand in front of the hearth. "We should have let Norcross bring his bloody bow and arrows."

Ashen, Edna put on her coat. Norcross grabbed a stick of firewood. It wasn't particularly heavy, but it was better than nothing.

"Right, let's go." Rowland opened the front door, and he and Milton stepped out.

A man got out from behind the wheel of the Plymouth and opened the passenger door. Molly Cartwright stepped out in her white mink coat. Her hair had been beautifully coiffed beneath a stylish hat, and her hands were protected from the cold by a matching mink muff. Three men escorted her across the road.

"Rowly, Milton," she said sweetly.

"Hello, Molly. What are you doing here?"

"I thought it was time you and I had an honest to goodness chat, Rowly."

"How did you know we were here?" Milton asked, playing for time.

"Jim and Tommy followed you from Manchester. We followed them."

Rowland regarded Jim and Tommy, who Edna had recognised as her abductors. It was everything he could do to hold back. Molly observed the restrained fury with interest. "So, you've figured that out." She smiled. "I suppose Clyde is trying to head out the back with Norcross and that whore. Don't you worry, lover, I had some boys meet them. They'll be waiting for us inside, so perhaps we should join them."

Rowland did not let the dismay reach his eyes. "What would Danny think of what you're doing, Molly?"

"I think we need to talk about your precious friend, Danny. I think it's about time you knew who he was, Rowly." She took her hand out of the muff and waved a revolver at him. "Now invite us in...it's cold."

Rowland opened the door and stood aside to allow Molly to enter.

"You have lovely manners, Rowly, but you and Milton first." She pressed her weapon into his side.

They walked in to find their companions had been captured. Clyde had his arm around Edna. The young lawyer from Burr, Mayfair and Wilkes, and two other men in flat caps held them and Norcross at gunpoint. Clyde was bleeding rather profusely from a gash above his ear. He'd obviously not gone quietly. Norcross's eyes were fixed on Molly.

For a time she returned his gaze. The loathing was plain, unmitigated, and Rowland was afraid she would kill Otis Norcross there and then. So he spoke.

"Molly—what are you doing? This is in no one's interest."

She turned. "Don't you dare! You're no better than him… Danny's beloved Rowly! You used me! Courted me until she called you back like a trained dog!"

Rowland didn't flinch. He didn't want her to turn around again. He didn't want Edna in her line of sight. "If I don't administer Danny's estate," he said, "for any reason, all of it goes to Yale. This is not going to achieve anything."

"You're so wrong." She smiled. "I don't suppose you've been introduced to Percy Herbert—wave to Rowly, Percy." The lawyer looked over and nodded. "Percy is one of Burr, Mayfair and Wilkes's brightest young attorneys," Molly said brightly.

"Mr. Herbert." Rowland was calm, almost casual. "I take it Mr. Burr is unaware of your second job."

Herbert handed his weapon to one of his compatriots and moved to stand next to Molly. "Mr. Burr is barely aware that I exist." He extracted a sheaf of papers from inside his jacket. Molly nodded and Herbert proffered the document to Rowland.

Rowland read quickly. A letter for his signature, stating that he had found Otis Norcross, but that he had come to realise that Norcross had killed his benefactor, Daniel Cartwright, and as such could not inherit. Consequently, the gift made to Otis Norcross would form part of the residual estate and was therefore conferred on the Manchester Seaside Gallery, in accordance with Daniel Cartwright's last will and testament.

He looked up. This was about some misguided quest for justice on her brother's behalf. A misunderstanding... monumental, vindictive, but not beyond the reach of reason. "Molly, Otis Norcross didn't kill your brother. Danny was dead before Norcross returned to Boston."

"You know this, do you?" Molly's laugh was harsh.

"I do, Molly. I promise you Otis Norcross had nothing to do with Danny's murder."

"Again you're wrong, Rowly." Molly tilted her head to one side, studying him intently. "Otis had everything to do with Danny's death. If not for Otis, I would not have shot Danny."

Chapter Thirty-Six

TWO HELD WITHOUT BAIL IN DOUBLE
GANG KILLING

GUSTIN GANG LEADER AND HENCHMAN
SLAIN

...Police say the sensational murder of Frank
Gustin spells doom to the Gustin gang, which
has caused more trouble in Boston in recent
years than any other outlaw group.

FEAR OF REPRISALS

About midnight, when police were searching
a downtown hotel for suspects, a report was
received at Headquarters that members of the
Gustin gang were organising at 9th St and
Broadway, South Boston, for a reprisal...

LOMBARDI IS SOUGHT

Police also were ordered to pick up Joseph
Lombardi, in whose office the gang war broke
out and arrest him on sight on the charge of
suspicion of murder.

—*Boston Globe*,
December 23, 1931

❧

For a moment Rowland thought that surely she'd misspoken
or that he'd misunderstood. And then he saw that Molly
Cartwright was in deadly earnest.

"Why?" It was Norcross who asked. A cry of horror and
agony and loss. "Why did you kill him?"

Molly spun towards him. "Because of you, you unnatural
son of a bitch!" She lifted the revolver. "God, what fun it
would be to drop you right here."

Rowland tried to get her attention away from Norcross, who
was so agitated now that he could well draw her fire by speaking
unwisely. "You killed Danny because he loved Norcross?"

"If only that was all it was." Molly turned back to
Rowland. "Danny was my confidant. He knew I was in
love with Otis when he seduced him, corrupted him, stole
him!" She stamped her foot. "Otis wooed me so that no one
would suspect what he and Danny were up to."

"Molly, Danny would never have meant to—" Rowland
began.

"Oh, but he did." Angrily, Molly wiped the tears from
her cheeks. "Kneel!" she demanded. She glanced at Milton.
"Both of you—kneel."

Slowly, they complied. "I read your letters to Danny," Rowland said. "He introduced you to many men, Molly—how was he to know you'd fall in love with Norcross?"

"Because I told him, you idiot!" Molly lifted the gun and smashed it against the side of his head. Because he could still not move his left arm quickly enough to catch himself, Rowland went down, his injured shoulder taking the impact.

"Rowly!" Edna cried as Molly screeched at her to stay back.

For a moment the pain was disabling and Rowland could only curse. Milton started towards him, and one of Molly's men pressed a gun against the poet's forehead. "You move and I'll blow your feckin' head off."

"I'm all right!" Rowland gasped, warning his friends to stand down.

"Get up!" Molly hissed.

Rowland struggled back to his knees.

"Do you know why Danny asked me to meet him in the Harvard Yard that evening? Do you, Rowly?"

Rowland was still trying to clear his head.

"He wanted to give me the opportunity to redeem myself."

"Redeem yourself for what?" Milton asked, trying to give Rowland a chance to at least get his breath.

"For telling Otis's parents about Highland Hospital. For suggesting a solution."

Norcross made a strange sound.

Rowland spoke quickly now before she turned back to Norcross again. "You told the Norcrosses to have Otis committed?"

"Yes." She was smiling again. "I did, and I was never sorry."

"Jesus, Molly!" Norcross shouted. "Do you know what they did to me in there? All because I couldn't love you?"

"All because you made me love you, you bastard. You and Danny used me. And what's more, my dear brother wanted to do it again."

"What did he want, Molly?" Rowland asked. "What chance did he offer you?"

Molly spat out the answer as if she were choking on the words. "Danny wanted me to marry Otis."

"Why?" Edna gasped, horror surpassing fear and good sense.

"Because Mrs. Otis Norcross would be Mr. Otis Norcross's next of kin. She could have Otis legally released from Highland. She could prevent his parents ever sending him back." Molly's face was white as she recounted the deal Danny had offered her. "He told me that he would cut me off—that if I wanted to carry on living in the manner to which I'd become accustomed, I'd have to marry Otis."

"And so you shot him?" Rowland said quietly.

"Yes. Three times. Maybe four... I can't really remember. It was not something I planned, only I was so angry—"

"But you'd brought the gun to the boathouse with you?" Milton said pointedly.

"Thanks to Percy, I knew Danny had changed his will." Molly smiled at the young lawyer who winked in return. "And I knew Otis had escaped Highland Hospital. It was self-defence in every sense of the term." Her eyes became a little distant. "Danny looked so surprised when I pulled the trigger, like he never expected I would stand up for myself, like it was inconceivable that I would defy him." She giggled. "'Molly, what are you doing?'" she said with mock horror. "'I'm killing you, Danny.'"

Rowland saw his friend's last moments in his mind's eye. "And the lipstick?" he asked.

"I wanted the world to know what he was. I wasn't going to let him die a respectable victim."

"But why try to convince me that Mr. Norcross had killed Danny rather than joining your brothers in having the will struck out in its entirety?" Rowland asked. "Surely Mr.

Herbert informed you that you stood more to gain from the latter course?"

"Danny thought he was so clever with his codicils and residual clauses." She laughed. "A couple of days before I shot Danny, I bought the Manchester Seaside Gallery."

Rowland understood then. The purpose of the document she'd handed him was to declare the will valid as Danny's executor and then remove the primary heir. But he also realised that she would have to kill him the moment he signed; she would have to kill all of them for her scheme to work. He played for time. "This isn't going to work, Molly," he said. "For one thing, this letter is typed. Who's going to believe I found and captured a murderer, and then went looking for a typewriter to make it all official? I assume you want this to have the power of a dying declaration of some sort... It'll need to be in my handwriting."

"And you'd be willing to do that, would you?"

"Molly, whatever you've done, you're Danny's sister. He'd want me to help you get out of this mess."

"Oh, yes." She pressed her lips together, nodding. "Help me. Like when you took me dancing and then tried to seduce me?"

"Molly, that's not what—" Rowland said, alarmed.

"It's exactly what happened...till she called you back." Molly walked over to Edna and, removing the sculptress's hat, ran her hand over the ragged remains of her hair. Edna froze.

"Don't touch her!" Rowland snarled.

Molly ignored him. "What's it like being ugly, Edna? What's it like not to be able to steal any man you want? Did you learn your lesson?"

"I'll write the letter!" Rowland said, desperate to distract her from Edna.

Molly turned. She smiled and collected the fire iron that

had been wrested from Clyde by one of her men, strode over to Rowland, and swung it as hard as she could into his stomach. "I know you're not stupid, Rowly. Don't treat me like I am." She regarded him furiously as he lay crumpled on the boards. "I know you know that I can't allow any of you to survive this. Otis Norcross will have to kill you all."

"I won't do it!" Norcross shouted as Clyde held Edna back.

"Of course you won't, Otis. You won't have to."

"For God's sake, Molly," Rowland groaned, straightening painfully and struggling back onto his knees, "if it's money you want, my fortune is nearly as large as your brother's. Just take me to a bank, and I'll organise for you to receive whatever funds you want a darn sight sooner than waiting for any letter to be given effect! Don't you think Frank and Geoffrey are going to fight this as hard as they've fought everything else?"

The man who had his gun on Milton turned at this. "Actually, Molly, that sounds to me like a grand idea. Why shouldn't we take a little something for our trouble?"

"There'll be plenty of money when Danny's estate is settled on the gallery, Sean. Percy is sure the letter will crystallise the gift. Frank and Geoffrey will get their ten thousand, and the rest is ours."

"Crystals? Feckin' crystals! You're putting too much faith in the boy, Molly," Sean spat. "You're losing the run of yourself. We're trying to keep Lombardo from getting his mitts on your brother's money, and you're worried about whether Sinclair here fancies you."

"You're the Gustins?" Clyde said suddenly. He looked at Molly. "You aligned yourself with the gang the Italians forced out."

"Oh, they haven't forced us out yet, sonny," Sean said.

Rowland saw a chance to drive home a wedge. "I could give you a fortune, enough to fight Lombardo and his men. And if I refuse to continue as executor, then Danny's estate goes to Yale, and Lombardo has no chance of getting his hands on it. And you won't need to murder anybody."

"You think we have a problem with murder?"

"You murder this many people, and you will have a problem."

"No!" Molly screamed. "We stick to the plan! We agreed!"

"Jaysus, Molly," Sean replied. "The man makes a bit of sense. There's no point—"

Molly shot him. Edna screamed. Rowland and Milton pulled back as they were splattered with the Irishman's blood.

Silence. The moment of shock before hell broke loose. And then it did.

The next shot was aimed at Molly as the men of the Gustin Gang took exception to the execution of one of their own. Milton knocked Rowland to the ground as the bullets started to fly in both directions. Again Rowland's shoulder crashed into the boards, but this time he barely noticed.

"Stay down, Rowly," Milton growled.

"Ed—"

"Clyde's got her." Milton dragged Rowland back behind a trunk and away from the line of fire. "Bloody hell, Rowly, you're bleeding. Have you been—"

"No." Rowland glanced down at the blood on his shirt. His ears were ringing. "I think that's just the old wound. I'm all right."

The gunshots ceased, replaced instead by profanity and panic. Molly was down. Percy Herbert was kneeling beside her trying to stop the bleeding. Two other Gustins were also dead. The remaining three backed towards the door; the youngest of them was crying. Again events poised as the desperate men made choices. It was possibly the sirens that predicated the decision to cut losses and run. They bolted through the back door, leaving the Australians, the carnage, and Percy Herbert behind.

"Clyde... Ed..."

"We're all right, Rowly."

"Mr. Norcross."

"I'm not hurt, Mr. Sinclair."

Rowland stood slowly. Someone would have to go out to talk to the police.

Herbert snapped around, Molly's gun in his hand.

"Mr. Herbert," Rowland said carefully. "It's over. You've not killed anyone yet—"

"Molly's dead," Herbert said. "My God, she's dead!"

"Put the gun down, Mr. Herbert."

"This is your fault!" Herbert lifted the gun to aim at Rowland's head.

Norcross made his move, hurling himself at the grieving lawyer from behind. The revolver discharged as it was knocked out of Herbert's hand, the bullet flying wild. Rowland didn't wait to see where it went, adding his weight to Norcross's as Herbert fought them in a kind of deranged grief.

"Stop, or I'll shoot." Edna had the revolver, a fact that had more effect on Rowland than Herbert.

"Ed, no!" The last time Edna had picked up a gun, she'd shot him, so his concern was not entirely unfounded.

Milton put his arm around the sculptress. Slowly, he removed the revolver from her hand. Clyde stepped in to help Rowland and Norcross subdue Herbert, removing his own tie to bind the lawyer's hands behind his back.

The police banged at the front door of the loft, demanding entry.

"Clyde," Rowland said quietly. "Get Mr. Norcross out of here. Hide him somewhere until we come for him."

"What?"

"We can't let anyone know where he is until we can make sure he won't be sent back to Highland Hospital."

"But—" Norcross began.

"Trust us, Mr. Norcross. Go."

Clyde nodded and took Norcross out the back door. They were aided by the fact that the officers who'd been despatched to that exit were pursuing the three members of the Gustin Gang. Rowland and Milton opened the front door with their hands up.

Chapter Thirty-Seven

INTERESTED IN GOLF

Miss Harriot S. Curtis and Miss Margaret Curtis of 28 Mr Vernon St and Sharksmouth Manchester, arrived in Philadelphia yesterday for the opening of the women's national golf championship play. They have been guests of honor at the women's international Curtis Cup tournament played last week at the Chevy Chase Club, Washington, D.C. Distinguished guests at the Chevy Chase Club for the presentation of the trophy, which was donated by the Misses Curtis, included Sir Ronald Lindsay, the British Ambassador.

—*Boston Globe*,
October 2, 1934

The Australians and Percy Herbert were taken into custody. The Rockport Police had, after all, found them in a sailor's loft with four bodies, three of whom were members of the notorious Gustin Gang, and the fourth the daughter of one of Boston's most prominent families. Percy Herbert was initially uncommunicative and then hysterical.

Rowland telephoned Oliver Burr. "Mr. Burr, Rowland Sinclair. I think I may require your assistance."

Burr arrived with a number of colleagues and Detective O'Brien of the Boston Police Department. The lawyer unleashed righteous anger in legal parlance, demanding to know why his clients had not been taken to a hospital. A doctor was called to the station and much made of Rowland Sinclair's injury, though how he sustained an arrow wound in a gunfight was difficult to explain.

The druggist Harrison came in to explain that Rowland Sinclair and his party had taken residence at the loft the day before with his permission. The Australians said nothing to the police about Clyde or Norcross, and Harrison was quick enough to avoid any mention of him. Herbert was too distraught to make a coherent point that there were two men missing.

Oliver Burr made up for the fact that a member of his firm had tried to kill them by ensuring his clients were released without charge. As they left the station, Rowland briefed the lawyer in full so that he understood why they wished to remain in the area rather than returning to the Copley.

"All things considered, Mr. Sinclair, with three Gustins still at large and the fact that you may want to keep the presence of certain members of your party to yourselves for now, I wouldn't recommend a hotel in Rockport. News of the shootings will be rife, and people will be curious."

"What do you suggest, Mr. Burr?" Rowland asked.

"A private home. I have old friends half an hour away in

Manchester who I'm sure would be willing to take you in. They are the most discreet of people."

Burr escorted them out there himself and introduced the somewhat bedraggled Australians to Harriot and Margaret Curtis, the current mistresses of Sharksmouth, a magnificent granite construction which overlooked the sea. The waterfront estate was large enough to grant its inhabitants the privacy afforded by space. The Curtis sisters seemed more intrigued than alarmed by the state of them. Margaret had long been involved in social work and possibly considered her new houseguests refugees, which in some sense they were.

Burr explained that there were another two gentlemen he wished to impose upon his old friends, one of whose identity and presence required the utmost discretion. He glanced at Rowland and informed the Curtises that he expected these additional gentlemen would also turn up that evening.

All this, Harriot and Margaret took in their stride, more interested in whether their guests could play golf than why they might be in hiding. Milton, Rowland, and Edna were made welcome, assigned guest rooms, and lent clothes and razors and everything else that was required to make them fit for residence at Sharksmouth. Edna was given a golf lesson in the gallery while Rowland and Milton took the Cadillac back down to Artist's Row, where they drove onto Bradley Wharf, parked near the red fish shack, and waited. Though it was now dark, they turned the motorcar's headlights off, lest they attract more than the attention they intended.

"Are you sure Clyde will think to look for us here?" Milton asked.

"I hope so." Rowland kept his eyes open for any sign of them. "Both the loft and Harrison's place could be being watched. It's really the only other place in Rockport we all know."

When Clyde and Norcross eventually climbed into the

back seat, they were near frozen. Milton passed back his flask, before he started the car.

"My God, you're blue," Rowland said as the two men shivered behind him. "Where the dickens did you hide?"

"Dingy...canvas...bloody cold..." was all Clyde could manage to get out.

"Drink!" Milton instructed. "If you look or sound cold when we reach the roadblock, you're going to rouse suspicions."

Rowland cranked up the Madame X's heater, and they gave Clyde and Norcross a few minutes to thaw before trying to get through the roadblock. The officer peered into the cabin. They all wished him a good evening, relying on their accents to demonstrate that were unlikely to be members of the Irish gang. And so they were passed through.

"What happened at the police station?" Clyde asked once they were on the road to Manchester. "Are we fugitives?"

"No," Rowland assured him. "The police are looking for the Gustins. They know we didn't shoot anybody."

"Mightn't have been the case if I hadn't disarmed Ed, of course," Milton said, grinning at Rowland. "But you can thank me later."

"We're just making sure we know we can protect Mr. Norcross before we tell anyone we've found him," Rowland said, ignoring the poet. Rowland explained quickly about the Curtis sisters, their current sanctuary at Sharksmouth.

"And if there is no way to prevent my parents insisting I return to Highland Hospital?" Norcross said wearily.

"How old are your parents, Mr. Norcross?" Milton asked.

"My father's eighty-four; my mother is seventy-nine."

"So they're unlikely to be around too much longer...say five years at a stretch."

"Bloody hell, Milt!" Clyde exploded. "You're talking about his mum and dad."

"Who buried him alive and then incarcerated him in that madhouse—"

"You can't expect the man to wait around hoping his parents will die."

Milton smiled faintly. "Comrade, you're not suggesting we take more affirmative action?"

"Milt!" Rowland stopped the poet before his sometimes wicked sense of humour took things too far.

But Norcross took no offence. "You can't wait that long to settle Danny's estate," he said.

"Probably not," Rowland admitted. "But we'll think of something."

◦◦◦

Edna was helping Harriot and Margaret Curtis hang Christmas decorations when the men returned. There was a flurry of fuss as Clyde and Norcross were welcomed and warmed and fed. And for a moment, it felt like they were ordinary holiday visitors come to enjoy the seaside and the festivities of the season. It was only after their elderly hostesses had retired, leaving them to enjoy brandy by the fire, that they spoke of what had happened.

Norcross wept as he spoke of what Daniel Cartwright had done. "How could he ask his sister to marry me? How could he be so cruel?"

"He'd discovered that she'd betrayed you both, comrade— that she'd as good as sent you to that asylum." Milton shook his head. "He knew what had happened to you there. I expect he was bloody angry."

"But Molly was his sister. He loved her. We both did in our way."

"Oh, Mr. Norcross," Edna said gently. "Danny was desperate. Perhaps he thought this was a way of taking care of both of you. As your wife, Molly could have had you released from that hospital, and you could have looked after her financially."

Rowland swirled the brandy in his glass absently. "He made a mistake, Mr. Norcross. We all do. I don't think he meant to be cruel to Molly, but perhaps he was in this instance. And she shot him before he could realise or be sorry or take it back."

Edna leaned her head against his shoulder and then pulled back as she realised what she was doing. "I forgot about your shoulder. I'm so sorry, Rowly."

Norcross grimaced. "So am I."

Rowland smiled. "It's fine. Really. I can barely feel it now."

"In that case…" Edna returned her cheek to rest against his shoulder, enjoying the warmth of the fire, the closeness of Rowland.

"So all this has been Molly." Clyde sighed. He glanced at Edna. "Even what happened to you?"

"She nearly blew everything then," Milton muttered. "If Rowly had called it quits, her whole plan would have amounted to nothing."

"I wonder why she would risk everything like that?" Clyde murmured.

"Because Molly thought Mr. Norcross had been stolen from her. She wasn't going to let Ed steal Rowly," Milton said. "Hell hath no fury…"

"I wasn't stealing Rowly," Ed said drowsily.

Edna's eyes were closed so she didn't see the look Clyde and Milton exchanged.

"So what now, Rowly?" Clyde asked.

"We start thinking seriously about how we're going to make sure Mr. Norcross is never returned to Highland Hospital."

Edna opened her eyes. "I have an idea about that."

Rowland looked down at her. "Carry on."

Edna turned to Norcross. "Do you trust us, Mr. Norcross?"

"Yes, of course."

"Do you trust me? This is only a solution if you trust me...and I understand you barely know me."

"I'd trust you with my life, Miss Higgins."

"Ed..." Rowland began.

"What if I were to marry you, Mr. Norcross? I could give you the protection Danny wanted Molly to give you. I'd be your next of kin, and you could never be confined to a hospital again without my consent...which I simply would not give."

Clyde and Milton sat up, shocked. Rowland's face was unreadable.

Norcross swallowed. "I couldn't ask you to do that, Miss Higgins. It's too much."

"You're not asking, Mr. Norcross, I'm offering. It would be a marriage to protect you—that's all. When your parents are no longer able to commit you, we'll simply have the marriage annulled."

"My parents may not pass away for years."

"I understand that."

"It'll mean you can't marry anyone else in that time."

"I understand that too."

"It doesn't seem fair, Miss Higgins."

"I'm the only one of the four of us who can marry you, Mr. Norcross. And none of this is fair."

Milton spoke up. "Ed, this is a bit drastic, don't you think?"

"Yes." The sculptress nodded. "If we can find another way, let's definitely do that, but if we can't, then perhaps this is the lesser of evils. Mr. Burr can tell us the least we need to do to make me Mr. Norcross's next of kin. And then we carry on as we were, in the knowledge that if anyone tries to commit Mr. Norcross again, I can stop them."

Norcross rubbed his face. "How can I let you do this?"

Edna smiled. "Mr. Norcross, I promise you, I will be the most negligent, absent, and unfaithful wife. Your mother will hate me, and your friends will feel sorry for you, but you will be safe."

Norcross laughed though there were tears as well. "My mother hates me, and you are the only friends I have, aside from Zelda." He looked up at the Australian men. "Gentlemen, would you let her do this?"

Clyde sighed. "Miss Higgins doesn't answer to any of us, Mr. Norcross."

"If she did, would you stop her?" He wiped his eyes. "Please, gentlemen, think only of her interests, for it seems she is too kind to do so."

Clyde sat back. He glanced at Rowland, recognising that, however inscrutable he remained, Rowland was struggling.

Milton shook his head. "It's always been Rowly who'd try to solve problems by proposing."

"Jesus, Mary, and Joseph!" Clyde glared at the poet, appalled by his insensitivity.

But Rowland smiled. He laughed softly, sadly. Only a year ago he'd offered marriage to save a lady's reputation—marriage that would have been in more than just name and with no prospect of release. How could he object to this? "I'm not going to tell you that I'm happy about this, Mr. Norcross, but,"—he glanced at Edna—"whether I'm happy is irrelevant. It is a temporary solution." He took Edna's hand and kissed it. She had always reminded him what kindness was.

Norcross studied the two of them for a moment. "I give you all my word as a gentleman that if Miss Higgins changes her mind, if she wants to be released, for whatever reason, even if it puts me in danger, then I will release her immediately and without question."

The Australian men looked to Edna. She nodded.

Rowland swallowed. "Then we'd better speak to Mr. Burr."

Chapter Thirty-Eight

AMERICAN MEN TO BLAME FOR GOLD
DIGGERS

If They Put the Same Premium on Women
That They Do on Business, Marriage Would
Be More Successful, Says Dr. A. J. Cronin,
British Novelist

What is Marriage?

When I observe the marriages about me I
must say that marriage is a messy state. It has
become nothing more or less than a traveling
circus.

Marriage is a necessity. It is the best institution that has been devised for the needs of
the man and one which permits him to grow
and develop.

It naturally has tremendous difficulties and
hardships. But when you attempt by divorce to
improve it, you are attempting the impossible.

You are misunderstanding the very principle of marriage which involves a certain amount of boredom, submission and a certain give and take.

Dr. A. J. Cronin

—*The Nebraska State Journal*
(Lincoln, Nebraska), May 5, 1935

∿᷂◌᷂∿

Rowland hesitated before he tapped on Edna's door, but he tapped nevertheless. "Ed, it's me."

"Come in, Rowly."

He opened the door and stopped, for a moment unable to do anything but gaze at her.

The Curtis sisters had insisted that Edna have a dress and veil. They'd found a gown that one or the other had worn to a ball many years ago, that was close enough to white and required only a few strategic tacking stitches to make it fit. The veil was borrowed from their sister, Elinor, who lived in a separate house on the estate. It fell softly around Edna's shoulders and all but hid what had been done to her hair.

She smiled nervously. "I feel like I'm in fancy dress."

"You are, in a way. But you're so beautiful." He took her hand. It was cold. "Sweetheart, are you having second thoughts? Because if you are—"

"No. I'm not." She pulled her surviving curl absently. "This won't change anything will it, Rowly?"

"It's a legal formality, Ed, that's all. But if you don't want—"

"It's not me, Rowly. I'm worried about you."

"Me?"

"You haven't said a lot."

"There's not a lot to say." Gently he pushed the stray curl behind her ear. "It's a bit strange watching you get married... I always thought..." He stopped before he blurted, "it would be me." "I always thought you wouldn't."

Her eyes softened. "You know that I'm not...not really."

He smiled. "Yes, I know."

And so the marriage of Mr. Otis Norcross to Miss Edna Higgins took place at Sharksmouth, in a private ceremony attended by Harriot and Margaret Curtis, the bride's friends, and several lawyers. It was a short proceeding.

Milton gave away the bride, and Rowland stood up for the groom. The sense of relief that followed the formalities made them all a little giddy, or perhaps that was the champagne, or the thought that they would finally be able to settle Daniel Cartwright's estate and go home.

Oliver Burr ensured that all the legal details and requirements were addressed so that Edna Higgins would become Otis Norcross's next of kin. He hoped that the embarrassment of having the son they buried return would be enough to hold the greater Norcrosses at bay for the immediate future at least. On his recommendation, Norcross decided to travel abroad for a time.

Despite its awkward beginnings, the wedding party became quite festive. Milton recited sonnets, Clyde and Norcross made progressively more inebriated toasts, and Rowland danced with the bride.

∽✺∾

There were footprints in the snow by Molly Cartwright's grave. Unmarked but for a temporary wooden cross, she lay beside Daniel Cartwright. Rowland was surprised by his grief for her. Even after everything she'd orchestrated, her terrible anger, her ruthless vengeance, he remembered the raw hurt in her voice when she spoke of what Daniel had asked.

Now Daniel and Molly lay beside each other in death and tragedy and the enormity of what they had done to each other. He wondered if they would make their peace.

Otis Norcross had wept so inconsolably at Danny's grave that Edna had pulled him away. Rowland could see them in the distance, Edna comforting her new husband.

They'd all become firm friends in the time they'd been at Sharksmouth waiting for the Cartwright estate to be finally settled. Out of the public eye, Edna and Norcross had begun to laugh about their matrimonial status—she had taken to calling him "Mr. Norcross, dear," and he would ask about what she had prepared for his supper, after which they would giggle like naughty children. Aside from that, little seemed to have changed among them. Edna had not pulled away from Rowland, or Clyde or Milton, and though she played the part of a devoted young wife when it was called for, she was in all other instances simply herself. Occasionally, she had night-mares about the abduction and at those times she still turned to Rowland—though not quite as she had before. She kept her side of a bargain, as he did his.

Margaret and Harriot Curtis had introduced them all to the eminent artist Charles Hopkinson, who had married their sister, Elinor. Consequently, the last month had been one of artistic exchange. Indeed, Hopkinson had been so taken with Rowland's painting of Edna, which Bradford had sent over from New York, that he'd shown the work to Robert Vose, who'd accepted it immediately for exhibition. Hopkinson had invited Rowland and Clyde into his studio at Fenway in Boston, and from him the Australians learned much about watercolour technique and the art scene of New England and the Boston School.

Determined to remove the stain of Percy Herbert's actions from the reputation of his firm, Oliver Burr had worked tirelessly to ensure that both Norcross and Edna were protected from lawsuits that might be initiated by the Cartwrights. Norcross settled generously with Frank and Geoffrey Cartwright, and the challenges to their brother's will were dropped. But neither were men to be trusted.

They all had passages on a flight to New York that afternoon. The *Boston Globe* would be on hand to photograph Mr. and Mrs. Otis Norcross setting off on an extended round-the-world honeymoon. From New York, Norcross and Burr would proceed to London, where Norcross intended to settle for a while, and the Australians would go home.

Rowland placed a paintbrush on Daniel Cartwright's grave. "Goodbye, Danny. *Tu vas me manquer, mon ami.*"

Clyde and Milton walked up from the path. "Are you ready to go, Rowly?" Clyde asked.

Rowland nodded. "We might get home for the last days of summer," he said apologetically.

"We spent the Australian winter in Shanghai," Clyde replied. "It's probably a fair trade."

Milton glanced down at Daniel Cartwright's grave. A number of brushes laid in tribute now. "Do you think he had any idea what he was unleashing? What his people would do for money?"

"I don't know that this was ever about the Cartwright fortune," Rowland said, looking back at Edna and Norcross. "Not for Danny or for Molly."

"Do you think this marriage will work?" Clyde asked carefully. He still wondered how Rowland was really dealing with this.

"To keep Norcross from being committed, yes." Rowland frowned. "He could still go to prison for indecency if he is discovered at any time…but there's not a lot we can do about that. He'll just have to be careful."

"This is going to be an awkward one to explain to Wilfred," Clyde observed. "He thinks the length of Milt's hair is a scandal."

Rowland grimaced. That much was true. "We might just tell Wilfred it was about money."

Epilogue

Otis Norcross bought an estate in London near Oxford. He lived quietly and privately behind high hedges, always aware that his natural inclinations remained illegal, but his home was always open to the four Australians who'd resurrected him. Daniel Cartwright's apartment at the Warwick was sold and the proceeds divided amongst his staff, who though they were now out of work, had means. The remainder of the vast Cartwright empire was ably managed by Oliver Burr.

Rather than explain to Boston Society why they had buried a son who was very much alive, Otis Norcross's fictitiously bereaved parents left Massachusetts and settled in Washington. The elder Mr. Norcross spent much of his remaining fortune on lawyers in an attempt to bring his son back under control of doctors. In this, he was consistently thwarted by the steadfast refusal of Otis's Australian wife to believe he was in any way insane.

∿◎∿

Joseph Kennedy became the first chairman of the U.S. Maritime Commission in 1937. In 1938, President Roosevelt appointed him as the United States' ambassador to the Court of

Saint Otis (United Kingdom). Rejecting Winston Churchill's belief that any compromise with Hitler was impossible, Kennedy supported Chamberlain's policy of appeasement. He consistently sought meetings with Adolf Hitler in order to "bring about a better understanding between the United States and Germany." Kennedy argued strongly against providing military and economic aid to the United Kingdom stating in the *Boston Sunday Globe* (November 10, 1940), "Democracy is finished in England. It may be here." He resigned as ambassador in October 1940, and returned to the United States. He never made another movie.

༄༅

Father Coughlin's rhetoric became progressively more anti-Semitic, and in the late 1930s, he came to openly support the Fascist policies of Adolf Hitler, Benito Mussolini, and Emperor Hirohito of Japan, views he broadcast to millions via his weekly radio show. In 1938, after the Nazis attacked Austrian Jews, their synagogues, and businesses in what became known as Kristallnacht, Coughlin claimed that "Jewish persecution only followed after Christians first were persecuted." The speech led to some radio stations refusing to air his broadcasts. Thousands of the "Radio Priest's" followers picketed the studios in protest, shouting anti-Semitic slogans. With the outbreak of war in Europe in 1939, the Roosevelt administration forced him off the air.

༄༅

F. Scott Fitzgerald continued to holiday and write at the Grove Park Inn in Asheville, North Carolina. The part he'd played in the escape of John Smith from Highland Hospital, and his encounter with the Australians, became material for a book he intended to write once he finished *The Love of the Last Tycoon*. In 1937, he signed a lucrative contract with Metro-Goldwyn-Mayer and moved to Hollywood, where he wrote for the screen. He began a public, live-in affair with movie columnist Sheilah Graham and continued to drink. In 1939, Metro-Goldwyn-Mayer terminated his contract. F. Scott Fitzgerald died of a heart attack in 1940 at the age of forty-four. The unfinished manuscript, *The Love of the Last Tycoon*, was published posthumously as *The Last Tycoon*. Fitzgerald's story of an Australian millionaire and his quixotic love for a beautiful sculptress never quite made it beyond a few scribbled notes.

~☙~

Zelda Fitzgerald remained in various states of mental distress and in and out of the Highland Hospital for the remainder of her life. In 1938, she travelled to Cuba with her husband. On their return, F. Scott Fitzgerald was hospitalized for intoxication and exhaustion, and Zelda never saw him again. After he died, however, she was instrumental in seeing *The Last Tycoon* was published and began working again on her own novel, *Caesar's Things*. When fire broke out at the Highland Hospital in 1948, Zelda Fitzgerald was one of nine women who died in the inferno.

~☙~

Rowland Sinclair, Clyde Watson Jones, Milton Isaacs, and Edna Higgins arrived in Sydney after nearly a year abroad, most of which time they'd spent outside the British Empire. With the passing of George V, they returned to an Australia under Edward VIII. Edna had slipped off her wedding ring as they left the U.S., but she wrote to her husband every month, as he did her, and they confided in each other about all manner of things, including the men they loved.

**Don't miss a single adventure with
Rowland Sinclair!**

EXCERPTED FROM *SHANGHAI SECRETS*, BOOK 9 IN THE ROWLAND SINCLAIR WWII MYSTERIES

Rowland Sinclair's Chrysler Airflow was a magnet for attention, both admiring and aghast in equal measure, and so the presence of three men loitering curiously by the motorcar was not particularly unusual. The automobile's revolutionary design and all-metal body, not to mention its yellow paintwork, made it distinctive amongst the black Austins and Ford Tudors also parked in Druitt Lane.

Rowland handed his seven-year-old nephew the key to the Airflow's door. "Let yourself in, Ernie, while I have a word with these gentlemen."

Rowland had become accustomed to explaining his automobile to inquisitive strangers. He was, himself, still enamoured enough with the vehicle not to find the interest tedious. Still, on this occasion, he was in a hurry, and the men in question had placed themselves in the way of the car... They'd probably want him to show them the engine.

Ernest Sinclair ran directly to the driver's side door with the key clutched tightly in his fist while Rowland strode over to the men leaning on the Airflow's bonnet.

"Afternoon, gentlemen."

"Flash car. She yours?"

"She is."

The man who'd asked glanced at his companions. "You Sinclair?"

At the mention of his name, Rowland tensed instinctively. Apparently, the reaction was reply enough, and they fell upon him, fists leading. In the face of the onslaught, Rowland gave no quarter and responded in kind. He'd been in this kind of situation often enough that he knew to keep the three men in front of him—if one was to grab and hold him from behind, the situation would become grim indeed. His assailants, too, were clearly not novices in the dubious arts of street fighting. They forced him away from the car, raining blow after blow and using their number to bypass his defences. Eventually Rowland went down.

The surface of Druitt Lane was warm and hard against his face. He used it to steady the world, to focus on fighting back. Rowland wanted to shout at Ernest to run, but he was not sure if that would simply alert what might be a band of kidnappers to the boy's location.

He was almost relieved when one of the men—he could not see which—called him a "Commie-loving traitor." This was about him, not Ernest. Whatever their purpose, it was probably not child abduction. The jagged impact of a boot against his ribs drove the breath from his lungs. And then another.

"Oi! What the hell's going on here?"

From the ground Rowland knew only that it was a voice he'd not heard before, followed by several moments when he could almost hear the indecision, and then the pounding feet of men in flight.

"Are you all right, mate?" A concerned hand on his shoulder.

Rowland pushed himself gingerly off the road. "Yes, I think so."

"Mongrels! Bloody mongrels! Did they rob yer?"

Rowland shook his head slowly.

The Samaritan—a large man with a strong and steady grip—helped him stand. "They were giving you one hell of a kicking, you sure you're—"

Rowland's head began to clear. "Dammit! Ernie!"

"I beg yer pardon, mate?"

"Ernie, my nephew. He was..." Rowland stepped unsteadily towards the Airflow, panicked now. He couldn't see the boy. "Ernie!"

A tousled head rose hesitantly above the dash, blue eyes wide.

Rowland stopped to breathe. He opened the front passenger door. "Ernie, thank God!"

Ernest was pale and obviously shaken. "I wanted to help, Uncle Rowly, but you told me to stay in the car."

"I'm glad you did, mate." Rowland leant against the doorframe still trying to get his breath.

"You're bleeding, Uncle Rowly." Ernest remained in the protection of the Airflow's cabin.

"It's just a scratch, Ernie. I'll be all right."

"Who were those men?"

"To be perfectly honest, I'm not really sure."

"Why were they cross with you?"

To that, Rowland did not respond. He could guess why, but there was no point frightening Ernest. "We should get home to Woodlands."

"Are you up to driving that contraption, mate?" The man who'd stopped the attack regarded first the Airflow then Rowland Sinclair with equal scepticism, before drawing back sharply. "Hold your horses there a minute..." He rummaged inside his jacket to extract a newspaper.

Rowland grimaced. He really didn't want to get into another fight, but at least there was only one man this time.

The man held the front page beside Rowland's face. "That's you!" he said. "That's you with that fella, Keesch."

Rowland glanced back at Ernest in the car. Egon Kisch was regarded as either a peace advocate or a dangerous Communist subversive. The three men who'd just tried to pound Rowland into the ground were indisputably of the latter opinion. Still, Rowland had never been a man to deny his friends. "Yes, that's me."

"Well, whaddaya know, from the front page! The wife will never believe it."

Rowland smiled and put out his hand. He introduced himself, relieved that the gentleman seemed more starstruck than offended by the picture. "I appreciate your assistance, sir."

"Barry Love," he said, shaking Rowland's hand solemnly. "Always pleased to help a gentleman. You'd best be on your way, lest those jokers come back. There's some folk pretty worked up over your mate Keesch."

"It would seem so."

Rowland farewelled Love with more thanks and slipped behind the steering wheel, wincing as he settled.

ACKNOWLEDGMENTS

I, Sulari Gentill, being of sound mind, do hereby make the following acknowledgments and bequests:

To my husband, Michael, my gratitude for all you do to allow me to write.

To my sons, Edmund and Atticus, my apologies for all you have to live with and without because I write.

To my dad, whose faith in me defies logic, and my sister, Devini, whose support is unwavering: thank you.

Leith Henry, to whom I turn when I am uncertain that I have the words, who knows Rowland Sinclair as well as I do, and who is there when my courage fails.

Larry Vincent, friend and colleague, whose generosity allowed me to set this novel in a place I did not know—my sincere thanks.

Diane DiBiase, whose editorial guidance ensures I am writing the words I need and no more.

Beth Deveny and the incredible team from Poisoned Pen Press and Sourcebooks, who have turned my story into a book. Thank you.

My friends and colleagues who have kept eye-rolling to a minimum while I talk to Rowland. My thanks.

The remainder of my gratitude I give, in its entirety and without reservation, to the greater community of readers, reviewers, bloggers, and booksellers who have so cared about my gentleman artist that there are now ten books. Thank you.

ABOUT THE AUTHOR

Photo by Edmund Blenkins

Sulari Gentill is the author of the multi-award-winning Rowland Sinclair WWII Mysteries, a series of historical crime novels set in 1930s Australia about Rowland Sinclair, the wealthy gentleman artist cum amateur detective. The tenth in series, *Where There's a Will*, was published in the United States by Poisoned Pen Press in January 2022.

Under the name S. D. Gentill, Sulari wrote the acclaimed fantasy adventure series The Hero Trilogy: *Chasing Odysseus*, *Trying War*, and *The Blood of Wolves*.

Her widely praised standalone novel *After She Wrote Him* was chosen as a "Target Recommends" book for 2020 and Apple's Best Book of the Month for April 2020. In Australia, where Sulari lives, it won the Ned Kelly Award for Best Crime Novel and was short-listed for the Davitt Award.

Sulari was part of an Australia Council–sponsored delegation of Australian mystery writers who toured the U.S. in 2019 to represent Australian crime fiction to a U.S. readership. Most recently, she was awarded a Copyright Agency fellowship for a new literary mystery titled *The Woman in the Library*.

Sulari lives in a small country town in the Australian Snowy Mountains on a truffle-growing farm, which she shares with her family and several beloved animals. She remains in love with the art of storytelling.